THE
VIRAGO BOOK
OF
GHOST
STORIES

EDITED BY
RICHARD DALBY

virago

VIRAGO

First published in Great Britain in 2006 by Virago Press
This edition published in 2008 by Virago Press
Reprinted 2008, 2009

A CIP catalogue record for this book
is available from the British Library.

ISBN 978-1-84408-538-5

Typeset in Goudy by M Rules
Printed and bound in Great Britain by
Clays Ltd, St Ives plc

Papers used by Virago are natural, renewable and recyclable
products sourced from well-managed forests and certified
in accordance with the rules of the Forest Stewardship Council.

Mixed Sources
Product group from well-managed
forests and other controlled sources
www.fsc.org Cert no. SGS-COC-004081
© 1996 Forest Stewardship Council

Virago Press
An imprint of
Little, Brown Book Group
100 Victoria Embankment
London EC4Y 0DY

An Hachette UK Company
www.hachette.co.uk

www.virago.co.uk

CONTENTS

PREFACE

'Besides this earth, and besides the race of men, there is an invisible world and a kingdom of spirits; that world is round us, for it is everywhere.'

These lines come from Charlotte Brontë's *Jane Eyre* and are spoken by Helen Burns, the tragic and saintly character said to be based on Charlotte's two elder sisters who both died at a very young age in 1825.

A very large number of the Victorian population, including the Queen herself, became obsessed with the supernatural and the after-life, reflected in an endless run of literary fiction (and non-fiction) works.

Over the past 150 years Britain has led the world in the art of the classic ghost story, and it is no exaggeration to state that at least fifty per cent of quality examples in the genre were by women writers. This is especially true of the nineteenth century, which began with the classic Gothic novels of Ann Radcliffe, Clara Reeve and Mary Shelley.

The ghost story reached a high peak in magazines like Dickens's *Household Words* and *All the Year Round*, and became an essential annual ingredient of the best-selling Christmas numbers. Most of the greatest women writers of the Victorian era contributed marvellous tales to these magazines, and most of the leading names (Mrs Gaskell, Mrs Riddell, Mrs Oliphant) are represented in the present anthology.

This great tradition has endured triumphantly from the Edwardian era up to the present day, not only with specialists in the genre but also with other mainstream writers who experimented successfully, but rarely, with the form.

Edith Wharton freely admitted that it is not easy to write a thoroughly convincing ghost story, adding: 'It is luckier for a ghost to be vividly imagined than dully 'experienced'; and nobody knows better than a ghost how hard it is to put him or her into words shadowy, yet transparent enough . . . If a ghost story sends a cold shiver down one's spine, it has done its job and done it well.'

The present volume includes over thirty of the best ghostly tales from *The Virago Book of Ghost Stories: The Twentieth Century* (two volumes, 1987 & 1991) and *The Virago Book of Victorian Ghost Stories* (1988). The stories are arranged in chronological order, so the reader can easily perceive how the form of the ghost story has developed over the past 150 years. All are examples of fine, imaginative story-telling with a supreme command of the supernatural.

Richard Dalby

ACKNOWLEDGEMENTS

Permission to reproduce the following extracts has been kindly granted by the following: 'The Token', May Sinclair, copyright © May Sinclair 1923, by Curtis Brown Ltd, London on behalf of the Estate of May Sinclair; 'Roaring Tower' Stella Gibbons, copyright © Stella Gibbons 1937, by David Higham Associates; 'The Happy Autumn Fields', Elizabeth Bowen, copyright © Elizabeth Bowen 1945, by Curtis Brown Ltd on behalf of the Estate of Elizabeth Bowen; 'Diamond Jim', Lisa St Aubin de Terán, copyright © Lisa St Aubin de Terán 1987, by Ed Victor Ltd; 'Ashputtle', Angela Carter, copyright © Angela Carter 1987, by Rogers, Coleridge and White Ltd; 'The July Ghost', A.S. Byatt, copyright © A.S. Byatt 1987. This story first appeared in *Sugar and Other Stories*, C&W. Reproduced by permission of the author c/o Rogers, Coleridge & White Ltd, 20 Powis Mews, London W11 1JN; 'The Eyes', Edith Wharton, copyright © Edith Wharton 1910, by Abner Stein, London; 'The Black Dog', Penelope Lively, from *Pack of Cards*, William Heinemann Ltd and Penguin Books Ltd, copyright © Penelope Lively 1986, by David Higham Associates; 'Don't Tell Cissie', Celia Fremlin, from *By Horror Haunted*, copyright © Celia Fremlin 1974, by Gregory & Company; 'Who's Been Sitting in My Car?', copyright © Antonia Fraser 1976, by Curtis Brown Ltd; 'The Haunting of Shawley Rectory', Ruth Rendell, by PFD; 'The Ghosts of Calagou', Elizabeth Fancett, copyright © Elizabeth Fancett 1991, by the author; 'Rosalind', Richmal Crompton, from *Mist and Other Stories*, copyright © Richmal Crompton 1928, by A.P. Watt Ltd; 'Redundant', Dorothy K. Haynes, copyright © Dorothy K. Haynes

CHARLOTTE BRONTË

NAPOLEON AND THE SPECTRE

Well, as I was saying, the Emperor got into bed.

'Chevalier,' says he to his valet, 'let down those window-curtains, and shut the casement before you leave the room.'

Chevalier did as he was told, and then, taking up his candlestick, departed.

In a few minutes the Emperor felt his pillow becoming rather hard, and he got up to shake it. As he did so a slight rustling noise was heard near the bed-head. His Majesty listened, but all was silent as he lay down again.

Scarcely had he settled into a peaceful attitude of repose, when he was disturbed by a sensation of thirst. Lifting himself on his elbow, he took a glass of lemonade from the small stand which was placed beside him. He refreshed himself by a deep draught. As he returned the goblet to its station a deep groan burst from a kind of closet in one corner of the apartment.

'Who's there?' cried the Emperor, seizing his pistols. 'Speak, or I'll blow your brains out.'

This threat produced no other effect than a short, sharp laugh, and a dead silence followed.

The Emperor started from his couch, and, hastily throwing on a *robe-de-chambre* which hung over the back of a chair, stepped coura-geously to the haunted closet. As he opened the door something rustled. He sprang forward sword in hand. No soul or even sub-stance appeared, and the rustling, it was evident, proceeded from the falling of a cloak, which had been suspended by a peg from the door.

Half ashamed of himself he returned to bed.

Just as he was about once more to close his eyes, the light of the three wax tapers, which burned in a silver branch over the mantel-piece, was suddenly darkened. He looked up. A black, opaque shadow obscured it. Sweating with terror, the Emperor put out his hand to seize the bell-rope, but some invisible being snatched it rudely from his grasp, and at the same instant the ominous shade vanished.

'Pooh!' exclaimed Napoleon, 'it was but an ocular delusion.'

'Was it?' whispered a hollow voice, in deep mysterious tones, close to his ear. 'Was it a delusion, Emperor of France? No! all thou hast heard and seen is sad forewarning reality. Rise, lifter of the Eagle Standard! Awake, swayer of the Lily Sceptre! Follow me, Napoleon, and thou shalt see more.'

As the voice ceased, a form dawned on his astonished sight. It was that of a tall, thin man, dressed in a blue surtout edged with gold lace. It wore a black cravat very tightly round its neck, and confined by two little sticks placed behind each ear. The countenance was livid; the tongue protruded from between the teeth, and the eyes all glazed and bloodshot started with frightful prominence from their sockets.

'Mon Dieu!' exclaimed the Emperor, 'what do I see? Spectre, whence cometh thou?'

The apparition spoke not, but gliding forward beckoned Napoleon with uplifted finger to follow.

Controlled by a mysterious influence, which deprived him of the capability of either thinking or acting for himself, he obeyed in silence.

The solid wall of the apartment fell open as they approached, and, when both had passed through, it closed behind them with a noise like thunder.

They would now have been in total darkness had it not been for a dim light which shone round the ghost and revealed the damp walls of a long, vaulted passage. Down this they proceeded with mute rapidity. Ere long a cool, refreshing breeze, which rushed wailing up the vault and caused the Emperor to wrap his loose nightdress closer round, announced their approach to the open air.

This they soon reached, and Nap found himself in one of the principal streets of Paris.

'Worthy Spirit,' said he, shivering in the chill night air, 'permit me to return and put on some additional clothing. I will be with you again presently.'

'Forward,' replied his companion sternly.

He felt compelled, in spite of the rising indignation which almost choked him, to obey.

On they went through the deserted streets till they arrived at a lofty house built on the banks of the Seine. Here the Spectre stopped, the gates rolled back to receive them, and they entered a large marble hall which was partly concealed by a curtain drawn across, through the half transparent folds of which a bright light might be seen burning with dazzling lustre. A row of fine female figures, richly attired, stood before this screen. They wore on their heads garlands of the most beautiful flowers, but their faces were concealed by ghastly masks representing death's-heads.

'What is all this mummery?' cried the Emperor, making an effort to shake off the mental shackles by which he was so unwillingly restrained, 'Where am I, and why have I been brought here?'

'Silence,' said the guide, lolling out still further his black and bloody tongue. 'Silence, if thou wouldst escape instant death.'

The Emperor would have replied, his natural courage overcoming the temporary awe to which he had at first been subjected, but just then a strain of wild, supernatural music swelled behind the huge curtain, which waved to and fro, and bellied slowly out as if agitated by some internal commotion or battle of waving winds. At the same moment an overpowering mixture of the scents of mortal corruption, blent with the richest Eastern odours, stole through the haunted hall.

A murmur of many voices was now heard at a distance, and something grasped his arm eagerly from behind.

He turned hastily round. His eyes met the well-known countenance of Marie Louise.

'What! are you in this infernal place, too?' said he. 'What has brought you here?'

'Will your Majesty permit me to ask the same question of yourself?' said the Empress, smiling.

He made no reply; astonishment prevented him.

No curtain now intervened between him and the light. It had been removed as if by magic, and a splendid chandelier appeared suspended over his head. Throngs of ladies, richly dressed, but without death's-head masks, stood round, and a due proportion of gay cavaliers was mingled with them. Music was still sounding, but it was seen to proceed from a band of mortal musicians stationed in an orchestra near at hand. The air was yet redolent of incense, but it was incense unblended with stench.

'*Mon Dieu!*' cried the Emperor, 'how is all this come about? Where in the world is Piche?'

'Piche?' replied the Empress. 'What does your Majesty mean? Had you not better leave the apartment and retire to rest?'

'Leave the apartment? Why, where am I?'

'In my private drawing-room, surrounded by a few particular persons of the Court whom I had invited this evening to a ball. You entered a few minutes since in your nightdress with your eyes fixed and wide open. I suppose from the astonishment you now testify that you were walking in your sleep.'

The Emperor immediately fell into a fit of catalepsy, in which he continued during the whole of that night and the greater part of the next day.

ELIZABETH GASKELL

THE OLD NURSE'S STORY

You know, my dears, that your mother was an orphan, and an only child; and I dare say you have heard that your grandfather was a clergyman up in Westmoreland, where I come from. I was just a girl in the village school, when, one day, your grandmother came in to ask the mistress if there was any scholar there who would do for a nurse-maid; and mighty proud I was, I can tell ye, when the mistress called me up, and spoke to my being a good girl at my needle, and a steady honest girl, and one whose parents were very respectable, though they might be poor. I thought I should like nothing better than to serve the pretty young lady, who was blushing as deep as I was, as she spoke of the coming baby, and what I should have to do with it. However, I see you don't care so much for this part of my story, as for what you think is to come, so I'll tell you at once. I was engaged and settled at the parsonage before Miss Rosamond (that was the baby, who is now your mother) was born. To be sure, I had little enough to do with her when she came, for she was never out of her mother's arms, and slept by her all night long; and proud enough was I sometimes when missis trusted her to me. There never was such a baby before or since, though you've all of you been fine enough in your turns; but for sweet, winning ways, you've none of you come up to your mother. She took after her mother, who was a real lady born; a Miss Furnivall, a granddaughter of Lord Furnivall's, in Northumberland. I believe she had neither brother nor sister, and had been brought up in my lord's family till she had married your grandfather, who was just a curate, son to a shopkeeper in Carlisle – but a clever, fine gentleman as ever was – and one who was a right-down hard worker in his parish, which was very wide, and scattered all abroad over the Westmoreland Fells. When your mother, little Miss Rosamond, was about four or five years old, both her parents died in a fortnight – one after the other. Ah! that was a sad time. My pretty young mistress and me was looking for another baby, when my master came home from one of his long rides, wet, and tired, and took the fever he died of; and then she never held up her head again, but just lived to see her dead baby, and have it laid on her breast before she sighed away her life. My mistress had asked me, on her death-bed, never to leave Miss Rosamond; but if she had never spoken a word, I would have gone with the little child to the end of the world.

The next thing, and before we had well stilled our sobs, the executors and guardians came to settle the affairs. They were my poor young mistress's own cousin, Lord Furnivall, and Mr Esthwaite, my master's brother, a shopkeeper in Manchester; not so well-to-do then as he was afterwards, and with a large family rising about him. Well! I don't know if it were their settling, or because of a letter my mistress wrote on her death-bed to her cousin, my lord; but somehow it was settled that Miss Rosamond and me were to go to Furnivall Manor House, in Northumberland, and my lord spoke as if it had been her mother's wish that she should live with his family, and as if he had no objections, for that one or two more or less could make no difference in so grand a household. So though that was not the way in which I should have wished the coming of my bright and pretty pet to have been looked at – who was like a sunbeam in any family, be it never so grand – I was well pleased that all the folks in the Dale should stare and admire, when they heard I was going to be young lady's maid at my Lord Furnivall's at Furnivall Manor.

But I made a mistake in thinking we were to go and live where my lord did. It turned out that the family had left Furnivall Manor

House fifty years or more. I could not hear that my poor young mistress had ever been there, though she had been brought up in the family; and I was sorry for that, for I should have liked Miss Rosamond's youth to have passed where her mother's had been.

My lord's gentleman, from whom I asked so many questions as I durst, said that the Manor House was at the foot of the Cumberland Fells, and a very grand place; that an old Miss Furnivall, a great-aunt of my lord's, lived there, with only a few servants; but that it was a very healthy place, and my lord had thought that it would suit Miss Rosamond very well for a few years, and that her being there might perhaps amuse his old aunt.

I was bidden by my lord to have Miss Rosamond's things ready by a certain day. He was a stern proud man, as they say all the Lords Furnivall were; and he never spoke a word more than was necessary. Folk did say he had loved my young mistress; but that, because she knew that his father would object, she would never listen to him, and married Mr Esthwaite; but I don't know. He never married, at any rate. But he never took much notice of Miss Rosamond; which I thought he might have done if he had cared for her dead mother. He sent his gentleman with us to the Manor House, telling him to join him at Newcastle that same evening; so there was no great length of time for him to make us known to all the strangers before he, too, shook us off; and we were left, two lonely young things (I was not eighteen), in the great old Manor House. It seems like yesterday that we drove there. We had left our own dear parsonage very early, and we had both cried as if our hearts would break, though we were travelling in my lord's carriage, which I thought so much of once. And now it was long past noon on a September day, and we stopped to change horses for the last time at a little smoky town, all full of colliers and miners. Miss Rosamond had fallen asleep, but Mr Henry told me to waken her, that she might see the park and the Manor House as we drove up. I thought it rather a pity; but I did what he bade me, for fear he should complain of me to my lord. We had left all signs of a town, or even a village, and were then inside the gates of a large wild park – not like the parks here in the north, but with rocks, and the noise of running water, and gnarled thorn-trees, and old oaks, all white and peeled with age.

The road went up about two miles, and then we saw a great and stately house, with many trees close around it, so close that in some places their branches dragged against the walls when the wind blew; and some hung broken down; for no one seemed to take much charge of the place; – to lop the wood, or to keep the moss-covered carriageway in order. Only in front of the house all was clear. The great oval drive was without a weed; and neither tree nor creeper was allowed to grow over the long, many-windowed front; at both sides of which a wing projected, which were each the ends of other side fronts; for the house, although it was so desolate, was even grander than I expected. Behind it rose the Fells, which seemed unenclosed and bare enough; and on the left hand of the house, as you stood facing it, was a little, old-fashioned flower-garden, as I found out afterwards. A door opened out upon it from the west front; it had been scooped out of the thick dark wood for some old Lady Furnivall; but the branches of the great forest trees had grown and overshadowed it again, and there were very few flowers that would live there at that time.

When we drove up to the great front entrance, and went into the hall, I thought we should be lost – it was so large, and vast, and grand. There was a chandelier all of bronze, hung down from the middle of the ceiling; and I had never seen one before, and looked at it all in amaze. Then, at one end of the hall, was a great fireplace, as large as the sides of the houses in my country, with massy andirons and dogs to hold the wood; and by it were heavy old-fashioned sofas. At the opposite end of the hall, to the left as you went in – on the western side – was an organ built into the wall, and so large that it filled up the best part of that end. Beyond it, on the same side, was a door; and opposite, on each side of the fire-place, were also doors leading to the east front; but those I never went through as long as I stayed in the house, so I can't tell you what lay beyond.

The afternoon was closing in, and the hall, which had no fire lighted in it, looked dark and gloomy, but we did not stay there a moment. The old servant, who had opened the door for us, bowed to Mr Henry, and took us in through the door at the further side of the great organ, and led us through several smaller halls and passages into the west drawing-room, where he said that Miss Furnivall was sitting. Poor little Miss Rosamond held very tight to me, as if she were scared and lost in that great place, and as for myself, I was not much better. The west drawing-room was very cheerful-looking, with a warm fire in it, and plenty of good, comfortable furniture about. Miss Furnivall was an old lady not far from eighty, I should think, but I do not know. She was thin and tall, and had a face as full of fine wrinkles as if they had been drawn all over it with a needle's point. Her eyes were very watchful, to make up, I suppose, for her being so deaf as to be obliged to use a trumpet. Sitting with her, working at the same great piece of tapestry, was Mrs Stark, her maid and companion, and almost as old as she was. She had lived with Miss Furnivall ever since they were both young, and now she seemed more like a friend than a servant; she looked so cold and grey, and stony as if she had never loved or cared for any one; and I don't suppose she did care for any one, except her mistress; and, owing to the great deafness of the latter, Mrs Stark treated her very much as if she were a child. Mr Henry gave some message from my lord, and then he bowed goodbye to us all – taking no notice of my sweet little Miss Rosamond's outstretched hand – and left us standing there, being looked at by the two old ladies through their spectacles.

I was right glad when they rung for the old footman who had shown us in at first, and told him to take us to our rooms. So we went out of that great drawing-room, and into another sitting-room, and out of that, and then up a great flight of stairs, and along a broad gallery – which was something like a library, having books all down one side, and windows and writing-tables all down the other – till we came to our rooms, which I was not sorry to hear were just over the kitchens; for I began to think I should be lost in that wilderness of a house. There was an old nursery that had been used

for all the little lords and ladies long ago, with a pleasant fire burning in the grate, and the kettle boiling on the hob, and tea-things
spread out on the table; and out of that room was the night-nursery,
with a little crib for Miss Rosamond close to my bed. And old James
called up Dorothy, his wife, to bid us welcome; and both he and she
were so hospitable and kind, that by and by Miss Rosamond and me
felt quite at home; and by the time tea was over, she was sitting on
Dorothy's knee, and chattering away as fast as her little tongue
could go. I soon found out that Dorothy was from Westmoreland,
and that bound her and me together, as it were; and I would never
wish to meet with kinder people than were old James and his wife.
James had lived pretty nearly all his life in my lord's family, and
thought there was no one so grand as they. He even looked down a
little on his wife; because, till he had married her, she had never
lived in any but a farmer's household. But he was very fond of her,
as well he might be. They had one servant under them, to do all the
rough work. Agnes they called her; and she and me, and James and
Dorothy, with Miss Furnivall and Mrs Stark, made up the family;
always remembering my sweet little Miss Rosamond! I used to
wonder what they had done before she came, they thought so much
of her now. Kitchen and drawing-room, it was all the same. The
hard, sad Miss Furnivall, and the cold Mrs Stark, looked pleased
when she came fluttering in like a bird, playing and pranking hither
and thither, with a continual murmur, and pretty prattle of gladness.
I am sure, they were sorry many a time when she flitted away into
the kitchen, though they were too proud to ask her to stay with
them, and were a little surprised at her taste; though to be sure, as
Mrs Stark said it was not to be wondered at, remembering what
stock her father had come of. The great, old rambling house was a
famous place for little Miss Rosamond. She made expeditions all
over it, with me at her heels; all, except the east wing, which was
never opened, and whither we never thought of going. But in the
western and northern part was many a pleasant room; full of things
that were curiosities to us, though they might not have been to
people who had seen more. The windows were darkened by the

sweeping boughs of the trees, and the ivy which had overgrown them: but, in the green gloom, we could manage to see old China jars and carved ivory boxes, and great heavy books, and, above all, the old pictures!

Once, I remember, my darling would have Dorothy go with us to tell us who they all were; for they were all portraits of some of my lord's family, though Dorothy could not tell us the names of every one. We had gone through most of the rooms, when we came to the old state drawing-room over the hall, and there was a picture of Miss Furnivall; or, as she was called in those days, Miss Grace, for she was the younger sister. Such a beauty she must have been! but with such a set, proud look, and such scorn looking out of her handsome eyes, with her eyebrows just a little raised, as if she were wondering how any one could have the impertinence to look at her; and her lip curled at us, as we stood there gazing. She had a dress on, the like of which I had never seen before, but it was all the fashion when she was young: a hat of some soft white stuff like beaver, pulled a little over her brows, and a beautiful plume of feathers sweeping round it on one side; and her gown of blue satin was open in front to a quilted white stomacher.

'Well, to be sure!' said I, when I had gazed my fill. 'Flesh is grass, they do say; but who would have thought that Miss Furnivall had been such an out-and-out beauty, to see her now?'

'Yes,' said Dorothy. 'Folks change sadly. But if what my master's father used to say was true, Miss Furnivall, the elder sister, was handsomer than Miss Grace. Her picture is here somewhere; but, if I show it you, you must never let on, even to James, that you have seen it. Can the little lady hold her tongue, think you?' asked she.

I was not so sure, for she was such a little sweet, bold, open-spoken child, so I set her to hide herself; and then I helped Dorothy to turn a great picture, that leaned with its face towards the wall, and was not hung up as the others were. To be sure, it beat Miss Grace for beauty; and, I think, for scornful pride, too, though in that matter it might be hard to choose. I could have looked at it an hour, but Dorothy seemed half frightened at having shown it to me, and hurried it back again, and bade me run and find Miss Rosamond, for that there were some ugly places about the house, where she should like ill for the child to go. I was a brave, high-spirited girl, and thought little of what the old woman said, for I liked hide-and-seek as well as any child in the parish; so off I ran to find my little one.

As winter drew on, and the days grew shorter, I was sometimes almost certain that I heard a noise as if some one was playing on the great organ in the hall. I did not hear it every evening; but, certainly, I did very often; usually when I was sitting with Miss Rosamond, after I had put her to bed, and keeping quite still and silent in the bedroom. Then I used to hear it booming and swelling away in the distance. The first night, when I went down to my supper, I asked Dorothy who had been playing music, and James said very shortly that I was a gowk to take the wind soughing among the trees for music: but I saw Dorothy look at him very fearfully, and Bessy, the kitchen-maid, said something beneath her breath, and went quite white. I saw they did not like my question, so I held my peace till I was with Dorothy alone, when I knew I could get a good deal out of her. So, the next day, I watched my time, and I coaxed and asked her who it was that played the organ; for I knew that it was the organ and not the wind well enough, for all I had kept silence before James. But Dorothy had had her lesson, I'll warrant, and never a word could I get from her. So then I tried Bessy, though I had always held my head rather above her, as I was evened to James and Dorothy, and she was little better than their servant. So she said I must never, never tell; and if I ever told, I was never to say *she* had told me; but it was a very strange noise, and she had heard it many a time, but most of all on winter nights, and before storms; and folks did say, it was the old lord playing on the great organ in the hall, just as he used to when he was alive; but who the old lord was, or why he played, and why he played on stormy winter evenings in particular, she either could not or would not tell me. Well! I told you I had a brave heart; and I thought it was rather pleasant to have that grand music rolling about the house, let who would be the player; for now it rose above the great gusts of wind, and wailed and triumphed just like a living creature, and then it fell to a softness most complete; only it was always music and tunes, so it was nonsense to call it the wind. I thought at first that it might be Miss Furnivall who played, unknown to Bessy; but one day when I was in the hall by myself, I opened the organ and peeped all about it and around it, as I had done to the organ in Crosthwaite Church once before, and I saw it was all broken and destroyed inside, though it looked so brave and fine; and then, though it was noonday, my flesh began to creep a little, and I shut it up, and ran away pretty quickly to my own bright nursery; and I did not like hearing the music for some time after that, any more than James and Dorothy did. All this time Miss Rosamond was making herself more and more beloved. The old ladies liked her to dine with them at their early dinner; James stood behind Miss Furnivall's chair, and I behind Miss Rosamond's all in state; and, after dinner, she would play about in a corner of the great drawing-room, as still as any mouse, while Miss Furnivall slept, and I had my dinner in the kitchen. But she was glad enough to come to me in the nursery afterwards; for, as she said, Miss Furnivall was so sad, and Mrs Stark so dull; but she and I were merry enough; and, by-and-by, I got not to care for that weird rolling music, which did one no harm, if we did not know where it came from.

That winter was very cold. In the middle of October the frosts began, and lasted many, many weeks. I remember, one day at dinner, Miss Furnivall lifted up her sad, heavy eyes, and said to Mrs Stark, 'I am afraid we shall have a terrible winter,' in a strange kind of meaning way. But Mrs Stark pretended not to hear, and talked very loud of something else. My little lady and I did not care for the frost; not we! As long as it was dry we climbed up the steep brows, behind the house, and went up on the Fells, which were bleak, and bare enough, and there we ran races in the fresh, sharp air; and once we came down by a new path that took us past the two old gnarled holly-trees, which grew about half-way down by the east side of the house. But the days grew shorter and shorter; and the old lord, if it was he, played more and more stormily and sadly on the great organ. One Sunday afternoon – it must have been towards the end of November – I asked Dorothy to take charge of little Missey when she came out of the drawing-room, after Miss Furnivall had had her nap; for it was too cold to take her with me to church, and yet I wanted to go. And Dorothy was glad enough to promise, and was so fond of the child that all seemed well; Bessy and I set off very briskly, though the sky hung heavy and black over the white earth, as if the night had never fully gone away; and the air, though still, was very biting and keen.

'We shall have a fall of snow,' said Bessy to me. And sure enough, even while we were in church, it came down thick, in great large flakes, so thick it almost darkened the windows. It had stopped snowing before we came out, but it lay soft, thick and deep beneath our feet, as we tramped home. Before we got to the hall the moon rose, and I think it was lighter then, – what with the moon, and what with the white dazzling snow – than it had been when we went to church, between two and three o'clock. I have not told you that Miss Furnivall and Mrs Stark never went to church: they used to read the prayers together, in their quiet gloomy way; they seemed to feel the Sunday very long without their tapestry-work to be busy at. So when I went to Dorothy in the kitchen, to fetch Miss Rosamond and take her upstairs with me, I did not much wonder when the old woman told me that the ladies had kept the child with them, and that she had never come to the kitchen, as I had bidden her, when she was tired of behaving pretty in the drawing-room. So I took off my things and went to find her, and bring her to her supper in the nursery. But when I went into the best drawing-room there sat the two old ladies, very still and quiet, dropping out a word now and then but looking as if nothing so bright and merry as Miss Rosamond had ever been near them. Still I thought she might be hiding from me; it was one of her pretty ways; and that she had per-suaded them to look as if they knew nothing about her, so I went softly peeping under this sofa, and behind that chair, making believe I was sadly frightened at not finding her.

'What's the matter, Hester?' said Mrs Stark, sharply. I don't know if Miss Furnivall had seen me, for, as I told you, she was very deaf, and she sat quite still, idly staring into the fire, with her hopeless face. 'I'm only looking for my little Rosy-Posy,' replied I, still thinking that the child was there, and near me, though I could not see her.

'Miss Rosamond is not here,' said Mrs Stark. 'She went away more than an hour ago to find Dorothy.' And she too turned and went on looking into the fire.

My heart sank at this, and I began to wish I had never left my darling. I went back to Dorothy and told her. James was gone out for the day, but she and me and Bessy took lights and went up into the nursery first, and then we roamed over the great large house, calling and entreating Miss Rosamond to come out of her hiding-place, and not frighten us to death in that way. But there was no answer; no sound.

'Oh!' said I at last, 'Can she have got into the east wing and hidden there?'

But Dorothy said it was not possible, for that she herself had never been there; that the doors were always locked, and my lord's steward had the keys, she believed; at any rate, neither she nor James had ever seen them: so I said I would go back, and see if, after all, she was not hidden in the drawing-room, unknown to the old ladies; and if I found her there, I said, I would whip her well for the fright she had given me; but I never meant to do it. Well, I went back to the west drawing-room, and I told Mrs Stark we could not find her anywhere, and asked for leave to look all about the furniture there, for I thought now, that she might have fallen asleep in some warm hidden corner; but no! we looked, Miss Furnivall got up and looked, trembling all over, and she was nowhere there; then we set off again, every one in the house, and looked in all the places we had searched before, but we could not find her. Miss Furnivall shivered and shook so much that Mrs Stark took her back into the warm drawing-room; but not before they had made me promise to bring her to them when she was found. Well-a-day! I began to think she never would be found, when I bethought me to look out into the great front court, all covered with snow. I was upstairs when I looked out; but it was such clear moonlight, I could see, quite plain, two little footprints, which might be traced from the hall door, and round the corner of the east wing. I don't know how I got down, but I tugged open the great, stiff hall door; and, throwing the skirt of my gown over my head for a cloak, I ran out. I turned the east corner, and there a black shadow fell on the snow; but when I came again into the moonlight, there were the little footmarks going up – up to the Fells. It was bitter cold; so cold that the air almost took the skin off my face as I ran, but I ran on, crying to think how my poor little darling must be perished, and frightened. I was within sight of the holly-trees when I saw a shepherd coming down the hill, bearing something in his arms wrapped in his maud. He shouted to me, and asked me if I had lost a bairn; and, when I could not speak for crying, he bore towards me, and I saw my wee bairnie lying still, and white, and stiff, in his arms, as if she had been dead. He told me he had been up the Fells to gather in his sheep, before the deep cold of night came on, and that under the holly-trees (black marks on the hillside, where no other bush was for miles around) he had found my little lady – my lamb – my queen – my darling – stiff and cold, in the terrible sleep which is frost-begotten. Oh! the joy, and the tears of having her in my arms once again! for I would not let him carry her, but took her, maud and all, into my own arms, and held her near my own warm neck and heart, and felt the life stealing slowly back again into her little gentle limbs. But she was still insensible when we reached the hall, and I had no breath for speech. We went in by the kitchen door.

'Bring the warming-pan,' said I; and I carried her upstairs and began undressing her by the nursery fire, which Bessy had kept up. I called my little lammie all the sweet and playful names I could think of – even while my eyes were blinded by my tears; and at last, oh! at length she opened her large blue eyes. Then I put her into her warm bed, and sent Dorothy down to tell Miss Furnivall that all was well; and I made up my mind to sit by my darling's bedside the live-long night. She fell away into a soft sleep as soon as her pretty head had touched the pillow, and I watched her until morning light; when she wakened up bright and clear – or so I thought at first – and, my dears, so I think now.

She said that she had fancied that she should like to go to Dorothy, for that both the old ladies were asleep, and it was very dull in the drawing-room; and that, as she was going through the west lobby, she saw the snow through the high window falling – falling – soft and steady; but she wanted to see it lying pretty and white on the ground; so she made her way into the great hall; and then, going to the window, she saw it bright and soft upon the drive; but while she stood there, she saw a little girl, not so old as she was, 'but so pretty,' said my darling, 'and this little girl beckoned to me to come out; and oh, she was so pretty and so sweet, I could not choose but to go.' And then this other little girl had taken her by the hand, and side by side the two had gone round the east corner.

'Now you are a naughty little girl, and telling stories,' said I. 'What would your good mamma, that is in heaven, and never told a story in her life, say to her little Rosamond, if she heard her – and I dare say she does – telling stories!'

'Indeed, Hester,' sobbed out my child, 'I'm telling you true. Indeed I am.'

'Don't tell me!' said I, very stern. 'I tracked you by your footmarks through the snow; there were only yours to be seen: and if you had had a little girl to go hand-in-hand with you up the hill, don't you think the footprints would have gone along with yours?'

'I can't help it, dear, dear Hester,' said she, crying, 'if they did not; I never looked at her feet, but she held my hand fast and tight in her little one, and it was very, very cold. She took me up the Fell-path, up to the holly-trees; and there I saw a lady weeping and crying; but when she saw me, she hushed her weeping, and smiled very proud and grand, and took me on her knee, and began to lull me to sleep; and that's all, Hester – but that is true; and my dear mamma knows it is,' said she, crying. So I thought the child was in a fever, and pretended to believe her, as she went over her story – over and over again, and always the same. At last Dorothy knocked at the door with Miss Rosamond's breakfast, and she told me the old ladies were down in the eating parlour, and that they wanted to speak to me. They had both been into the night-nursery the evening before, but it was after Miss Rosamond was asleep; so they had only looked at her – not asked me any questions.

'I shall catch it,' thought I to myself, as I went along the north gallery. 'And yet,' I thought, taking courage, 'it was in their charge I left her; and it's they that's to blame for letting her steal away unknown and unwatched.' So I went in boldly, and told my story. I told it all to Miss Furnivall, shouting close to her ear; but when I came to the mention of the other little girl out in the snow, coaxing and tempting her out, and willing her up to the grand and beautiful lady by the holly-tree, she threw her arms up – her old and withered arms – and cried aloud, 'Oh! Heaven, forgive! Have mercy!'

Mrs Stark took hold of her; roughly enough, I thought; but she was past Mrs Stark's management, and spoke to me, in a kind of wild warning and authority.

'Hester! keep her from that child! It will lure her to her death! That evil child! Tell her it is a wicked, naughty child.' Then Mrs Stark hurried me out of the room; where, indeed, I was glad enough to go; but Miss Furnivall kept shrieking out, 'Oh! have mercy! Wilt Thou never forgive! It is many a long year ago'—

I was very uneasy in my mind after that. I durst never leave Miss Rosamond, night or day, for fear lest she might slip off again, after some fancy or other; and all the more because I thought I could make out that Miss Furnivall was crazy, from the odd ways about her; and I was afraid lest something of the same kind (which might be in the family, you know) hung over my darling. And the great frost never ceased all this time; and whenever it was a more stormy night than usual, between the gusts, and through the wind, we heard the old lord playing on the great organ. But, old lord, or not, wherever Miss Rosamond went, there I followed; for my love for her, pretty helpless orphan, was stronger than my fear for the grand

and terrible sound. Besides, it rested with me to keep her cheerful and merry, as beseemed her age. So we played together, and wandered together, here and there, and everywhere; for I never dared to lose sight of her again in that large and rambling house. And so it happened, that one afternoon, not long before Christmas Day, we were playing together on the billiard-table in the great hall (not that we knew the way of playing, but she liked to roll the smooth ivory balls with her pretty hands, and I liked to do whatever she did); and, by-and-by, without our noticing it, it grew dusk indoors, though it was still light in the open air, and I was thinking of taking her back into the nursery, when, all of a sudden, she cried out:

'Look, Hester! Look! there is my poor little girl out in the snow!'

I turned towards the long narrow windows, and there, sure enough, I saw a little girl, less than my Miss Rosamond – dressed all unfit to be out-of-doors such a bitter night – crying, and beating against the window-panes, as if she wanted to be let in. She seemed to sob and wail, till Miss Rosamond could bear it no longer, and was flying to the door to open it, when, all of a sudden, and close up upon us, the great organ pealed out so loud and thundering, it fairly made me tremble; and all the more when I remembered me that, even in the stillness of that dead-cold weather, I had heard no sound of little battering hands upon the window-glass, although the Phantom Child had seemed to put forth all its force; and, although I had seen it wail and cry, no faintest touch of sound had fallen upon my ears. Whether I remembered all this at the very moment, I do not know; the great organ sound had so stunned me into terror; but this I know, I caught up Miss Rosamond before she got the hall door opened, and clutched her, and carried her away, kicking and screaming, into the large bright kitchen, where Dorothy and Agnes were busy with their mince-pies.

'What is the matter with my sweet one?' cried Dorothy, as I bore in Miss Rosamond, who was sobbing as if her heart would break.

'She won't let me open the door for my little girl to come in; and she'll die if she is out on the Fells all night. Cruel, naughty Hester,' she said, slapping me; but she might have struck harder, for I had seen a look of ghastly terror on Dorothy's face, which made my very blood run cold.

'Shut the back-kitchen door fast, and bolt it well,' said she to Agnes. She said no more; she gave me raisins and almonds to quiet Miss Rosamond: but she sobbed about the little girl in the snow, and would not touch any of the good things. I was thankful when she cried herself to sleep in bed. Then I stole down to the kitchen, and told Dorothy I had made up my mind. I would carry my darling back to my father's house in Applethwaite; where, if we lived humbly, we lived at peace. I said I had been frightened enough with the old lord's organ-playing; but now, that I had seen for myself this little moaning child, all decked out as no child in the neighbourhood could be, beating and battering to get in, yet always without any sound or noise – with the dark wound on its right shoulder; and that Miss Rosamond had known it again for the phantom that had nearly lured her to her death (which Dorothy knew was true); I would stand it no longer.

I saw Dorothy change colour once or twice. When I had done, she told me she did not think I could take Miss Rosamond with me, for that she was my lord's ward, and I had no right over her; and she asked me, would I leave the child that I was so fond of, just for sounds and sights that could do me no harm; and that they had all had to get used to in their turns? I was all in a hot, trembling passion; and I said it was very well for her to talk, that knew what these sights and noises betokened, and that had, perhaps, had something to do with the Spectre-Child while it was alive. And I taunted her so, that she told me all she knew, at last; and then I wished I had never been told, for it only made me afraid more than ever.

She said she had heard the tale from old neighbours, that were alive when she was first married; when folks used to come to the hall sometimes, before it had got such a bad name on the countryside: it might not be true, or it might, what she had been told.

The old lord was Miss Furnivall's father – Miss Grace as Dorothy called her, for Miss Maude was the elder, and Miss Furnivall by rights. The old lord was eaten up with pride. Such a proud man was never seen or heard of; and his daughters were like him. No one was good enough to wed them, although they had choice enough; for they were the great beauties of their day, as I had seen by their portraits, where they hung in the state drawing-room. But, as the old saying is, 'Pride will have a fall'; and these two haughty beauties fell in love with the same man, and he no better than a foreign musician, whom their father had down from London to play music with him at the Manor House. For, above all things, next to his pride, the old lord loved music. He could play on nearly every instrument that ever was heard of: and it was a strange thing it did not soften him; but he was a fierce dour old man, and had broken his poor wife's heart with his cruelty, they said. He was mad after music, and would pay any money for it. So he got this foreigner to come; who made such beautiful music, that they said the very birds on the trees stopped their singing to listen. And, by degrees, this foreign gentleman got such a hold over the old lord, that nothing would serve him but that he must come every year; and it was he that had the great organ brought from Holland, and built up in the hall, where it stood now. He taught the old lord to play on it; but many and many a time, when Lord Furnivall was thinking of nothing but his fine organ, and his finer music, the dark foreigner was walking abroad in the woods with one of the young ladies; now Miss Maude, and then Miss Grace.

Miss Maude won the day and carried off the prize, such as it was; and he and she were married, all unknown to any one; and before he made his next yearly visit, she had been confined of a little girl at a farm-house on the Moors, while her father and Miss Grace thought she was away at Doncaster Races. But though she was a wife and a mother, she was not a bit softened, but as haughty and as passionate as ever, and perhaps more so, for she was jealous of Miss Grace, to whom her foreign husband paid a deal of court – by way of blinding her – as he told his wife. But Miss Grace triumphed over Miss Maude, and Miss Maude grew fiercer and fiercer, both with her husband and with her sister; and the former – who could easily shake off what was disagreeable, and hide himself in foreign countries – went away a month before his usual time that summer, and half-threatened that he would never come back again. Meanwhile, the little girl was left at the farm-house, and her mother used to have her horse saddled and gallop wildly over the hills to see her once every week, at the very least – for where she loved, she loved; and where she hated, she hated. And the old lord went on playing – playing on his organ; and the servants thought the sweet music he made had soothed down his awful temper, of which (Dorothy said) some terrible tales could be told. He grew infirm too, and had to walk with a crutch; and his son – that was the present Lord Furnivall's father – was with the army in America, and the other son at sea; so Miss Maude had it pretty much her own way, and she and Miss Grace grew colder and bitterer to each other every day; till at last they hardly ever spoke, except when the old lord was by. The foreign musician came again the next summer, but it was for the last time; for they led him such a life with their jealousy and their passions, that he grew weary, and went away, and never was heard of again. And Miss Maude, who had always meant to have her marriage acknowledged when her father should be dead, was left now a deserted wife – whom nobody knew to have been married – with a child that she dared not own, although she loved it to distraction; living with a father whom she feared, and a sister whom she hated. When the next summer passed over and the dark foreigner never came, both Miss Maude and Miss Grace grew gloomy and sad; they had a haggard look about them, though they looked handsome as ever. But by-and-by Miss Maude brightened; for her father grew more and more infirm, and more than ever carried away by his music; and she and Miss Grace lived almost entirely apart, having separate rooms, the one on the west side, Miss Maude on the east – those very rooms which were now shut up. So she thought she might have her little girl with her, and no one need ever know except those who dared not speak about it, and were bound to believe that it was, as she said, a cottager's child she had taken a fancy to. All this, Dorothy said, was pretty well known; but what came afterwards no one knew, except Miss Grace, and Mrs Stark, who was even then her maid, and much more of a friend to her than ever her sister had been. But the servants supposed, from words that were dropped, that Miss Maude had triumphed over Miss Grace, and told her that all the time the dark foreigner had been mocking her with pretended love – he was her own husband; the colour left Miss Grace's cheek and lips that very day for ever, and she was heard to say many a time that sooner or later she would have her revenge; and Mrs Stark was for ever spying about the east rooms.

One fearful night, just after the New Year had come in, when the snow was lying thick and deep, and the flakes were still falling – fast enough to blind any one who might be out and abroad – there was a great and violent noise heard, and the old lord's voice above all, cursing and swearing awfully – and the cries of a little child – and the proud defiance of a fierce woman – and the sound of a blow – and a dead stillness – and moans and wailings dying away on the hill-side! Then the old lord summoned all his servants, and told them, with terrible oaths, and words more terrible, that his daughter had disgraced herself, and that he had turned her out of doors – her, and her child – and that if ever they gave her help – or food – or shelter – he prayed that they might never enter Heaven. And, all the while, Miss Grace stood by him, white and still as any stone; and when he had ended she heaved a great sigh, as much as to say her work was done, and her end was accomplished. But the old lord never touched his organ again, and died within the year; and no wonder! for, on the morrow of that wild and fearful night, the shepherds, coming down the Fell side, found Miss Maude sitting, all crazy and smiling, under the holly-trees, nursing a dead child – with a terrible mark on its right shoulder. 'But that was not what killed it,' said Dorothy; 'it was the frost and the cold; – every wild creature was in its hole, and every beast in its fold – while the child and its mother were turned out to wander on the Fells! And now you know all! and I wonder if you are less frightened now?'

I was more frightened than ever; but I said I was not. I wished Miss Rosamond and myself well out of that dreadful house for ever;

but I would not leave her, and I dared not take her away. But oh! how I watched her, and guarded her! We bolted the doors and shut the window-shutters fast, an hour or more before dark, rather than leave them open five minutes too late. But my little lady still heard the weird child crying and mourning; and not all we could do or say could keep her from wanting to go to her, and let her in from the cruel wind and the snow. All this time, I kept away from Miss Furnivall and Mrs Stark, as much as ever I could; for I feared them – I knew no good could be about them, with their grey hard faces, and their dreamy eyes, looking back into the ghastly years that were gone. But, even in my fear, I had a kind of pity – for Miss Furnivall, at least. Those gone down to the pit can hardly have a more hopeless look than that which was ever on her face. At last I even got so sorry for her – who never said a word but what was quite forced from her – that I prayed for her; and I taught Miss Rosamond to pray for one who had done a deadly sin; but often when she came to those words, she would listen, and start up from her knees, and say, 'I hear my little girl plaining and crying very sad – Oh! let her in, or she will die!'

One night – just after New Year's Day had come at last, and the long winter had taken a turn, as I hoped – I heard the west drawing-room bell ring three times, which was a signal for me. I would not leave Miss Rosamond alone, for all she was asleep – for the old lord had been playing wilder than ever – and I feared lest my darling should waken to hear the Spectre-Child; see her I knew she could not. I had fastened the windows too well for that. So I took her out of her bed and wrapped her up in such outer clothes as were most handy, and carried her down to the drawing-room, where the old ladies sat at their tapestry-work as usual. They looked up when I came in, and Mrs Stark asked, quite astounded, 'Why did I bring Miss Rosamond there, out of her warm bed?' I had begun to whisper, 'Because I was afraid of her being tempted out while I was away, by the wild child in the snow,' when she stopped me short (with a glance at Miss Furnivall), and said Miss Furnivall wanted me to undo some work she had done wrong, and which neither of them could see to unpick. So I laid my pretty dear on the sofa, and sat down on a stool by them, and hardened my heart against them, as I heard the wind rising and howling.

Miss Rosamond slept on sound, for all the wind blew so; and Miss Furnivall said never a word, nor looked round when the gusts shook the windows. All at once she started up to her full height, and put up one hand, as if to bid us listen.

'I hear voices!' said she, 'I hear terrible screams – I hear my father's voice!'

Just at that moment my darling wakened with a sudden start: 'My little girl is crying, oh, how she is crying!' and she tried to get up and go to her, but she got her feet entangled in the blanket, and I caught her up; for my flesh had begun to creep at these noises, which they heard while we could catch no sound. In a minute or two the noises came, and gathered fast, and filled our ears; we, too, heard voices and screams, and no longer heard the winter's wind that raged abroad. Mrs Stark looked at me, and I at her, but we dared not speak. Suddenly Miss Furnivall went towards the door, out into the ante-room, through the west lobby, and opened the door into the great hall. Mrs Stark followed, and I durst not be left, though my heart almost stopped beating for fear. I wrapped my darling tight in my arms, and went out with them. In the hall the screams were louder than ever; they sounded to come from the east wing – nearer and nearer – close on the other side of the locked-up doors – close behind them. Then I noticed that the great bronze chandelier seemed all alight, though the hall was dim, and that a fire was blazing in the vast hearth-place, though it gave no heat; and I shuddered up with terror, and folded my darling closer to me. But as I did so, the east door shook, and she, suddenly struggling to get free from me, cried, 'Hester, I must go! My little girl is there; I hear her; she is coming! Hester, I must go!'

I held her tight with all my strength; with a set will, I held her. If I had died, my hands would have grasped her still, I was so resolved in my mind. Miss Furnivall stood listening, and paid no regard to my darling, who had got down to the ground, and whom I, upon my knees now, was holding with both my arms clasped round her neck; she still striving and crying to get free.

All at once the east door gave way with a thundering crash, as if torn open in a violent passion, and there came into that broad and mysterious light, the figure of a tall old man, with grey hair and gleaming eyes. He drove before him, with many a relentless gesture of abhorrence, a stern and beautiful woman, with a little child clinging to her dress.

'O Hester! Hester!' cried Miss Rosamond. 'It's the lady! the lady below the holly-trees; and my little girl is with her. Hester! Hester! let me go to her; they are drawing me to them. I feel them – I feel them. I must go!'

Again she was almost convulsed by her efforts to get away; but I held her tighter and tighter, till I feared I should do her a hurt; but rather that than let her go towards those terrible phantoms. They passed along towards the great hall-door, where the winds howled and ravened for their prey; but before they reached that, the lady turned; and I could see that she defied the old man with a fierce and proud defiance; but then she quailed – and then she threw up her arms wildly and piteously to save her child – her little child – from a blow from his uplifted crutch.

And Miss Rosamond was torn as if by a power stronger than mine, and writhed in my arms, and sobbed (for by this time the poor darling was growing faint).

'They want me to go with them on to the Fells – they are drawing me to them. Oh, my little girl! I would come, but cruel, wicked Hester holds me very tight.' But when she saw the uplifted crutch she swooned away, and I thanked God for it. Just at this moment – when the tall old man, his hair streaming as in the blast of a furnace, was going to strike the little shrinking child – Miss Furnivall, the old woman by my side, cried out, 'Oh, father! father! spare the little innocent child!' But just then I saw – we all saw – another phantom shape itself, and grow clear out of the blue and misty light that filled the hall; we had not seen her till now, for it was another lady who stood by the old man, with a look of relentless hate and triumphant scorn. That figure was very beautiful to look upon, with a soft white hat drawn down over the proud brows and a red and curling lip. It was dressed in an open robe of blue satin. I had seen that figure before. It was the likeness of Miss Furnivall in her youth; and the terrible phantoms moved on, regardless of old Miss Furnivall's wild entreaty – and the uplifted crutch fell on the right shoulder of the little child, and the younger sister looked on, stony and deadly serene. But at that moment the dim lights, and the fire that gave no heat, went out of themselves, and Miss Furnivall lay at our feet stricken down by the palsy – death-stricken.

Yes! she was carried to her bed that night never to rise again. She lay with her face to the wall muttering low but muttering away: 'Alas! Alas! what is done in youth can never be undone in age! What is done in youth can never be undone in age!'

Amelia B. Edwards

THE STORY OF SALOME

A few years ago, no matter how many, I, Harcourt Blunt, was travelling with my friend Coventry Turnour, and it was on the steps of our hotel that I received from him the announcement – he sent one to me – that he was again in love.

'I tell you, Blunt,' said my fellow-traveller, 'she's the loveliest creature I ever beheld in my life.'

I laughed outright.

'My dear fellow,' I replied, 'you've so often seen the loveliest creature you ever beheld in your life.'

'Ay, but I am in earnest now for the first time.'

'And you have so often been in earnest for the first time! Remember the innkeeper's daughter at Cologne.'

'A pretty housemaid, whom no training could have made presentable.'

'Then there was the beautiful American at Interlachen.'

'Yes; but—'

'And the Bella Marchesa at Prince Torlonia's ball.'

'Not one of them worthy to be named in the same breath with my imperial Venetian. Come with me to the Merceria and be convinced. By taking a gondola to St Mark's Place we shall be there in a quarter of an hour.'

I went, and he raved of his new flame all the way. She was a

Jewess – he would convert her. Her father kept a shop in the Merceria – what of that? He dealt only in costliest Oriental merchandise, and was as rich as a Rothschild. As for any probable injury to his own prospects, why need he hesitate on that account? What were 'prospects' when weighed against the happiness of one's whole life? Besides, he was not ambitious. He didn't care to go into Parliament. If his uncle Sir Geoffrey cut him off with a shilling, what then? He had a moderate independence of which no one living could deprive him, and what more could any reasonable man desire?

I listened, smiled, and was silent. I knew Coventry Turnour too well to attach the smallest degree of importance to anything that he might say or do in a matter of this kind. To be distractedly in love was his normal condition. We had been friends from boyhood; and since the time when he used to cherish a hopeless attachment to the young lady behind the counter of the tart-shop at Harrow, I had never known him 'fancy-free' for more than a few weeks at a time. He had gone through every phase of no less than three *grandes passions* during the five months that we had now been travelling together; and having left Rome about eleven weeks before with every hope laid waste, and a heart so broken that it could never by any possibility be put together again, he was now, according to the natural course of events, just ready to fall in love again.

We landed at the traghetto San Marco. It was a cloudless morning towards the middle of April, just ten years ago. The ducal palace glowed in the hot sunshine; the boatmen were clustered, gossiping, about the Molo; the orange-vendors were busy under the arches of the piazzetta; the flâneurs were already eating ices and smoking cigarettes outside the cafés. There was an Austrian military band, strapped, buckled, moustachioed, and white-coated, playing just in front of St Mark's; and the shadow of the great bell-tower slept all across the square.

Passing under the low round archway leading to the Merceria, we plunged at once into that cool labyrinth of narrow, intricate, and picturesque streets, where the sun never penetrates – where no wheels are heard, and no beast of burden is seen – where every house is a shop, and every shop-front is open to the ground, as in an Oriental bazaar – where the upper balconies seem almost to meet overhead, and are separated by only a strip of burning sky – and where more than three people cannot march abreast in any part. Pushing our way as best we might through the motley crowd that here chatters, cheapens, buys, sells, and perpetually bustles to and fro, we came presently to a shop for the sale of Eastern goods. A few glass jars filled with spices, and some pieces of stuff, untidily strewed the counter next the street; but within, dark and narrow though it seemed, the place was crammed with costliest merchandise. Cases of gorgeous Oriental jewellery, embroideries and fringes of massive gold and silver bullion, precious drugs and spices, exquisite toys in filigree, miracles of carving in ivory, sandal-wood, and amber, jewelled yataghans, scimitars of state rich with 'barbaric pearl and gold', bales of Cashmere shawls, China silks, India muslins, gauzes, and the like, filled every inch of available space from floor to ceiling, leaving only a narrow lane from the door to the counter, and a still narrower passage to the rooms beyond the shop.

We went in. A young woman, who was sitting reading on a low seat behind the counter, laid aside her book, and rose slowly. She was dressed wholly in black. I cannot describe the fashion of her garments. I only know that they fell about her in long, soft, trailing folds, leaving a narrow band of fine cambric visible at the throat and wrists; and that, however graceful and unusual this dress may have been, I scarcely observed it, so entirely was I taken up with admiration of her beauty.

For she was indeed very beautiful – beautiful in a way that I had not anticipated. Coventry Turnour, with all his enthusiasm, had failed to do her justice. He had raved of her eyes – her large, lustrous, melancholy eyes – of the transparent paleness of her complexion, of the faultless delicacy of her features; but he had not prepared me for the unconscious dignity, the perfect nobleness and refinement, that informed her every look and gesture. My friend requested to see a bracelet at which he had been looking the day before. Proud, stately, silent, she unlocked the case in which it was kept, and laid it before him on the counter. He asked permission to take it over to the light. She bent her head, but answered not a word. It was like being waited upon by a young empress.

Turnour took the bracelet to the door and affected to examine it. It consisted of a double row of gold coins linked together at intervals by a bean-shaped ornament, studded with pink coral and diamonds. Coming back into the shop he asked me if I thought it would please his sister, to whom he had promised a remembrance of Venice.

'It is a pretty trifle,' I replied; 'but surely a remembrance of Venice should be of Venetian manufacture. This, I suppose, is Turkish.'

The beautiful Jewess looked up. We spoke in English; but she understood and replied:

'E Greco, signore,' she said coldly.

At this moment an old man came suddenly forward from some dark counting-house at the back – a grizzled, bearded, eager-eyed Shylock, with a pen behind his ear.

'Go in, Salome – go in, my daughter,' he said hurriedly. 'I will serve these gentlemen.'

She lifted her eyes to his for one moment – then moved silently away, and vanished in the gloom of the room beyond.

We saw her no more. We lingered awhile, looking over the contents of the jewel-cases; but in vain. Then Turnour bought his bracelet, and we went out again into the narrow streets, and back to the open daylight of the Gran' Piazza.

'Well,' he said breathlessly, 'what do you think of her?'

'She is very lovely.'

'Lovelier than you expected?'

'Much lovelier. But—'

'But what?'

'The sooner you succeed in forgetting her, the better.'

He vowed, of course, that he never would and never could forget her. He would hear of no incompatibilities, listen to no objections, believe in no obstacles. That the beautiful Salome was herself not only unconscious of his passion and indifferent to his person, but ignorant of his very name and station, were facts not even to be admitted on the list of difficulties. Finding him thus deaf to reason, I said no more.

It was all over, however, before the week was out.

'Look here, Blunt,' he said, coming up to me one morning in the coffee-room of our hotel just as I was sitting down to answer a pile of home-letters; 'would you like to go on to Trieste tomorrow? There, don't look at me like that – you can guess how it is with me. I was a fool ever to suppose she would care for me – a stranger, a foreigner, a Christian. Well, I'm horribly out of sorts anyhow – and – and I wish I was a thousand miles off at this moment!'

We travelled on together to Athens, and there parted, Turnour being bound for England, and I for the East. My own tour lasted many months longer. I went first to Egypt and the Holy Land; then joined an exploring party on the Euphrates; and at length, after just twelve months of Oriental life, found myself back again at Trieste about the middle of April in the year following that during which occurred the events I have just narrated. There I found that batch of letters and papers to which I had been looking forward for many weeks past; and amongst the former, one from Coventry Turnour. This time he was not only irrecoverably in love, but on the eve of matrimony. The letter was rapturous and extravagant enough. The writer was the happiest of men; his destined bride the loveliest and most amiable of her sex; the future a paradise; the past a melancholy series of mistakes. As for love, he had never, of course, known what it was till now.

And what of the beautiful Salome?

Not one word of her from beginning to end. He had forgotten her as utterly as if she had never existed. And yet how desperately in love and how desperately in despair he was 'one little year ago'! Ah, yes; but then it *was* 'one little year ago'; and who that had ever known Coventry Turnour would expect him to remember *la plus grande des grandes passions* for even half that time?

I slept that night at Trieste, and went on next day to Venice.

Somehow, I could not get Turnour and his love affairs out of my head. I remembered our visit to the Merceria. I was haunted by the image of the beautiful Jewess. Was she still so lovely? Did she still sit reading in her wonted seat by the open counter, with the gloomy shop reaching away behind, and the cases of rich robes and jewels all around?

An irresistible impulse prompted me to go to the Merceria and see her once again. I went. It had been a busy morning with me, and I did not get there till between three and four o'clock in the afternoon. The place was crowded. I passed up the well-remembered street, looking out on both sides for the gloomy little shop with its unattractive counter; but in vain. When I had gone so far that I thought I must have passed it, I turned back. House by house I retraced my steps to the very entrance, and still could not find it. Then, concluding that I had not gone far enough at first, I turned back again till I reached a spot where several streets diverged. Here I came to a standstill, for beyond this point I knew I had not passed before.

It was now only too evident that the Jew no longer occupied his former shop in the Merceria, and that my chance of discovering his whereabouts was exceedingly slender. I could not inquire of his successor, because I could not identify the house. I found it impossible even to remember what trades were carried on by his neighbours on either side. I was ignorant of his very name. Convinced, therefore, of the inutility of making any further effort, I gave up the search, and comforted myself by reflecting that my own heart was not made of adamant, and that it was, perhaps, better for my peace not to see the beautiful Salome again. I was destined to see her again, however, and that ere many days had passed over my head.

A year of more than ordinarily fatiguing Eastern travel had left me in need of rest, and I had resolved to allow myself a month's sketching in Venice and its neighbourhood before turning my face homewards. As, therefore, it is manifestly the first object of a sketcher to select his points of view, and as no more luxurious machine than a Venetian gondola was ever invented for the use of man, I proceeded to employ the first days of my stay in endless boatings to and fro: now exploring all manner of canals and canaletti; rowing out in the direction of Murano; now making for the islands beyond San Pietro Castello, and in the course of these pilgrimages noting down an infinite number of picturesque sites, and smoking an infinite number of cigarettes. It was, I think, about the fourth or fifth day of this pleasant work, when my gondolier proposed to take me as far as the Lido. It wanted about two hours to sunset, and the great sandbank lay not more than three or four miles away; so I gave the word, and in another moment we had changed our route and were gliding farther and farther from Venice at each dip of the oar. Then the long dull distant ridge that had all day bounded the shallow horizon rose gradually above the placid level of the Lagune, assumed a more broken outline, resolved itself into hillocks and hollows of tawny sand, showed here and there a patch of parched grass and tangled brake, and looked like the coasts of some inhospitable desert beyond which no traveller might penetrate. My boatman made straight for a spot where some stakes at the water's edge gave token of a landing-place; and here, though with some difficulty, for the tide was low, ran the gondola aground. I landed. My first step was among graves.

'E'l cimeterio giudaico, signore,' said my gondolier, with a touch of his cap.

The Jewish cemetery! The ghetto of the dead! I remembered now to have read or heard long since how the Venetian Jews, cut off in death as in life from the neighbourhood of their Christian rulers, had been buried from immemorial time upon this desolate waste. I stooped to examine the headstone at my feet. It was but a shattered fragment, crusted over with yellow lichens, and eaten away by the salt sea air. I passed on to the next, and the next. Some were completely matted over with weeds and brambles; some were half-buried in the drifting sand; of some, only a corner remained above the surface. Here and there a name, a date, a fragment of heraldic carving, or part of a Hebrew inscription, was yet legible; but all were more or less broken and effaced.

Wandering on thus among graves and hillocks, ascending at every step, and passing some three or four glassy pools overgrown with gaunt-looking reeds, I presently found that I had reached the central and most elevated part of the Lido, and that I commanded an uninterrupted view on every side. On the one hand lay the broad, silent Lagune bounded by Venice and the Euganean hills – on the other, stealing up in long, lazy folds, and breaking noiselessly against the endless shore, the blue Adriatic. An old man gathering shells on the seaward side, a distant gondola on the Lagune, were the only signs of life for miles around.

Standing on the upper ridge of this narrow barrier, looking upon both waters, and watching the gradual approach of what promised to be a gorgeous sunset, I fell into one of those wandering trains of thought in which the real and unreal succeed each other as capriciously as in a dream. I remembered how Goethe here conceived his vertebral theory of the skull – how Byron, too lame to walk, kept his horse on the Lido, and here rode daily to and fro – how Shelley loved the wild solitude of the place, wrote of it in *Julian and Maddalo*, listened, perhaps from this very spot, to the mad-house bell on the island of San Giorgio. Then I wondered if Titian had ever come hither from his gloomy house on the other side of Venice, to study the gold and purple of these western skies – if Othello had walked here with Desdemona – if Shylock was buried yonder, and Leah whom he loved 'when he was a bachelor'.

And then in the midst of my reverie, I came suddenly upon another Jewish cemetery.

Was it indeed another, or but an outlying portion of the first? It was evidently another, and a more modern one. The ground was better kept. The monuments were newer. Such dates as I had succeeded in deciphering on the broken sepulchres lower down were all of the fourteenth and fifteenth centuries; but the inscriptions upon these bore reference to quite recent interments.

I went on a few steps farther. I stopped to copy a quaint Italian couplet on one tomb – to gather a wild forget-me-not from the foot of another – to put aside a bramble that trailed across a third – and then I became aware for the first time of a lady sitting beside a grave not a dozen yards from the spot on which I stood.

I had believed myself so utterly alone, and was so taken by surprise, that for the first moment I could almost have persuaded myself that she also was 'of the stuff that dreams are made of'. She was dressed from head to foot in the deepest mourning; her face turned from me, looking towards the sunset; her cheek resting in the palm of her hand. The grave by which she sat was obviously recent. The scant herbage round about had been lately disturbed, and the marble headstone looked as if it had not yet undergone a week's exposure to wind and weather.

Persuaded that she had not observed me, I lingered for an instant looking at her. Something in the grace and sorrow of her attitude, something in the turn of her head and the flow of her sable draperies, arrested my attention. Was she young? I fancied so. Did she mourn a husband? – a lover? – a parent? I glanced towards the headstone. It was covered with Hebrew characters; so that, had I even been nearer, it could have told me nothing.

But I felt that I had no right to stand there, a spectator of her sorrow, an intruder on his privacy. I proceeded to move noiselessly away. At that moment she turned and looked at me.

It was Salome.

Salome, pale and worn as from some deep and wasting grief, but more beautiful, if that could be, than ever. Beautiful, with a still more spiritual beauty than of old; with cheeks so wan and eyes so unutterably bright and solemn, that my very heart seemed to stand still as I looked upon them. For one second I paused, half fancying, half hoping that there was recognition in her glance; then, not daring to look or linger longer, turned away. When I had gone far enough to do so without discourtesy, I stopped and gazed back. She had resumed her former attitude, and was looking over towards Venice and the setting sun. The stone by which she watched was not more motionless.

The sun went down in glory. The last flush faded from the domes and bell-towers of Venice; the western peaks changed from rose to purple, from gold to grey; a scarcely perceptible film of mist became all at once visible upon the surface of the Lagune; and overhead, the first star trembled into light. I waited and watched till the shadows had so deepened that I could no longer distinguish one distant object from another. Was that the spot? Was she still there? Was she moving? Was she gone? I could not tell. The more I looked, the more uncertain I became. Then, fearing to miss my way in the fast gathering twilight, I struck down towards the water's edge, and made for the point at which I had landed.

I found my gondolier fast asleep, with his head on a cushion, and his bit of gondola-carpet thrown over him for a counterpane. I asked if he had seen any other boat put off from the Lido since I left? He rubbed his eyes, started up, and was awake in a moment.

'*Per Bacco, signore*, I have been asleep,' he said apologetically: 'I have seen nothing.'

'Did you observe any other boat moored hereabouts when we landed?'

'None, *signore*.'

'And you have seen nothing of a lady in black?'

He laughed and shook his head.

'*Consolatevi, signore*,' he said archly. 'She will come tomorrow.'

Then, finding that I looked grave, he touched his cap, and with a gentle, '*Scusate, signore*,' took his place at the stern, and there waited. I bade him row to my hotel; and then, leaning dreamily back in my little dark cabin, I folded my arms, closed my eyes, and thought of Salome.

How lovely she was! How infinitely more lovely than even my first remembrance of her! How was it that I had not admired her more that day in the Merceria? Was I blind, or had she become indeed more beautiful? It was a sad and strange place in which to meet her again. By whose grave was she watching? By her father's? Yes, surely by her father's. He was an old man when I saw him, and in the course of nature had not long to live. He was dead: hence my unavailing search in the Merceria. He was dead. His shop was let to another occupant. His stock-in-trade was sold and dispersed. And

Salome – was she left alone? Had she no mother? no brother? – no lover? Would her eyes have had that look of speechless woe in them if she had any very near or dear tie left on earth? Then I thought of Coventry Turnour, and his approaching marriage. Did he ever really love her? I doubted it. 'True love,' saith an old song, 'can ne'er forget'; but he had forgotten, as though the past had been a dream. And yet he was in earnest while it lasted – would have risked all for her sake, if she would have listened to him. Ah, if she *had* listened to him! And then I remembered that he had never told me the particulars of that affair. Did she herself reject him, or did he lay his suit before her father? And was he rejected only because he was a Christian? I had never cared to ask these things while we were together; but now I would have given the best hunter in my stables to know every minute detail connected with the matter.

Pondering thus, travelling over the same ground again and again, wondering whether she remembered me, whether she was poor, whether she was indeed alone in the world, how long the old man had been dead, and a hundred other things of the same kind – I scarcely noticed how the watery miles glided past, or how the night closed in. One question, however, recurred oftener than any other: How was I to see her again?

I arrived at my hotel; I dined at the *table d'hôte*; I strolled out, after dinner, to my favourite café in the piazza; I dropped in for half an hour at the Fenice, and heard one act of an extremely poor opera; I came home restless, uneasy, wakeful; and sitting for hours before my bedroom fire, asked myself the same perpetual question, How was I to see her again?

Fairly tired out at last, I fell asleep in my chair, and when I awoke the sun was shining upon my window.

I started to my feet. I had it now. It flashed upon me, as if it came with the sunlight. I had but to go again to the cemetery, copy the inscription upon the old man's tomb, ask my learned friend Professor Nicolai, of Padua, to translate it for me, and then, once in possession of names and dates, the rest would be easy.

In less than an hour, I was once more on my way to the Lido.

I took a rubbing of the stone. It was the quickest way, and the surest; for I knew that in Hebrew everything depended on the pointing of the characters, and I feared to trust my own untutored skill. This done, I hastened back, wrote my letter to the professor, and dispatched both letter and rubbing by the midday train.

The professor was not a prompt man. On the contrary he was a pre-eminently slow man; dreamy, indolent, buried in Oriental lore. From any other correspondent one might have looked for a reply in the course of the morrow; but from Nicolai of Padua it would have been folly to expect one under two or three days. And in the meanwhile? Well, in the meanwhile there were churches and palaces to be seen, sketches to be made, letters of introduction to be delivered. It was, at all events, of no use to be impatient.

And yet I was impatient – so impatient that I could neither sketch, nor read, nor sit still for ten minutes together. Possessed by an uncontrollable restlessness, I wandered from gallery to gallery, from palace to palace, from church to church. The imprisonment of even a gondola was irksome to me. I was, as it were, impelled to be moving and doing; and even so, the day seemed endless.

The next was even worse. There was just the possibility of a reply from Padua, and the knowledge of that possibility unsettled me for the day. Having watched and waited for every post from eight to four, I went down to the traghetto of St Mark's, and was there hailed by my accustomed gondolier.

He touched his cap and waited for orders.

'Where to, *signore*?' he asked, finding that I remained silent.

'To the Lido.'

It was an irresistible temptation, and I yielded to it; but I yielded in opposition to my judgment. I knew that I ought not to haunt the place. I had resolved that I would not. And yet I went.

Going along, I told myself that I had only come to reconnoitre. It was not unlikely that she might be going to the same spot about the same hour as before; and in that case I might overtake her gondola by the way, or find it moored somewhere along the shore. At all events, I was determined not to land. But we met no gondola beyond San Pietro Castello; saw no sign of one along the shore. The afternoon was far advanced; the sun was near going down; we had the Lagune and the Lido to ourselves.

My boatman made for the same landing-place, and moored his gondola to the same stake as before. He took it for granted that I meant to land; and I landed. After all, however, it was evident that Salome could not be there, in which case I was guilty of no intrusion. I might stroll in the direction of the cemetery, taking care to avoid her, if she were anywhere about, and keeping well away from that part where I had last seen her. So I broke another resolve, and went up towards the top of the Lido. Again I came to the salt pools and the reeds; again stood with the sea upon my left hand and the Lagune upon my right, and the endless sandbank reaching on for miles between the two. Yonder lay the new cemetery. Standing thus I overlooked every foot of the ground. I could even distinguish the headstone of which I had taken the rubbing the morning before. There was no living thing in sight. I was, to all appearance, as utterly alone as Enoch Arden on his desert island.

Then I strolled on, a little nearer, and a little nearer still; and then, contrary to all my determinations, I found myself standing upon the very spot, beside the very grave, which I had made my mind on no account to approach.

The sun was now just going down – had gone down, indeed, behind a bank of golden-edged cumuli – and was flooding earth, sea, and sky with crimson. It was at this hour that I saw her. It was upon this spot that she was sitting. A few scant blades of grass had sprung up here and there upon the grave. Her dress must have touched them as she sat there – her dress; perhaps her hand. I gathered one, and laid it carefully between the leaves of my note-book.

At last I turned to go, and, turning, met her face to face!

She was distant about six yards, and advancing slowly towards the spot on which I was standing. Her head drooped slightly forward; her hands were clasped together; her eyes were fixed upon the ground. It was the attitude of a nun. Startled, confused, scarcely knowing what I did, I took off my hat, and drew aside to let her pass.

She looked up – hesitated – stood still – gazed at me with a strange, steadfast, mournful expression – then dropped her eyes again, passed me without another glance, and resumed her former place and attitude beside her father's grave.

I turned away. I would have given worlds to speak to her; but I had not dared, and the opportunity was gone. Yet I might have spoken! She looked at me – looked at me with so strange and piteous an expression in her eyes – continued looking at me as long as one might have counted five . . . I might have spoken. I surely might have spoken! And now – ah! now it was impossible. She had fallen into the old thoughtful attitude with her cheek resting on her hand. Her thoughts were far away. She had forgotten my very presence.

I went back to the shore, more disturbed and uneasy than ever. I spent all the remaining daylight in rowing up and down the margin of the Lido, looking for her gondola – hoping, at all events, to see her put off – to follow her, perhaps, across the waste of waters. But the dusk came quickly on, and then darkness, and I left at last without having seen any further sign or token of her presence.

Lying awake that night, tossing uneasily upon my bed, and thinking over the incidents of the last few days, I found myself perpetually recurring to that long, steady, sorrowful gaze which she fixed upon me in the cemetery. The more I thought of it, the more I seemed to feel that there was in it some deeper meaning than I, in my confusion, had observed at the time. It was such a strange look – a look almost of entreaty, of asking for help or sympathy; like the dumb appeal in the eyes of a sick animal. Could this really be? What, after all, more possible than that, left alone in the world – with, perhaps, not a single male relation to advise her – she found herself in some position of present difficulty, and knew not where to turn for help? All this might well be. She had even, perhaps, some instinctive feeling that she might trust me. Ah! if she would indeed trust me . . .

I had hoped to receive my Paduan letter by the morning delivery; but morning and afternoon went by as before, and still no letter came. As the day began to decline, I was again on my way to the Lido; this time for the purpose, and with the intention, of speaking to her. I landed, and went direct to the cemetery. It had been a dull day. Lagune and sky were both one leaden uniform grey, and a mist hung over Venice.

I saw her from the moment I reached the upper ridge. She was walking slowly to and fro among the graves, like a stately shadow. I had felt confident, somehow, that she would be there; and now, for some reason that I could not have defined for my life, I felt equally confident that she expected me.

Trembling and eager, yet half dreading the moment when she should discover my presence, I hastened on, printing the loose sand at every noiseless step. A few moments more, and I should overtake her, speak to her, hear the music of her voice – that music which I remembered so well, though a year had gone by since I last heard it. But how should I address her? What had I to say? I knew not. I had no time to think. I could only hurry on till within some ten feet of her trailing garments; stand still when she turned, and uncover before her as if she were a queen.

She paused and looked at me, just as she had paused and looked at me the evening before. With the same sorrowful meaning in her eyes; with even more than the same entreating expression. But she waited for me to speak.

I did speak. I cannot recall what I said; I only know that I faltered something of an apology – mentioned that I had had the honour of meeting her before, many months ago; and, trying to say more – trying to express how thankfully and proudly I would devote myself to any service, however humble, however laborious, I failed both in voice and words, and broke down utterly.

Having come to a stop, I looked up, and found her eyes still fixed upon me.

'You are a Christian,' she said.

A trembling came upon me at the first sound of her voice. It was the same voice; distinct, melodious, scarce louder than a whisper – and yet it was not quite the same. There was a melancholy in the music, and, if I may use a word which, after all, fails to express my meaning, a *remoteness*, that fell upon my ear like the plaintive cadence in an autumnal wind.

I bent my head, and answered that I was.

She pointed to the headstone of which I had taken a rubbing a day or two before.

'A Christian soul lies there,' she said, 'laid in earth without one Christian prayer – with Hebrew rites – in a Hebrew sanctuary. Will you, stranger, perform an act of piety towards the dead?'

'The Signora has but to speak,' I said. 'All that she wishes shall be done.'

'Read one prayer over this grave; trace a cross upon this stone.'

'I will.'

She thanked me with a gesture, slightly bowed her head, drew her outer garment more closely round her, and moved away to a rising ground at some little distance. I was dismissed. I had no excuse for lingering – no right to prolong the interview – no business to remain there one moment longer. So I left her there, nor once looked back till I reached the last point from which I knew I should be able to see her. But when I turned for that last look she was no longer in sight.

I had resolved to speak to her, and this was the result. A stranger interview never, surely, fell to the lot of man! I had said nothing that I meant to say – had learnt nothing that I sought to know. With regard to her circumstances, her place of residence, her very name, I was no wiser than before. And yet I had, perhaps, no reason to be dissatisfied. She had honoured me with her confidence, and entrusted to me a task of some difficulty and importance. It now only remained for me to execute that task as thoroughly and as quickly as possible. That done, I might fairly hope to win some place in her remembrance – by and by, perhaps, in her esteem.

Meanwhile, the old question rose again – whose grave could it be? I had settled this matter so conclusively in my own mind from the first, that I could scarcely believe even now that it was not her father's. Yet that he should have died a secret convert to

Christianity was incredible. Whose grave could it be? A lover's? a Christian lover's? Alas! it might be. Or a sister's? In either of these cases it was more than probable that Salome was herself a convert. But I had no time to waste in conjecture. I must act, and act promptly.

I hastened back to Venice as fast as my gondolier could row me; and as we went along I promised myself that all her wishes should be carried out before she visited the spot again. To at once secure the services of a clergyman who would go with me to the Lido at early dawn, and there read some portion, at least, of the burial-service! and at the same time to engage a stonemason to cut the cross – to have all done before she, or anyone, should have approached the place next day, was my especial object. And that object I was resolved to carry out, though I had to search Venice through before I laid my head upon the pillow.

I found my clergyman without difficulty. He was a young man occupying rooms in the same hotel, and on the same floor as myself. I had met him each day at the *table d'hôte*, and conversed with him once or twice in the reading-room. He was a North countryman, had not long since taken orders, and was both gentlemanly and obliging. He promised in the readiest manner to do all that I required, and to breakfast with me at six the next morning, in order that we might reach the cemetery by eight.

To find my stonemason, however, was not so easy; and yet I went to work methodically enough. I began with the Venetian Directory; then copied a list of stonemasons' names and addresses; then took a gondola *a due rame*, and started upon my voyage of discovery.

But a night's voyage of discovery among the intricate back canaletti of Venice is no very easy and no very safe enterprise. Narrow, tortuous, densely populated, often blocked by huge hay, wood, and provision barges, almost wholly unlighted, and so perplexingly alike that no mere novice in Venetian topography need ever hope to distinguish one from another, they baffle the very gondoliers, and are a *terra incognita* to all but the dwellers therein.

I succeeded, however, in finding three of the places entered on my list. At the first I was told that the workman of whom I was in quest was working by the week somewhere over by Murano, and would not be back again till Saturday night. At the second and third, I found the men at home, supping with their wives and children at the end of the day's work; but neither would consent to undertake my commission. One, after a whispered consultation with his son, declined reluctantly. The other told me plainly that he dared not do it, and that he did not believe I should find a stonemason in Venice who would be bolder than himself.

The Jews, he said, were rich and powerful; no longer an oppressed people; no longer to be insulted even in Venice with impunity. To cut a Christian cross upon a Jewish headstone in the Jewish cemetery, would be 'a sort of sacrilege', and punishable, no doubt, by the law. This sounded like truth; so finding that my rowers were by no means confident of their way, and that the canaletti were dark as the catacombs, I prevailed upon the stonemason to sell me a small mallet and a couple of chisels, and made up my mind to commit the sacrilege myself.

With this single exception, all was done next morning as I had planned to do. My new acquaintance breakfasted with me, accompanied me to the Lido, read such portions of the burial-service as seemed proper to him, and then, having business in Venice, left me to my task. It was by no means an easy one. To a skilled hand it would have been, perhaps, the work of half an hour; but it was my first effort, and rude as the thing was – a mere grooved attempt at a Latin cross, about two inches and a half in length, cut close at the bottom of the stone, where it could be easily concealed by a little piling of the sand – it took me nearly four hours to complete. While I was at work, the dull grey morning grew duller and greyer; a thick sea fog drove up from the Adriatic, and a low moaning wind came and went like the echo of a distant requiem. More than once I started, believing that she had surprised me there – fancying I saw the passing of a shadow – heard the rustling of a garment – the breathing of a sigh. But no. The mists and the moaning wind deceived me. I was alone.

When at length I got back to my hotel, it was just two o'clock. The hall-porter put a letter into my hand as I passed through. One glance at that crabbed superscription was enough. It was from Padua. I hastened to my room, tore open the envelope, and read these words:

'CARO SIGNORE, – The rubbing you send is neither ancient nor curious, as I fear you suppose it to be. *Altro*; it is of yesterday. It merely records that one Salome, the only and beloved child of a certain Isaac da Costa, died last autumn on the eighteenth of October, aged twenty-one years, and that by the said Isaac da Costa this monument is erected to the memory of her virtues and his grief.

'I pray you *caro signore*, to receive the assurance of my sincere esteem.

NICOLO NICOLAI.

'Padua, April 27th, 1857.'

The letter dropped from my hand. I seemed to have read without understanding it. I picked it up; went through it again, word by word; sat down; rose up; took a turn across the room; felt confused, bewildered, incredulous.

Could there, then, be two Salomes? or was there some radical and extraordinary mistake?

I hesitated; I knew not what to do. Should I go down to the Merceria, and see whether the name of da Costa was known in the *quartier*? Or find out the registrar of births and deaths for the Jewish district? Or call upon the principal rabbi, and learn from him who this second Salome had been, and in what degree of relationship she stood towards the Salome whom I knew? I decided upon the last course. The chief rabbi's address was easily obtained. He lived in an ancient house on the Giudecca, and there I found him – a grave, stately old man, with a grizzled beard reaching nearly to his waist.

I introduced myself, and stated my business. I came to ask if he could give me any information respecting the late Salome da Costa, who died on the 18th of October last, and was buried on the Lido.

The rabbi replied that he had no doubt he could give me any information I desired, as he had known the lady personally, and was the intimate friend of her father.

'Can you tell me,' I asked, 'whether she had any dear friend or female relative of the same name – Salome?' The rabbi shook his head. 'I think not,' he said. 'I remember no other maiden of that name.'

'Pardon me, but I know there was another,' I replied. 'There was a very beautiful Salome living in the Merceria when I was last in Venice, just this time last year.'

'Salome da Costa was very fair,' said the rabbi; 'and she dwelt with her father in the Merceria. Since her death, he hath removed to the neighbourhood of the Rialto.'

'This Salome's father was a dealer in Oriental goods,' I said, hastily.

'Isaac da Costa is a dealer in Oriental goods,' replied the old man very gently. 'We are speaking, my son, of the same persons.'

'Impossible!'

He shook his head again.

'But she lives!' I exclaimed, becoming greatly agitated. 'She lives. I have seen her. I have spoken to her. I saw her only last evening.'

'Nay,' he said compassionately, 'this is some dream. She of whom you speak is indeed no more.'

'I saw her only last evening,' I replied.

'Where did you suppose you beheld her?'

'On the Lido.'

'On the Lido?'

'And she spoke to me. I heard her voice – heard it as distinctly as I hear my own at this moment.'

The rabbi stroked his beard thoughtfully, and looked at me. 'You think you heard her voice!' he ejaculated. 'That is strange. What said she?'

I was about to answer. I checked myself – a sudden thought

flashed upon me – I trembled from head to foot. 'Have you – have you any reason for supposing that she died a Christian?' I faltered.

The old man started, and changed colour.

'I – I – that is a strange question,' he stammered. 'Why do you ask it?'

'Yes or no?' I cried wildly. 'Yes or no?'

He frowned, looked down, hesitated. 'I admit,' he said, after a moment or two – 'I admit that I may have heard something tending that way. It may be that the maiden cherished some secret doubt. Yet she was no professed Christian.'

'*Laid in earth without one Christian prayer; with Hebrew rites; in a Hebrew sanctuary!*' I repeated to myself.

'But I marvel how you come to have heard of this,' continued the rabbi. 'It was known only to her father and myself.'

'Sir,' I said solemnly, 'I know now that Salome da Costa is dead; I have seen her spirit thrice, haunting the spot where—'

My voice broke. I could not utter the words.

'Last evening, at sunset,' I resumed, 'was the third time. Never doubting that – that I indeed beheld her in the flesh, I spoke to her. She answered me. She – she told me this.'

The rabbi covered his face with his hands, and so remained for some time, lost in meditation. 'Young man,' he said at length, 'your story is strange, and you bring strange evidence to bear upon it. It may be as you say; it may be that you are the dupe of some waking dream – I know not.'

He knew not; but I – ah! I knew, only too well. I knew now why she had appeared to me clothed with such unearthly beauty. I understood now that look of dumb entreaty in her eyes – that tone of strange remoteness in her voice. The sweet soul could not rest amid the dust of its kinsfolk, 'unhousel'd, unanointed, unaneal'd', lacking even 'one Christian prayer' above its grave. And now – was it all over? Should I never see her more?

Never – ah! never. How I haunted the Lido at sunset for many a month, till spring had blossomed into autumn, and autumn had ripened into summer; how I wandered back to Venice year after year, at the same season, while yet any vestige of that wild hope remained alive; how my heart has never throbbed, my pulse never leaped, for love of mortal woman since that time – are details into which I need not enter here. Enough that I watched and waited but that her gracious spirit appeared to me no more. I wait still, but I watch no longer. I know now that our place of meeting will not be here.

MRS HENRY WOOD

REALITY OR DELUSION?

This is a ghost story. Every word of it is true. And I don't mind confessing that for ages afterwards some of us did not care to pass the spot alone at night. Some people do not care to pass it yet.

It was autumn, and we were at Crabb Cot. Lena had been ailing; and in October Mrs Todhetley proposed to the Squire that they should remove with her there, to see if the change would do her good.

We Worcestershire people call North Crabb a village; but one might count the houses in it, little and great, and not find four-and-twenty. South Crabb, half a mile off, is ever so much larger; but the church and school are at North Crabb.

John Ferrar had been employed by Squire Todhetley as a sort of overlooker on the estate, or working bailiff. He had died the previous winter; leaving nothing behind him except some debts; for he was not provident; and his handsome son Daniel. Daniel Ferrar, who was rather superior as far as education went, disliked work: he would make a show of helping his father, but it came to little. Old Ferrar had not put him to any particular trade or occupation, and Daniel, who was as proud as Lucifer, would not turn to it himself. He liked to be a gentleman. All he did now was to work in his garden, and feed his fowls, ducks, rabbits, and pigeons, of which he kept a great quantity, selling them to the houses around and sending them to market.

But, as every one said, poultry would not maintain him. Mrs Lease, in the pretty cottage hard by Ferrar's, grew tired of saying it. This Mrs Lease and her daughter, Maria, must not be confounded with Lease the pointsman: they were in a better condition of life, and not related to him. Daniel Ferrar used to run in and out of their house at will when a boy, and he was now engaged to be married to Maria. She would have a little money, and the Leases were respected in North Crabb. People began to whisper a query as to how Ferrar got his corn for the poultry: he was not known to buy much: and he would have to go out of his house at Christmas, for its owner, Mr Coney, had given him notice. Mrs Lease, anxious about Maria's prospects, asked Daniel what he intended to do then, and he answered, 'Make his fortune: he should begin to do it as soon as he could turn himself round.' But the time was going on, and the turning round seemed to be as far off as ever.

After Midsummer, a niece of the schoolmistress's, Miss Timmens, had come to the school to stay: her name was Harriet Roe. The father, Humphrey Roe, was half-brother to Miss Timmens. He had married a Frenchwoman, and lived more in France than in England until his death. The girl had been christened Henriette; but North Crabb, not understanding much French, converted it into Harriet. She was a showy, free-mannered, good-looking girl, and made speedy acquaintance with Daniel Ferrar; or he with her. They improved upon it so rapidly that Maria Lease grew jealous, and North Crabb began to say he cared for Harriet more than for Maria. When Tod and I got home the latter end of October, to spend the Squire's birthday, things were in this state. James Hill, the bailiff who had been taken on by the Squire in John Ferrar's place (but a far inferior man to Ferrar gave us an account of matters in general. Daniel Ferrar had been drinking lately, Hill added, and his head was not strong enough to stand it; and he was also beginning to look as if he had some care upon him.

'A nice lot, he, for them two women to be fighting for,' cried Hill, who was no friend to Ferrar. 'There'll be mischief between 'em if they don't draw in a bit. Maria Lease is next door to mad over it, I know; and t'other, finding herself the best liked, crows over her. It's something like the Bible story of Leah and Rachel, young gents, Dan Ferrar likes the one, and he's bound by promise to the t'other. As to the French jade,' concluded Hill, giving his head a toss, 'she'd make a show of liking any man that followed her, she would; a dozen of 'em on a string.'

It was all very well for surly Hill to call Daniel Ferrar a 'nice lot', but he was the best-looking fellow in the church on Sunday morning – well-dressed too. But his colour seemed brighter; and his hands shook as they were raised, often, to push back his hair, that the sun shone upon through the south-window, turning it to gold. He scarcely looked up, not even at Harriet Roe, with her dark eyes roving everywhere, and her streaming pink ribbons. Maria Lease was pale, quiet, and nice, as usual; she had no beauty, but her face was sensible, and her deep grey eyes had a strange and curious earnestness. The new parson preached, a young man just appointed to the parish of Crabb. He went in for great observances of Saints' days, and told his congregation that he should expect to see them at church on the morrow, which would be the Feast of All Saints.

Daniel Ferrar walked home with Mrs Lease and Maria after service, and was invited to dinner. I ran across to shake hands with the old dame, who had once nursed me through an illness, and promised to look in and see her later. We were going back to school on the morrow. As I turned away, Harriet Roe passed, her pink ribbons and her cheap gay silk dress gleaming in the sunlight. She stared at me, and I stared back again. And now, the explanation of matters being over, the real story begins. But I shall have to tell some of it as it was told by others.

The tea-things waited on Mrs Lease's table in the afternoon; waited for Daniel Ferrar. He had left them shortly before to go and attend to his poultry. Nothing had been said about his coming back for tea: that he would do so had been looked upon as a matter of course. But he did not make his appearance, and the tea was taken without him. At half-past five the church-bell rang out for evening service, and Maria put her things on. Mrs Lease did not go out at night.

'You are starting early, Maria. You'll be in church before other people.'

'That won't matter, mother.'

A jealous suspicion lay on Maria – that the secret of Daniel Ferrar's absence was his having fallen in with Harriet Roe: perhaps he had gone of his own accord to seek her. She walked slowly along. The gloom of dusk, and a deep dusk, had stolen over the evening, but the moon would be up later. As Maria passed the school-house, she halted to glance in at the little sitting-room window: the shutters were not closed yet, and the room was lighted by the blazing fire. Harriet was not there. She only saw Miss Timmens, the mistress, who was putting on her bonnet before a hand-glass propped upright on the mantelpiece. Without warning, Miss Timmens turned and threw open the window. It was only for the purpose of pulling-to the shutters, but Maria thought she must have been observed, and spoke.

'Good evening, Miss Timmens.'

'Who is it?' cried out Miss Timmens, in answer, peering into the dusk. 'Oh, it's you, Maria Lease! Have you seen anything of Harriet? She went off somewhere this afternoon, and never came in to tea.'

'I have not seen her.'

'She's gone to the Batleys', I'll be bound. She knows I don't like her to be with the Batley girls: they make her ten times flightier than she would otherwise be.'

Miss Timmens drew in her shutters with a jerk, without which they would not close, and Maria Lease turned away.

'Not at the Batleys', not at the Batleys', but with *him*,' she cried, in bitter rebellion, as she turned away from the church. From the church, not to it. Was Maria to blame for wishing to see whether she was right or not? – for walking about a little in the thought of meeting them? At any rate it is what she did. And had her reward; such as it was.

As she was passing the top of the withy walk, their voices

reached her ear. People often walked there, and it was one of the ways to South Crabb. Maria drew back amidst the trees, and they came on: Harriet Roe and Daniel Ferrar, walking arm-in-arm.

'I think I had better take it off,' Harriet was saying. 'No need to invoke a storm upon my head. And that would come in a shower of hail from stiff old Aunt Timmens.'

The answer seemed one of quick accent, but Ferrar spoke low. Maria Lease had hard work to control herself: anger, passion, jealousy, all blazed up. With her arms stretched out to a friendly tree on either side, – with her heart beating, – with her pulses coursing on to fever-heat, she watched them across the bit of common to the road. Harriet went one way then; he another, in the direction of Mrs Lease's cottage. No doubt to fetch her – Maria – to church, with a plausible excuse of having been detained. Until now she had had no proof of his falseness; had never perfectly believed in it.

She took her arms from the trees and went forward, a sharp faint cry of despair breaking forth on the night air. Maria Lease was one of those silent-natured girls who can never speak of a wrong like this. She had to bury it within her; down, down, out of sight and show; and she went into church with her usual quiet step. Harriet Roe with Miss Timmens came next, quite demure, as if she had been singing some of the infant scholars to sleep at their own homes. Daniel Ferrar did not go to church at all: he stayed, as was found afterwards, with Mrs Lease.

Maria might as well have been at home as at church: better perhaps that she had been. Not a syllable of the service did she hear: her brain was a sea of confusion; the tumult within it rising higher and higher. She did not hear even the text, 'Peace, be still', or the sermon; both so singularly appropriate. The passions in men's minds, the preacher said, raged and foamed just like the angry waves of the sea in a storm, until Jesus came to still them.

I ran after Maria when church was over, and went in to pay the promised visit to old Mother Lease. Daniel Ferrar was sitting in the parlour. He got up and offered Maria a chair at the fire, but she turned her back and stood at the table under the window, taking off her gloves. An open Bible was before Mrs Lease: I wondered whether she had been reading aloud to Daniel.

'What was the text, child?' asked the old lady.

No answer.

'Do you hear, Maria! What was the text?'

Maria turned at that, as if suddenly awakened. Her face was white; her eyes had in them an uncertain terror.

'The text?' she stammered. 'I – I forget it, mother. It was from Genesis, I think.'

'Was it, Master Johnny?'

'It was from the fourth chapter of St Mark, "Peace, be still."'

Mrs Lease stared at me. 'Why, that is the very chapter I've been reading. Well now, that's curious. But there's never a better in the Bible, and never a better text was taken from it than those three words. I have been telling Daniel here, Master Johnny, that when once that peace, Christ's peace, is got into the heart, storms can't hurt us much. And you are going away again tomorrow, sir?' she added, after a pause. 'It's a short stay?'

I was not going away on the morrow. Tod and I, taking the Squire in a genial moment after dinner, had pressed to be let stay until Tuesday, Tod using the argument, and laughing while he did it, that it must be wrong to travel on All Saints' Day, when the parson had specially enjoined us to be at church. The Squire told us we were a couple of encroaching rascals, and if he did let us stay it should be upon condition that we did go to church. This I said to them.

'He may send you all the same, sir, when the morning comes,' remarked Daniel Ferrar.

'Knowing Mr Todhetley as you do Ferrar, you may remember that he never breaks his promises.'

Daniel laughed. 'He grumbles over them, though, Master Johnny.'

'Well, he may grumble tomorrow about our staying, say it is wasting time that ought to be spent in study, but he will not send us back until Tuesday.'

Until Tuesday! If I could have foreseen then what would have happened before Tuesday! If all of us could have foreseen! Seen the few hours between now and then depicted, as in a mirror, event by event! Would it have saved the calamity, the dreadful sin that could never be redeemed? Why, yes; surely it would. Daniel Ferrar turned and looked at Maria.

'Why don't you come to the fire?'

'I am very well here, thank you.'

She had sat down where she was, her bonnet touching the curtain. Mrs Lease, not noticing that anything was wrong, had begun talking about Lena, whose illness was turning to low fever, when the house door opened and Harriet Roe came in.

'What a lovely night it is!' she said, taking of own accord the chair I had not cared to take, for I kept saying I must go. 'Maria, what went with you after church? I hunted for you everywhere.'

Maria gave no answer. She looked black and angry; and her bosom heaved as if a storm were brewing. Harriet Roe slightly laughed.

'Do you intend to take holiday tomorrow, Mrs Lease?'

'Me take holiday! what is there in tomorrow to take holiday for?' returned Mrs Lease.

'I shall,' continued Harriet, not answering the question: 'I have been used to it in France. All Saints' Day is a grand holiday there; we go to church in our best clothes, and pay visits afterwards. Following it, like a dark shadow, comes the gloomy Jour des Morts.'

'The what?' cried Mrs Lease, bending her ear.

'The day of the dead. All Souls' Day. But you English don't go to the cemeteries to pray.'

Mrs Lease put on her spectacles, which lay upon the open pages of the Bible, and stared at Harriet. Perhaps she thought they might help her to understand. The girl laughed.

'On All Souls' Day, whether it be wet or dry, the French cemeteries are full of kneeling women draped in black; all praying for the repose of their dead relatives, after the manner of the Roman Catholics.'

Daniel Ferrar, who had not spoken a word since she came in, but sat with his face to the fire, turned and looked at her. Upon which she tossed back her head and her pink ribbons, and smiled till all her teeth were seen. Good teeth they were. As to reverence in her tone, there was none.

'I have seen them kneeling when the slosh and wet have been ankle-deep. Did you ever see a ghost?' added she, with energy. 'The French believe that the spirits of the dead come abroad on the night of All Saints' Day. You'd scarcely get a French woman to go out of her house after dark. It is their chief superstition.'

'What *is* the superstition?' questioned Mrs Lease.

'Why, *that*,' said Harriet. 'They believe that the dead are allowed to revisit the world after dark on the Eve of All Souls; that they hover in the air, waiting to appear to any of their living relatives, who may venture out, lest they should forget to pray on the morrow for the rest of their souls.'*

'Well, I never!' cried Mrs Lease, staring excessively. 'Did you ever hear the like of that, sir?' turning to me.

'Yes; I have heard of it.'

Harriet Roe looked up at me; I was standing at the corner of the mantelpiece. She laughed a free laugh.

'I say, wouldn't it be fun to go out tomorrow night, and meet the ghosts? Only, perhaps they don't visit this country, as it is not under Rome.'

'Now just you behave yourself before your betters, Harriet Roe,' put in Mrs Lease, sharply. 'That gentleman is young Mr Ludlow of Crabb Cot.'

'And very happy I am to make young Mr Ludlow's acquaintance,' returned easy Harriet, flinging back her mantle from her shoulders. 'How hot your parlour is, Mrs Lease.'

The hook of the cloak had caught in a thin chain of twisted gold that she wore round her neck, displaying it to view. She hurriedly

*A superstition obtaining amongst some of the lower orders in France.

folded her cloak together, as if wishing to conceal the chain. But Mrs Lease's spectacles had seen it.

'What's that you've got on, Harriet? A gold chain?'

A moment's pause, and then Harriet Roe flung back her mantle again, defiance upon her face, and touched the chain with her hand.

'That's what it is, Mrs Lease: a gold chain. And a very pretty one, too.'

'Was it your mother's?'

'It was never anybody's but mine. I had it made a present to me this afternoon; for a keepsake.'

Happening to look at Maria, I was startled at her face, it was so white and dark: white with emotion, dark with an angry despair that I for one did not comprehend. Harriet Roe, throwing at her a look of saucy triumph, went out with as little ceremony as she had come in, just calling back a general good night; and we heard her footsteps outside getting gradually fainter in the distance. Daniel Ferrar rose.

'I'll take my departure too, I think. You are very unsociable tonight, Maria.'

'Perhaps I am. Perhaps I have cause to be.'

She flung his hand back when he held it out; and in another moment, as if a thought struck her, ran after him into the passage to speak. I, standing near the door in the small room, caught the words.

'I must have an explanation with you, Daniel Ferrar. Now. Tonight. We cannot go on thus for a single hour longer.'

'Not tonight, Maria; I have no time to spare. And I don't know what you mean.'

'You do know. Listen. I will not go to my rest, no, though it were for twenty nights to come, until we have had it out. I *vow* I will not. There. You are playing with me. Others have long said so, and I know it now.'

He seemed to speak some quieting words to her, for the tone was low and soothing; and then went out, closing the door behind him. Maria came back and stood with her face and its ghastliness turned from us. And still the old mother noticed nothing.

'Why don't you take your things off, Maria?' she asked.

'Presently,' was the answer.

I said goodnight in my turn, and went away. Half-way home I met Tod with the two young Lexoms. The Lexoms made us go in and stay to supper, and it was ten o'clock before we left them.

'We shall catch it,' said Tod, setting off at a run. They never let us stay out late on a Sunday evening, on account of the reading.

But, as it happened, we escaped scot-free this time, for the house was in a commotion about Lena. She had been better in the afternoon, but at nine o'clock the fever returned worse than ever. Her little cheeks and lips were scarlet as she lay on the bed, her wide-open eyes were bright and glistening. The Squire had gone up to look at her, and was fuming and fretting in his usual fashion.

'The doctor has never sent the medicine,' said patient Mrs Todhetley, who must have been worn out with nursing. 'She ought to take it; I am sure she ought.'

'These boys are good to run over to Cole's for that,' cried the Squire. 'It won't hurt them; it's a fine night.'

Of course we were good for it. And we got our caps again; being charged to enjoin Mr Cole to come over the first thing in the morning.

'Do you care much about my going with you, Johnny?' Tod asked as we were turning out at the door. 'I am awfully tired.'

'Not a bit. I'd as soon go alone as not. You'll see me back in half-an-hour.'

I took the nearest way; flying across the fields at a canter, and startling the hares. Mr Cole lived near South Crabb, and I don't believe more than ten minutes had gone by when I knocked at his door. But to get back as quickly was another thing. The doctor was not at home. He had been called out to a patient at eight o'clock, and had not yet returned.

I went in to wait: the servant said he might be expected to come in from minute to minute. It was of no use to go away without the medicine; and I sat down in the surgery in front of the shelves, and fell asleep counting the white jars and physic bottles. The doctor's entrance awoke me.

'I am sorry you should have had to come over and to wait,' he said. 'When my other patient, with whom I was detained a considerable time, was done with, I went on to Crabb Cot with the child's medicine, which I had in my pocket.'

'They think her very ill tonight, sir.'

'I left her better, and going quietly to sleep. She will soon be well again I hope.'

'Why! is that the time?' I exclaimed, happening to catch sight of the clock as I was crossing the hall. It was nearly twelve. Mr Cole laughed saying time passed quickly when folk were asleep.

I went back slowly. The sleep, or the canter before it, had made me feel as tired as Tod had said he was. It was a night to be abroad in and to enjoy; calm, warm, light. The moon, high in the sky, illumined every blade of grass; sparkled on the water of the little rivulet, brought out the moss on the grey walls of the old church; played on its round-faced clock, then striking twelve.

Twelve o'clock at night at North Crabb answers to about three in the morning in London, for country people are mostly in bed and asleep at ten. Therefore, when loud and angry voices struck up in dispute, just as the last stroke of the hour was dying away on the midnight air, I stood still and doubted my ears.

I was getting near home then. The sounds came from the back of a building standing alone in a solitary place on the left-hand side of the road. It belonged to the Squire, and was called the yellow barn, its walls being covered with a yellow wash; but it was in fact used as a storehouse for corn. I was passing in front of it when the voices rose upon the air. Round the building I ran, and saw – Maria Lease: and something else that I could not at first comprehend. In the pursuit of her vow, not to go to rest until she had 'had it out' with Daniel Ferrar, Maria had been abroad searching for him. What ill fate brought her looking for him up near our barn? – perhaps because she had fruitlessly searched in every other spot.

At the back of this barn, up some steps, was an unused door. Unused partly because it was not required, the principal entrance being in front; partly because the key of it had been for a long time missing. Stealing out at this door, a bag of corn upon his shoulders, had come Daniel Ferrar in a smock-frock. Maria saw him, and stood back in the shade. She watched him lock the door and put the key in his pocket; she watched him give the heavy bag a jerk as he turned to come down the steps. Then she burst out. Her loud reproaches petrified him, and he stood there as one suddenly turned to stone. It was at that moment that I appeared.

I understood it all soon; it needed not Maria's words to enlighten me. Daniel Ferrar possessed the lost key and could come in and out at will in the midnight hours when the world was sleeping, and help himself to the corn. No wonder his poultry throve; no wonder there had been grumblings at Crabb Cot at the mysterious disappearance of the good grain.

Maria Lease was decidedly mad in those few first moments. Stealing is looked upon in an honest village as an awful thing; a disgrace, a crime; and there was the night's earlier misery besides. Daniel Ferrar was a thief! Daniel Ferrar was false to her! A storm of words and reproaches poured forth from her in confusion, none of it very distinct. 'Living upon theft! Convicted felon! Transportation for life! Squire Todhetley's corn! Fattening poultry on stolen goods! Buying gold chains with the profits for that bold, flaunting French girl, Harriet Roe! Taking his stealthy walks with her!'

My going up to them stopped the charge. There was a pause; and then Maria, in her mad passion, denounced him to me, as representative (so she put it) of the Squire – the breaker-in upon our premises! the robber of our stored corn!

Daniel Ferrar came down the steps; he had remained there still as a statue, immovable; and turned his white face to me. Never a word in defence said he: the blow had crushed him; he was a proud man (if any one can understand that), and to be discovered in this ill-doing was worse than death to him.

'Don't think of me more hardly than you can help, Master

Johnny,' he said in a quiet tone. 'I have been almost tired of my life this long while.'

Putting down the bag of corn near the steps, he took the key from his pocket and handed it to me. The man's aspect had so changed; there was something so grievously subdued and sad about him altogether, that I felt as sorry for him as if he had not been guilty. Maria Lease went on in her fiery passion.

'You'll be more tired of it tomorrow when the police are taking you to Worcester gaol. Squire Todhetley will not spare you, though your father was his many-years bailiff. He could not, you know, if he wished; Master Ludlow has seen you in the act.'

'Let me have the key again for a minute, sir,' he said, as quietly as though he had not heard a word. And I gave it to him. I'm not sure but I should have given him my head had he asked for it.

He swung the bag on his shoulders, unlocked the granary door, and put the bag beside the other sacks. The bag was his own, as we found afterwards, but he left it there. Locking the door again, he gave me the key, and went away with a weary step.

'Goodbye, Master Johnny.'

I answered back goodnight civilly, though he had been stealing. When he was out of sight, Maria Lease, her passion full upon her still, dashed off towards her mother's cottage, a strange cry of despair breaking from her lips.

'Where have you been lingering, Johnny?' roared the Squire, who was sitting up for me. 'You have been throwing at the owls, sir, that's what you've been at; you have been scudding after the hares.'

I said I had waited for Mr Cole, and had come back slower than I went; but I said no more, and went up to my room at once. And the Squire went to his.

I know I am only a muff; people tell me so, often: but I can't help it; I did not make myself. I lay awake till nearly daylight, first wishing Daniel Ferrar could be screened, and then thinking it might perhaps be done. If he would only take the lesson to heart and go straight for the future, what a capital thing it would be. We had liked old Ferrar; he had done me and Tod many a good turn: and, for the matter of that, we liked Daniel. So I never said a word when morning came of the past night's work.

'Is Daniel at home?' I asked, going to Ferrar's the first thing before breakfast. I meant to tell him that if he would keep right, I would keep counsel.

'He went out at dawn, sir,' answered the old woman who did for him, and sold his poultry at market. 'He'll be in presently: he have had no breakfast yet.'

'Then tell him when he comes, to wait in, and see me: tell him it's all right. Can you remember, Goody? "It is all right."'

'I'll remember, safe enough, Master Ludlow.'

Tod and I, being on our honour, went to church, and found about ten people in the pews. Harriet Roe was one, with her pink ribbons, the twisted gold chain showing outside a short-cut velvet jacket.

'No, sir; he has not been home yet; I can't think where he can have got to,' was the old Goody's reply when I went again to Ferrar's. And so I wrote a word in pencil, and told her to give it him when he came in, for I could not go dodging there every hour of the day.

After luncheon, strolling by the back of the barn: a certain reminiscence I suppose taking me there, for it was not a frequented spot: I saw Maria Lease coming along.

Well, it was a change! The passionate woman of the previous night had subsided into a poor, wild-looking, sorrow-stricken thing, ready to die of remorse. Excessive passion had wrought its usual consequences; a reaction: a reaction in favour of Daniel Ferrar. She came up to me, clasping her hands in agony – beseeching that I would spare him; that I would not tell of him; that I would give him a chance for the future: and her lips quivered and trembled, and there were dark circles round her hollow eyes.

I said that I had not told and did not intend to tell. Upon which she was going to fall down on her knees, but I rushed off.

'Do you know where he is?' I asked, when she came to her sober senses.

'Oh, I wish I did know! Master Johnny, he is just the man to go and do something desperate. He would never face shame; and I was a mad, hard-hearted, wicked girl to do what I did last night. He might run away to sea; he might go and enlist for a soldier.'

'I dare say he is at home by this time. I have left a word for him there, and promised to go in and see him tonight. If he will undertake not to be up to wrong things again, no one shall ever know of this from me.'

She went away easier, and I sauntered on towards South Crabb. Eager as Tod and I had been for the day's holiday, it did not seem to be turning out much of a boon. In going home again – there was nothing worth staying out for – I had come to the spot by the three-cornered grove where I saw Maria, when a galloping policeman overtook me. My heart stood still; for I thought he must have come after Daniel Ferrar.

'Can you tell me if I am near to Crabb Cot – Squire Todhetley's?' he asked, reining-in his horse.

'You will reach it in a minute or two. I live there. Squire Todhetley is not at home. What do you want with him?'

'It's only to give in an official paper, sir. I have to leave one personally upon all the county magistrates.'

He rode on. When I got in I saw the folded paper upon the hall-table; the man and horse had already gone onwards. It was worse indoors than out; less to be done. Tod had disappeared after church; the Squire was abroad; Mrs Todhetley sat upstairs with Lena: and I strolled out again. It was only three o'clock then.

An hour, or more, was got through somehow; meeting one, talking to another, throwing at the ducks and geese; anything. Mrs Lease had her head, smothered in a yellow shawl, stretched out over the palings as I passed her cottage.

'Don't catch cold, mother.'

'I am looking for Maria, sir. I can't think what has come to her today, Master Johnny,' she added, dropping her voice to a confidential tone. 'The girl seems demented: she has been going in and out ever since daylight like a dog in a fair.'

'If I meet her I will send her home.'

And in another minute I did meet her. For she was coming out of Daniel Ferrar's yard. I supposed he was at home again.

'No,' she said looking more wild, worn, haggard than before; 'that's what I have been to ask. I am just out of my senses, sir. He has gone for certain. Gone!'

I did not think it. He would not be likely to go away without clothes.

'Well, I know he is, Master Johnny; something tells me. I've been all about everywhere. There's a great dread upon me, sir; I never felt anything like it.'

'Wait until night, Maria; I dare say he will go home then. Your mother is looking out for you; I said if I met you I'd send you in.'

Mechanically she turned towards the cottage, and I went on. Presently, as I was sitting on a gate watching the sunset, Harriet Roe passed towards the withy walk, and gave me a nod in her free but good-natured way.

'Are you going there to look out for the ghosts this evening?' I asked: and I wished not long afterwards I had not said it. 'It will soon be dark.'

'So it will,' she said, turning to the red sky in the west. 'But I have no time to give to the ghosts tonight.'

'Have you seen Ferrar today?' I cried, an idea occurring to me.

'No. And I can't think where he has got to; unless he is off to Worcester. He told me he should have to go there some day this week.'

She evidently knew nothing about him, and went on her way with another free-and-easy nod. I sat on the gate till the sun had gone down, and then thought it was time to be getting homewards.

Close against the yellow barn, the scene of last night's trouble, whom should I come upon but Maria Lease. She was standing still, and turned quickly at the sound of my footsteps. Her face was bright again, but had a puzzled look upon it.

'I have just seen him: he has not gone,' she said in a happy whisper. 'You were right, Master Johnny, and I was wrong.'

'Where did you see him?'

'Here; not a minute ago. I saw him twice. He is angry, very, and will not let me speak to him; both times he got away before I could reach him. He is close by somewhere.'

I looked round, naturally; but Ferrar was nowhere to be seen. There was nothing to conceal him except the barn, and that was locked up. The account she gave was this – and her face grew puzzled again as she related it.

Unable to rest indoors, she had wandered up here again, and saw Ferrar standing at the corner of the barn, looking very hard at her. She thought he was waiting for her to come up, but before she got close to him he had disappeared, and she did not see which way. She hastened past the front of the barn, ran round to the back, and there he was. He stood near the steps looking out for her; waiting for her, as it again seemed; and was gazing at her with the same fixed stare. But again she missed him before she could get quite up; and it was at that moment that I arrived on the scene.

I went all round the barn, but could see nothing of Ferrar. It was an extraordinary thing where he could have got to. Inside the barn he could not be: it was securely locked; and there was no appearance of him in the open country. It was, so to say, broad daylight yet, or at least not far short of it; the red light was still in the west. Beyond the field at the back of the barn, was a grove of trees in the form of a triangle; and this grove was flanked by Crabb Ravine, which ran right and left. Crabb Ravine had the reputation of being haunted; for a light was sometimes seen dodging about its deep descending banks at night that no one could account for. A lively spot altogether for those who liked gloom.

'Are you sure it was Ferrar, Maria?'

'Sure!' she returned in surprise. 'You don't think I could mistake him, Master Johnny, do you? He wore that ugly seal-skin winter-cap of his tied over his ears, and his thick grey coat. The coat was buttoned closely round him. I have not seen him wear either since last winter.'

That Ferrar must have gone into hiding somewhere seemed quite evident; and yet there was nothing but the ground to receive him.

Maria said she lost sight of him the last time in a moment; both times in fact; and it was absolutely impossible that he could have made off to the triangle or elsewhere, as she must have seen him cross the open land. For that matter I must have seen him also.

On the whole, not two minutes had elapsed since I came up, though it seems to have been longer in telling it: when, before we could look further, voices were heard approaching from the direction of Crabb Cot; and Maria, not caring to be seen, went away quickly. I was still puzzling about Ferrar's hiding-place, when they reached me – the Squire, Tod, and two or three men. Tod came slowly up, his face dark and grave.

'I say, Johnny, what a shocking thing this is!'

'What is a shocking thing?'

'You have not heard of it? – But I don't see how you could hear it.'

I had heard nothing. I did not know what there was to hear. Tod told me in a whisper.

'Daniel Ferrar's dead, lad.'

'*What?*'

'He has destroyed himself. Not more than half-an-hour ago. Hung himself in the grove.'

I turned sick, taking one thing with another, comparing this recollection with that; which I dare say you will think no one but a muff would do.

Ferrar was indeed dead. He had been hiding all day in the three-cornered grove: perhaps waiting for night to get away – perhaps only waiting for night to go home again. Who can tell? About half-past two, Luke Macintosh, a man who sometimes worked for us, sometimes for old Coney, happening to go through the grove, saw him there, and talked with him. The same man, passing back a little before sunset, found him hanging from a tree, dead. Macintosh ran with the news to Crabb Cot, and they were now flocking to the scene. When facts came to be examined there appeared only too much reason to think that the unfortunate appearance of the galloping policeman had terrified Ferrar into the act; perhaps – we all hoped it! – had scared his senses quite away. Look at it as we would, it was very dreadful.

But what of the appearance Maria Lease saw? At that time, Ferrar had been dead at least half-an-hour. Was it reality or delusion? That is (as the Squire put it), did her eyes see a real, spectral Daniel Ferrar; or were they deceived by some imagination of the brain? Opinions were divided. Nothing can shake her own steadfast belief in its reality; to her it remains an awful certainty, true and sure as heaven.

If I say that I believe in it too, I shall be called a muff and a double muff. But there is no stumbling-block difficult to be got over. Ferrar, when found, was wearing the seal-skin cap tied over the ears and the thick grey coat buttoned up round him, just as Maria Lease had described to me; and he had never worn them since the previous winter, or taken them out of the chest where they were kept. The old woman at his home did not know he had done it then. When told that he had died in these things, she protested that they were in the chest, and ran up to look for them. But the things were gone.

CHARLOTTE RIDDELL

THE OLD HOUSE IN VAUXHALL WALK

I

'Houseless – homeless – hopeless!'

Many a one who had before him trodden that same street must have uttered the same words – the weary, the desolate, the hungry, the forsaken, the waifs and strays of struggling humanity that are always coming and going, cold, starving and miserable, over the pavements of Lambeth Parish; but it is open to question whether they were ever previously spoken with a more thorough conviction of their truth, or with a feeling of keener self-pity, than by the young man who hurried along Vauxhall Walk one rainy winter's night, with no overcoat on his shoulders and no hat on his head.

A strange sentence for one-and-twenty to give expression to – and it was stranger still to come from the lips of a person who looked like and who was a gentleman. He did not appear either to have sunk very far down in the good graces of Fortune. There was no sign or token which would have induced a passer-by to imagine he had been worsted after a long fight with calamity. His boots were not worn down at the heels or broken at the toes, as many,

many boots were which dragged and shuffled and scraped along the pavement. His clothes were good and fashionably cut, and innocent of the rents and patches and tatters that slunk wretchedly by, crouched in doorways, and held out a hand mutely appealing for charity. His face was not pinched with famine or lined with wicked wrinkles, or brutalised by drink and debauchery, and yet he said and thought he was hopeless, and almost in his young despair spoke the words aloud.

It was a bad night to be about with such a feeling in one's heart. The rain was cold, pitiless and increasing. A damp, keen wind blew down the cross streets leading from the river. The fumes of the gas works seemed to fall with the rain. The roadway was muddy; the pavement greasy; the lamps burned dimly; and that dreary district of London looked its very gloomiest and worst.

Certainly not an evening to be abroad without a home to go to, or a sixpence in one's pocket, yet this was the position of the young gentleman who, without a hat, strode along Vauxhall Walk, the rain beating on his unprotected head.

Upon the houses, so large and good – once inhabited by well-to-do citizens, now let out for the most part in floors to weekly tenants – he looked enviously. He would have given much to have had a room, or even part of one. He had been walking for a long time, ever since dark in fact, and dark falls soon in December. He was tired and cold and hungry, and he saw no prospect save of pacing the streets all night.

As he passed one of the lamps, the light falling on his face revealed handsome young features, a mobile, sensitive mouth, and that particular formation of the eyebrows – not a frown exactly, but a certain draw of the brows – often considered to bespeak genius, but which more surely accompanies an impulsive organisation easily pleased, easily depressed, capable of suffering very keenly or of enjoying fully. In his short life he had not enjoyed much, and he had suffered a good deal. That night, when he walked bareheaded through the rain, affairs had come to a crisis. So far as he in his despair felt able to see or reason, the best thing he could do was to die. The world did not want him; he would be better out of it.

The door of one of the houses stood open, and he could see in the dimly lighted hall some few articles of furniture waiting to be removed. A van stood beside the curb, and two men were lifting a table into it as he, for a second, paused.

'Ah,' he thought, 'even those poor people have some place to go to, some shelter provided, while I have not a roof to cover my head, or a shilling to get a night's lodging.' And he went on fast, as if memory were spurring him, so fast that a man running after had some trouble to overtake him.

'Master Graham! Master Graham!' this man exclaimed, breathlessly; and, thus addressed, the young fellow stopped as if he had been shot.

'Who are you that know me?' he asked, facing round.

'I'm William; don't you remember William, Master Graham? And, Lord's sake, sir, what are you doing out a night like this without your hat?'

'I forgot it,' was the answer; 'and I did not care to go back and fetch it.'

'Then why don't you buy another, sir? You'll catch your death of cold; and besides, you'll excuse me, sir, but it does look odd.'

'I know that,' said Master Graham grimly; 'but I haven't a halfpenny in the world.'

'Have you and the master, then—' began the man, but there he hesitated and stopped.

'Had a quarrel? Yes, and one that will last us our lives,' finished the other, with a bitter laugh.

'And where are you going now?'

'Going! Nowhere, except to seek out the softest paving stone, or the shelter of an arch.'

'You are joking, sir.'

'I don't feel much in a mood for jesting either.'

'Will you come back with me, Master Graham? We are just at the last of our moving, but there is a spark of fire still in the grate, and it would be better talking out of this rain. Will you come, sir?'

'Come! Of course I will come,' said the young fellow, and, turning, they retraced their steps to the house he had looked into as he passed along.

An old, old house, with long, wide hall, stairs low, easy of ascent, with deep cornices to the ceilings, and oak floorings, and mahogany doors, which still spoke mutely of the wealth and stability of the original owner, who lived before the Tradescants and Ashmoles were thought of, and had been sleeping far longer than they, in St Mary's churchyard, hard by the archbishop's palace.

'Step upstairs, sir,' entreated the departing tenant; 'it's cold down here, with the door standing wide.'

'Had you the whole house, then, William?' asked Graham Coulton, in some surprise.

'The whole of it, and right sorry I, for one, am to leave it; but nothing else would serve my wife. This room, sir,' and with a little conscious pride, William, doing the honours of his late residence, asked his guest into a spacious apartment occupying the full width of the house on the first floor.

Tired though he was, the young man could not repress an exclamation of astonishment.

'Why, we have nothing so large as this at home, William,' he said.

'It's a fine house,' answered William, raking the embers together as he spoke and throwing some wood upon them; 'but, like many a good family, it has come down in the world.'

There were four windows in the room, shuttered close; they had deep, low seats, suggestive of pleasant days gone by; when, well-curtained and well-cushioned, they formed snug retreats for the children, and sometimes for adults also; there was no furniture left, unless an oaken settle beside the hearth, and a large mirror let into the panelling at the opposite end of the apartment, with a black marble console table beneath it could be so considered; but the very absence of chairs and tables enabled the magnificent proportions of the chamber to be seen to full advantage, and there was nothing to distract the attention from the ornamented ceiling, the panelled walls, the old-world chimney-piece so quaintly carved, and the fireplace lined with tiles, each one of which contained a picture of some scriptural or allegorical subject.

'Had you been staying on here, William,' said Coulton, flinging himself wearily on the settle, 'I'd have asked you to let me stop where I am for the night.'

'If you can make shift, sir, there is nothing as I am aware of to prevent you stopping,' answered the man, fanning the wood into a flame. 'I shan't take the key back to the landlord till tomorrow, and this would be better for you than the cold streets at any rate.'

'Do you really mean what you say?' asked the other eagerly. 'I should be thankful to lie here; I feel dead beat.'

'Then stay, Master Graham, and welcome. I'll fetch a basket of coals I was going to put in the van, and make up a good fire, so that you can warm yourself; then I must run round to the other house for a minute or two, but it's not far, and I'll be back as soon as ever I can.'

'Thank you, William; you were always good to me,' said the young man gratefully. 'This is delightful,' and he stretched his numbed hands over the blazing wood, and looked round the room with a satisfied smile.

'I did not expect to get into such quarters,' he remarked, as his friend in need reappeared, carrying a half-bushel basket full of coals, with which he proceeded to make up a roaring fire. 'I am sure the last thing I could have imagined was meeting with anyone I knew in Vauxhall Walk.'

'Where were you coming from, Master Graham?' asked William curiously.

'From old Melfield's. I was at his school once, you know, and he has now retired, and is living upon the proceeds of years of robbery in Kennington Oval. I thought, perhaps he would lend me a pound, or offer me a night's lodging, or even a glass of wine; but, oh dear, no. He took the moral tone, and observed he could have nothing to say to a son who defied his father's authority. He gave me plenty of advice, but nothing else, and showed me out into the rain with a bland courtesy, for which I could have struck him.'

William muttered something under his breath which was not a blessing, and added aloud:

'You are better here, sir, I think, at any rate. I'll be back in less than half an hour.'

Left to himself, young Coulton took off his coat, and shifting the settle a little, hung it over the end to dry. With his handkerchief he rubbed some of the wet out of his hair; then, perfectly exhausted, he lay down before the fire and, pillowing his head on his arm, fell fast asleep.

He was awakened nearly an hour afterwards by the sound of someone gently stirring the fire and moving quietly about the room. Starting into a sitting posture, he looked around him, bewildered for a moment, and then, recognising his humble friend, said laughingly:

'I had lost myself; I could not imagine where I was.'

'I am sorry to see you here, sir,' was the reply; 'but still this is better than being out of doors. It has come on a nasty night. I brought a rug round with me that, perhaps, you would wrap yourself in.'

'I wish, at the same time, you had brought me something to eat,' said the young man, laughing.

'Are you hungry, then, sir?' asked William, in a tone of concern.

'Yes; I have had nothing to eat since breakfast. The governor and I commenced rowing the minute we sat down to luncheon, and I rose and left the table. But hunger does not signify; I am dry and warm, and can forget the other matter in sleep.'

'And it's too late now to buy anything,' soliloquised the man; 'the shops are all shut long ago. Do you think, sir,' he added, brightening, 'you could manage some bread and cheese?'

'Do I think – I should call it a perfect feast,' answered Graham Coulton. 'But never mind about food tonight, William; you have had trouble enough, and to spare, already.'

William's only answer was to dart to the door and run downstairs. Presently he reappeared, carrying in one hand bread and cheese wrapped up in paper, and in the other a pewter measure full of beer.

'It's the best I could do, sir,' he said apologetically. 'I had to beg this from the landlady.'

'Here's to her good health!' exclaimed the young fellow gaily, taking a long pull at the tankard. 'That tastes better than champagne in my father's house.'

'Won't he be uneasy about you?' ventured William, who, having by this time emptied the coals, was now seated on the inverted basket, looking wistfully at the relish with which the son of the former master was eating his bread and cheese.

'No,' was the decided answer. 'When he hears it pouring cats and dogs he will only hope I am out in the deluge, and say a good drenching will cool my pride.'

'I do not think you are right there,' remarked the man.

'But I am sure I am. My father always hated me, as he hated my mother.'

'Begging your pardon, sir; he was over fond of your mother.'

'If you had heard what he said about her today, you might find reason to alter your opinion. He told me I resembled her in mind as well as body; that I was a coward, a simpleton, and a hypocrite.'

'He did not mean it, sir.'

'He did, every word. He does think I am a coward, because I – I—' And the young fellow broke into a passion of hysterical tears.

'I don't half like leaving you here alone,' said William, glancing round the room with a quick trouble in his eyes; 'but I have no place fit to ask you to stop, and I am forced to go myself, because I am night watchman, and must be on at twelve o'clock.'

'I shall be right enough,' was the answer. 'Only I mustn't talk any more of my father. Tell me about yourself, William. How did you manage to get such a big house, and why are you leaving it?'

'The landlord put me in charge, sir; and it was my wife's fancy not to like it.'

'Why did she not like it?'

'She felt desolate alone with the children at night,' answered William, turning away his head; then added, next minute: 'Now, sir, if you think I can do no more for you, I had best be off. Time's getting on. I'll look round tomorrow morning.'

'Goodnight,' said the young fellow, stretching out his hand, which the other took as freely and frankly as it was offered. 'What should I have done this evening if I had not chanced to meet you?'

'I don't think there is much chance in the world, Master Graham,' was the quiet answer. 'I do hope you will rest well, and not be the worse for your wetting.'

'No fear of that,' was the rejoinder, and the next minute the young man found himself all alone in the Old House in Vauxhall Walk.

II

Lying on the settle, with the fire burnt out, and the room in total darkness, Graham Coulton dreamed a curious dream. He thought he awoke from deep slumber to find a log smouldering away upon the hearth, and the mirror at the end of the apartment reflecting fitful gleams of light. He could not understand how it came to pass that, far away as he was from the glass, he was able to see everything in it; but he resigned himself to the difficulty without astonishment, as people generally do in dreams.

Neither did he feel surprised when he beheld the outline of a female figure seated beside the fire, engaged in picking something out of her lap and dropping it with a despairing gesture.

He heard the mellow sound of gold, and knew she was lifting and dropping sovereigns. He turned a little so as to see the person engaged in such a singular and meaningless manner, and found that, where there had been no chair on the previous night, there was a chair now, on which was seated an old, wrinkled hag, her clothes poor and ragged, a mob cap barely covering her scant white hair, her cheeks sunken, her nose hooked, her fingers more like talons than aught else as they dived down into the heap of gold, portions of which they lifted but to scatter mournfully.

'Oh! my lost life,' she moaned, in a voice of the bitterest anguish. 'Oh! my lost life – for one day, for one hour of it again!'

Out of the darkness – out of the corner of the room where the shadows lay deepest – out from the gloom abiding near the door – out from the dreary night, with their sodden feet and wet dripping from their heads, came the old men and the young children, the worn women and the weary hearts, whose misery that gold might have relieved, but whose wretchedness it mocked.

Round that miser, who once sat gloating as she now sat lamenting, they crowded – all those pale, sad shapes – the aged of days, the infant of hours, the sobbing outcast, honest poverty, repentant vice; but one low cry proceeded from those pale lips – a cry for help she might have given, but which she withheld.

They closed about her, all together, as they had done singly in life; they prayed, they sobbed, they entreated; with haggard eyes the figure regarded the poor she had repulsed, the children against whose cry she had closed her ears, the old people she had suffered to starve and die for want of what would have been the merest trifle to her; then, with a terrible scream, she raised her lean arms above her head, and sank down – down – the gold scattering as it fell out of her lap, and rolling along the floor, till its gleam was lost in the outer darkness beyond.

Then Graham Coulton awoke in good earnest, with the perspiration oozing from every pore, with a fear and an agony upon him such as he had never before felt in all his existence, and with the sound of the heart-rending cry – 'Oh! my lost life' – still ringing in his ears.

Mingled with all, too, there seemed to have been some lesson for him which he had forgotten, that, try as he would, eluded his memory, and which, in the very act of waking, glided away.

He lay for a little thinking about all this, and then, still heavy with sleep, retraced his way into dreamland once more.

It was natural, perhaps, that, mingling with the strange fantasies which follow in the train of night and darkness, the former vision should recur, and the young man ere long found himself toiling through scene after scene wherein the figure of the woman he had seen seated beside a dying fire held principal place.

He saw her walking slowly across the floor munching a dry crust – she who could have purchased all the luxuries wealth can command; on the hearth, contemplating her, stood a man of commanding presence, dressed in the fashion of long ago. In his eyes there was a dark look of anger, on his lips a curling smile of disgust, and somehow, even in his sleep, the dreamer understood it was the ancestor to the descendant he beheld – that the house put to mean uses in which he lay had never so far descended from its high estate, as the woman possessed of so pitiful a soul, contaminated with the most despicable and insidious vice poor humanity knows, for all other vices seem to have connection with the flesh, but the greed of the miser eats into the very soul.

Filthy of person, repulsive to look at, hard of heart as she was, he yet beheld another phantom, which, coming into the room, met her almost on the threshold, taking her by the hand, and pleading, as it seemed, for assistance. He could not hear all that passed, but a word now and then fell upon his ear. Some talk of former days; some mention of a fair young mother – an appeal, as it seemed, to a time when they were tiny brother and sister, and the accursed greed for gold had not divided them. All in vain; the hag only answered him as she had answered the children, and the young girls, and the old people in his former vision. Her heart was as invulnerable to natural affection as it had proved to human sympathy. He begged, as it appeared, for aid to avert some bitter misfortune or terrible disgrace, and adamant might have been found more yielding to his prayer. Then the figure standing on the hearth changed to an angel, which folded its wings mournfully over its face, and the man, with bowed head, slowly left the room.

Even as he did so the scene changed again; it was night once more, and the miser wended her way upstairs. From below, Graham Coulton fancied he watched her toiling wearily from step to step.

She had aged strangely since the previous scenes. She moved with difficulty; it seemed the greatest exertion for her to creep from step to step, her skinny hand traversing the balusters with slow and painful deliberateness. Fascinated, the young man's eyes followed the progress of that feeble, decrepit woman. She was solitary in a desolate house, with a deeper blackness than the darkness of night waiting to engulf her.

It seemed to Graham Coulton that after that he lay for a time in a still, dreamless sleep, upon awaking from which he found himself entering a chamber as sordid and unclean in its appointments as the woman of his previous vision had been in her person. The poorest labourer's wife would have gathered more comforts around her than that room contained. A four-poster bedstead without hangings of any kind – a blind drawn up awry – an old carpet covered with dust, and dirt on the floor – a rickety washstand with all the paint worn off it – an ancient mahogany dressing-table, and a cracked glass spotted all over – were all the objects he could at first discern, looking at the room through that dim light which oftentimes obtains in dreams.

By degrees, however, he perceived the outline of someone lying huddled on the bed. Drawing nearer, he found it was that of the person whose dreadful presence seemed to pervade the house. What a terrible sight she looked, with her thin white locks scattered over the pillow, with what were mere remnants of blankets gathered about her shoulders, with her claw-like fingers clutching the clothes, as though even in sleep she was guarding her gold!

An awful and a repulsive spectacle, but not with half the terror in it of that which followed. Even as the young man looked he heard stealthy footsteps on the stairs. Then he saw first one man and then his fellow steal cautiously into the room. Another second, and the pair stood beside the bed, murder in their eyes.

Graham Coulton tried to shout – tried to move, but the deterrent power which exists in dreams only tied his tongue and paralysed his limbs. He could but hear and look, and what he heard and saw was this: aroused suddenly from sleep, the woman started, only to receive a blow from one of the ruffians, whose fellow followed his lead by plunging a knife into her breast.

Then, with a gurgling scream, she fell back on the bed, and at the same moment, with a cry, Graham Coulton again awoke, to thank heaven it was but an illusion.

III

'I hope you slept well, sir.' It was William, who, coming into the hall with the sunlight of a fine bright morning streaming after him, asked this question: 'Had you a good night's rest?'

Graham Coulton laughed, and answered:

'Why, faith, I was somewhat in the case of Paddy, "who could not slape for dhraming". I slept well enough, I suppose, but whether it was in consequence of the row with my dad, or the hard bed, or the cheese – most likely the bread and cheese so late at night – I dreamt all the night long, the most extraordinary dreams. Some old woman kept cropping up, and I saw her murdered.'

'You don't say that, sir?' said William nervously.

'I do, indeed,' was the reply. 'However, that is all gone and past. I have been down in the kitchen and had a good wash, and I am as fresh as a daisy, and as hungry as a hunter, and, oh, William, can you get me any breakfast?'

'Certainly, Master Graham. I have brought round a kettle, and I will make the water boil immediately. I suppose, sir' – this tentatively – 'you'll be going home today?'

'Home!' repeated the young man. 'Decidedly not. I'll never go home again till I return with some medal hung to my coat, or a leg or arm cut off. I've thought it all out, William. I'll go and enlist. There's a talk of war, and, living or dead, my father shall have reason to retract his opinion about my being a coward.'

'I am sure the admiral never thought you anything of the sort, sir,' said William. 'Why, you have the pluck of ten!'

'Not before him,' answered the young fellow sadly.

'You'll do nothing rash, Master Graham; you won't go 'listing, or aught of that sort, in your anger?'

'If I do not, what is to become of me?' asked the other. 'I cannot dig – to beg I am ashamed. Why, but for you, I should not have had a roof over my head last night.'

'Not much of a roof, I am afraid, sir.'

'Not much of a roof!' repeated the young man. 'Why, who could desire a better? What a capital room this is,' he went on, looking around the apartment, where William was now kindling a fire; 'one might dine twenty people here easily!'

'If you think so well of the place, Master Graham, you might stay here for a while, till you have made up your mind what you are going to do. The landlord won't make any objection, I am very sure.'

'Oh! nonsense; he would want a long rent for a house like this.'

'I dare say; *if he could get it*,' was William's significant answer.

'What do you mean? Won't the place let?'

'No, sir. I did not tell you last night, but there was a murder done here, and people are shy of the house ever since.'

'A murder! What sort of a murder? Who was murdered?'

'A woman, Master Graham – the landlord's sister, she lived here all alone, and was supposed to have money. Whether she had or not, she was found dead from a stab in her breast, and if there ever was any money, it must have been taken at the same time, for none ever was found in the house from that day to this.'

'Was that the reason your wife would not stop here?' asked the young man, leaning against the mantelshelf, and looking thoughtfully down on William.

'Yes, sir. She could not stand it any longer; she got that thin and nervous no one would have believed it possible; she never saw anything, but she said she heard footsteps and voices, and then when she walked through the hall, or up the staircase, someone always seemed to be following her. We put the children to sleep in that big room you had last night, and they declared they often saw an old woman sitting by the hearth. Nothing ever came my way,' finished

William, with a laugh; 'I was always ready to go to sleep the minute my head touched the pillow.'

'Were not the murderers discovered?' asked Graham Coulton.

'No, sir; the landlord, Miss Tynan's brother, had always lain under the suspicion of it – quite wrongfully, I am very sure – but he will never clear himself now. It was known he came and asked her for help a day or two before the murder, and it was also known he was able within a week or two to weather whatever trouble had been harassing him. Then, you see, the money was never found; and, altogether, people scarce knew what to think.'

'Humph!' ejaculated Graham Coulton, and he took a few turns up and down the apartment. 'Could I go and see this landlord?'

'Surely, sir, if you had a hat,' answered William, with such a serious decorum that the young man burst out laughing.

'That is an obstacle, certainly,' he remarked, 'and I must make a note do instead. I have a pencil in my pocket, so here goes.'

Within half an hour from the dispatch of that note William was back again with a sovereign; the landlord's compliments, and he would be much obliged if Mr Coulton could 'step round'.

'You'll do nothing rash, sir,' entreated William.

'Why, man,' answered the young fellow, 'one may as well be picked off by a ghost as a bullet. What is there to be afraid of!'

William only shook his head. He did not think his young master was made of the stuff likely to remain alone in a haunted house and solve the mystery it assuredly contained by dint of his own unassisted endeavours. And yet when Graham Coulton came out of the landlord's house he looked more bright and gay than usual, and walked up the Lambeth road to the place where William awaited his return, humming an air as he paced along.

'We have settled the matter,' he said. 'And now if the dad wants his son for Christmas, it will trouble him to find him.'

'Don't say that, Master Graham, don't,' entreated the man, with a shiver, 'maybe after all it would have been better if you had never happened to chance upon Vauxhall Walk.'

'Don't croak, William,' answered the young man; 'if it was not the best day's work I ever did for myself, I'm a Dutchman.'

During the whole of that forenoon and afternoon, Graham Coulton searched diligently for the missing treasure Mr Tynan assured him had never been discovered. Youth is confident and self-opinionated, and this fresh explorer felt satisfied that, though others had failed, he would be successful. On the second floor he found one door locked, but he did not pay much attention to that at the moment, as he believed if there was anything concealed it was more likely to be found in the lower than the upper part of the house. Late into the evening he pursued his researches in the kitchen and cellars and old-fashioned cupboards, of which the basement had an abundance.

It was nearly eleven, when, engaged in poking about amongst the empty bins of a wine cellar as large as a family vault, he suddenly felt a rush of cold air at his back. Moving, his candle was instantly extinguished, and in the very moment of being left in darkness he saw, standing in the doorway, a woman, resembling her who had haunted his dreams overnight.

He rushed with outstretched hands to seize her, but clutched only air. He relit his candle, and closely examined the basement, shutting off communication with the ground floor ere doing so. All in vain. Not a trace could he find of living creature – not a window was open – not a door unbolted.

'It is very odd,' he thought, as, after securely fastening the door at the top of the staircase, he searched the whole upper portion of the house, with the exception of the one room mentioned.

'I must get the key of that tomorrow,' he decided, standing gloomily with his back to the fire and his eyes wandering about the drawing-room, where he had once again taken up his abode.

Even as the thought passed through his mind, he saw standing in the open doorway a woman with white dishevelled hair, clad in mean garments, ragged and dirty. She lifted her hand and shook it at him with a menacing gesture, and then, just as he was darting towards her, a wonderful thing occurred.

From behind the great mirror there glided a second female figure, at the sight of which the first turned and fled, uttering piercing shrieks as the other followed her from storey to storey.

Sick almost with terror, Graham Coulton watched the dreadful pair as they fled upstairs past the locked room to the top of the house.

It was a few minutes before he recovered his self-possession. When he did so, and searched the upper apartments, he found them totally empty.

That night, ere lying down before the fire, he carefully locked and bolted the drawing-room door; before he did more he drew the heavy settle in front of it, so that if the lock were forced no entrance could be effected without considerable noise.

For some time he lay awake, then dropped into a deep sleep, from which he was awakened suddenly by a noise as if of something scuffling stealthily behind the wainscot. He raised himself on his elbow and listened, and, to his consternation, beheld seated at the opposite side of the hearth the same woman he had seen before in his dreams, lamenting over her gold.

The fire was not quite out, and at that moment shot up a last tongue of flame. By the light, transient as it was, he saw that the figure pressed a ghostly finger to its lips, and by the turn of its head and the attitude of its body seemed to be listening.

He listened also – indeed, he was too much frightened to do aught else; more and more distinct grew the sounds which had aroused him, a stealthy rustling coming nearer and nearer – up and up it seemed, behind the wainscot.

'It is rats,' thought the young man, though, indeed, his teeth were almost chattering in his head with fear. But then in a moment he saw what disabused him of that idea – *the gleam of a candle or lamp through a crack in the panelling*. He tried to rise, he strove to shout – all in vain; and, sinking down, remembered nothing more till he awoke to find the grey light of an early morning stealing through one of the shutters he had left partially unclosed.

For hours after his breakfast, which he scarcely touched, long after William had left him at mid-day, Graham Coulton, having in the morning made a long and close survey of the house, sat thinking before the fire, then, apparently having made up his mind, he put on the hat he had bought, and went out.

When he returned the evening shadows were darkening down, but the pavements were full of people going marketing, for it was Christmas Eve, and all who had money to spend seemed bent on shopping.

It was terribly dreary inside the old house that night. Through the deserted rooms Graham could feel that ghostly semblance was wandering mournfully. When he turned his back he knew she was flitting from the mirror to the fire, from the fire to the mirror; but he was not afraid of her now – he was far more afraid of another matter he had taken in hand that day.

The horror of the silent house grew and grew upon him. He could hear the beating of his own heart in the dead quietude which reigned from garret to cellar.

At last William came; but the young man said nothing to him of what was in his mind. He talked to him cheerfully and hopefully enough wondered where his father would think he had got to, and hoped Mr Tynan might send him some Christmas pudding. Then the man said it was time for him to go, and, when Mr Coulton went downstairs to the hall-door, remarked the key was not in it.

'No,' was the answer, 'I took it out today, to oil it.'

'It wanted oiling,' agreed William, 'for it worked terribly stiff.' Having uttered which truism he departed.

Very slowly the young man retraced his way to the drawing-room, where he only paused to lock the door on the outside; then taking off his boots he went up to the top of the house, where, entering the front attic, he waited patiently in darkness and in silence.

It was a long time, or at least it seemed long to him, before he heard the same sound which had aroused him on the previous night – a stealthy rustling – then a rush of cold air – then cautious footsteps – then the quiet opening of a door below.

It did not take as long in action as it has required to tell. In a moment the young man was out on the landing and had closed a portion of the panelling on the wall which stood open; noiselessly he crept back to the attic window, unlatched it, and sprung a rattle, the sound of which echoed far and near through the deserted streets, then rushing down the stairs, he encountered a man who, darting past him, made for the landing above; but perceiving the way of escape closed, fled down again, to find Graham struggling desperately with his fellow.

'Give him the knife – come along,' he said savagely; and next instant Graham felt something like a hot iron through his shoulder, and then heard a thud, as one of the men, tripping in his rapid flight, fell from the top of the stairs to the bottom.

At the same moment there came a crash, as if the house was falling, and faint, sick, and bleeding, young Coulton lay insensible on the threshold of the room where Miss Tynan had been murdered.

When he recovered he was in the dining-room, and a doctor was examining his wound.

Near the door a policeman stiffly kept guard. The hall was full of people; all the misery and vagabondism the streets contain at that hour was crowding in to see what had happened.

Through the midst two men were being conveyed to the station-house; one, with his head dreadfully injured, on a stretcher, the other handcuffed, uttering frightful imprecations as he went.

After a time the house was cleared of the rabble, the police took possession of it, and Mr Tynan was sent for.

'What was that dreadful noise?' asked Graham feebly, now seated on the floor, with his back resting against the wall.

'I do not know. Was there a noise?' said Mr Tynan, humouring his fancy, as he thought.

'Yes, in the drawing-room, I think; the key is in my pocket.'

Still humouring the wounded lad, Mr Tynan took the key and ran upstairs.

When he unlocked the door, what a sight met his eyes! The mirror had fallen – it was lying all over the floor shivered into a thousand pieces; the console table had been borne down by its weight, and the marble slab was shattered as well. But this was not what chained his attention. Hundreds, thousands of gold pieces were scattered about, and an aperture behind the glass contained boxes filled with securities and deeds and bonds, the possession of which had cost his sister her life.

'Well, Graham, and what do you want?' asked Admiral Coulton that evening as his eldest born appeared before him, looking somewhat pale but otherwise unchanged.

'I want nothing,' was the answer, 'but to ask your forgiveness. William has told me all the story I never knew before; and, if you let me, I will try to make it up to you for the trouble you have had. I am provided for,' went on the young fellow, with a nervous laugh; 'I have made my fortune since I left you, and another man's fortune as well.'

'I think you are out of your senses,' said the Admiral shortly.

'No, sir, I have found them,' was the answer; 'and I mean to strive and make a better thing of my life than I should ever have done had I not gone to the Old House in Vauxhall Walk.'

'Vauxhall Walk! What is the lad talking about?'

'I will tell you, sir, if I may sit down,' was Graham Coulton's answer, and then he told his story.

MARGARET OLIPHANT

THE OPEN DOOR

I took the house of Brentwood on my return from India in 18—, for the temporary accommodation of my family, until I could find a permanent home for them. It had many advantages which made it peculiarly appropriate. It was within reach of Edinburgh, and my boy Roland, whose education had been considerably neglected, could go in and out to school, which was thought to be better for him than either leaving home altogether or staying there always with a tutor. The first of these expedients would have seemed preferable to me, the second commended itself to his mother. The doctor, like a judicious man, took the midway between. 'Put him on his pony, and let him ride into the High School every morning; it will do him all the good in the world,' Dr Simson said; 'and when it is bad weather there is the train.' His mother accepted the solution of the difficulty more easily than I could have hoped; and our pale-faced boy, who had never known anything more invigorating than Simla, began to encounter the brisk breezes of the North in the subdued severity of the month of May. Before the time of the vacation in July we had the satisfaction of seeing him begin to acquire something of the brown and ruddy complexion of his schoolfellows. The English system did not commend itself to Scotland in those days. There was no little Eton at Fettes; nor do I think, if there had been, that a genteel exotic of that class would have tempted either my wife or me. The lad was doubly precious to us, being the only one left us of many; and he was fragile in body, we believed, and deeply sensitive in mind. To keep him at home, and yet to send him to school – to combine the advantages of the two systems – seemed to be everything that could be desired. The two girls also found at Brentwood everything they wanted. They were near enough to Edinburgh to have masters and lessons as many as they required for completing that never-ending education which the young people seem to require nowadays. Their mother married me when she was younger than Agatha, and I should like to see them improve upon their mother! I myself was then no more than twenty-five – an age at which I see the young fellows now groping about them, with no notion what they are going to do with their lives. However, I suppose every generation has a conceit of itself which elevates it, in its own opinion, above that which comes after it.

Brentwood stands on that fine and wealthy slope of country, one of the richest in Scotland, which lies between the Pentland Hills and the Firth. In clear weather you could see the blue gleam – like a bent bow, embracing the wealthy fields and scattered houses – of the great estuary on one side of you; and on the other the blue heights, not gigantic like those we had been used to, but just high enough for all the glories of the atmosphere, the play of clouds, and sweet reflections, which give to a hilly country an interest and a charm which nothing else can emulate. Edinburgh, with its two lesser heights – the Castle and the Calton Hill – its spires and towers piercing through the smoke, and Arthur's Seat lying crouched behind, like a guardian no longer very needful, taking his repose beside the well-beloved charge, which is now, so to speak, able to take care of itself without him – lay at our right hand. From the lawn and drawing-room windows we could see all these varieties of landscape. The colour was sometimes a little chilly, but sometimes, also, as animated and full of vicissitude as a drama. I was never tired of it. Its colour and freshness revived the eyes which had grown weary of arid plains and blazing skies. It was always cheery, and fresh, and full of repose.

The village of Brentwood lay almost under the house, on the other side of the deep little ravine, down which a stream – which ought to have been a lovely, wild, and frolicsome little river – flowed between its rocks and trees. The river, like so many in that district, had, however, in its earlier life been sacrificed to trade, and was grimy with paper-making. But this did not affect our pleasure in it so much as I have known it to affect other streams. Perhaps our water was more rapid – perhaps less clogged with dirt and refuse. Our side of the dell was charmingly *accidenté*, and clothed with fine trees, through which various paths wound down to the river-side and to the village bridge which crossed the stream. The village lay in the hollow, and climbed, with very prosaic houses, the other side. Village architecture does not flourish in Scotland. The blue slates and the grey stone are sworn foes to the picturesque; and though I do not, for my own part, dislike the interior of an old-fashioned pewed and galleried church, with its little family settlements on all sides, the square box outside, with its bit of a spire like a handle to lift it by, is not an improvement to the landscape. Still, a cluster of houses on differing elevations – with scraps of garden coming in between, a hedgerow with clothes laid out to dry, the opening of a street with its rural sociability, the women at their doors, the slow waggon lumbering along – gives a centre to the landscape. It was cheerful to look at, and convenient in a hundred ways. Within ourselves we had walks in plenty, the glen being always beautiful in all its phases, whether the woods were green in the spring or ruddy in the autumn. In the park which surrounded the house were the ruins of the former mansion of Brentwood, a much smaller and less important house than the solid Georgian edifice which we inhabited. The ruins were picturesque, however, and gave importance to the place. Even we, who were but tempo-rary tenants, felt a vague pride in them, as if they somehow reflected a certain consequence upon ourselves. The old building had the remains of a tower, an indistinguishable mass of mason-work, overgrown with ivy, and the shells of walls attached to this were half filled up with soil. I had never examined it closely, I am ashamed to say. There was a large room, or what had been a large room, with the lower part of the windows still existing, on the principal floor, and underneath other windows, which were perfect, though half filled up with fallen soil, and waving with a wild growth of brambles and chance growths of all kinds. This was the oldest part of all. At a little distance were some very common-place and disjointed fragments of the building, one of them suggesting a certain pathos by its very commonness and the complete wreck which it showed. This was the end of a low gable, a bit of grey wall, all encrusted with lichens, in which was a common doorway. Probably it had been a servants' entrance, a back-door, or opening into what are called 'the offices' in Scotland. No offices remained to be entered – pantry and kitchen had all been swept out of being; but there stood the doorway open and vacant, free to all the winds, to the rabbits, and every wild creature. It struck my eye, the first time I went to Brentwood, like a melancholy comment upon a life that was over. A door that led to nothing – closed once perhaps with anxious care, bolted and guarded, now void of any meaning. It impressed me, I remember, from the first; so perhaps it may be said that my mind was prepared to attach to it an importance, which nothing justified.

The summer was a very happy period of repose for us all. The warmth of Indian suns was still in our veins. It seemed to us that we could never have enough of the greenness, the dewiness, the freshness of the northern landscape. Even its mists were pleasant to us, taking all the fever out of us, and pouring in vigour and refreshment. In autumn we followed the fashion of the time, and went away for change which we did not in the least require. It was when the family had settled down for the winter, when the days were short and dark, and the rigorous reign of frost upon us, that the incidents occurred which alone could justify me in intruding upon the world my private affairs. These incidents were, however, of so curious a character, that I hope my inevitable references to my own family and pressing personal interests will meet with a general pardon.

I was absent in London when these events began. In London an old Indian plunges back into the interests with which all his previous life has been associated, and meets old friends at every step. I had been circulating among some half-dozen of these – enjoying the return to my former life in shadow, though I had been so thankful in substance to throw it aside – and had missed some of my home letters, what with going down from Friday to Monday to old Benbow's place in the country, and stopping on the way back to dine and sleep at Sellar's and to take a look into Cross's stables, which occupied another day. It is never safe to miss one's letters. In this transitory life, as the Prayer-book says, how can one ever be certain what is going to happen? All was well at home. I knew exactly (I thought) what they would have to say to me: 'The weather has been so fine, that Roland has not once gone by train, and he enjoys the ride beyond anything.' 'Dear papa, be sure that you don't forget anything, but bring us so-and-so and so-and-so' – a list as long as my arm. Dear girls and dearer mother! I would not for the world have forgotten their commissions, or lost their little letters, for all the Benbows and Crosses in the world.

But I was confident in my home-comfort and peacefulness. When I got back to my club, however, three or four letters were lying for me, upon some of which I noticed the 'immediate', 'urgent', which old-fashioned people and anxious people still believe will influence the post-office and quicken the speed of the mails. I was about to open one of these, when the club porter brought me two telegrams, one of which, he said, had arrived the night before. I opened, as was to be expected, the last first, and this was what I read: 'Why don't you come or answer? For God's sake, come. He is much worse.' This was a thunderbolt to fall upon a man's head who had only one son, and he the light of his eyes! The other telegram, which I opened with hands trembling so much that I lost time by my haste, was to much the same purport: 'No better; doctor afraid of brain-fever. Calls for you day and night. Let nothing detain you.' The first thing I did was to look up the time-tables to see if there was any way of getting off sooner than by the night-train, though I knew well enough there was not! and then I read the letters, which furnished, alas! too clearly, all the details. They told me that the boy had been pale for some time, with a scared look. His mother had noticed it before I left home, but would not say anything to alarm me. This look had increased day by day; and soon it was observed that Roland came home at a wild gallop through the park, his pony panting and in foam, himself 'as white as a sheet', but with the perspiration streaming from his forehead. For a long time he had resisted all questioning, but at length had developed such strange changes of mood, showing a reluctance to go to school, a desire to be fetched in the carriage at night – which was a ridiculous piece of luxury – an unwillingness to go out into the grounds, and nervous start at every sound, that his mother had insisted upon an explanation. When the boy – our boy Roland, who had never known what fear was – began to talk to her of voices he had heard in the park, and shadows that had appeared to him among the ruins, my wife promptly put him to bed and sent for Dr Simson – which, of course, was the only thing to do.

I hurried off that evening, as may be supposed, with an anxious heart. How I got through the hours before the starting of the train, I cannot tell. We must all be thankful for the quickness of the railway when in anxiety; but to have thrown myself into a post-chaise as soon as horses could be put to, would have been a relief. I got to Edinburgh very early in the blackness of the winter morning, and scarcely dared look the man in the face at whom I gasped 'What news?' My wife had sent the brougham for me, which I concluded, before the man spoke, was a bad sign. His answer was that stereotyped answer which leaves the imagination so wildly free – 'Just the same.' Just the same! What might that mean? The horses seemed to me to creep along the long dark country-road. As we dashed through the park, I thought I heard someone moaning among the trees, and clenched my fist at him (whoever he might be) with fury. Why had the fool of a woman at the gate allowed anyone to come in to disturb the quiet of the place? If I had not been in such hot haste to get home, I think I should have stopped the carriage and got out to see what tramp it was that had made an entrance and chosen my grounds, of all places in the world – when my boy was ill! – to grumble and groan in. But I had no reason to complain of our slow pace here. The horses flew like lightning along the intervening path, and drew up at the door all panting, as if they had run a race. My wife stood waiting to receive me with a pale face, and a candle in her hand, which made her look paler still as the wind blew the flame about. 'He is sleeping,' she said in a whisper, as if her voice might wake him. And I replied, when I could find my voice, also in a whisper, as though the jingling of the horses' furniture and the sound of their hoofs must not have been more dangerous. I stood on the steps with her a moment, almost afraid to go in, now that I was here; and it seemed to me that I saw without observing, if I may say so, that the horses were unwilling to turn round, though their stables lay that way, or that the men were unwilling. These things occurred to me afterwards, though at the moment I was not capable of anything but to ask questions and to hear of the condition of the boy.

I looked at him from the door of his room, for we were afraid to go near, lest we should disturb that blessed sleep. It looked like actual sleep – not the lethargy into which my wife told me he would sometimes fall. She told me everything in the next room, which communicated with his, rising now and then and going to the door of communication; and in this there was much that was very startling and confusing to the mind. It appeared that ever since the winter began, since it was early dark and night had fallen before his return from school, he had been hearing voices among the ruins – at first only a groaning, he said, at which his pony was as much alarmed as he was, but by degrees a voice. The tears ran down my wife's cheeks as she described to me how he would start up in the night and cry out, 'Oh, mother, let me in! oh, mother, let me in!' with a pathos which rent her heart. And she sitting there all the time, only longing to do everything his heart could desire! But though she would try to soothe him, crying, 'You are at home, my darling. I am here. Don't you know me? Your mother is here,' he would only stare at her, and after a while spring up again with the same cry. At other times he would be quite reasonable, she said, asking eagerly when I was coming, but declaring that he must go with me as soon as I did so, 'to let them in'. 'The doctor thinks his nervous system must have received a shock,' my wife said. 'Oh, Henry, can it be that we have pushed him on too much with his work – a delicate boy like Roland? – and what is his work in comparison with his health? Even you would think little of honours or prizes if it hurt the boy's health.' Even I! as if I were an inhuman father sacrificing my child to my ambition. But I would not increase her trouble by taking any notice. After a while they persuaded me to lie down, to rest, and to eat – none of which things had been possible since I received their letters. The mere fact of being on the spot, of course, in itself was a great thing; and when I knew that I would be called in a moment, as soon as he was awake and wanted me, I felt capable, even in the dark, chill morning twilight, to snatch an hour or two's sleep. As it happened, I was so worn out with the strain of anxiety, and he so quieted and consoled by knowing I had come, that I was not disturbed till the afternoon, when the twilight had again settled down. There was just daylight enough to see his face when I went to him; and what a change in a fortnight! He was paler and more worn, I thought, than even in those dreadful days in the plains before we left India. His hair seemed to me to have grown long and lank; his eyes were like blazing lights projecting out of his white face. He got hold of my hand in a cold and tremulous clutch, and waved to everybody to go away. 'Go away – even mother,' he said – 'go away.' This went to her heart, for she did not like that even I should have more of the boy's confidence than herself; but my wife has never been a woman to think of herself, and she left us alone. 'Are they all gone?' he said, eagerly. 'They would not let me speak. The doctor treated me as if I were a fool. You know I am not a fool, papa.'

'Yes, yes my boy, I know; but you are ill, and quiet is so necessary. You are not only not a fool, Roland, but you are reasonable and understand. When you are ill you must deny yourself; you must not do everything that you might do being well.'

He waved his thin hand with a sort of indignation. 'Then, father, I am not ill,' he cried. 'Oh, I thought when you came you would not stop me – you would see the sense of it! What do you think is the matter with me, all of you? Simson is well enough, but he is only a doctor. What do you think is the matter with me? I am no more ill than you are. A doctor, of course, he thinks you are ill the moment he looks at you – that's what he's there for – and claps you into bed.'

'Which is the best place for you at present, my dear boy.'

'I made up my mind,' cried the little fellow, 'that I would stand it till you came home. I said to myself, I won't frighten mother and the girls. But now, father,' he cried, half jumping out of the bed, 'it's not illness – it's a secret.'

His eyes shone so wildly, his face was so swept with strong feeling, that my heart sank within me. It could be nothing but fever that did it, and fever had been so fatal. I got him into my arms to put him back into bed. 'Roland,' I said, humouring the poor child, which I knew was the only way, 'if you are going to tell me this secret to do any good, you know you must be quite quiet, and not excite yourself. If you excite yourself, I must not let you speak.'

'Yes, father,' said the boy. He was quiet directly, like a man, as if he quite understood. When I had laid him back on his pillow, he looked up at me with that grateful, sweet look with which children, when they are ill, break one's heart, the water coming into his eyes in his weakness. 'I was sure as soon as you were here you would know what to do,' he said.

'To be sure, my boy. Now keep quiet, and tell it all out like a man.' To think I was telling lies to my own child! for I did it only to humour him, thinking, poor little fellow, his brain was wrong.

'Yes, father. Father, there is some one in the park – some one that has been badly used.'

'Hush, my dear; you remember, there is to be no excitement. Well, who is this somebody, and who has been ill-using him? We will soon put a stop to that.'

'Ah,' cried Roland, 'but it is not so easy as you think. I don't know who it is. It is just a cry. Oh, if you could hear it! It gets into my head in my sleep. I heard it as clear as clear; and they think that I am dreaming – or raving perhaps,' the boy said, with a sort of disdainful smile.

This look of his perplexed me; it was less like fever than I thought. 'Are you quite sure you have not dreamt it, Roland?' I said.

'Dreamt? – that!' He was springing up again when he suddenly bethought himself, and lay down flat with the same sort of smile on his face. 'The pony heard it too,' he said. 'She jumped as if she had been shot. If I had not grasped at the reins – for I was frightened, father—'

'No shame to you, my boy,' said I, though I scarcely knew why.

'If I hadn't held to her like a leech, she'd have pitched me over her head, and she never drew breath till we were at the door. Did the pony dream it?' he said, with a soft disdain, yet indulgence for my foolishness. Then he added slowly: 'It was only a cry the first time, and all the time before you went away. I wouldn't tell you, for it was so wretched to be frightened. I thought it might be a hare or a rabbit snared, and I went in the morning and looked, but there was nothing. It was after you went I heard it really first, and this is what he says.' He raised himself on his elbow close to me, and looked me in the face. '"Oh, mother, let me in! oh, mother, let me in!"' As he said the words a mist came over his face, the mouth quivered, the soft features all melted and changed, and when he had ended these pitiful words, dissolved in a shower of heavy tears.

Was it a hallucination? Was it the fever of the brain? Was it the disordered fancy caused by great bodily weakness? How could I tell? I thought it wisest to accept it as if it were all true.

'This is very touching, Roland,' I said.

'Oh, if you had just heard it, father! I said to myself, "if father heard it he would do something"; but mamma, you know, she's given over to Simson, and that fellow's a doctor, and never thinks of anything but clapping you into bed.'

'We must not blame Simson for being a doctor, Roland.'

'No, no,' said my boy, with delightful toleration and indulgence; 'oh, no; that's the good of him – that's what he's for; I know that. But you – you are different; you are just father: and you'll do something – directly, papa, directly – this very night.'

'Surely,' I said. 'No doubt, it is some little lost child.'

He gave me a sudden, swift look, investigating my face as though to see whether, after all, this was everything my eminence as 'father' came to – no more than that? Then he got hold of my shoulder, clutching it with his thin hand: 'Look here,' he said, with a quiver in his voice; 'suppose it wasn't – living at all!'

'My dear boy, how then could you have heard it?' I said.

He turned away from me, with a pettish exclamation – 'As if you didn't know better than that!'

'Do you want to tell me it is a ghost?' I said.

Roland withdrew his hand; his countenance assumed an aspect of great dignity and gravity; a slight quiver remained about his lips. 'Whatever it was – you always said we were not to call names. It was something – in trouble. Oh, father, in terrible trouble!'

'But, my boy,' I said – I was at my wits' end – 'if it was a child that was lost, or any poor human creature— But, Roland, what do you want me to do?'

'I should know if I was you,' said the child, eagerly. 'That is what I always said to myself – "Father will know." Oh, papa, papa, to have to face it night after night, in such terrible, terrible trouble! and never to be able to do it any good. I don't want to cry; it's like a baby, I know; but what can I do else? – out there all by itself in the ruin, and nobody to help it. I can't bear it, I can't bear it!' cried my generous boy. And in his weakness he burst out, after many attempts to restrain it, into a great childish fit of sobbing and tears.

I do not know that I ever was in a greater perplexity in my life; and afterwards, when I thought of it, there was something comic in it too. It is bad enough to find your child's mind possessed with the conviction that he has seen – or heard – a ghost. But that he should require you to go instantly and help that ghost, was the most bewildering experience that had ever come my way. I am a sober man myself, and not superstitious – at least any more than everybody is superstitious. Of course I do not believe in ghosts; but I don't deny, any more than other people, that there are stories which I cannot pretend to understand. My blood got a sort of chill in my veins at the idea that Roland should be a ghost-seer; for that generally means a hysterical temperament and weak health and all that men most hate and fear for their children. But that I should take up his ghost and right its wrongs, and save it from its trouble, was such a mission as was enough to confuse any man. I did my best to console my boy without giving any promise of this astonishing kind; but he was too sharp for me. He would have none of my caresses. With sobs breaking in at intervals upon his voice, and the raindrops hanging on his eye-lids, he yet returned to the charge.

'It will be there now – it will be there all the night. Oh think, papa, think, if it was me! I can't rest for thinking of it. Don't!' he cried, putting away my hand – 'don't! You go and help it, and mother can take care of me.'

'But, Roland, what can I do?'

My boy opened his eyes, which were large with weakness and fever, and gave me a smile such, I think, as sick children only know the secret of. 'I was sure you would know as soon as you came. I always said – "Father will know"; and mother,' he cried, with a softening of repose upon his face, his limbs relaxing, his form sinking with a luxurious ease in his bed – 'mother can come and take care of me.'

I called her, and saw him turn to her with the complete dependence of a child, and then I went away and left them, as perplexed a man as any in Scotland. I must say, however, I had this consolation, that my mind was greatly eased about Roland. He might be under a hallucination, but his head was clear enough, and I did not think him so ill as everybody else did. The girls were astonished even at the ease with which I took it. 'How do you think he is?' they said in a breath, coming round me, laying hold of me. 'Not half so ill as I expected,' I said; 'not very bad at all.' 'Oh, papa, you are a darling,' cried Agatha, kissing me, and crying upon my shoulder; while little Jeanie, who was as pale as Roland, clasped both her arms around mine, and could not speak at all. I knew nothing about it, not half so much as Simson; but they believed in me; they had a feeling that all would go right now. God is very good to you when your children look to you like that. It makes one humble, not proud. I was not worthy of it; and then I recollected that I had to act the part of a father to Roland's ghost, which made me almost laugh, though I might just as well have cried. It was the strangest mission that ever was entrusted to mortal man.

It was then I remembered suddenly the looks of the men when they turned to take the brougham to the stables in the dark that morning: they had not liked it, and the horses had not liked it. I remembered that even in my anxiety about Roland I had heard them tearing along the avenue back to the stables, and had made a memorandum mentally that I must speak of it. It seemed to me that the best thing I could do was to go to the stables now and make a few inquiries. It is impossible to fathom the minds of rustics; there might be some devilry of practical joking, for anything I knew; or they might have some interest in getting up a bad reputation for the Brentwood avenue. It was getting dark by the time I went out, and nobody who knows the country will need to be told how black is the darkness of a November night under high laurel-bushes and yew-trees. I walked into the heart of the shrubberies two or three times, not seeing a step before me, till I came out upon the broader carriage-road, where the trees opened a little, and there was a faint grey glimmer of sky visible, under which the great limes and elms stood darkling like ghosts; but it grew black again as I approached the corner where the ruins lay. Both eyes and ears were on the alert, as may be supposed; but I could see nothing in the absolute gloom, and, so far as I can recollect, I heard nothing. Nevertheless, there came a strong impression upon me that somebody was there. It is a sensation which most people have felt. I have seen when it has been strong enough to awake me out of sleep, the sense of someone looking at me. I suppose my imagination had been affected by Roland's story; and the mystery of the darkness is always full of suggestions. I stamped my feet violently on the gravel to rouse myself, and called out sharply, 'Who's there?' Nobody answered, nor did I expect anyone to answer, but the impression had been made. I was so foolish that I did not like to look back, but went sideways, keeping an eye on the gloom behind. It was with great relief that I spied the light in the stables, making a sort of oasis in the darkness. I walked very quickly into the midst of that lighted and cheerful place, and thought the clank of the groom's pail one of the pleasantest sounds I had ever heard. The coachman was the head of this little colony, and it was to his house I went to pursue my investigations. He was a native of the district, and had taken care of the place in the absence of the family for years; it was impossible but that he must know everything that was going on, and all the traditions of the place. The men, I could see, eyed me anxiously when I thus appeared at such an hour among them, and followed me with their eyes to Jarvis's house, where he lived alone with his old wife, their children being all married and out in the world. Mrs Jarvis met me with anxious questions. How was the poor young gentleman? but the others knew, I could see by their faces, that not even this was the foremost thing in my mind.

'Noises? – ou ay, there'll be noises – the wind in the trees, and the water soughing down the glen. As for tramps, Cornel, no, there's little o' that kind of cattle about here; and Merran at the gate's a careful body.' Jarvis moved about with some embarrassment from one leg to another as he spoke. He kept in the shade, and did not look at me more than he could help. Evidently his mind was perturbed, and he had reasons for keeping his own counsel. His wife sat by, giving him a quick look now and then, but saying nothing. The kitchen was very snug, and warm, and bright – as different as could be from the chill and mystery of the night outside.

'I think you are trifling with me, Jarvis,' I said.

'Triflin', Cornel? no me. What would I trifle for? If the deevil himsel' was in the auld hoose, I have no interest in't one way or another—'

'Sandy, hold your peace!' cried his wife imperatively.

'And what am I to hold my peace for, wi' the Cornel standing there asking a' thae questions? I'm saying, if the deevil himsel'—'

'And I'm telling ye hold your peace!' cried the woman, in great excitement. 'Dark November weather and lang nichts, and us that ken a' we ken. How daur ye name – a name that shouldna be spoken?' She threw down her stocking and got up, also in great agitation. 'I tell't ye you never could keep it. It's no a thing that will hide; and the haill toun kens as weel as you or me. Tell the Cornel straight out – or see, I'll do it. I dinna hold wi' your secrets; and a secret that the haill toun kens!' She snapped her fingers with an air of large disdain. As for Jarvis, ruddy and big as he was, he shrank to nothing before this decided woman. He repeated to her two or three times her own adjuration, 'Hold your peace!' then, suddenly changing his tone, cried out, 'Tell him then, confound ye! I'll wash my hands o't. If a' the ghosts in Scotland were in the auld hoose, is that any concern o' mine?'

After this I elicited without much difficulty the whole story. In the opinion of the Jarvises, and of everybody about, the certainty that the place was haunted was beyond all doubt. As Sandy and his wife warmed to the tale, one tripping up another in their eagerness to tell everything, it gradually developed as distinct a superstition as I ever heard, and not without poetry and pathos. How long it was since the voice had been heard first, nobody could tell with certainty. Jarvis's opinion was that his father, who had been coachman at Brentwood before him, had never heard anything about it, and that the whole thing had arisen within the last ten years, since the complete dismantling of the old house: which was a wonderfully modern date for a tale so well authenticated. According to these witnesses, and to several whom I questioned afterwards, and who were all in perfect agreement, it was only in the months of November and December that 'the visitation' occurred. During these months, the darkest of the year, scarcely a night passed without the recurrence of these inexplicable cries. Nothing, it was said, had ever been seen – at least nothing that could be identified. Some people, bolder or more imaginative than the others, had seen the darkness moving, Mrs Jarvis said, with unconscious poetry. It began when night fell and continued, at intervals, till day broke. Very often it was only an inarticulate cry and moaning, but sometimes the words which had taken possession of my poor boy's fancy had been distinctly audible – 'Oh, mother, let me in!' The Jarvises were not aware that there had ever been any investigation into it. The estate of Brentwood had lapsed into the hands of a distant branch of the family, who had lived but little there; and of the many people who had taken it, as I had done, few had remained through two Decembers. And nobody had taken the trouble to make a very close examination into the facts. 'No, no,' Jarvis said, shaking his head. 'No, no, Cornel. Wha wad set themsels up for a laughin'-stock to a' the country-side, making a wark about a ghost? Naebody believes in ghosts. It bid to be the wind in the trees, the last gentleman said, or some effec' o' the water wrastlin' among the rocks. He said it was a' quite easy explained: but he gave up the hoose. And when you cam, Cornel, we were awfu' anxious you should never hear. What for should I have spoiled the bargain and hairmed the property for nothing?'

'Do you call my child's life nothing?' I said in the trouble of the moment, unable to restrain myself. 'And instead of telling this all to me, you have told it to him – to a delicate boy, a child unable to sift evidence, or judge for himself, a tender-hearted young creature—'

I was walking about the room with an anger all the hotter that I felt it to be most likely quite unjust. My heart was full of bitterness against the stolid retainers of a family who were content to risk other people's children and comfort rather than let the house lie empty. If I had been warned I might have taken precautions, or left the place, or sent Roland away, a hundred things which now I could not do; and here I was with my boy in a brain-fever, and his life, the most precious life on earth, hanging in the balance, dependent on whether or not I could get to the reason of a commonplace ghost story! I paced about in high wrath, and seeing what I was to do; for, to take Roland away, even if he were able to travel, would not settle his agitated mind; and I feared even that a scientific explanation of refracted sound, or reverberation, or any other of the easy certainties with which we elder men are silenced, would have very little effect upon the boy.

'Cornel,' said Jarvis, solemnly, 'and *she'll* bear me witness – the young gentleman never heard a word from me – no, nor from either groom or gardener; I'll gie ye my word for that. In the first place, he's no a lad that invites ye to talk. There are some that are, and some that arena. Some will draw ye on, till ye've tellt them a' the clatter of the toun, and a' ye ken, and whiles mair. But Maister Roland, his mind's fu' of his books. He's aye civil and kind, and a fine lad; but no that sort. And ye see it's for a' our interest, Cornel, that you should stay at Brentwood. I took it upon me mysel' to pass the word – "No a syllable to Maister Roland, nor to the young leddies – no a sylla-ble." The women-servants, that have little reason to be out at night, ken little or nothing about it. And some think it grand to have a ghost so long as they're no in the way of coming across it. If you had been tellt the story to begin with, maybe ye would have thought so yourself.'

This was true enough, though it did not throw any light upon my perplexity. If we had heard of it to start with, it is possible that all the family would have considered the possession of a ghost a distinct advantage. It is the fashion of the times. We never think what a risk it is to play with young imaginations, but cry out, in the fashionable jargon, 'A ghost – nothing else was wanted to make it perfect.' I should not have been above this myself. I should have smiled, of course, at the idea of the ghost at all, but then to feel that it was mine would have pleased my vanity. Oh, yes, I claim no exemption. The girls would have been delighted. I could fancy their eagerness, their interest, and excitement. No; if we had been told, it would have done no good – we should have made the bargain all the more eagerly, the fools that we are. 'And there has been no attempt to investigate it,' I said, 'to see what it really is?'

'Eh, Cornel,' said the coachman's wife, 'wha would investigate, as ye call it, a thing that nobody believes in? Ye would be the laughing-stock of a' the country-side, as my man says.'

'But you believe in it,' I said, turning upon her hastily. The woman was taken by surprise. She made a step backward out of my way.

'Lord, Cornel, how ye frichten a body! Me! – there's awful strange things in this world. An unlearned person doesna ken what to think. But the minister and the gentry they just laugh in your face. Inquire into the thing that is not! Na, na, we just let it be.'

'Come with me, Jarvis,' I said, hastily, 'and we'll make an attempt at least. Say nothing to the men or to anybody. I'll come back after dinner, and we'll make a serious attempt to see what it is, if it is anything. If I hear it – which I doubt – you may be sure I shall never rest till I make it out. Be ready for me about ten o'clock.'

'Me, Cornel!' Jarvis said, in a faint voice. I had not been looking at him in my own preoccupation, but when I did so, I found that the greatest change had come over the fat and ruddy coachman. 'Me, Cornel!' he repeated, wiping the perspiration from his brow. His ruddy face hung in flabby folds, his knees knocked together, his voice seemed half extinguished in his throat. Then he began to rub his hands and smile upon me in a deprecating, imbecile way. 'There's nothing I wouldna do to pleasure ye, Cornel,' taking a step further back. 'I'm sure *she* kens I've aye said I never had to do with a mair fair, weelspoken gentleman—' Here Jarvis came to a pause, again looking at me, rubbing his hands.

Well?' I said.

'But eh, sir!' he went on, with the same imbecile yet insinuating smile, 'if ye'll reflect that I am no used to my feet. With a horse atween my legs, or the reins in my hand, I'm maybe nae worse than other men; but on fit, Cornel – It's no the – bogles; – but I've been cavalry, ya see,' with a little hoarse laugh, 'a' my life. To face a thing ye didna understan' – on your feet, Cornel—'

'Well, sir, if *I* do it,' said I tartly, 'why shouldn't you?'

'Eh, Cornel, there's an awfu' difference. In the first place, ye tramp about the haill country-side, and think naething of it; but a walk tires me mair than a hunard miles' drive; and then ye'e a gentleman, and do your ain pleasure; and you're no so auld as me; and it's for your ain bairn, ye see, Cornel; and then—'

'He believes in it, Cornel, and you dinna believe in it,' the woman said.

'Will you come with me?' I said, turning to her.

She jumped back, upsetting her chair in her bewilderment. 'Me!' with a scream, and then fell into a sort of hysterical laugh. 'I wouldna say but what I would go; but what would the folk say to hear of Cornel Mortimer with an auld silly woman at his heels?'

The suggestion made me laugh too, though I had little inclination for it. 'I'm sorry you have so little spirit, Jarvis,' I said. 'I must find someone else, I suppose.'

Jarvis, touched by this, began to remonstrate, but I cut him short. My butler was a soldier who had been with me in India, and was not supposed to fear anything – man or devil – certainly not the former; and I felt that I was losing time. The Jarvises were too thankful to get rid of me. They attended me to the door with the most anxious courtesies. Outside, the two grooms stood close by, a little confused by my sudden exit. I don't know if perhaps they had been listening – at least standing as near as possible, to catch any scrap of the conversation. I waved my hand to them as I went past, in answer to their salutations, and it was very apparent to me that they also were glad to see me go.

And it will be thought very strange, but it would be weak not to add, that I myself, though bent on the investigation I have spoken of, pledged to Roland to carry it out, and feeling that my boy's health, perhaps his life, depended on the result of my inquiry – I felt the most unaccountable reluctance to pass these ruins on my way home. My curiosity was intense; and yet it was all my mind could do to pull my body along. I dare say the scientific people would describe it the other way, and attribute my cowardice to the state of my stomach. I went on; but if I had followed my impulse, I should have turned and bolted. Everything in me seemed to cry out against it; my heart thumped, my pulses all began, like sledge-hammers, beating against my ears and every sensitive part. It was very dark, as I have said; the old house, with its shapeless tower, loomed a heavy mass through the darkness, which was only not entirely so solid as itself. On the other hand, the great dark cedars of which we were so proud seemed to fill up the night. My foot strayed out of the path in my confusion and the gloom together, and I brought myself up with a cry as I felt myself knock against something solid. What was it? The contact with hard stone and lime, and prickly bramblebushes, restored me a little to myself. 'Oh, it's only the old gable,' I said aloud, with a little laugh to reassure myself. The rough feeling of the stones reconciled me. As I groped about thus, I shook off my visionary folly. What so easily explained as that I should have strayed from the path in the darkness? This brought me back to common existence, as if I had been shaken by a wise hand out of all the silliness of superstition. How silly it was, after all! What did it matter which path I took? I laughed again, this time with better heart – when suddenly, in a moment, the blood was chilled in my veins, a shiver stole along my spine, my faculties seemed to forsake me. Close by me at my side, at my feet, there was a sigh. No, not a groan, not a moaning, not anything so tangible – a perfectly soft, faint, inarticulate sigh. I sprang back, and my heart stopped beating. Mistaken! no, mistake was impossible. I heard it as clearly as I hear myself speak; a long, soft, weary sigh, as if drawn to the utmost, and emptying out a load of sadness that filled the breast. To hear this in the solitude, in the dark, in the night (though it was still early), had an effect which I cannot describe. I feel it now – something cold creeping over me, up into my hair, and down to my feet, which refused to move. I cried out with a trembling voice, 'Who is there?' as I had done before – but there was no reply.

I got home – I don't quite know how; but in my mind there was no longer any indifference as to the thing, whatever it was, that haunted these ruins. My scepticism disappeared like a mist. I was as firmly determined that there was something as Roland was. I did not for a moment pretend to myself that it was possible I could be deceived; there were movements and noises which I understood all about, cracklings of small branches in the frost, and little rolls of gravel on the path, such as have a very eerie sound sometimes, and perplex you with wonder as to who has done it, *when there is no real mystery*; but I assure you all these little movements of nature don't affect you one bit *when there is something*. I understood *them*. I did not understand the sigh. That was not simple nature; there was meaning in it – feeling, the soul of a creature invisible. This is the thing that human nature trembles at – a creature invisible, yet with sensations, feelings, a power somehow of expressing itself. I had not the same sense of unwillingness to turn my back upon the scene of the mystery which I had experienced in going to the stables; but I almost ran home, impelled by eagerness to get everything done that had to be done in order to apply myself to finding it out. Bagley was in the hall as usual when I went in. He was always there in the afternoon, always with the appearance of perfect occupation, yet, so far as I know, never doing anything. The door was open, so that I hurried in without any pause, breathless; but the sight of his calm regard, as he came to help me off with my overcoat, subdued me in a moment. Anything out of the way, anything incomprehensible, faded to nothing in the presence of Bagley. You saw and wondered how *he* was made: the parting of his hair, the tie of his white neck-cloth, the fit of his trousers, all perfect as works of art; but you could see how they were done, which makes all the difference. I flung myself upon him, so to speak, without waiting to note the extreme unlikeness of the man to anything of the kind I meant. 'Bagley,' I said, 'I want you to come out with me tonight to watch for—'

'Poachers, Colonel,' he said, a gleam of pleasure running all over him.

'No, Bagley; a great deal worse,' I cried.

'Yes, Colonel; at what hour, sir?' the man said; but then I had not told him what it was.

It was ten o'clock when we set out. All was perfectly quiet

indoors. My wife was with Roland, who had been quite calm, she said, and who (though, no doubt, the fever must run its course) had been better since I came. I told Bagley to put on a thick greatcoat over his evening coat, and did the same myself – with strong boots; for the soil was like a sponge, or worse. Talking to him, I almost forgot what we were going to do. It was darker even than it had been before, and Bagley kept very close to me as we went along. I had a small lantern in my hand, which gave us a partial guidance. We had come to the corner where the path turns. On one side was the bowling-green, which the girls had taken possession of for their croquet-ground – a wonderful enclosure surrounded by high hedges of holly, three hundred years old and more; on the other, the ruins. Both were black as night; but before we got so far, there was a little opening in which we could just discern the trees and the lighter line of the road. I thought it best to pause there and take breath. 'Bagley,' I said, 'there is something about these ruins I don't understand. It is there I am going. Keep your eyes open and your wits about you. Be ready to pounce upon any stranger you see – anything, man or woman. Don't hurt, but seize – anything you see.' 'Colonel,' said Bagley, with a little tremor in his breath, 'they do say there's things there – as is neither man nor woman.' There was no time for words. 'Are you game to follow me, my man? that's the question,' I said. Bagley fell in without a word, and saluted. I knew then I had nothing to fear.

We went, so far as I could guess, exactly as I had come, when I heard that sigh. The darkness, however, was so complete that all marks, as of trees or paths, disappeared. One moment we felt our feet on the gravel, another sinking noiselessly into the slippery grass, that was all. I had shut up my lantern, not wishing to scare anyone, whoever it might be. Bagley followed, it seemed to me, exactly in my footsteps as I made my way, as I supposed, towards the mass of the ruined house. We seemed to take a long time groping along seeking this; the squash of the wet soil under our feet was the only thing that marked our progress. After a while I stood still to see, or rather feel, where we were. The darkness was very still, but

no stiller than is usual in a winter's night. The sounds I have mentioned – the crackling of twigs, the roll of a pebble, the sound of
some rustle in the dead leaves, or creeping creature on the grass –
were audible when you listened, all mysterious enough when your
mind is disengaged, but to me cheering now as signs of the living-
ness of nature, even in the death of the frost. As we stood still
there came up from the trees in the glen the prolonged hoot of an
owl. Bagley started with alarm, being in a state of general nervousness, and not knowing what he was afraid of. But to me the sound
was encouraging and pleasant, being so comprehensible. 'An owl,'
I said, under my breath. 'Y-es, Colonel,' said Bagley, his teeth chattering. We stood still about five minutes, while it broke into the still
brooding of the air, the sound widening out in circles, dying upon
the darkness. This sound, which is not a cheerful one, made me
almost gay. It was natural, and relieved the tension of the mind. I
moved on with new courage, my nervous excitement calming
down.

When all at once, quite suddenly, close to us, at our feet, there
broke out a cry. I made a spring backwards in the first moment of
surprise and horror, and in doing so came sharply against the same
rough masonry and brambles that had struck me before. This new
sound came upwards from the ground – a low, moaning, wailing
voice, full of suffering and pain. The contrast between it and the
hoot of the owl was indescribable; the one with a wholesome wildness and naturalness that hurt nobody – the other a sound that
made one's blood curdle, full of human misery. With a great deal of
fumbling – for in spite of everything I could do to keep up my
courage my hands shook – I managed to remove the slide of my
lantern. The light leaped out like something living, and made the
place visible in a moment. We were what would have been inside
the ruined building had anything remained but the gable-wall
which I have described. It was close to us, the vacant doorway in it
going out straight into the blackness outside. The light showed the
bit of wall, the ivy glistening upon it in clouds of dark green, the
bramble-branches waving, and below, the open door – a door that

led to nothing. It was from this the voice came which died out just as the light flashed upon this strange scene. There was a moment's silence, and then it broke forth again. The sound was so near, so penetrating, so pitiful, that, on the nervous start I gave, the light fell out of my hand. As I groped for it in the dark my hand was clutched by Bagley, who I think must have dropped upon his knees; but I was too much perturbed myself to think much of this. He clutched at me in the confusion of his terror, forgetting all his usual decorum. 'For God's sake, what is it, sir?' he gasped. If I yielded, there was evidently an end of both of us. 'I can't tell,' I said, 'any more than you; that's what we've got to find out: up, man, up!' I pulled him to his feet. 'Will you go round and examine the other side, or will you stay here with the lantern?' Bagley gasped at me with a face of horror. 'Can't we stay together, Colonel?' he said – his knees were trembling under him. I pushed him against the corner of the wall, and put the light into his hands. 'Stand fast till I come back; shake yourself together, man; let nothing pass you,' I said. The voice was within two or three feet of us, of that there could be no doubt.

I went myself to the other side of the wall, keeping close to it. The light shook in Bagley's hand, but tremulous though it was, shone out through the vacant door, one oblong block of light marking all the crumbling corners and hanging masses of foliage. Was that something dark huddled in a heap by the side of it? I pushed forward across the light in the doorway, and fell upon it with my hands; but it was only a juniper-bush growing close against the wall. Meanwhile, the sight of my figure crossing the doorway had brought Bagley's nervous excitement to a height: he flew at me, gripping my shoulder. 'I've got him, Colonel! I've got him!' he cried, with a voice of sudden exultation. He thought it was a man, and was at once relieved. But at that moment the voice burst forth again between us, at our feet – more close to us than any separate being could be. He dropped off from me, and fell against the wall, his jaw dropping as if he were dying. I suppose, at the same moment, he saw that it was me whom he had clutched. I, for my part, had scarcely more command of myself. I snatched the light out of his hand, and flashed it all about me wildly. Nothing – the juniper-bush which I thought I had never seen before, the heavy growth of the glistening ivy, the brambles waving. It was close to my ears now, crying, crying, pleading as if for life. Either I heard the same words Roland had heard, or else, in my excitement, his imagination got possession of mine. The voice went on, growing into distinct articulation, but wavering about, now from one point, now from another, as if the owner of it were moving slowly back and forward – 'Mother! Mother!' and then an outburst of wailing. As my mind steadied, getting accustomed (as one's mind gets accustomed to anything), it seemed to me as if some uneasy, miserable creature was pacing up and down before a closed door. Sometimes – but that must have been excitement – I thought I heard a sound like knocking, and then another burst, 'Oh, Mother! Mother!' All this close, close to the space where I was standing with my lantern – now before me, now behind me: a creature restless, unhappy, moaning, crying, before the vacant doorway, which no one could either shut or open more.

'Do you hear it, Bagley? do you hear what it is saying?' I cried, stepping in through the doorway. He was lying against the wall – his eyes glazed, half dead with terror. He made a motion of his lips as if to answer me, but no sounds came; then lifted his hand with a curious imperative movement as if ordering me to be silent and listen. And how long I did so I cannot tell. It began to have an interest, an exciting hold upon me, which I could not describe. It seemed to call up visibly a scene anyone could understand – a something shut out, restlessly wandering to and fro; sometimes the voice dropped, as if throwing itself down – sometimes wandered off a few paces, growing sharp and clear. 'Oh, Mother, let me in! oh, Mother, Mother, let me in! oh, let me in!' every word was clear to me. No wonder the boy had gone wild with pity. I tried to steady my mind upon Roland, upon his conviction that I could do something, but my head swam with the excitement, even when I partially overcame the terror. At last the words died away, and there was a sound of sobs and moaning. I cried out, 'In the name of God who are you?' with a kind of feeling in my mind that to use the name of God was profane, seeing that I did not believe in ghosts or anything supernatural; but I did it all the same, and waited, my heart giving a leap of terror lest there should be a reply. Why this should have been I cannot tell, but I had a feeling that if there was an answer, it would be more than I could bear. But there was no answer; the moaning went on, and then, as if it had been real, the voice rose, a little higher again, the words recommenced, 'Oh, mother, let me in! oh, mother, let me in!' with an expression that was heart-breaking to hear.

As if it had been real! What do I mean by that? I suppose I got less alarmed as the thing went on. I began to recover the use of my senses – I seemed to explain it all to myself by saying that this had once happened, that it was a recollection of a real scene. Why there should have seemed something quite satisfactory and composing in this explanation I cannot tell, but so it was. I began to listen almost as if it had been a play, forgetting Bagley, who, I almost think, had fainted, leaning against the wall. I was startled out of this strange spectatorship that had fallen upon me by the sudden rush of something which made my heart jump once more, a large black figure in the doorway waving its arms. 'Come in! come in! come in!' it shouted out hoarsely at the top of a deep bass voice, and then poor Bagley fell down senseless across the threshold. He was less sophisticated than I – he had not been able to bear it any longer. I took him for something supernatural, as he took me, and it was some time before I awoke to the necessities of the moment. I remembered only after, that from the time I began to give my attention to the man, I heard the other voice no more. It was some time before I brought him to. It must have been a strange scene; the lantern making a luminous spot in the darkness, the man's white face lying on the black earth, I over him, doing what I could for him. Probably I should have been thought to be murdering him had anyone seen us. When at last I succeeded in pouring a little brandy down his throat he sat up and looked about him wildly. 'What's up?' he said;

then recognising me, tried to struggle to his feet with a faint 'Beg your pardon, Colonel.' I got him home as best I could, making him lean upon my arm. The great fellow was as weak as a child. Fortunately he did not for some time remember what had happened. From the time Bagley fell the voice had stopped, and all was still.

'You've got an epidemic in your house, Colonel,' Simson said to me next morning. 'What's the meaning of it all? Here's your butler raving about a voice. This will never do, you know, and so far as I can make out, you are in it too.'

'Yes, I am in it, doctor. I thought I had better speak to you. Of course you are treating Roland all right – but the boy is not raving, he is as sane as you or me. It's all true.'

'As sane as – I – or you. I never thought the boy insane. He's got cerebral excitement, fever. I don't know what you've got. There's something very queer about the look of your eyes.'

'Come,' said I, 'you can't put us all to bed, you know. You had better listen and hear the symptoms in full.'

The doctor shrugged his shoulders, but he listened to me patiently. He did not believe a word of the story, that was clear; but he heard it all from beginning to end. 'My dear fellow,' he said, 'the boy told me just the same. It's an epidemic. When one person falls a victim to this sort of thing, it's as safe as can be – there's always two or three.'

'Then how do you account for it?' I said.

'Oh, account for it! – that's a different matter; there's no accounting for the freaks our brains are subject to. If it's delusion; if it's some trick of the echoes or the winds – some phonetic disturbance or other—'

'Come with me tonight, and judge for yourself,' I said.

Upon this he laughed aloud, then said, 'That's not such a bad idea; but it would ruin me for ever if it were known that John Simson was ghost-hunting.'

'There it is,' said I; 'you dart down on us who are unlearned with your phonetic disturbances, but you daren't examine what the thing really is for fear of being laughed at. That's science!'

'It's not science – it's common sense,' said the doctor. 'The thing has delusion on the front of it. It is encouraging an unwholesome tendency even to examine. What good could come of it? Even if I am convinced, I shouldn't believe.'

'I should have said so yesterday; and I don't want you to be convinced or to believe,' said I. 'If you prove it to be a delusion, I shall be very much obliged to you for one. Come; somebody must go with me.'

'You are cool,' said the doctor. 'You've disabled this poor fellow of yours, and made him – on that point – a lunatic for life; and now you want to disable me. But for once, I'll do it. To save appearance, if you'll give me a bed, I'll come over after my last rounds.'

It was agreed that I should meet him at the gate, and that we should visit the scene of last night's occurrences before we came to the house, so that nobody might be the wiser. It was scarcely possible to hope that the cause of Bagley's sudden illness should not somehow steal into the knowledge of the servants at least, and it was better that all should be done as quietly as possible. The day seemed to me a very long one. I had to spend a certain part of it with Roland, which was a terrible ordeal for me – for what could I say to the boy? The improvement continued, but he was still in a very precarious state, and the trembling vehemence with which he turned to me when his mother left the room filled me with alarm. 'Father!' he said, quietly. 'Yes, my boy; I am giving my best attention to it – all is being done that I can do. I have not come to any conclusion – yet. I am neglecting nothing you said,' I cried. What I could not do was to give his active mind any encouragement to dwell upon the mystery. It was a hard predicament, for some satisfaction had to be given him. He looked at me very wistfully, with the great blue eyes which shone so large and brilliant out of his white and worn face. 'You must trust me,' I said. 'Yes, father. Father understands,' he said to himself, as if to soothe some inward doubt. I left him as soon as I could. He was about the most precious thing I had on earth, and his health my first thought; but yet somehow, in the excitement of this other subject, I put that aside, and preferred not to dwell upon Roland, which was the most curious part of it all.

That night at eleven I met Simson at the gate. He had come by train, and I let him in gently myself. I had been so much absorbed in the coming experiment that I passed the ruins in going to meet him, almost without thought, if you can understand that. I had my lantern; and he showed me a coil of taper which he had ready for use. 'There is nothing like light,' he said, in his scoffing tone. It was a very still night, scarcely a sound, but not so dark. We could keep the path without difficulty as we went along. As we approached the spot we could hear a low moaning, broken occasionally by a bitter cry. 'Perhaps that is your voice,' said the doctor; 'I thought it must be something of the kind. That's a poor brute caught in some of these infernal traps of yours; you'll find it among the bushes somewhere.' I said nothing. I felt no particular fear, but a triumphant satisfaction in what was to follow. I led him to the spot where Bagley and I had stood on the previous night. All was silent as a winter night could be – so silent that we heard far off the sound of the horses in the stables, the shutting of a window at the house. Simson lighted his taper and went peering about, poking into all the corners. We looked like two conspirators lying in wait for some unfortunate traveller, but not a sound broke the quiet. The moaning had stopped before we came up; a star or two shone over us in the sky, looking down as if surprised at our strange proceedings. Dr Simson did nothing but utter subdued laughs under his breath. 'I thought as much,' he said. 'It is just the same with tables and all other kinds of ghostly apparatus; a sceptic's presence stops everything. When I am present nothing ever comes off. How long do you think it will be necessary to stay here? Oh, I don't complain; only, when *you* are satisfied, *I* am – quite.'

I will not deny that I was disappointed beyond measure by this result. It made me look like a credulous fool. It gave the doctor such a pull over me as nothing else could. I should point all his morals for years to come, and his materialism, his scepticism, would be increased beyond endurance. 'It seems, indeed,' I said, 'that there is to be no—' 'Manifestation,' he said, laughing; 'that is what all the mediums say. No manifestations, in consequence of the presence of an unbeliever.' His laugh sounded very uncomfortable to me in the silence; and it was now near midnight. But that laugh seemed the signal; before it died away the moaning we had heard before was resumed. It started from some distance off, and came towards us, nearer and nearer, like someone walking along and moaning to himself. There could be no idea now that it was a hare caught in a trap. The approach was slow, like that of a weak person, with little halts and pauses. We heard it coming along the grass straight towards the vacant doorway. Simson had been a little startled by the first sound. He said hastily, 'That child has no business to be out so late.' But he felt, as well as I, that this was no child's voice. As it came nearer, he grew silent, and, going to the doorway with his taper, stood looking out towards the sound. The taper being unprotected blew about in the night air, though there was scarcely any wind. I threw the light of my lantern steady and white across the same space. It was a blaze of light in the midst of the blackness. A little icy thrill had gone over me at the first sound, but as it came close, I confess that my only feeling was satisfaction. The scoffer could scoff no more. The light touched his own face, and showed a very perplexed countenance. If he was afraid, he concealed it with great success, but he was perplexed. And then all that had happened on the previous night was enacted once more. It fell strangely upon me with a sense of repetition. Every cry, every sob seemed the same as before. I listened almost without any emotion at all in my own person, thinking of its effect upon Simson. He maintained a very bold front on the whole. All that coming and going of the voice was, if our ears could be trusted, exactly in front of the vacant, blank doorway, blazing full of light, which caught and shone in the glistening leaves of the great hollies at a little distance. Not a rabbit could have crossed the turf without being seen; but there was nothing. After a time, Simson, with a certain caution and bodily reluctance, as it seemed to me, went out with his roll of taper into this space. His figure showed against the holly in full outline. Just at this moment the voice sank, as was its custom, and seemed to fling itself down at the door. Simson recoiled violently, as if someone had come up against him, then turned, and held his taper low as if examining something. 'Do you see anybody?' I cried in a whisper, feeling the chill of nervous panic steal over me at this action. 'It's nothing but a – confounded juniper-bush,' he said. This I knew very well to be nonsense, for the juniper-bush was on the other side. He went about after this round and round, poking his taper everywhere, then returned to me on the inner side of the wall. He scoffed no longer; his face was contracted and pale. 'How long does this go on?' he whispered to me, like a man who does not wish to interrupt someone who is speaking. I had become too much perturbed myself to remark whether the successions and changes of the voice were the same as last night. It suddenly went out in the air almost as he was speaking, with a soft, reiterated sob dying away. If there had been anything to be seen, I should have said that the person was at that moment crouching on the ground close to the door.

We walked home very silent afterwards. It was only when we were in sight of the house that I said, 'What do you think of it?' 'I can't tell what to think of it,' he said, quickly. He took – though he was a very temperate man – not the claret I was going to offer him, but some brandy from the tray, and swallowed it almost undiluted. 'Mind you, I don't believe a word of it,' he said, when he had lighted his candle; 'but I can't tell what to think,' he turned round to add, when he was half-way upstairs.

All of this, however, did me no good with the solution of my problem. I was to help this weeping, sobbing thing, which was already to me as distinct a personality as anything I knew – or what should I say to Roland? It was on my heart that my boy would die if I could not find some way of helping this creature. You may be surprised that I should speak of it in this way. I did not know if it was man or woman; but I no more doubted that it was a soul in pain than I doubted my own being; and it was my business to soothe this pain – to deliver it, if that was possible. Was ever such a task given to an anxious father trembling for his only boy? I felt in my heart, fantastic as it may appear, that I must fulfil this somehow, or part with my child; and you may conceive that rather than do that I was ready to die. But even my dying would not have advanced me – unless by bringing me into the same world with that seeker at the door.

Next morning Simson was out before breakfast, and came in with evident signs of the damp grass on his boots, and a look of worry and weariness, which did not say much for the night he had passed. He improved a little after breakfast, and visited his two patients, for Bagley was still an invalid. I went out with him on his way to the train, to hear what he had to say about the boy. 'He is going on very well,' he said; 'there are no complications as yet. But mind you, that's not a boy to be trifled with, Mortimer. Not a word to him about last night.' I had to tell him then of my last interview with Roland, and of the impossible demand he had made upon me – by which, though he tried to laugh, he was much discomposed, as I could see. 'We must just perjure ourselves all round,' he said, 'and swear you exorcised it'; but the man was too kind-hearted to be satisfied with that. 'It's frightfully serious for you, Mortimer. I can't laugh as I should like to. I wish I saw a way out of it, for your sake. By the way,' he added shortly, 'didn't you notice that juniper-bush on the left-hand side?' 'There was one on the right hand of the door. I noticed you made that mistake last night.' 'Mistake!' he cried, with a curious low laugh, pulling up the collar of his coat as though he felt the cold – 'there's no juniper there this morning, left or right. Just go and see.' As he stepped into the train a few minutes after, he looked back upon me and beckoned me for a parting word. 'I'm coming back tonight,' he said.

I don't think I had any feeling about this as I turned away from that common bustle of the railway, which made my private preoccupations feel so strangely out of date. There had been a distinct satisfaction in my mind before that his scepticism had been so entirely defeated. But the more serious part of the matter pressed upon me now. I went straight from the railway to the manse, which stood on a little plateau on the side of the river opposite to the woods of Brentwood. The minister was one of a class which is not so common in Scotland as it used to be. He was a man of good family, well educated in the Scotch way, strong in philosophy, not so strong in Greek, strongest of all in experience – a man who had 'come across', in the course of his life, most people of note that had ever been in Scotland – and who was said to be very sound in doctrine, without infringing the toleration with which old men, who are good men, are generally endowed. He was old-fashioned; perhaps he did not think so much about the troublous problems of theology as many of the young men, nor ask himself any hard questions about the Confession of Faith – but he understood human nature, which is perhaps better. He received me with a cordial welcome. 'Come away, Colonel Mortimer,' he said; 'I'm all the more glad to see you, that I feel it's a good sign for the boy. He's doing well? – God be praised – and the Lord bless him and keep him. He has many a poor body's prayers – and that can do nobody harm.'

'He will need them all, Dr Moncrieff,' I said, 'and your counsel too.' And I told him the story – more than I had told Simson. The old clergyman listened to me with many suppressed exclamations, and at the end the water stood in his eyes.

'That's just beautiful,' he said. 'I do not mind to have heard anything like it; it's as fine as Burns when he wished deliverance to one – that is prayed for in no kirk. Ay, ay! so he would have you console the poor lost spirit? God bless the boy! There's something more than common in that, Colonel Mortimer. And also the faith of him in his father! – I would like to put that into a sermon.' Then the old gentleman gave me an alarmed look, and said, 'No, no; I was not meaning a sermon; but I must write it down for the *Children's Record*.' I saw the thought that passed through his mind. Either he thought, or he feared I would think, of a funeral sermon. You may believe this did not make me more cheerful.

I can scarcely say that Dr Moncrieff gave me any advice. How could anyone advise on such a subject? But he said, 'I think I'll come too. I'm an old man; I'm less liable to be frightened than those that are further off the world unseen. It behoves me to think of my own journey there. I've no cut-and-dry beliefs on the subject. I'll come too; and maybe at the moment the Lord will put into our heads what to do.'

This gave me a little comfort – more than Simson had given me. To be clear about the cause of it was not my grand desire. It was another thing that was in my mind – my boy. As for the poor soul at the open door, I had no more doubt, as I have said, of its existence than I had of my own. It was no ghost to me. I knew the creature, and it was in trouble. That was my feeling about it, as it was Roland's. To hear it first was a great shock to my nerves, but not now; a man will get accustomed to anything. But to do something for it was the great problem; how was I to be serviceable to a being that was invisible, that was mortal no longer? 'Maybe at the moment the Lord will put it into our heads.' This is very old-fashioned phraseology, and a week before, most likely, I should have smiled (though always with kindness) at Dr Moncrieff's credulity; but there was a great comfort, whether rational or otherwise I cannot say, in the mere sound of the words.

The road to the station and the village lay through the glen – not by the ruins; but though the sunshine and the fresh air, and the beauty of the trees, and the sound of the water were all very soothing to the spirits, my mind was so full of my own subject that I could not refrain from turning to the right hand as I got to the top of the glen, and going straight to the place which I may call the scene of all my thoughts. It was lying full in the sunshine, like all the rest of the world. The ruined gable looked due east, and in the present aspect of the sun the light streamed down through the doorway as our lantern had done, throwing a flood of light upon the damp grass beyond. There was a strange suggestion in the open door – so futile, a kind of emblem of vanity – all free around, so that you could go where you pleased, and yet that semblance of an enclosure – that way of entrance, unnecessary, leading to nothing. And why any creature should pray and weep to get in – to nothing: or be kept out – by nothing! You could not dwell upon it, or it made your brain go round. I remembered however, what Simson said about the juniper, with a little smile on my own mind as to the inaccuracy of recollection, which even a scientific man will be guilty of. I could see now the light of my lantern gleaming upon the wet glistening surface of the spiky leaves at the right hand – and he ready to go to the stake for it that it was the left! I went round to make sure. And then I saw what he had said. Right or left there was no juniper at all. I was confounded by this, though it was entirely a matter of detail: nothing at all: a bush of brambles waving, the grass growing up to the very walls. But after all, though it gave me a shock for a moment, what did that matter? There were marks as if a number of footsteps had been up and down in front of the door; but these might have been our steps; and all was bright, peaceful, and still. I poked about the other ruin – the larger ruins of the old house – for some time, as I had done before. There were marks upon the grass here and there, I could not call them footsteps, all about; but that told for nothing one way or another. I had examined the ruined rooms closely the first day. They were half filled up with soil and *débris*, withered brackens and bramble – no refuge for anyone there. It vexed me that Jarvis should see me coming from that spot when he came up to me for his orders. I don't know whether my nocturnal expeditions had got wind among the servants. But there was a significant look in his face. Something in it I felt was like my own sensation when Simson in the midst of his scepticism was struck dumb. Jarvis felt satisfied that his veracity had been put beyond question. I never spoke to a servant of mine in such a peremptory tone before. I sent him away 'with a flea in his lug', as the man described it afterwards. Interference of any kind was intolerable to me at such a moment.

But what was strangest of all was that I could not face Roland. I did not go up to his room as I would have naturally done at once. This the girls could not understand. They saw there was some mystery in it. 'Mother has gone to lie down,' Agatha said; 'he had such a good night.' 'But he wants you so, papa!' cried little Jeanie, always with her two arms embracing mine in a pretty way she had. I was obliged to go at last – but what could I say? I could only kiss him, and tell him to keep still – that I was doing all I could. There is something mystical about the patience of a child. 'It will come all right won't it, father?' he said. 'God grant it may! I hope so, Roland,' 'Oh yes, it will come all right.' Perhaps he understood that in the midst of my anxiety I could not stay with him as I should have done otherwise. But the girls were more surprised than it is possible to describe. They looked at me with wondering eyes. 'If I were ill, papa, and you only stayed with me a moment, I should break my heart,' said Agatha. But the boy had a sympathetic feeling. He knew that of my own will I would not have done it. I shut myself up in the library, where I could not rest, but kept pacing up and down like a caged beast. What could I do? and if I could do nothing, what would become of my boy? These were the questions that, without ceasing, pursued each other through my mind.

Simson came out to dinner, and when the house was all still, and most of the servants in bed, we went out and met Dr Moncrieff, as we had appointed, at the head of the glen. Simson, for his part, was disposed to scoff at the doctor. 'If there are to be any spells, you know, I'll cut the whole concern,' he said. I did not make him any reply. I had not invited him; he could go or come as he pleased. He was very talkative, far more than suited my humour, as we went on. 'One thing is certain, you know, there must be some human agency,' he said. 'It is all bosh about apparitions. I never have investigated the laws of sound to any great extent, and there's a great deal in ventriloquism that we don't know much about.' 'If it's the same to you,' I said, 'I wish you'd keep all that to yourself, Simson. It doesn't suit my state of mind.' 'Oh, I hope I know how to respect idiosyncrasy,' he said. The very tone of his voice irritated me beyond measure. These scientific fellows, I wonder people put up with them as they do, when you have no mind for their cold-blooded confidence. Dr Moncrieff met us about eleven o'clock, the same time as on the previous night. He was a large man, with a venerable countenance and white hair – old, but in full vigour, and thinking less of a cold night walk than many a younger man. He had his lantern as I had. We were fully provided with means of lighting the place, and we were all of us resolute men. We had a rapid consultation as we went up, and the result was that we divided to different posts. Dr Moncrieff remained inside the wall – if you can call that inside where there was no wall but one. Simson placed himself on the side next the ruins, so as to intercept any communication with the old house, which was what his mind was fixed upon. I was posted on the other side. To say that nothing could come near without being seen was self-evident. It had been so also on the previous night. Now, with our three lights in the midst of the darkness, the whole place seemed illuminated. Dr Moncrieff's lantern, which was a large one, without any means of shutting up – an old-fashioned lantern with a pierced and ornamental top – shone steadily, the rays shooting out of it upward into the gloom. He placed it on the grass, where the middle of the room, if this had been a room, would have been. The usual effect of the light streaming out of the doorway was prevented by the illumination which Simson and I on either side supplied. With these differences, everything seemed as on the previous night.

And what occurred was exactly the same, with the same air of repetition, point for point, as I had formerly remarked. I declare that it seemed to me as if I were pushed against, put aside, by the owner of the voice as he paced up and down in his trouble – though these are perfectly futile words, seeing that the stream of light from my lantern, and that from Simson's taper, lay broad and clear, without a shadow, without the smallest break, across the entire breadth of the grass. I had ceased even to be alarmed, for my part. My heart was rent with pity and trouble – pity for the poor suffering human creature that moaned and pleaded so, and trouble for myself and my boy.

God! if I could not find any help – and what help could I find? – Roland would die.

We were all perfectly still till the first outburst was exhausted, as I knew (by experience) it would be. Dr Moncrieff, to whom it was new, was quite motionless on the other side of the wall, as we were in our places. My heart had remained almost at its usual beating during the voice. I was used to it; it did not rouse all my pulses as it did at first. But just as it threw itself sobbing at the door (I cannot use other words), there suddenly came something which sent the blood coursing through my veins and my heart into my mouth. It was a voice inside the wall – the minister's well-known voice. I would have been prepared for it in any kind of adjuration, but I was not prepared for what I heard. It came out with a sort of stammering, as if too much moved for utterance. 'Willie, Willie! Oh, God preserve us! is it you?'

These simple words had an effect upon me that the voice of the invisible creature had ceased to have. I thought the old man, whom I had brought into this danger, had gone mad with terror. I made a dash round to the other side of the wall, half crazed myself with the thought. He was standing where I had left him, his shadow thrown vague and large upon the grass by the lantern which stood at his feet. I lifted my own light to see his face as I rushed forward. He was very pale, his eyes wet and glistening, his mouth quivering with parted lips. He neither saw nor heard me. We that had gone through this experience before, had crouched towards each other to get a little strength to bear it. But he was not even aware that I was there. His whole being seemed absorbed in anxiety and tenderness. He held out his hands, which trembled, but it seemed to me with eagerness, not fear. He went on speaking all the time. 'Willie, if it is you – and it's you, if it is not a delusion of Satan – Willie, lad! why come ye here frighting them that know you not? Why came ye not to me?'

He seemed to wait for an answer. When his voice ceased, his countenance, every line moving, continued to speak. Simson gave me another terrible shock, stealing into the open doorway with his light, as much awe-stricken, as wildly curious, as I. But the minister resumed, without seeing Simson, speaking to someone else. His voice took a tone of expostulation –

'Is this right to come here? Your mother's gone with your name on her lips. Do you think she would ever close her door on her own lad? Do ye think the Lord will close the door, ye faint-hearted creature? No! – I forbid ye! I forbid ye!' cried the old man. The sobbing voice had begun to resume its cries. He made a step forward, calling out the last words in a voice of command. 'I forbid ye! Cry out no more to man. Go home, ye wandering spirit! go home! Do you hear me? – me that christened ye, that have struggled with ye, that have wrestled for ye with the Lord!' Here the loud tones of his voice sank into tenderness. 'And her too, poor woman! poor woman; her you are calling upon. She's no here. You'll find her with the Lord. Go there and seek her, not here. Do you hear me, lad? go after her there. He'll let you in, though it's late. Man, take heart! if you will lie and sob and greet, let it be at heaven's gate, and no your poor mother's ruined door.'

He stopped to get his breath: and the voice had stopped, not as it had done before, when its time was exhausted and all its repetitions said, but with a sobbing catch in the breath as if overruled. Then the minister spoke again, 'Are you hearing me, Will? Oh, laddie, you've liked the beggarly elements all your days. Be done with them now. Go home to the Father – the Father! Are you hearing me?' Here the old man sank down upon his knees, his face raised upwards, his hands held up with a tremble in them, all white in the light in the midst of the darkness. I resisted as long as I could, although I cannot tell why – then I, too, dropped upon my knees. Simson all the time stood in the doorway with an expression in his face such as words could not tell, his underlip drooped, his eyes wild, staring. It seemed to be to him, that image of blank ignorance and wonder, that we were praying. All the time the voice, with a low arrested sobbing, lay just where he was standing, as I thought.

'Lord,' the minister said – 'Lord, take him into Thy everlasting habitations. The mother he cries to is with Thee. Who can open to him but Thee? Lord, when is it too late for Thee, or what is too hard for Thee? Lord, let that woman there draw him inower! Let her draw him inower!'

I sprang forward to catch something in my arms that flung itself wildly within the door. The illusion was so strong, that I never paused till I felt my forehead graze against the wall and my hands clutch the ground – for there was nobody there to save from falling, as in my foolishness I thought. Simson held out his hand to me to help me up. He was trembling and cold, his lower lip hanging, his speech almost inarticulate. 'It's gone,' he said, stammering – 'it's gone!' We leant upon each other for a moment, trembling so much both of us that the whole scene trembled as if it were going to dissolve and disappear; and yet as long as I live I will never forget it – the shining of the strange lights, the blackness all round, the kneeling figure with all the whiteness of the light concentrated on its white venerable head and uplifted hands. A strange solemn stillness seemed to close all round us. By intervals a single syllable, 'Lord! Lord!' came from the old minister's lips. He saw none of us, nor thought of us. I never knew how long we stood, like sentinels guarding him at his prayers, holding our lights in a confused dazed way, not knowing what we did. But at last he rose from his knees, and standing up at his full height, raised his arms, as the Scotch manner is at the end of a religious service, and solemnly gave the apostolical benediction – to what? to the silent earth, the dark woods, the wide breathing atmosphere – for we were but spectators gasping an Amen!

It seemed to me that it must be the middle of the night, as we all walked back. It was in reality very late. Dr Moncrieff put his arm into mine. He walked slowly, with an air of exhaustion. It was as if we were coming from a death-bed. Something hushed and solemnised the very air. There was that sense of relief in it which there always is at the end of a death-struggle. And nature persistent, never daunted, came back in all of us, as we returned into the ways of life. We said nothing to each other, indeed, for a time; but when we got clear of the trees and reached the opening near the house, where we could see the sky, Dr Moncrieff himself was the first to speak. 'I must be going,' he said; 'it's very late, I'm afraid. I will go down the glen, as I came.'

'But not alone. I am going with you, doctor.'

'Well, I will not oppose it. I am an old man, and agitation wearies more than work. Yes; I'll be thankful of your arm. Tonight, Colonel, you've done me more good turns than one.'

I pressed his hand on my arm, not feeling able to speak. But Simson, who turned with us, and who had gone along all this time with his taper flaring, in entire unconsciousness, came to himself, apparently at the sound of our voices, and put out that wild little torch with a quick movement, as if of shame. 'Let me carry your lantern,' he said; 'it is heavy.' He recovered with a spring, and in a moment, from the awe-stricken spectator he had been, became himself sceptical and cynical. 'I should like to ask you a question,' he said. 'Do you believe in Purgatory, doctor? It's not in the tenets of the Church, so far as I know.'

'Sir,' said Dr Moncrieff, 'an old man like me is sometimes not very sure what he believes. There is just one thing I am certain of – and that is the loving-kindness of God.'

'But I thought that was in this life. I am no theologian—'

'Sir,' said the old man, again with a tremor in him which I could feel going over all his frame, 'if I saw a friend of mine within the gates of hell, I would not despair but his Father would take him by the hand still – if he cried like yon.'

'I allow it is very strange – very strange. I cannot see through it. That there must be human agency, I feel sure. Doctor, what made you decide upon the person and the name?'

The minister put out his hand with the impatience which a man might show if he were asked how he recognised his brother. 'Tuts!' he said, in familiar speech – then more solemnly, 'how should I not recognise a person that I know better – far better – than I know you?'

'Then you saw the man?'

Dr Moncrieff made no reply. He moved his hand again with a

little impatient movement, and walked on, leaning heavily on my arm. And we went on for a long time without another word, threading the dark paths, which were steep and slippery with the damp of the winter. The air was very still – not more than enough to make a faint sighing in the branches, which mingled with the sound of the water to which we were descending. When we spoke again, it was about indifferent matters – about the height of the river, and the recent rains. We parted with the minister at his own door, where his old housekeeper appeared in great perturbation, waiting for him. 'Eh, me, minister! the young gentleman will be worse?' she cried.

'Far from that – better. God bless him!' Dr Moncrieff said.

I think if Simson had begun again to me with his questions, I should have pitched him over the rocks as we returned up the glen; but he was silent, by a good inspiration. And the sky was clearer than it had been for many nights, shining high over the trees, with here and there a star faintly gleaming through the wilderness of dark and bare branches. The air, as I have said, was very soft in them, with a subdued and peaceful cadence. It was real, like every natural sound, and came to us like a hush of peace and relief. I thought there was a sound in it as of the breath of a sleeper, and it seemed clear to me that Roland must be sleeping, satisfied and calm. We went up to his room when we went in. There we found the complete hush of rest. My wife looked up out of a doze, and gave me a smile; 'I think he is a great deal better: but you are very late,' she said in a whisper, shading the light with her hand that the doctor might see his patient. The boy had got back something like his own colour. He woke as we stood all round his bed. His eyes had the happy half-awakened look of childhood, glad to shut again, yet pleased with the interruption and glimmer of the light. I stooped over him and kissed his forehead, which was moist and cool. 'All is well, Roland,' I said. He looked up at me with a glance of pleasure, and took my hand and laid his cheek upon it, and so went to sleep.

*

For some nights after, I watched among the ruins, spending all the dark hours up to midnight patrolling about the bit of wall which was associated with so many emotions; but I heard nothing, and saw nothing beyond the quiet course of nature: nor, so far as I am aware, has anything been heard again. Dr Moncrieff gave me the history of the youth, whom he never hesitated to name. I did not ask, as Simson did, how he recognised him. He had been a prodigal – weak, foolish, easily imposed upon, and 'led away', as people say. All that we had heard had passed actually in life, the Doctor said. The young man had come home thus a day or two after his mother died – who was no more than the housekeeper in the old house – and distracted with the news, had thrown himself down at the door and called upon her to let him in. The old man could scarcely speak of it for tears. To me it seemed as if – heaven help us, how little do we know about anything! – a scene like that might impress itself somehow upon the hidden heart of nature. I do not pretend to know how, but the repetition had struck me at the time as, in its terrible strangeness and incomprehensibility, almost mechanical – as if the unseen actor could not exceed or vary, but was bound to re-enact the whole. One thing that struck me, however, greatly, was the likeness between the old minister and my boy in the manner of regarding these strange phenomena. Dr Moncrieff was not terrified, as I had been myself, and all the rest of us. It was no 'ghost', as I fear we all vulgarly considered it, to him – but a poor creature whom he knew under these conditions, just as he had known him in the flesh, having no doubt of his identity. And to Roland it was the same. This spirit in pain – if it was a spirit – this voice out of the unseen – was a poor fellow-creature in misery, to be succoured and helped out of his trouble, to my boy. He spoke to me quite frankly about it when he got better. 'I knew father would find out some way,' he said. And this was when he was strong and well, and all idea that he would turn hysterical or become a seer of visions had happily passed away.

I must add one curious fact which does not seem to me to have any relation to the above, but which Simson made great use of, as the human agency which he was determined to find somehow. We had examined the ruins very closely at the time of these occurrences; but afterwards, when all was over, as we went casually about them one Sunday afternoon in the idleness of that unemployed day, Simson with his stick penetrated an old window which had been entirely blocked up with fallen soil. He jumped down into it in great excitement, and called me to follow. There we found a little hole – for it was more a hole than a room – entirely hidden under the ivy ruins, in which there was a quantity of straw laid in a corner, as if someone had made a bed there, and some remains of crusts about the floor. Someone had lodged there, and not very long before, he made out; and that this unknown being was the author of all the mysterious sounds we heard he is convinced. 'I told you it was human agency,' he said, triumphantly. He forgets, I suppose, how he and I stood with our lights seeing nothing, while the space between us was audibly traversed by something that could speak, and sob, and suffer. There is no argument with men of this kind. He is ready to get up a laugh against me on this slender ground. 'I was puzzled myself – I could not make it out – but I always felt convinced human agency was at the bottom of it. And here it is – and a clever fellow he must have been,' the doctor says.

Bagley left my service as soon as he got well. He assured me it was no want of respect; but he could not stand 'them kind of things', and the man was so shaken and ghastly that I was glad to give him a present and let him go. For my own part, I made a point of staying out the time, two years, for which I had taken Brentwood; but I did not renew my tenancy. By that time we had settled, and found ourselves a pleasant home of our own.

I must add that when the doctor defies me, I can always bring back gravity to his countenance, and a pause in his railing, when I remind him of the juniper-bush. To me that was a matter of little importance. I could believe it was mistaken. I did not care about it one way or other; but on his mind the effect was different. The miserable voice, the spirit in pain, he could think of as the result of ventriloquism, or reverberation, or – anything you please: an elaborate prolonged hoax executed somehow by the tramp that had found a lodging in the old tower. But the juniper-bush staggered him. Things have effects so different on the minds of different men.

ELLA D'ARCY

THE VILLA LUCIENNE

Madame Koetlegon told the story, and told it so well that her audience seemed to know the sombre alley, the neglected garden, the shuttered house, as intimately as though they had visited it themselves, seemed to feel a faint reverberation of the incommunicable thrill which she had felt – which the surly guardian, the torn rag of lace, the closed pavilion had made her feel. And yet, as you will see, there is in reality no story at all; it is merely an account of how, when in the Riviera two winters ago, she went with some friends to look over a furnished villa, which one of them thought of taking.

It was afternoon when we started on our expedition, Madame de M—, Cécile her widowed daughter-in-law, and I. Cécile's little girl Renée, the nurse, and Médor, the boarhound of which poor Guy had been so inordinately fond, dawdled after us up the steep and sunny road.

The December day was deliciously blue and warm. Cecile took off her furs and carried them over her arm. We only put down our sunshades when a screen of olive-trees on the left interposed their grey-green foliage between us and the sunshine.

Up in these trees barefooted men armed with bamboos were beating the branches to knock down the fruit; and three generations of women, grandmothers, wives, and children, knelt in the grass, gathering up the little purplish olives into baskets. All these paused to follow us with black persistent eyes, as we passed by; but the men went on working, unmoved. The tap-tapping, swish-swishing, of their light sticks against the boughs played a characteristically southern accompaniment to our desultory talk.

We were reasonably happy, pleasantly exhilarated by the beauty of the weather and the scene. Renée and Médor, with shrill laughter and deep-mouthed joy-notes, played together the whole way. And when the garden wall, which now replaced the olive-trees upon our right, gave place to a couple of iron gates standing open upon a broad straight drive, and we, looking up between the overarching palm-trees and cocoanuts, saw a white, elegant, sun-bathed house at the end, Cécile jumped to the conclusion that here was the Villa Lucienne, and that nowhere else could she find a house which on the face of it would suit her better.

But the woman who came to greet us, the jocund, brown-faced young woman, with the superb abundance of bosom beneath her crossed neckerchief of orange-coloured wool, told us no; this was the Villa Soleil (appropriate name!) and belonged to Monsieur Morgera, the deputy, who was now in Paris. The Villa Lucienne was higher up; she pointed vaguely behind her through the house; a long walk round by the road. But if these ladies did not mind a path which was a trifle damp perhaps, owing to Monday's rain, they would find themselves in five minutes at the Villa, for the two houses in reality were not more than a stone's throw apart.

She conducted us across a spacious garden golden with sunshine, lyric with bird-song, brilliant with flowers, where eucalyptus, mimosa, and tea-roses interwove their strong and subtle perfumes through the air, to an angle in a remote laurel hedge. Here she stooped to pull aside some ancient pine-boughs which ineffectually closed the entrance to a dark and trellised walk. Peering up at it, it seemed to stretch away interminably into green gloom, the ground rising a little all the while, and the steepness of the ascent being modified every here and there by a couple of rotting wooden steps.

We were to go up this alley, our guide told us, and we would be sure to find Laurent at the top. Laurent, she explained to us, was the gardener who lived at the Villa Lucienne and showed it to visitors. But there were not many who came, although it had been to let an immense time, ever since the death of old Madame Gray, and that had occurred before she, the speaker, had come south with the Morgeras. We were to explain to Laurent that we had been sent up from the Villa Soleil, and then it would be all right. For he sometimes used the alley himself, as it gave him a short cut into Antibes; but the passage had been blocked up many years ago, to prevent the Morgera children running into it.

Oh, Madame was very kind, it was no trouble at all, and of course if these ladies liked they could return by the alley also; but once they found themselves at the Villa they would be close to the upper road, which they would probably prefer. Then came her cordial voice calling after Cécile, 'Madame had best put on her furs again, it is cold in there.'

It was cold and damp too, with the damp coldness of places where sun and wind never penetrate. It was so narrow that we had to walk in single file. The walls on either hand, the low roof above our heads, were formed of trellised woodwork dropping into complete decay. But roof and walls might have been removed altogether, and the tunnel nevertheless would still have retained its shape; for the creepers which overgrew it had with time developed gnarled trunks and branches, which formed a second natural tunnelling outside. Through the broken places in the woodwork we could see the thick, inextricably twisted stems; and beyond again was a tangled matting of greenery, that suffered no drop of sunlight to trickle through. The ground was covered with lichens, deathstools, and a spongy moss exuding water beneath the foot, and one had the consciousness that the whole place, floor, walls, and roof, must creep with the repulsive, slimy, running life, which pullulates in dark and solitary places.

The change from the gay and scented garden to this dull alley, heavy with the smells of moisture and decay, was curiously depressing.

We followed each other in silence; first Cécile; then Renée clinging to her nurse's hand, with Médor pressing close against them; Madame de M— next; and I brought up the rear.

You would have pronounced it impossible to find in any southern garden so sombre a place, but that, after all, it is only in the south that such extraordinary contrasts of gaiety and gloom ever present themselves.

The sudden tearing away of a portion of one of the wooden steps beneath my tread startled us all, and the circular scatter of an immense colony of woodlice that had formed its habitat in the crevices of the wood, filled me with shivering disgust. I was exceedingly glad when we emerged from the tunnel upon daylight again and the Villa.

Upon daylight, but not upon sunlight, for the small garden in which we found ourselves was ringed round by the compact tops of the umbrella-pines which climbed the hill on every side. The site had been chosen, of course, on account of the magnificent view which we knew must be obtainable from the Villa windows, though from where we stood we could see nothing but the dark trees, the wild garden, the overshadowed house. And we saw none of these things very distinctly, for our attention was focussed on a man standing there in the middle of the garden, knee-deep in the grass, evidently awaiting us.

He was a short, thick-set peasant, dressed in the immensely wide blue velveteen trousers, the broad crimson sash, and the flannel shirt, open at the throat, which are customary in these parts. He was strong-necked as a bull, dark as a mulatto, and his curling, grizzled hair was thickly matted over his head and face and breast. He wore a flat knitted cap, and held the inevitable cigarette between his lips, but he made no attempt to remove one or the other at our approach. He stood stolid, silent, his hands thrust deep into his pockets, staring at us, and shifting from one to another his suspicious and truculent little eyes.

So far as I was concerned, and though the Villa had proved a palace, I should have preferred abandoning the quest at once to going over it in his company; but Cécile addressed him with intrepid politeness.

'We had been permitted to come up from the Villa Soleil. We understood that the Villa Lucienne was to let furnished; if so, might we look over it?'

From his heavy, expressionless expression, one might have supposed that the very last thing he expected or desired was to find a tenant for the Villa, and I thought with relief that he was going to refuse Cécile's request. But, after a longish pause:

'Yes, you can see it,' he said, grudgingly, and turned from us, to disappear into the lower part of the house.

We looked into each other's disconcerted faces, then round the grey and shadowy garden: a garden long since gone to ruin, with paths and flower-beds inextricably mingled, with docks and nettles choking up the rose-trees run wild, with wind-planted weeds growing from the stone vases on the terrace, with grasses pushing between the marble steps leading up to the hall door.

In the middle of the lawn a terra-cotta faun, tumbled from his pedestal, grinned sardonically up from amidst the tangled greenery, and Madame de M— began to quote:

> 'Un vieux faune en terre-cuite
> Rit au centre des boulingrins,
> Présageant sans doute une fuite
> De ces instants sereins
> Qui m'ont conduit et t'ont conduit . . .'

The Villa itself was as dilapidated, as mournful-looking as the garden. The ground-floor alone gave signs of occupation, in a checked shirt spread out upon a window-ledge to dry, in a worn besom, an earthenware pipkin, and a pewter jug, ranged against the wall. But the upper part, with the yellow plaster crumbling from the walls, the grey painted persiennes all monotonously closed, said with a thousand voices it was never opened, never entered, had not been lived in for years.

Our surly gardener reappeared, carrying some keys. He led the way up the steps. We exchanged mute questions; all desire to inspect the Villa was gone. But Cécile is a woman of character: she devoted herself.

'I'll just run up and see what it is like,' she said; 'it's not worth while you should tire yourself too, Mamma. You, all, wait here.'

We stood at the foot of the steps; Laurent was already at the top. Cécile began to mount lightly towards him, but before she was half-way she turned, and to our surprise, 'I wish you would come up, all of you,' she said, and stopped there until we joined her.

Laurent fitted a key to the door, and it opened with a shriek of rusty hinges. As he followed us, pulling it to behind him, we found ourselves in total darkness. I assure you I went through a bad quarter of a minute. Then we heard the turning of a handle, an inner door was opened, and in the semi-daylight of closed shutters we saw the man's squat figure going from us down a long, old-fashioned, vacant drawing-room towards two windows at the further end.

At the same instant Renée burst into tears:

'Oh, I don't like it. Oh, I'm frightened!' she sobbed.

'Little goosie!' said her grandmother, 'see, it's quite light now!' for Laurent had pushed back the persiennes, and a magical panorama had sprung into view: the whole range of the mountains behind Nice, their snow-caps suffused with a heavenly rose colour by the setting sun.

But Renée only clutched tighter at Madame de M—'s gown and wept:

'Oh, I don't like it, Bonnemaman! She is looking at me still. I want to go home!'

'No one is looking at you,' her grandmother told her: 'talk to your friend Médor. He'll take care of you.'

But Renée whispered:

'He wouldn't come in; he's frightened too.'

And, listening, we heard the dog's impatient and complaining bark calling to us from the garden.

Cécile sent Renée and the nurse to join him, and while Laurent let them out, we stepped on to the terrace, and for a moment our hearts were eased by the incomparable beauty of the view, for, raised now above the tree-tops, we looked over the admirable bay, the illimitable sky; we feasted our eyes upon unimaginable colour, upon matchless form. We were almost prepared to declare that the possession of the Villa was a piece of good fortune not to be let slip, when we heard a step behind us, and turned to see Laurent surveying us morosely from the window threshold, and again to experience the oppression of his ungenial personality.

Under his guidance we now inspected the century-old furniture, the faded silks, the tarnished gilt, the ragged brocades which had once embellished the room. The oval mirrors were dim with mildew, the parquet floor might have been a mere piece of grey drugget, so thick was the overlying dust. Curtains, yellowish, ropey, of undeterminable material, hung forlornly where once they had draped windows and doors. Originally they may have been of rose satin, for there were traces of rose colour still on the walls and the ceiling, painted in gay southern fashion with loves and doves, festoons of flowers, and knots of ribbons. But these paintings were all fragmentary, indistinct, seeming to lose sequence and outline the more diligently you tried to decipher them.

Yet you could not fail to see that when first furnished the room must have been charming and coquettish. I wondered for whom it had been thus arranged, why it had been thus abandoned. For there grew upon me, I cannot tell you why, the curious conviction that the last inhabitant of the room having casually left it, had, from some unexpected obstacle, never again returned. They were but the merest trifles that created this idea: the tiny heap of brown ash which lay on a marble gueridon, the few withered twigs in the vase beside it, speaking of the last rose plucked from the garden; the big berceuse chair drawn out beside the sculptured mantelpiece which seemed to retain the impression of the last occupant; and in the dark recesses of the unclosed hearth the smouldering heat which my fancy detected in the half-charred logs of wood.

The other rooms in the Villa resembled the *salon*; each time our surly guide opened the shutters we saw a repetition of the ancient furniture, of the faded decoration; everything dust-covered and time-decayed. Nor in these other rooms was any sign of former occupation to be seen, until, caught upon the girandole of a pier-glass, a long ragged fragment of lace took my eye; an exquisitely fine and cobwebby piece of lace, as though caught and torn from some gala shawl or flounce, as the wearer had hurried by.

It was odd perhaps to see this piece of lace caught thus, but not odd enough surely to account for the strange emotion which seized hold of me: an overwhelming pity, succeeded by an overwhelming fear. I had had a momentary intention to point the lace out to the others, but a glance at Laurent froze the words on my lips. Never in my life have I experienced such a paralysing fear. I was filled with an intense desire to get away from the man and from the Villa.

But Madame de M——, looking from the window, had noticed a pavilion standing isolated in the garden. She inquired if it were to be let with the house. He gave a surly assent. Then she supposed we could visit it. No, said the man, that was impossible. Cécile pointed out it was only right that tenants should see the whole of the prem-ises for which they would have to pay, but he refused this time with so much rudeness, his little brutish eyes narrowed with so much malignancy, that the panic which I had just experienced now seized the others, and it was a *sauve-qui-peut*.

We gathered up Renée, nurse, and Médor in our hasty passage through the garden, and found our way unguided to the gate upon the upper road.

At once at large beneath the serene evening sky, winding slowly westward down the olive-bordered ways: 'What an odious old ruf-fian!' said one; 'What an eerie, uncanny place!' said another. We compared notes. We found that each of us had been conscious of the same immense, the same inexplicable sense of fear.

Cécile, the least nervous of women, had felt it the first. It had laid hold of her when going up the steps to the door, and it had been so real a terror, she explained to us, that if we had not joined her she would have turned back. Nothing could have induced her to enter the Villa alone.

Madame de M—'s account was that her mind had been more or less troubled from the first moment of entering the garden, but that when the man refused us access to the pavilion, it had been suddenly invaded by a most intolerable sense of wrong. Being very imaginative (poor Guy undoubtedly derived his extraordinary gifts from her), Madame de M— was convinced that the gardener had murdered someone and buried the body inside the pavilion.

But for me it was not so much the personality of the man – although I admitted he was unprepossessing enough – as the Villa itself which inspired fear. Fear seemed to exude from the walls, to dim the mirrors with its clammy breath, to stir shudderingly among the tattered draperies, to impregnate the whole atmosphere as with an essence, a gas, a contagious disease. You fought it off for a shorter or longer time, according to your powers of resistance, but you were bound to succumb to it at last. The oppressive and invisible fumes had laid hold of us one after the other, and the incident of the closed pavilion had raised our terrors to a ludicrous pitch.

Nurse's experiences, which she gave us a day or two later, supported this view. For she told us that when Renée began to cry, and she took her hand to lead her out, all at once she felt quite nervous and uncomfortable too, as though the little one's trouble had passed by touch into her.

'And what is very strange,' said she, 'when we reached the garden, there was Médor, his forepaws planted firmly on the ground, his whole body rigid, and his hair bristling all along his backbone from end to end.'

Nurse was convinced that both the child and the dog had seen something which we others could not see.

This reminded us of a word of Renée's, a very curious word:

'I don't like it, *she* is looking at me still,' – and Cécile undertook to question her.

'You remember, Renée, when mother took you the other day to look over the pretty Villa—'

Renée opened wide apprehensive eyes.

'Why did you cry?'

'I was frightened at the lady,' she whispered.

'The lady . . . where was the lady?' Cécile asked her.

'She was in the drawing-room, sitting in the big chair.'

'Was she an old lady like grandmamma, or a young lady like mother?'

'She was like Bonnemaman,' said Renée, and her little mouth began to quiver.

'And what did she do?'

'She got up and began to – to come—'

But here Renée again burst into tears. And as she is a very nervous, a very excitable child, we had to drop the subject.

But what it all meant, whether there was anything in the history of the house or of its guardian which could account for our sensations, we never knew. We made inquiries, of course, concerning Laurent and the Villa Lucienne, but we learned very little, and that little was so vague, so remote, so irrelevant, that it does not seem worth while repeating.

The indisputable fact is the overwhelming fear which the adventure awoke in each and all of us; and this effect is impossible to describe, being just the crystallisation of one of those subtle, unformulated emotions in which only poor Guy himself could have hoped to succeed.

MARY E. WILKINS

THE VACANT LOT

When it became generally known in Townsend Centre that the Townsends were going to move to the city, there was great excitement and dismay. For the Townsends to move was about equivalent to the town's moving. The Townsend ancestors had founded the village a hundred years ago. The first Townsend had kept a wayside hostelry for man and beast, known as the 'Sign of the Leopard'. The sign-board, on which the leopard was painted a bright blue, was still extant, and prominently so, being nailed over the present Townsend's front door. This Townsend, by name David, kept the village store. There had been no tavern since the railroad was built through Townsend Centre in his father's day. Therefore the family, being ousted by the march of progress from their chosen employment, took up with a general country store as being the next thing to a country tavern, the principal difference consisting in the fact that all the guests were transients, never requiring bedchambers, securing their rest on the tops of sugar and flour barrels and codfish boxes, and their refreshment from stray nibblings at the stock in trade, to the profitless deplenishment of raisins and loaf sugar and crackers and cheese.

The flitting of the Townsends from the home of their ancestors was due to a sudden access of wealth from the death of a relative and the desire of Mrs Townsend to secure better advantages for her son

George, sixteen years old, in the way of education, and for her daughter Adrianna, ten years older, better matrimonial opportunities. However, the last inducement for leaving Townsend Centre was not openly stated, only ingeniously surmised by the neighbours.

'Sarah Townsend don't think there's anybody in Townsend Centre fit for her Adrianna to marry, and so she's goin' to take her to Boston to see if she can't pick up somebody there,' they said. Then they wondered what Abel Lyons would do. He had been a humble suitor for Adrianna for years, but her mother had not approved, and Adrianna, who was dutiful, had repulsed him delicately and rather sadly. He was the only lover whom she had ever had, and she felt sorry and grateful; she was a plain, awkward girl, and had a patient recognition of the fact.

But her mother was ambitious, more so than her father, who was rather pugnaciously satisfied with what he had, and not easily disposed to change. However, he yielded to his wife and consented to sell out his business and purchase a house in Boston and move there.

David Townsend was curiously unlike the line of ancestors from whom he had come. He had either retrograded or advanced, as one might look at it. His moral character was certainly better, but he had not the fiery spirit and eager grasp at advantage which had distinguished them. Indeed, the old Townsends, though prominent and respected as men of property and influence, had reputations not above suspicions. There was more than one dark whisper regarding them handed down from mother to son in the village, and especially was this true of the first Townsend, he who built the tavern bearing the Sign of the Blue Leopard. His portrait, a hideous effort of contemporary art, hung in the garret of David Townsend's home. There was many a tale of wild roistering, if no worse, in that old roadhouse, and high stakes, and quarrelling in cups, and blows, and money gotten in evil fashion, and the matter hushed up with a high hand for inquirers by the imperious Townsends who terrorised everybody. David Townsend terrorised nobody. He had gotten his little competence from his store by honest methods – the exchanging of sterling goods and true weights for country produce and country shillings. He was sober and reliable, with intense self-respect and a decided talent for the management of money. It was principally for this reason that he took great delight in his sudden wealth by legacy. He had thereby greater opportunities for the exercise of his native shrewdness in a bargain. This he evinced in his purchase of a house in Boston.

One day in spring the old Townsend house was shut up, the Blue Leopard was taken carefully down from his lair over the front door, the family chattels were loaded on the train, and the Townsends departed. It was a sad and eventful day for Townsend Centre. A man from Barre had rented the store – David had decided at the last not to sell – and the old familiars congregated in melancholy fashion and talked over the situation. An enormous pride over their departed townsman became evident. They paraded him, flaunting him like a banner in the eyes of the new man. 'David is awful smart,' they said; 'there won't nobody get the better of him in the city if he has lived in Townsend Centre all his life. He's got his eyes open. Know what he paid for his house in Boston? Well, sir, that house cost twenty-five thousand dollars, and David he bought it for five. Yes, sir, he did.'

'Must have been some out about it,' remarked the new man, scowling over his counter. He was beginning to feel his disparaging situation.

'Not an out, sir. David he made sure on't. Catch him gettin' bit. Everythin' was in apple-pie order, hot an' cold water and all, and in one of the best locations of the city – real high-up street. David he said the rent in that street was never under a thousand. Yes, sir, David he got a bargain – five thousand dollars for a twenty-five-thousand-dollar house.'

'Some out about it!' growled the new man over the counter.

However, as his fellow townsmen and allies stated, there seemed to be no doubt about the desirableness of the city house which David Townsend had purchased and the fact that he had secured it for an absurdly low price. The whole family were at first suspicious.

It was ascertained that the house had cost a round sum only a few years ago; it was in perfect repair; nothing whatever was amiss with plumbing, furnace, anything. There was not even a soap factory within smelling distance, as Mrs Townsend had vaguely surmised. She was sure that she had heard of houses being undesirable for such reasons, but there was no soap factory. They all sniffed and peeked; when the first rainfall came they looked at the ceiling, confidently expecting to see dark spots where the leaks had commenced, but there were none. They were forced to confess that their suspicions were allayed, that the house was perfect, even overshadowed with the mystery of a lower price than it was worth. That, however, was an additional perfection in the opinion of the Townsends, who had their share of New England thrift. They had lived just one month in their new house, and were happy, although at times somewhat lonely from missing the society of Townsend Centre, when the trouble began. The Townsends, although they lived in a fine house in a genteel, almost fashionable, part of the city, were true to their antecedents and kept, as they had been accustomed, only one maid. She was the daughter of a farmer on the outskirts of their native village, was middle-aged, and had lived with them for the last ten years. One pleasant Monday morning she rose early and did the family washing before breakfast, which had been prepared by Mrs Townsend and Adrianna, as was their habit on washing-days. The family were seated at the breakfast table in their basement dining-room, and this maid, whose name was Cordelia, was hanging out the clothes in the vacant lot. This vacant lot seemed a valuable one, being on a corner. It was rather singular that it had not been built upon. The Townsends had wondered at it and agreed that they would have preferred their own house to be there. They had, however, utilised it as far as possible with their innocent, rural disregard of property rights in unoccupied land.

'We might just as well hang out our washing in that vacant lot,' Mrs Townsend had told Cordelia the first Monday of their stay in the house. 'Our little yard ain't half big enough for all our clothes, and it is sunnier there, too.'

So Cordelia had hung out the wash there for four Mondays, and this was the fifth. The breakfast was about half finished – they had reached the buckwheat cakes – when this maid came rushing into the dining-room and stood regarding them, speechless, with a countenance indicative of the utmost horror. She was deadly pale. Her hands, sodden with soapsuds, hung twitching at her sides in the folds of her calico gown; her very hair, which was light and sparse, seemed to bristle with fear. All the Townsends turned and looked at her. David and George rose with a half-defined idea of burglars.

'Cordelia Battles, what is the matter?' cried Mrs Townsend. Adrianna gasped for breath and turned as white as the maid. 'What is the matter?' repeated Mrs Townsend, but the maid was unable to speak. Mrs Townsend, who could be peremptory, sprang up, ran to the frightened woman and shook her violently. 'Cordelia Battles, you speak,' said she, 'and not stand there staring that way, as if you were struck dumb! What is the matter with you?'

Then Cordelia spoke in a fainting voice.

'There's – somebody else – hanging out clothes – in the vacant lot,' she gasped, and clutched at a chair for support.

'Who?' cried Mrs Townsend, rousing to indignation, for already she had assumed a proprietorship in the vacant lot. 'Is it the folks in the next house? I'd like to know what right they have! We are next to that vacant lot.'

'I – dunno – who it is,' gasped Cordelia.

'Why, we've seen that girl next door go to mass every morning,' said Mrs Townsend. 'She's got a fiery red head. Seems as if you might know her by this time, Cordelia.'

'It ain't that girl,' gasped Cordelia. Then she added in a horror-stricken voice, 'I couldn't see who 'twas.'

They all stared.

'Why couldn't you see?' demanded her mistress. 'Are you struck blind?'

'No, ma'am.'

'Then why couldn't you see?'

'All I could see was—' Cordelia hesitated, with an expression of the utmost horror.

'Go on,' said Mrs Townsend, impatiently.

'All I could see was the shadow of somebody, very slim, hanging out the clothes, and—'

'What?'

'I could see the shadows of the things flappin' on their line.'

'You couldn't see the clothes?'

'Only the shadow on the ground.'

'What kind of clothes were they?'

'Queer,' replied Cordelia, with a shudder.

'If I didn't know you so well, I should think you had been drinking,' said Mrs Townsend. 'Now, Cordelia Battles, I'm going out in that vacant lot and see myself what you're talking about.'

'I can't go,' gasped the woman.

With that Mrs Townsend and all the others, except Adrianna, who remained to tremble with the maid, sallied forth into the vacant lot. They had to go out the area gate into the street to reach it. It was nothing unusual in the way of vacant lots. One large poplar tree, the relic of the old forest which had once flourished there, twinkled in one corner; for the rest, it was overgrown with coarse weeds and a few dusty flowers. The Townsends stood just inside the rude board fence which divided the lot from the street and stared with wonder and horror, for Cordelia had told the truth. They all saw what she had described – the shadow of an exceedingly slim woman moving along the ground with upstretched arms, the shadows of strange, nondescript garments flapping from a shadowy line, but when they looked up for the substance of the shadows nothing was to be seen except the clear, blue October air.

'My goodness!' gasped Mrs Townsend. Her face assumed a strange gathering of wrath in the midst of her terror. Suddenly she made a determined move forward, although her husband strove to hold her back.

'You let me be,' said she. She moved forward. Then she recoiled and gave a loud shriek. 'The wet sheet flapped in my face,' she cried. 'Take me away, take me away!' Then she fainted. Between them they got her back to the house. 'It was awful,' she moaned when she came to herself, with the family all around her where she lay on the dining-room floor. 'Oh, David, what do you suppose it is?'

'Nothing at all,' replied David Townsend stoutly. He was remarkable for courage and staunch belief in actualities. He was now denying to himself that he had seen anything unusual.

'Oh, there was,' moaned his wife.

'I saw something,' said George, in a sullen, boyish bass.

The maid sobbed convulsivly and so did Adrianna for sympathy.

'We won't talk any about it,' said David. 'Here, Jane, you drink this hot tea – it will do you good; and Cordelia, you hang out the clothes in our own yard. George, you go and put up the line for her.'

'The line is out there,' said George, with a jerk of his shoulder.

'Are you afraid?'

'No, I ain't,' replied the boy resentfully, and went out with a pale face.

After that Cordelia hung the Townsend wash in the yard of their own house, standing always with her back to the vacant lot. As for David Townsend, he spent a good deal of his time in the lot watching the shadows, but he came to no explanation, although he strove to satisfy himself with many.

'I guess the shadows come from the smoke from our chimneys, or else the poplar tree,' he said.

'Why do the shadows come on Monday mornings, and no other?' demanded his wife.

David was silent.

Very soon new mysteries arose. One day Cordelia rang the dinner-bell at their usual dinner hour, the same as in Townsend Centre, high noon, and the family assembled. With amazement Adrianna looked at the dishes on the table.

'Why, that's queer!' she said.

'What's queer?' asked her mother.

Cordelia stopped short as she was about setting a tumbler of water beside a plate, and the water slopped over.

'Why,' said Adrianna, her face paling, 'I – thought there was boiled dinner. I – smelt cabbage cooking.'

'I knew there would be something else come up,' gasped Cordelia, leaning hard on the back of Adrianna's chair.

'What do you mean?' asked Mrs Townsend sharply, but her own face began to assume the shocked pallor which it was so easy nowadays for all their faces to assume at the merest suggestion of anything out of the common.

'I smelt cabbage cooking all the morning up in my room,' Adrianna said faintly, 'and here's codfish and potatoes for dinner.'

The Townsends all looked at one another. David rose with an exclamation and rushed out of the room. The others waited tremblingly. When he came back his face was lowering.

'What did you—' Mrs Townsend asked hesitatingly.

'There's some smell of cabbage out there,' he admitted reluctantly. Then he looked at her with a challenge. 'It comes from the next house,' he said. 'Blows over our house.'

'Our house is higher.'

'I don't care; you can never account for such things.'

'Cordelia,' said Mrs Townsend, 'you go over to the next house and you ask if they've got cabbage for dinner.'

Cordelia switched out of the room, her mouth set hard. She came back promptly.

'Says they never have cabbage,' she announced with gloomy triumph and a conclusive glance at Mr Townsend. 'Their girl was real sassy.'

'Oh, father, let's move away; let's sell the house,' cried Adrianna in a panic-stricken tone.

'If you think I'm going to sell a house that I got as cheap as this one because we smell cabbage in a vacant lot, you're mistaken,' replied David firmly.

'It isn't the cabbage alone,' said Mrs Townsend.

'And a few shadows,' added David. 'I am tired of such nonsense. I thought you had more sense, Jane.'

'One of the boys at school asked me if we lived in the house next to the vacant lot on Wells Street and whistled when I said "Yes",' remarked George.

'Let him whistle,' said Mr Townsend.

After a few hours the family, stimulated by Mr Townsend's calm common sense, agreed that it was exceedingly foolish to be disturbed by a mysterious odour of cabbage. They even laughed at themselves.

'I suppose we have got so nervous over those shadows hanging out clothes that we notice every little thing,' conceded Mrs Townsend.

'You will find out some day that that is no more to be regarded than the cabbage,' said her husband.

'You can't account for that wet sheet hitting my face,' said Mrs Townsend, doubtfully.

'You imagined it.'

'I *felt* it.'

That afternoon things went on as usual in the household until nearly four o'clock. Adrianna went downtown to do some shopping. Mrs Townsend sat sewing beside the bay window in her room, which was a front one in the third storey. George had not got home. Mr Townsend was writing a letter in the library. Cordelia was busy in the basement; the twilight, which was coming earlier and earlier every night, was beginning to gather, when suddenly there was a loud crash which shook the house from its foundations. Even the dishes on the sideboard rattled, and the glasses rang like bells. The pictures on the walls of Mrs Townsend's room swung out from the walls. But that was not all: every looking-glass in the house cracked simultaneously – as nearly as they could judge – from top to bottom, then shivered into fragments over the floors. Mrs Townsend was too frightened to scream. She sat huddled in her chair, gasping for breath, her eyes, rolling from side to side in incredulous terror, turned towards the street. She saw a great black group of people crossing it just in front of the vacant lot. There was something inexpressibly strange and gloomy about this moving group; there was an effect of sweeping, wavings and foldings of sable draperies and gleams of deadly white faces; then they passed. She twisted her head to see, and they disappeared in the vacant lot. Mr Townsend came hurrying into the room; he was pale, and looked at once angry and alarmed.

'Did you fall?' he asked inconsequently, as if his wife, who was small, could have produced such a manifestation by a fall.

'Oh, David, what is it?' whispered Mrs Townsend.

'Darned if I know!' said David.

'Don't swear. It's too awful. Oh, see the looking-glass, David!'

'I see it. The one over the library mantel is broken, too.'

'Oh, it is a sign of death!'

Cordelia's feet were heard as she staggered on the stairs. She almost fell into the room. She reeled over to Mr Townsend and clutched his arm. He cast a sidewise glance, half furious, half commiserating at her.

'Well, what is it all about?' he asked.

'I don't know. What is it? Oh, what is it? The looking-glass in the kitchen is broken. All over the floor. Oh, oh! What is it?'

'I don't know any more than you do. I didn't do it.'

'Lookin'-glasses broken is a sign of death in the house,' said Cordelia. 'If it's me, I hope I'm ready; but I'd rather die than be so scared as I've been lately.'

Mr Townsend shook himself loose and eyed the two trembling women with gathering resolution.

'Now, look here, both of you,' he said. 'This is nonsense. You'll die sure enough of fright if you keep on this way. I was a fool myself to be startled. Everything it is is an earthquake.'

'Oh, David!' gasped his wife, not much reassured.

'It is nothing but an earthquake,' persisted Mr Townsend. 'It acted just like that. Things are always broken on the walls, and the middle of the room isn't affected. I've read about it.'

Suddenly Mrs Townsend gave a loud shriek and pointed.

'How do you account for that,' she cried, 'if it's an earthquake? Oh, oh, oh!'

She was on the verge of hysterics. Her husband held her firmly by the arm as his eyes followed the direction of her rigid pointing finger. Cordelia looked also, her eyes seeming converged to a bright point of fear. On the floor in front of the broken looking-glass lay a mass of black stuff in a gruesome long ridge.

'It's something you dropped there,' almost shouted Mr Townsend. 'It ain't. Oh!'

Mr Townsend dropped his wife's arm and took one stride towards the object. It was a very long crepe veil. He lifted it, and it floated out from his arm as if imbued with electricity.

'It's yours,' he said to his wife.

'Oh, David, I never had one. You know, oh, you know I – shouldn't – unless you died. How came it there?'

'I'm darned if I know,' said David, regarding it. He was deadly pale, but still resentful rather than afraid.

'Don't hold it; don't!'

'I'd like to know what in thunder all this means?' said David. He gave the thing an angry toss and it fell on the floor in exactly the same long heap as before.

Cordelia began to weep with racking sobs. Mrs Townsend reached out and caught her husband's hand with ice-cold fingers.

'What's got into this house, anyhow?' he growled.

'You'll have to sell it. Oh, David, we can't live here.'

'As for my selling a house I paid only five thousand for when it's worth twenty-five, for any such nonsense as this, I won't!'

David gave one stride towards the black veil, but it rose from the floor and moved away before him across the room at exactly the same height as if suspended from a woman's head. He pursued it, clutching vainly, all around the room, then he swung himself on his heel with an exclamation and the thing fell to the floor again in the long heap. Then were heard hurrying feet on the stairs and Adrianna burst into the room. She ran straight to her father and clutched his arm; she tried to speak, but she chattered unintelligibly; her face was blue. Her father shook her violently.

'Adrianna, do have more sense!' he cried.

'Oh, David, how can you talk so?' sobbed her mother.

'I can't help it. I'm mad!' said he with emphasis. 'What has got into this house and you all, anyhow?'

'What is it, Adrianna, poor child,' asked her mother. 'Only look what has happened here.'

'It's an earthquake,' said her father staunchly; 'nothing to be afraid of.'

'How do you account for *that*?' said Mrs Townsend in an awful voice, pointing to the veil.

Adrianna did not look – she was too engrossed with her own terrors. She began to speak in a breathless voice.

'I – was – coming – by the vacant lot,' she panted, 'and – I – I – had my new hat in a paper bag and – a parcel of blue ribbon, and – I saw a crowd, an awful – oh! a whole crowd of people with white faces, as if – they were dressed all in black.'

'Where are they now?'

'I don't know. Oh!' Adrianna sank gasping feebly into a chair.

'Get her some water, David,' sobbed her mother.

David rushed with an impatient exclamation out of the room and returned with a glass of water which he held to his daughter's lips.

'Here, drink this!' he said roughly.

'Oh, David, how can you speak so?' sobbed his wife.

'I can't help it. I'm mad clean through,' said David.

Then there was a hard bound upstairs, and George entered. He was very white, but he grinned at them with an appearance of unconcern.

'Hullo!' he said in a shaking voice, which he tried to control. 'What on earth's to pay in that vacant lot now?'

'Well, what is it?' demanded his father.

'Oh, nothing, only – well, there are lights over it exactly as if there was a house there, just about where the windows would be. It looked as if you could walk right in, but when you look close there are those old dried-up weeds rattling away on the ground the same as ever. I looked at it and couldn't believe my eyes. A woman saw it, too. She came along just as I did. She gave one look, then she screeched and ran. I waited for someone else, but nobody came.'

Mr Townsend rushed out of the room.

'I dare say it'll be gone when he gets there,' began George, then he stared round the room. 'What's to pay here?' he cried.

'Oh, George, the whole house shook all at once, and all the looking-glasses broke,' wailed his mother, and Adrianna and Cordelia joined.

George whistled with pale lips. Then Mr Townsend entered.

'Well,' asked George, 'see anything?'

'I don't want to talk,' said his father. 'I've stood just about enough.'

'We've got to sell and go back to Townsend Centre,' cried his wife in a wild voice. 'Oh, David, say you'll go back.'

'I won't go back for any such nonsense as this, and sell a twenty-five-thousand-dollar house for five thousand,' said he firmly.

But that very night his resolution was shaken. The whole family watched together in the dining-room. They were all afraid to go to bed – that is, all except possibly Mr Townsend. Mrs Townsend declared firmly that she for one would leave that awful house and go back to Townsend Centre whether he came or not, unless they all stayed together and watched, and Mr Townsend yielded. They chose the dining-room for the reason that it was nearer the street should they wish to make their egress hurriedly, and they took up their station around the dining-table on which Cordelia had placed a luncheon.

'It looks exactly as if we were watching with a corpse,' she said in a horror-stricken whisper.

'Hold your tongue if you can't talk sense,' said Mr Townsend.

The dining-room was very large, finished in oak, with a dark blue paper above the wainscoting. The old sign of the tavern, the Blue Leopard, hung over the mantelshelf. Mr Townsend had insisted on hanging it there. He had a curious pride in it. The family sat together until after midnight and nothing unusual happened. Mrs Townsend began to nod; Mr Townsend read the paper ostentatiously. Adrianna and Cordelia stared with roving eyes about the room, then at each other as if comparing notes on terror. George had a book which he studied furtively. All at once Adrianna gave a startled exclamation and Cordelia echoed her. George whistled faintly. Mrs Townsend awoke with a start and Mr Townsend's paper rattled to the floor.

'Look!' gasped Adrianna.

The sign of the Blue Leopard over the shelf glowed as if a lantern hung over it. The radiance was thrown from above. It grew brighter and brighter as they watched. The Blue Leopard seemed to crouch and spring with life. Then the door into the front hall opened – the outer door, which had been carefully locked. It squeaked and they all recognised it. They sat staring. Mr Townsend was as transfixed as the rest. They heard the outer door shut, then the door into the room swung open and slowly that awful black group of people which they had seen in the afternoon entered. The Townsends with one accord rose and huddled together in a far corner; they all held to each other and stared. The people, their faces gleaming with a whiteness of death, their black robes waving and folding, crossed the room. They were a trifle above mortal height, or seemed so to the terrified eyes which saw them. They reached the mantelshelf where the sign-board hung, then a black-draped long arm was seen to rise and make a motion, as if plying a knocker. Then the whole company passed out of sight, as if through the wall, and the room was as before. Mrs Townsend was shaking in a nervous chill, Adrianna was almost fainting, Cordelia was in hysterics. David Townsend stood glaring in a curious way at the sign of the Blue Leopard. George stared at him with a look of horror. There was something in his father's face which made him forget everything else. At last he touched his arm timidly.

'Father,' he whispered.

David turned and regarded him with a look of rage and fury, then his face cleared; he passed his hand over his forehead.

'Good Lord! What *did* come to me?' he muttered.

'You looked like that awful picture of old Tom Townsend in the garret in Townsend Centre, father,' whimpered the boy, shuddering.

'Should think I might look like 'most any old cuss after such a darned work as this,' growled David, but his face was white. 'Go and pour out some hot tea for your mother,' he ordered the boy sharply. He himself shook Cordelia violently. 'Stop such actions!' he shouted in her ears, and shook her again. 'Ain't you a church member?' he demanded; 'what be you afraid of? You ain't done nothin' wrong, have ye?'

Then Cordelia quoted Scripture in a burst of sobs and laughter.

'Behold, I was shapen in iniquity; and in sin did my mother conceive me,' she cried out. 'If I ain't done wrong, mebbe them that's come before me did, and when the Evil One and the Powers of Darkness is abroad I'm liable, I'm liable!' Then she laughed loud and long and shrill.

'If you don't hush up,' said David, but still with that white terror and horror on his own face, 'I'll bundle you out in that vacant lot whether or no. I mean it.'

Then Cordelia was quiet, after one wild roll of her eyes at him. The colour was returning to Adrianna's cheeks; her mother was drinking hot tea in spasmodic gulps.

'It's after midnight,' she gasped, 'and I don't believe they'll come again tonight. Do you, David?'

'No, I don't,' said David conclusively.

'Oh, David, we mustn't stay another night in this awful house.'

'We won't. Tomorrow we'll pack off bag and baggage to Townsend Centre, if it takes all the fire department to move us,' said David.

Adrianna smiled in the midst of her terror. She thought of Abel Lyons.

The next day Mr Townsend went to the real estate agent who had sold him the house.

'It's no use,' he said, 'I can't stand it. Sell the house for what you can get. I'll give it away rather than keep it.'

Then he added a few strong words as to his opinion of parties who sold him such an establishment. But the agent pleaded innocent for the most part.

'I'll own I suspected something wrong when the owner, who pledged me to secrecy as to his name, told me to sell that place for what I could get, and did not limit me. I had never heard anything, but I began to suspect something was wrong. Then I made a few inquiries and found out that there was a rumour in the neighbourhood that there was something out of the usual about that vacant lot. I had wondered myself why it wasn't built upon. There was a story about its being undertaken once, and the contract made, and the contractor dying; then another man took it and one of the workmen was killed on his way to dig the cellar, and the others struck. I didn't pay much attention to it. I never believed much in that sort of thing anyhow, and then, too, I couldn't find out that there had ever been anything wrong about the house itself, except as the people who had lived there were said to have seen and heard queer things in the vacant lot, so I thought you might be able to get along, especially as you didn't look like a man who was timid, and the house was such a bargain as I never handled before. But this you tell me is beyond belief.'

'Do you know the names of the people who formerly owned the vacant lot?' asked Mr Townsend.

'I don't know for certain,' replied the agent, 'for the original owners flourished long before your or my day, but I do know that the lot goes by the name of the old Gaston lot. What's the matter? Are you ill?'

'No; it is nothing,' replied Mr Townsend. 'Get what you can for the house; perhaps another family might not be as troubled as we have been.'

'I hope you are not going to leave the city?' said the agent, urbanely.

'I am going back to Townsend Centre as fast as steam can carry me after we get packed up and out of that cursed house,' replied Mr David Townsend.

He did not tell the agent nor any of his family what had caused him to start when told the name of the former owners of the lot. He remembered all at once the story of a ghastly murder which had taken place in the Blue Leopard. The victim's name was Gaston and the murderer had never been discovered.

E. NESBIT

THE VIOLET CAR

Do you know the downs – the wide windy spaces, the rounded shoulders of the hills leaned against the sky, the hollows where farms and homesteads nestle sheltered, with trees round them pressed close and tight as a carnation in a button-hole? On long summer days it is good to lie on the downs, between short turf and pale, clear sky, to smell the wild thyme, and hear the tiny tinkle of the sheep-bells and the song of the skylark. But on winter evenings when the wind is waking up to its work, spitting rain in your eyes, beating the poor, naked trees and shaking the dusk across the hills like a grey pall, then it is better to be by a warm fireside, in one of the farms that lie lonely where shelter is, and oppose their windows glowing with candle light and firelight to the deepening darkness, as faith holds up its love-lamp in the night of sin and sorrow that is life.

I am unaccustomed to literary effort – and I feel that I shall not say what I have to say, or that it will convince you, unless I say it very plainly. I thought I could adorn my story with pleasant words, prettily arranged. But as I pause to think of what really happened, I see that the plainest words will be the best. I do not know how to weave a plot, nor how to embroider it. It is best not to try. These things happened. I have no skill to add to what happened; nor is any adding of mine needed.

I am a nurse – and I was sent for to go to Charlestown – a mental case. It was November – and the fog was thick in London, so that my cab went at a foot's pace, so I missed the train by which I should have gone. I sent a telegram to Charlestown, and waited in the dismal waiting room at London Bridge. The time was passed for me by a little child. Its mother, a widow, seemed too crushed to be able to respond to its quick questionings. She answered briefly, and not, as it seemed, to the child's satisfaction. The child itself presently seemed to perceive that its mother was not, so to speak, available. It leaned back on the wide, dusty seat and yawned. I caught its eye, and smiled. It would not smile, but it looked. I took out of my bag a silk purse, bright with beads and steel tassels, and turned it over and over. Presently, the child slid along the seat and said, 'Let me' – After that all was easy. The mother sat with eyes closed. When I rose to go, she opened them and thanked me. The child, clinging, kissed me. Later, I saw them get into a first-class carriage in my train. My ticket was a third-class one.

I expected, of course, that there would be a conveyance of some sort to meet me at the station – but there was nothing. Nor was there a cab or a fly to be seen. It was by this time nearly dark, and the wind was driving the rain almost horizontally along the unfrequented road that lay beyond the door of the station. I looked out, forlorn and perplexed.

'Haven't you engaged a carriage?' It was the widow lady who spoke.

I explained.

'My motor will be here directly,' she said, 'you'll let me drive you? Where is it you are going?'

'Charlestown,' I said, and as I said it, I was aware of a very odd change in her face. A faint change, but quite unmistakable.

'Why do you look like that?' I asked her bluntly. And, of course, she said, 'Like what?'

'There's nothing wrong with the house?' I said, for that, I found, was what I had taken that faint change to signify; and I was very young, and one has heard tales. 'No reason why I shouldn't go there, I mean?'

'No – oh no –' she glanced out through the rain, and I knew as well as though she had told me that there was a reason why *she* should not wish to go there.

'Don't trouble,' I said, 'it's very kind of you – but it's probably out of your way and . . .'

'Oh – but I'll take you – of *course* I'll take you,' she said, and the child said 'Mother, here comes the car.'

And come it did, though neither of us heard it till the child had spoken. I know nothing of motor cars, and I don't know the names of any of the parts of them. This was like a brougham – only you got in at the back, as you do in a waggonette (the seats were in the corners), and when the door was shut there was a little seat that pulled up, and the child sat on it between us. And it moved like magic – or like a dream of a train.

We drove quickly through the dark – I could hear the wind screaming, and the wild dashing of the rain against the windows, even through the whirring of the machinery. One could see nothing of the country – only the black night, and the shafts of light from the lamps in front.

After, as it seemed, a very long time, the chauffeur got down and opened a gate. We went through it, and after that the road was very much rougher. We were quite silent in the car, and the child had fallen asleep.

We stopped, and the car stood pulsating as though it were out of breath, while the chauffeur hauled down my box. It was so dark that I could not see the shape of the house, only the lights in the downstairs windows, and the low-walled front garden faintly revealed by their light and the light of the motor lamps. Yet I felt that it was a fair-sized house, that it was surrounded by big trees, and that there was a pond or river close by. In daylight next day I found that all this was so. I have never been able to tell how I knew it that first night, in the dark, but I did know it. Perhaps there was something in the way the rain fell on the trees and on the water. I don't know.

The chauffeur took my box up a stone path, whereon I got out, and said my goodbyes and thanks.

'Don't wait, please, don't,' I said. 'I'm all right now. Thank you a thousand times!'

The car, however, stood pulsating till I had reached the doorstep, then it caught its breath, as it were, throbbed more loudly, turned, and went.

And still the door had not opened. I felt for the knocker, and rapped smartly. Inside the door I was sure I heard whispering. The car light was fast diminishing to a little distant star, and its panting sounded now hardly at all. When it ceased to sound at all, the place was quiet as death. The lights glowed redly from curtained windows, but there was no other sign of life. I wished I had not been in such a hurry to part from my escort, from human companionship, and from the great, solid, competent presence of the motor car.

I knocked again, and this time I followed the knock by a shout.

'Hello!' I cried. 'Let me in. I'm the nurse!'

There was a pause, such a pause as would allow time for whisperers to exchange glances on the other side of a door.

Then a bolt ground back, a key turned, and the doorway framed no longer cold, wet wood, but light and a welcoming warmth – and faces.

'Come in, oh, come in,' said a voice, a woman's voice, and the voice of a man said: 'We didn't know there was anyone there.'

And I had shaken the very door with my knockings!

I went in, blinking at the light, and the man called a servant, and between them they carried my box upstairs.

The woman took my arm and led me into a low, square room, pleasant, homely, and comfortable, with solid mid-Victorian comfort – the kind that expressed itself in rep and mahogany. In the lamplight I turned to look at her. She was small and thin, her hair, her face, and her hands were of the same tint of greyish yellow.

'Mrs Eldridge?' I asked.

'Yes,' said she, very softly. 'Oh! I am so glad you've come. I hope you won't be dull here. I hope you'll stay. I hope I shall be able to make you comfortable.'

She had a gentle, urgent way of speaking that was very winning.

'I'm sure I shall be very comfortable,' I said; 'but it's I that am to take care of you. Have you been ill long?'

'It's not me that's ill, really,' she said, 'it's him—'

Now, it was Mr Robert Eldridge who had written to engage me to attend on his wife, who was, he said, slightly deranged.

'I see,' said I. One must never contradict them, it only aggravates their disorder.

'The reason . . .' she was beginning, when his foot sounded on the stairs, and she fluttered off to get candles and hot water.

He came in and shut the door. A fair, bearded, elderly man, quite ordinary.

'You'll take care of her,' he said. 'I don't want her to get talking to people. She fancies things.'

'What form do the illusions take?' I asked, prosaically.

'She thinks I'm mad,' he said, with a short laugh.

'It's a very usual form. Is that all?'

'It's about enough. And she can't hear things that I can hear, see things that I can see, and she can't smell things. By the way, you didn't see or hear anything of a motor as you came up, did you?'

'I came up *in* a motor car,' I said shortly. 'You never sent to meet me, and a lady gave me a lift.' I was going to explain about my missing the earlier train, when I found that he was not listening to me. He was watching the door. When his wife came in, with a steaming jug in one hand and a flat candlestick in the other, he went towards her, and whispered eagerly. The only words I caught were: 'She came in a real motor.'

Apparently, to these simple people a motor was as great a novelty as to me. My telegram, by the way, was delivered next morning.

They were very kind to me; they treated me as an honoured guest. When the rain stopped, as it did late the next day, and I was able to go out, I found that Charlestown was a farm, a large farm, but even to my inexperienced eyes, it seemed neglected and unprosperous. There was absolutely nothing for me to do but to follow Mrs Eldridge, helping her where I could in her household duties, and to sit with her while she sewed in the homely parlour. When I had been in the house a few days, I began to put together the little things that I had noticed singly, and the life at the farm seemed suddenly to come into focus, as strange surroundings do after a while.

I found that I had noticed that Mr and Mrs Eldridge were very fond of each other, and that it was a fondness, and their way of showing it, was a way that told that they had known sorrow, and had borne it together. That she showed no sign of mental derangement, save in the persistent belief of hers that *he* was deranged. That the morning found them fairly cheerful; that after the early dinner they seemed to grow more and more depressed; that after the 'early cup of tea' – that is just as dusk was falling – they always went for a walk together. That they never asked me to join them in this walk, and that it always took the same direction – across the downs towards the sea. That they always returned from this walk pale and dejected; that she sometimes cried afterwards alone in their bedroom, while he was shut up in the little room they called the office, where he did his accounts, and paid his men's wages, and where his hunting-crops and guns were kept. After supper, which was early, they always made an effort to be cheerful. I knew that this effort was for my sake, and I knew that each of them thought it was good for the other to make it.

Just as I had known before they showed it to me that Charlestown was surrounded by big trees and had a great pond beside it, so I knew, and in as inexplicable a way, that with these two fear lived. It looked at me out of their eyes. And I knew, too, that this fear was not her fear. I had not been two days in the place before I found that I was beginning to be fond of them both. They were so kind, so gentle, so ordinary, so homely – the kind of people who ought not to have known the name of fear – the kind of people to whom all honest, simple joys should have come by right, and no sorrows but such as come to us all, the death of old friends, and the slow changes of advancing years.

They seemed to belong to the land – to the downs, and the copses, and the old pastures, and the lessening cornfields. I found myself wishing that I, too, belonged to these, that I had been born a farmer's daughter. All the stress and struggle of cram and exam, of school, and college and hospital, seemed so loud and futile, compared with these open secrets of the down life. And I felt this the more, as more and more I felt that I must leave it all – that there was, honestly, no work for me here such as for good or ill I had been trained to do.

'I ought not to stay,' I said to her one afternoon, as we stood at the open door. It was February now, and the snowdrops were thick in tufts beside the flagged path. 'You are quite well.'

'I am,' she said.

'You are quite well, both of you,' I said. 'I oughtn't to be taking your money and doing nothing for it.'

'You're doing everything,' she said. 'You don't know how much you're doing.'

'We had a daughter of our own once,' she added vaguely, and then, after a very long pause, she said very quietly and distinctly:

'He has never been the same since.'

'How not the same?' I asked, turning my face up to the thin February sunshine.

She tapped her wrinkled, yellow-grey forehead, as country people do.

'Not right here,' she said.

'How?' I asked. 'Dear Mrs Eldridge, tell me; perhaps I could help somehow.'

Her voice was so sane, so sweet. It had come to this with me, that I did not know which of those two was the one who needed my help.

'He sees things that no one else sees, and hears things no one else hears, and smells things that you can't smell if you're standing there beside him.'

I remembered with a sudden smile his words to me on the morning of my arrival:

'She can't see, or hear, or smell.'

And once more I wondered to which of the two I owed my service.

'Have you any idea why?' I asked. She caught at my arm.

'It was after our Bessie died,' she said – 'the very day she was buried. The motor that killed her – they said it was an accident – it was on the Brighton Road. It was a violet colour. They go into mourning for Queens with violet, don't they?' she added; 'and my Bessie, she was a Queen. So the motor was violet: That was all right, wasn't it?'

I told myself now that I saw that the woman was not normal, and I saw why. It was grief that had turned her brain. There must have been some change in my look, though I ought to have known better, for she said suddenly, 'No. I'll not tell you any more.'

And then he came out. He never left me alone with her for very long. Nor did she ever leave him for very long alone with me.

I did not intend to spy upon them, though I am not sure that my position as nurse to one mentally afflicted would not have justified such spying. But I did not spy. It was chance. I had been to the village to get some blue sewing silk for a blouse I was making, and there was a royal sunset which tempted me to prolong my walk. That was how I found myself on the high downs where they slope to the broken edge of England – the sheer, white cliffs against which the English Channel beats for ever. The furze was in flower, and the skylarks were singing, and my thoughts were with my own life, my own hopes and dreams. So I found that I had struck a road, without knowing when I had struck it. I followed it towards the sea, and quite soon it ceased to be a road, and merged in the pathless turf as a stream sometimes disappears in sand. There was nothing but turf and furze bushes, the song of the skylarks, and beyond the slope that ended at the cliff's edge, the booming of the sea. I turned back, following the road, which defined itself again a few yards back, and presently sank to a lane, deep-banked and bordered with brown hedge stuff. It was there that I came upon them in the dusk. And I heard their voices before I saw them, and before it was possible for them to see me. It was her voice that I heard first.

'No, no, no, no, no,' it said.

'I tell you yes,' that was his voice; 'there – can't you hear it, that panting sound – right away – away? It must be at the very edge of the cliff.'

'There's nothing, dearie,' she said, 'indeed there's nothing.'

'You're deaf – and blind – stand back I tell you, it's close upon us.'

I came round the corner of the lane then, and as I came, I saw him catch her arm and throw her against the hedge – violently, as though the danger he feared were indeed close upon them. I stopped behind the turn of the hedge and stepped back. They had not seen me. Her eyes were on his face, and they held a world of pity, love, agony – his face was set in a mask of terror, and his eyes moved quickly as though they followed down the lane the swift passage of something – something that neither she nor I could see. Next moment he was cowering, pressing his body into the hedge – his face hidden in his hands, and his whole body trembling so that I could see it, even from where I was a dozen yards away, through the light screen of the over-grown hedge.

'And the smell of it!' – he said, 'do you mean to tell me you can't smell it?'

She had her arms round him.

'Come home, dearie,' she said. 'Come home! It's all your fancy – come home with your old wife that loves you.'

They went home.

Next day I asked her to come to my room to look at the new blue blouse. When I had shown it to her I told her what I had seen and heard yesterday in the lane.

'And now I know,' I said, 'which of you it is that wants care.'

To my amazement she said very eagerly, 'Which?'

'Why, he – of course', I told her, 'there was nothing there.'

She sat down in the chintz covered armchair by the window, and broke into wild weeping. I stood by her and soothed her as well as I could.

'It's a comfort to know,' she said at last, 'I haven't known what to believe. Many a time, lately, I've wondered whether after all it could be me that was mad, like he said. And there was nothing there? There always *was* nothing there – and it's on him the judgement, not on me. On him. Well, that's something to be thankful for.'

So her tears, I told myself, had been more of relief at her own escape. I looked at her with distaste, and forgot that I had been fond of her. So that her next words cut me like little knives.

'It's bad enough for him as it is,' she said, 'but it's nothing to what it would be for him, if I was really to go off my head and him left to think he'd brought it on me. You see, now I can look after him the same as I've always done. It's only once in the day it comes over him. He couldn't bear it, if it was all the time – like it'll be for me now. It's much better it should be him – I'm better able to bear it than he is.'

I kissed her then and put my arms around her, and said, 'Tell me what it is that frightens him so – and it's every day, you say?'

'Yes – ever since . . . I'll tell you. It's a sort of comfort to speak out. It was a violet-coloured car that killed our Bessie. You know our girl that I've told you about. And it's a violet-coloured car that he thinks he sees – every day up there in the lane. And he says he hears it, and that he smells the smell of the machinery – the stuff they put in it – you know.'

'Petrol?'

'Yes, and you can see he hears it, and you can *see* he sees it. It haunts him, as if it was a ghost. You see, it was he that picked her up after the violet car went over her. It was that that turned him. I only saw her as he carried her in, in his arms – and then he'd covered her face. But he saw her just as they'd left her, lying in the dust . . . you could see the place on the road where it happened for days and days.'

'Didn't they come back?'

'Oh yes . . . they came back. But Bessie didn't come back. But there was a judgement on them. The very night of the funeral, that violet car went over the cliff – dashed to pieces – every soul in it. That was the man's widow that drove you here the first night.'

'I wonder she uses a car after that,' I said – I wanted something commonplace to say.

'Oh,' said Mrs Eldridge, 'it's all what you're used to. We don't stop walking because our girl was killed on the road. Motoring comes as natural to them as walking to us. There's my old man calling – poor old dear. He wants me to go out with him.'

She went, all in a hurry, and in her hurry slipped on the stairs and twisted her ankle. It all happened in a minute and it was a bad sprain.

When I had bound it up, and she was on the sofa, she looked at him, standing as if he were undecided, staring out of the window, with his cap in his hand. And she looked at me.

'Mr Eldridge mustn't miss his walk,' she said. 'You go with him, my dear. A breath of air will do you good.'

So I went, understanding as well as though he had told me, that he did not want me with him, and that he was afraid to go alone, and that he yet had to go.

We went up the lane in silence. At that corner he stopped suddenly, caught my arm, and dragged me back. His eyes followed something that I could not see. Then he exhaled a held breath, and said, 'I thought I heard a motor coming.' He had found it hard to control his terror, and I saw beads of sweat on his forehead and temples. Then we went back to the house.

The sprain was a bad one. Mrs Eldridge had to rest, and again next day it was I who went with him to the corner of the lane.

This time he could not, or did not try to, conceal what he felt. 'There – listen!' he said. 'Surely you can hear it?'

I heard nothing.

'Stand back,' he cried shrilly, suddenly, and we stood back close against the hedge.

Again the eyes followed something invisible to me, and again the held breath exhaled.

'It will kill me one of these days,' he said, 'and I don't know that I care how soon – if it wasn't for her.'

'Tell me,' I said, full of that importance, that conscious competence, that one feels in the presence of other people's troubles. He looked at me.

'I will tell you, by God,' he said. 'I couldn't tell *her*. Young lady, I've gone so far as wishing myself a Roman, for the sake of a priest to tell it to. But I can tell *you*, without losing my soul more than it's lost already. Did you ever hear tell of a violet car that got smashed up – went over the cliff?'

'Yes,' I said. 'Yes.'

'The man that killed my girl was new to the place. And he hadn't any eyes or ears – or he'd have known me, seeing we'd been face to face at the inquest. And you'd have thought he'd have stayed at home that one day, with the blinds drawn down. But not he. He was swirling and swivelling all about the country in his cursed violet car, the very time we were burying her. And at dusk – there was a mist coming up – he comes up behind me in this very lane, and I stood back, and he pulls up, and he calls out, with his damned lights full in my face: "'Can you tell me the way to Hexham, my man?" says he.

'I'd have liked to shew him the way to hell. And that was the way for me, not him. I don't know how I came to do it. I didn't mean to do it. I didn't think I was going to – and before I knew anything, I'd said it. "Straight ahead," I said; "keep straight ahead." Then the motor-thing panted, chuckled, and he was off. I ran after him to try to stop him – but what's the use of running after these motor-devils? And he kept straight on. And every day since then, every dear day, the car comes by, the violet car that nobody can see but me – and it keeps straight on.'

'You ought to go away,' I said, speaking as I had been trained to speak. 'You fancy these things. You probably fancied the whole thing. I don't suppose you ever *did* tell the violet car to go straight ahead. I expect it was all imagination, and the shock of your poor daughter's death. You ought to go right away.'

'I can't,' he said earnestly. 'If I did, some one else would see the car. You see, somebody *has* to see it every day as long as I live. If it wasn't me, it would be someone else. And I'm the only person who *deserves* to see it. I wouldn't like any one else to see it – it's too horrible. *It's* much more horrible than you think,' he added slowly.

I asked him, walking beside him down the quiet lane, what it was that was so horrible about the violet car. I think I quite expected him to say that it was splashed with his daughter's blood . . . What he did say was, 'It's too horrible to tell you,' and he shuddered.

I was young then, and youth always thinks it can move mountains. I persuaded myself that I could cure him of his delusion by attacking – not the main fort – that is always, to begin with, impregnable, but one, so to speak, of the outworks. I set myself to persuade him not to go to that corner in the lane, at that hour in the afternoon.

'But if I don't, someone else will see it.'

'There'll be nobody there *to* see it,' I said briskly.

'Someone will be there. Mark my words, someone will be there – and then they'll know.'

'Then I'll be the someone,' I said. 'Come – you stay at home with your wife, and *I'll* go – and if I see it I'll promise to tell you, and if I don't – well, then I will be able to go away with a clear conscience.'

'A clear conscience,' he repeated.

I argued with him in every moment when it was possible to catch him alone. I put all my will and all my energy into my persuasions. Suddenly, like a door that you've been trying to open, and that has resisted every key till the last one, he gave way. Yes – I should go to the lane. And he would not go.

I went.

Being, as I said before, a novice in the writing of stories, I perhaps haven't made you understand that it was quite hard for me to go – that I felt myself at once a coward and a heroine. This business of an imaginary motor that only one poor old farmer could see, probably appears to you quite commonplace and ordinary. It was not so with me. You see, the idea of this thing had dominated my life for weeks and months, had dominated it even before I knew the nature of the domination. It was this that was the fear that I had known to walk with these two people, the fear that shared their bed and board, that lay down and rose up with them. The old man's fear of this and his fear of his fear. And the old man was terribly convincing. When one talked with him, it was quite difficult to believe that he was mad, and that there wasn't, and couldn't be, a mysteriously horrible motor that was visible to him, and invisible to other people. And when he said that, if he were not in the lane, someone else would see it – it was easy to say 'Nonsense,' but to think 'Nonsense' was not so easy, and to *feel* 'Nonsense' quite oddly difficult.

I walked up and down the lane in the dusk, wishing not to wonder what might be the hidden horror in the violet car. I would not let blood into my thoughts. I was not going to be fooled by thought transference, or any of those transcendental follies. I was not going to be hypnotised into seeing things.

I walked up the lane – I had promised him to stand near that corner for five minutes, and I stood there in the deepening dusk, looking up towards the downs and the sea. There were pale stars. Everything was very still. Five minutes is a long time. I held my watch in my hand. Four – four and a quarter – four and a half. Five. I turned instantly. And then I saw that *he* had followed me – he was standing a dozen yards away – and his face was turned from me. It was turned towards a motor car that shot up the lane. It came very swiftly, and before it came to where he was, I knew that it was very horrible. I crushed myself back into the crackling bare hedge, as I should have done to leave room for the passage of a real car – though I knew that this one was not real. It looked real – but I knew it was not.

As it neared him, he started back, then suddenly he cried out. I heard him. 'No, no, no, no – no more, no more,' was what he cried, with that he flung himself down on the road in front of the car, and its great tyres passed over him. Then the car shot past me and I saw what the full horror of it was. There was no blood – that was not the horror. The colour of it was, as she had said, violet.

I got to him and got his head up. He was dead. I was quite calm and collected now, and felt that to be so was extremely creditable to me. I went to a cottage where a labourer was having tea – he got some men and a hurdle.

When I had told his wife, the first intelligible thing she said was: 'It's better for him. Whatever he did he's paid for now –' So it looks as though she had known – or guessed – more than he thought.

I stayed with her till her death. She did not live long.

You think perhaps that the old man was knocked down and killed by a real motor, which happened to come that way of all ways, at that hour of all hours, and happened to be, of all colours, violet. Well, a real motor leaves its mark on you where it kills you, doesn't it? But when I lifted up that old man's head from the road, there was no mark on him, no blood – no broken bones – his hair was not disordered, nor his dress. I tell you there was not even a speck of mud on him, except where he had touched the road in falling. There were no tyre-marks in the mud.

The motor car that killed him came and went like a shadow. As he threw himself down, it swerved a little so that both its wheels should go over him.

He died, the doctor said, of heart failure. I am the only person to know that he was killed by a violet car, which, having killed him, went noiselessly away towards the sea. And that car was empty – there was no one in it. It was just a violet car that moved along the lanes swiftly and silently, and was empty.

EDITH WHARTON

THE EYES

I

We had been put in the mood for ghosts, that evening, after an excellent dinner at our old friend Culwin's, by a tale of Fred Murchard's – the narrative of a strange personal visitation.

Seen through the haze of our cigars, and by the drowsy gleam of a coal fire, Culwin's library, with its oak walls and dark old bindings, made a good setting for such avocations; and ghostly experiences at first hand being, after Murchard's opening, the only kind acceptable to us, we proceeded to take stock of our group and tax each member for a contribution. There were eight of us, and seven contrived, in a manner more or less adequate, to fulfil the condition imposed. It surprised us all to find that we could muster such a show of supernatural impressions, for none of us, excepting Murchard himself and young Phil Frenham – whose story was the slightest of the lot – had the habit of sending our souls into the invisible. So that, on the whole, we had every reason to be proud of our seven 'exhibits', and none of us would have dreamed of expecting an eighth from our host.

Our old friend, Mr Andrew Culwin, who had sat back in his armchair, listening and blinking through the smoke circles with the cheerful tolerance of a wise old idol, was not the kind of man likely to be favoured with such contacts, though he had imagination enough to enjoy, without envying, the superior privileges of his guests. By age and by education he belonged to the stout Positivist tradition, and his habit of thought had been formed in the days of the epic struggle between physics and metaphysics. But he had been, then and always, essentially a spectator, a humorous detached observer of the immense muddled variety show of life, slipping out of his seat now and then for a brief dip into the convivialities at the back of the house, but never, as far as one knew, showing the least desire to jump on the stage and do a 'turn'.

Among his contemporaries there lingered a vague tradition of his having, at a remote period, and in the romantic clime, been wounded in a duel; but this legend no more tallied with what we younger men knew of his character than my mother's assertion that he had once been 'a charming little man with nice eyes' corresponded to any possible reconstitution of his physiognomy.

'He never can have looked like anything but a bundle of sticks,' Murchard had once said of him. 'Or a phosphorescent log, rather,' someone else amended; and we recognized the happiness of this description of his small squat trunk, with the red blink of the eyes in a face like mottled bark. He had always been possessed of a leisure which he had nursed and protected, instead of squandering it in vain activities. His carefully guarded hours had been devoted to the cultivation of a fine intelligence and a few judiciously chosen habits; and none of the disturbances common to human experience seemed to have crossed his sky. Nevertheless, his dispassionate survey of the universe had not raised his opinion of that costly experiment, and his study of the human race seemed to have resulted in the conclusion that all men were superfluous, and women necessary only because someone had to do the cooking. On the importance of this point his convictions were absolute, and gastronomy was the only science which he revered as a dogma. It must be owned that his little dinners were a strong argument in favour of this view, besides being a reason – though not the main one – for the fidelity of his friends.

Mentally he exercised a hospitality less seductive but no less stimulating. His mind was like a forum, or some open meeting-place for the exchange of ideas; somewhat cold and draughty, but light, spacious, and orderly – a kind of academic grove from which all the leaves have fallen. In this privileged area a dozen of us were wont to stretch our muscles and expand our lungs; and, as if to prolong as much as possible the tradition of what we felt to be a vanishing institution, one or two neophytes were now and then added to our band.

Young Phil Frenham was the last, and the most interesting, of these recruits, and a good example of Murchard's somewhat morbid assertion that our old friend 'liked 'em juicy'. It was indeed a fact that Culwin, for all his dryness, specially tasted the lyric qualities in youth. As he was far too good an Epicurean to nip the flowers of soul which he gathered for his garden, his friendship was not a disintegrating influence: on the contrary, it forced the young idea to robuster bloom. And in Phil Frenham he had a good subject for experimentation. The boy was really intelligent, and the soundness of his nature was like the pure paste under a fine glaze. Culwin had fished him out of a fog of family dullness, and pulled him up to a peak in Darien; and the adventure hadn't hurt him a bit. Indeed, the skill with which Culwin had contrived to stimulate his curiosities without robbing them of their bloom of awe seemed to me a sufficient answer to Murchard's ogreish metaphor. There was nothing hectic in Frenham's efflorescence, and his old friend had not laid even a finger-tip on the sacred stupidities. One wanted no better proof of that than the fact that Frenham still reverenced them in Culwin.

'There's a side of him you fellows don't see. *I* believe that story about the duel!' he declared; and it was of the very essence of this belief that it should impel him – just as our little party was dispersing – to turn back to our host with the joking demand: 'And now you've got to tell us about *your* ghost!'

The outer door had closed on Murchard and the others; only Frenham and I remained; and the devoted servant who presided over Culwin's destinies, having brought a fresh supply of soda-water, had been laconically ordered to bed.

Culwin's sociability was a night-blooming flower, and we knew that he expected the nucleus of his group to tighten around him after midnight. But Frenham's appeal seemed to disconcert him comically, and he rose from the chair in which he had just reseated himself after his farewells in the hall.

'My ghost? Do you suppose I'm fool enough to go to the expense of keeping one of my own, when there are so many charming ones in my friends' closets? Take another cigar,' he said, revolving toward me with a laugh.

Frenham laughed, too, pulling up his slender height before the chimney-piece as he turned to face his short bristling friend.

'Oh,' he said, 'you'd never be content to share if you met one you really liked.'

Culwin had dropped back into his armchair, his head embedded in the hollow of worn leather, his little eyes glimmering over a fresh cigar.

'Liked – *liked*! Good Lord!' he growled.

'Ah, you *have*, then!' Frenham pounced on him in the same instant, with a side-glance of victory at me; but Culwin cowered gnome-like among his cushions, dissembling himself in a protective cloud of smoke.

'What's the use of denying it? You've seen everything, so of course you've seen a ghost!' his young friend persisted, talking intrepidly into the cloud. 'Or, if you haven't seen one, it's only because you've seen two!'

The form of the challenge seemed to strike our host. He shot his head out of the mist with a queer tortoise-like motion he sometimes had, and blinked approvingly at Frenham.

'That's it,' he flung at us on a shrill jerk of laughter; 'it's only because I've seen two!'

The words were so unexpected that they dropped down and down into a deep silence, while we continued to stare at each other over Culwin's head, and Culwin stared at his guests. At length

Frenham, without speaking, threw himself into the chair on the other side of the hearth, and leaned forward with his listening smile . . .

II

'Oh, of course they're not show ghosts – a collector wouldn't think anything of them . . . Don't let me raise your hopes . . . their one merit is their numerical strength: the exceptional fact of there being *two*. But, as against this, I'm bound to admit that at any moment I could probably have exorcised them both by asking my doctor for a prescription, or my oculist for a pair of spectacles. Only, as I never could make up my mind whether to go to the doctor or the oculist – whether I was afflicted by an optical or a digestive delusion – I left them to pursue their interesting double life, though at times they made mine exceedingly uncomfortable . . .

'Yes – uncomfortable; and you know how I hate to be uncomfortable! But it was part of my stupid pride, when the thing began, not to admit that I could be disturbed by the trifling matter of seeing two –

'And then I'd no reason, really, to suppose I was ill. As far as I knew I was simply bored – horribly bored. But it was part of my boredom – I remember – that I was feeling so uncommonly well, and didn't know how on earth to work off my surplus energy. I had come back from a long journey – down in South America and Mexico – and had settled down for the winter near New York, with an old aunt who had known Washington Irving and corresponded with N. P. Willis. She lived, not far from Irvington, in a damp Gothic villa, overhung by Norway spruces, and looking exactly like a memorial emblem done in hair. Her personal appearance was in keeping with this image, and her own hair – of which there was little left – might have been sacrificed to the manufacture of the emblem.

'I had just reached the end of an agitated year, with considerable arrears to make up in money and emotion; and theoretically it seemed as though my aunt's mild hospitality would be as beneficial to my nerves as to my purse. But the deuce of it was that, as soon as I felt myself safe and sheltered, my energy began to revive; and how was I to work it off inside of a memorial emblem? I had, at that time, the illusion that sustained intellectual effort could engage any man's whole activity; and I decided to write a great book – I forget about what. My aunt, impressed by my plan, gave up to me her Gothic library, filled with classics bound in black cloth and daguerreotypes of faded celebrities; and I sat down at my desk to win myself a place among their number. And to facilitate my task she lent me a cousin to copy my manuscript.

'The cousin was a nice girl, and I had an idea that a nice girl was just what I needed to restore my faith in human nature, and principally in myself. She was neither beautiful nor intelligent – poor Alice Nowell! – but it interested me to see any woman content to be so uninteresting, and I wanted to find out the secret of her content. In doing this I handled it rather rashly, and put it out of joint – oh, just for a moment! There's no fatuity in telling you this, for the poor girl had never seen anyone but cousins . . .

'Well, I was sorry for what I'd done, of course, and confoundedly bothered as to how I should put it straight. She was staying in the house, and one evening, after my aunt had gone to bed, she came down to the library to fetch a book she'd mislaid, like any artless heroine, on the shelves behind us. She was pink-nosed and flustered, and it suddenly occurrred to me that her hair, though it was fairly thick and pretty, would look exactly like my aunt's when she grew older. I was glad I had noticed this, for it made it easier for me to decide to do what was right; and when I had found the book she hadn't lost I told her I was leaving for Europe that week.

'Europe was terribly far off in those days, and Alice knew at once what I meant. She didn't take it in the least as I'd expected – it would have been easier if she had. She held her book very tight, and turned away a moment to wind up the lamp on my desk – it had a ground glass shade with vine leaves, and glass drops around the edge, I remember. Then she came back, held out her hand, and said: "Good-bye". And as she said it she looked straight at me and kissed me. I had never felt anything so fresh and shy and brave as her kiss. It was worse than any reproach, and it made me ashamed to deserve a reproach from her. I said to myself: "I'll marry her, and when my aunt dies she'll leave us this house, and I'll sit here at the desk and go on with my book; and Alice will sit over there with her embroidery and look at me as she's looking now. And life will go on like that for any number of years." The prospect frightened me a little, but at the time it didn't frighten me as much as doing any-thing to hurt her; and ten minutes later she had my seal ring on her finger, and my promise that when I went abroad she should go with me.

'You'll wonder why I'm enlarging on this incident. It's because the evening on which it took place was the very evening on which I first saw the queer sight I've spoken of. Being at that time an ardent believer in a necessary sequence between cause and effect, I naturally tried to trace some kind of link between what had just happened to me in my aunt's library, and what was to happen a few hours later on the same night; and so the coincidence between the two events always remained in my mind.

'I went up to bed with rather a heavy heart, for I was bowed under the weight of the first good action I had ever consciously committed; and young as I was, I saw the gravity of my situation. Don't imagine from this that I had hitherto been an instrument of destruction. I had been merely a harmless young man, who had fol-lowed his bent and declined all collaboration with Providence. Now I had suddenly undertaken to promote the moral order of the world, and I felt a good deal like the trustful spectator who had given his gold watch to the conjuror, and doesn't know in what shape he'll get it back when the trick is over . . . Still, a glow of self-righteousness tempered my fears, and I said to myself as I undressed that when I'd got used to being good it probably wouldn't make me as nervous as it did at the start. And by the time I was in bed, and had blown out my candle, I felt that I really *was* getting used to it, and that, as far as I'd got, it was not unlike sinking down into one of my aunt's very softest wool mattresses.

'I closed my eyes on this image, and when I opened them it must have been a good deal later, for my room had grown cold, and intensely still. I was waked by the queer feeling we all know – the feeling that there was something in the room that hadn't been there when I fell asleep. I sat up and strained my eyes into the darkness. The room was pitch black, and at first I saw nothing, but gradually a vague glimmer at the foot of the bed turned into two eyes staring back at me. I couldn't distinguish the features attached to them, but as I looked the eyes grew more and more distinct; they gave out a light of their own.

'The sensation of being thus gazed at was far from pleasant, and you might suppose that my first impulse would have been to jump out of bed and hurl myself on the invisible figure attached to the eyes. But it wasn't – my impulse was simply to lie still . . . I can't say whether this was due to an immediate sense of the uncanny nature of the apparition – to the certainty that if I did jump out of bed I should hurl myself on nothing – or merely to the benumbing effect of the eyes themselves. They were the very worst eyes I've ever seen: a man's, yes – but what a man! My first thought was that he must be frightfully old. The orbits were sunk, and the thick red-lined lids hung over the eyeballs like blinds of which the cords are broken. One lid drooped a little lower than the other, with the effect of a crooked leer; and between these folds of flesh, with their scant bristle of lashes, the eyes them-selves, small glassy discs with an agate-like rim, looked like sea-pebbles in the grip of a starfish.

'But the age of the eyes was not the most unpleasant thing about them. What turned me sick was their expression of vicious security. I don't know how else to describe the fact that they seemed to belong to a man who had done a lot of harm in his life, but had always kept just inside the danger lines. They were not the eyes of a coward, but of someone much too clever to take risks; and my gorge rose at their look of base astuteness. Yet even that wasn't the worst; for as we continued to scan each other I saw in them a tinge of derision, and felt myself to be its object.

'At that I was seized by an impulse of rage that jerked me to my feet and pitched me straight at the unseen figure. But, of course, there wasn't any figure there, and my fists struck at emptiness. Ashamed and cold, I groped about for a match and lit the candles. The room looked just as usual – as I had known it would; and I crawled back to bed, and blew out the lights.

'As soon as the room was dark again the eyes reappeared; and I now applied myself to explaining them on scientific principles. At first I thought the illusion might have been caused by the glow of the last embers in the chimney; but the fireplace was on the other side of my bed, and so placed that the fire could not be reflected in my toilet glass, which was the only mirror in the room. Then it struck me that I might have been tricked by the reflection of the embers in some polished bit of wood or metal; and though I couldn't discover any object of the sort in my line of vision, I got up again, groped my way to the hearth, and covered what was left of the fire. But as soon as I was back in bed, the eyes were back at its foot.

'They were an hallucination, then. That was plain. But the fact that they were not due to any external dupery didn't make them a bit pleasanter. For if they were a projection of my inner consciousness, what the deuce was the matter with that organ? I had gone deeply enough into the mystery of morbid pathological states to picture the conditions under which an exploring mind might lay itself open to such a midnight admonition; but I couldn't fit it to my present case. I had never felt more normal, mentally and physically; and the only unusual fact in my situation – that of having assured the happiness of an amiable girl – did not seem a kind to summon unclean spirits about my pillow. But there were the eyes still looking at me . . .

'I shut mine, and tried to evoke a vision of Alice Nowell's. They were not remarkable eyes, but they were as wholesome as fresh water, and if she had had more imagination – or longer lashes – their expression might have been interesting. As it was, they did not prove very efficacious, and in a few moments I perceived that they had mysteriously changed into the eyes at the foot of the bed. It exasperated me more to feel these glaring at me through my shut lids than to see them, and I opened my eyes again and looked straight into their hateful stare . . .

'And so it went on all night. I can't tell you what that night was like, nor how long it lasted. Have you ever lain in bed, hopelessly wide awake, and tried to keep your eyes shut, knowing that if you opened 'em you'd see something you dreaded and loathed? It sounds easy, but it's devilish hard. Those eyes hung there and drew me. I had the *vertige de l'abîme*, and their red lids were the edge of my abyss . . . I had known nervous hours before: hours when I'd felt the wind of danger in my neck; but never this kind of strain. It wasn't that the eyes were awful; they hadn't the majesty of the powers of darkness. But they had – how shall I say? – a physical effect that was the equivalent of a bad smell: their look left a smear like a snail's. And I didn't see what business they had with me, anyhow – and I stared and stared, trying to find out . . .

'I don't know what effect they were trying to produce; but the effect they *did* produce was that of making me pack my portmanteau and bolt to town early next morning. I left a note for my aunt, explaining that I was ill and had gone to see my doctor; and as a matter of fact I did feel uncommonly ill – the night seemed to have pumped all the blood out of me. But when I reached town I didn't go to the doctor's. I went to a friend's rooms, and threw myself on a bed, and slept for ten heavenly hours. When I woke it was the middle of the night, and I turned cold at the thought of what might be waiting for me. I sat up, shaking, and stared into the darkness; but there wasn't a break in its blessed surface, and when I saw that the eyes were not there I dropped back into another long sleep.

'I had left no word for Alice when I fled, because I meant to go back the next morning. But the next morning I was too exhausted to stir. As the day went on, the exhaustion increased, instead of wearing off like the fatigue left by an ordinary night of insomnia: the effect of the eyes seemed to be cumulative, and the thought of seeing them again grew intolerable. For two days I fought my dread; and on the third evening I pulled myself together and decided to go back the next morning. I felt a good deal happier as soon as I'd decided, for I knew that my abrupt disappearance, and the strangeness of my not writing, must have been very distressing to poor Alice. I went to bed with an easy mind, and I fell asleep at once; but in the middle of the night I woke, and there were the eyes . . .

'Well, I simply couldn't face them; and instead of going back to my aunt's, I bundled a few things into a trunk and jumped aboard the first steamer for England. I was so dead tired when I got on board that I crawled straight into my berth, and slept most of the way over; and I can't tell you the bliss it was to wake from those long dreamless stretches and look fearlessly into the dark, *knowing* that I shouldn't see the eyes . . .

'I stayed abroad for a year, and then I stayed for another; and during that time I never had a glimpse of them. That was enough reason for prolonging my stay if I'd been on a desert island. Another was, of course, that I had perfectly come to see, on the voyage over, the complete impossibility of marrying Alice Nowell. The fact that I had been so slow in making this discovery annoyed me, and made me want to avoid explanations. The bliss of escaping at one stroke from the eyes, and from this other embarrassment, gave my freedom an extraordinary zest; and the longer I savoured it the better I liked its taste.

'The eyes had burned such a hole in my consciousness that for a long time I went on puzzling over the nature of the apparition, and wondering if it would ever come back. But as time passed I lost this dread, and retained only the precision of the image. Then that faded in its turn.

'The second year found me settled in Rome, where I was planning, I believe, to write another great book – a definitive work on Etruscan influences in Italian art. At any rate, I'd found some pretext of the kind for taking a sunny apartment in the Piazza di Spagna and dabbling about in the Forum; and there, one morning, a charming youth came to me. As he stood there in the warm light, slender and smooth and hyacinthine, he might have stepped from a ruined altar – one to Antinous, say; but he'd come instead from New York, with a letter from (of all people) Alice Nowell. The letter – the first I'd had from her since our break – was simply a line introducing her young cousin, Gilbert Noyes, and appealing to me to befriend him. It appeared, poor lad, that he "had talent", and "wanted to write"; and, an obdurate family having insisted that his calligraphy should take the form of double entry, Alice had intervened to win him six months' respite, during which he was to travel abroad on a meagre pittance, and somehow prove his ability to increase it by his pen. The quaint conditions of the test struck me first: it seemed about as conclusive as a medieval "ordeal". Then I was touched by her having sent him to me. I had always wanted to do her some service, to justify myself in my own eyes rather than hers; and here was a beautiful occasion.

'I imagine it's safe to lay down the general principle that predestined geniuses don't, as a rule, appear before one in the spring sunshine of the Forum looking like one of its banished gods. At any rate, poor Noyes wasn't a predestined genius. But he *was* beautiful to see, and charming as a comrade. It was only when he began to talk literature that my heart failed me. I knew all the symptoms so well – the things he had "in him", and the things outside him that impinged! There's the real test, after all. It was always – punctually, inevitably, with the inexorableness of a mechanical law – it was *always* the wrong thing that struck him. I grew to find a certain fascination in deciding in advance exactly which wrong thing he'd select; and I acquired an astonishing skill at the game . . .

'The worst of it was that his *bêtise* wasn't of the too obvious sort. Ladies who met him at picnics thought him intellectual; and even at dinners he passed for clever. I, who had him under the microscope, fancied now and then that he might develop some kind of a slim talent, something that he could make "do" and be happy on; and wasn't that, after all, what I was concerned with? He was so charming – he continued to be so charming – that he called forth all my charity in support of this argument; and for the first few months I really believed there was a chance for him . . .

'Those months were delightful. Noyes was constantly with me, and the more I saw of him the better I liked him. His stupidity was a natural grace – it was as beautiful, really, as his eyelashes. And he was so gay, so affectionate, and so happy with me, that telling him the truth would have been about as pleasant as slitting the throat of some gentle animal. At first I used to wonder what had put into that radiant head the detestable delusion that it held a brain. Then I began to see it was simply protective mimicry – an instinctive ruse to get away from family and life and an office desk. Not that Gilbert didn't – dear lad! – believe in himself. There wasn't a trace of hypocrisy in him. He was sure that his "call" was irresistible, while to me it was the saving grace of the situation that it *wasn't*, and that a little money, a little leisure, a little pleasure, would have turned him into an inoffensive idler. Unluckily, however, there was no hope of money, and with the alternative of the office desk before him, he couldn't postpone his attempt at literature. The stuff he turned out was deplorable, and I see now that I knew it from the first. Still, the absurdity of deciding a man's whole future on a first trial seemed to justify me in withholding my verdict, and perhaps even in encouraging him a little, on the ground that the human plant generally needs warmth to flower.

'At any rate, I proceeded on that principle, and carried it to the point of getting his term of probation extended. When I left Rome he went with me, and we idled away a delicious summer between Capri and Venice. I said to myself: "If he has anything in him, it will come out now"; and it *did*. He was never more enchanting and enchanted. There were moments of our pilgrimage when beauty born of murmuring sound seemed actually to pass into his face – but only to issue forth in a flood of the palest ink . . .

'Well, the time came to turn off the tap; and I knew there was no hand but mine to do it. We were back in Rome, and I had taken him to stay with me, not wanting him to be alone in his *pension* when he had to face the necessity of renouncing his ambition. I hadn't, of course, relied solely on my own judgement in deciding to advise him to drop literature. I had sent his stuff to various people – editors and critics – and they had always sent it back with the same chilling lack of comment. Really there was nothing on earth to say –

'I confess I never felt more shabbily than I did on the day when I decided to have it out with Gilbert. It was not well enough to tell myself that it was my duty to knock the poor boy's hopes into splinters – but I'd like to know what act of gratuitous cruelty hasn't been justified on that plea? I've always shrunk from usurping the functions of Providence, and when I have to exercise them I decidedly prefer that it shouldn't be on an errand of destruction. Besides, in the last issue, who was I to decide, even after a year's trial, if poor Gilbert had it in him or not?

'The more I looked at the part I'd resolved to play, the less I liked it; and I liked it still less when Gilbert sat opposite me, with his head thrown back in the lamplight, just as Phil's is now . . . I'd been going over his last manuscript, and he knew it, and he knew that his future hung on my verdict – we'd tacitly agreed to that. The manuscript lay between us, on my table – a novel, his first novel, if you please! – and he reached over and laid his hand on it, and looked up at me with all his life in the look.

'I stood up and cleared my throat, trying to keep my eyes away from his face and on the manuscript.

'"The fact is, my dear Gilbert," I began –

'I saw him turn pale, but he was up and facing me in an instant.

'"Oh, look here, don't take on so, my dear fellow! I'm not so awfully cut up as all that!" His hands were on my shoulders, and he was laughing down on me from his full height, with a kind of mortally stricken gaiety that drove the knife into my side.

'He was too brutally brave for me to keep up any humbug about my duty. And it came over me suddenly how I should hurt others in hurting him: myself first, since sending him home meant losing him; but more particularly poor Alice Nowell, to whom I had so longed to prove my good faith and my desire to serve her. It really seemed like failing her twice to fail Gilbert –

'But my intuition was like one of those lightning flashes that encircle the whole horizon, and in the same instant I saw what I might be letting myself in for if I didn't tell the truth. I said to myself: "I shall have him for life" – and I'd never yet seen anyone, man or woman, whom I was quite sure of wanting on those terms. Well, this impulse of egotism decided me. I was ashamed of it, and to get away from it I took a leap that landed me straight in Gilbert's arms.

'"The thing's all right, and you're all wrong!" I shouted up at him; and as he hugged me, and I laughed and shook in his clutch, I had for a minute the sense of self-complacency that is supposed to attend the footsteps of the just. Hang it all, making people happy *has* its charms –

'Gilbert, of course, was for celebrating his emancipation in some spectacular manner; but I sent him away alone to explode his emotions, and I went to bed to sleep off mine. As I undressed I began to wonder what their aftertaste would be – so many of the finest don't keep. Still, I wasn't sorry, and I meant to empty the bottle, even if it *did* turn a trifle flat.

'After I got in bed I lay for a long time smiling at the memory of his eyes – his blissful eyes . . . Then I fell asleep, and when I woke the room was deathly cold, and I sat up with a jerk – and there were *the other eyes* . . .

'It was three years since I'd seen them, but I'd thought of them so often that I fancied they could never take me unawares again. Now, with their red sneer on me, I knew that I had really believed they would come back, and that I was as defenceless as ever against them . . . As before, it was the insane irrelevance of their coming that made it so horrible. What the deuce were they after, to leap out at me at such a time? I had lived more or less carelessly in the years since I'd seen them, though my worst indiscretions were not dark enough to invite the searchings of their infernal glare; but at this particular moment I was really in what might have been called a state of grace; and I can't tell you how the fact added to their horror . . .

'But it's not enough to say they were as bad as before: they were worse. Worse by just so much as I'd learned of life in the interval, by all the damnable implications my wider experience read into them. I saw now what I hadn't seen before; that they were eyes which had grown hideous gradually, which had built up their baseness coralwise, bit by bit, out of a series of small turpitudes slowly accumulated through the industrious years. Yes – it came to me that what made them so bad was that they'd grown bad so slowly . . .

'There they hung in the darkness, their swollen lids dropped across the little watery bulbs rolling loose in the orbits, and the puff of flesh making a muddy shadow underneath – and as their stare moved with my movements, there came over me a sense of their tacit complicity, of a deep hidden understanding between us that was worse than the first shock of their strangeness. Not that I understood them; but that they made it so clear that some day I should . . . Yes, that was the worst part of it, decidedly; and it was the feeling that became stronger each time they came back . . .

'For they got into the damnable habit of coming back. They reminded me of vampires with a taste for young flesh, they seemed so to gloat over the taste of a good conscience. Every night for a month they came to claim their morsel of mine: since I'd made Gilbert happy they simply wouldn't loosen their fangs. The coincidence almost made me hate him, poor lad, fortuitous as I felt it to be. I puzzled over it a good deal, but I couldn't find any hint of an explanation except in the chance of his association with Alice Nowell. But then the eyes had let up on me that moment I had abandoned her, so they could hardly be the emissaries of a woman scorned, even if one could have pictured poor Alice charging such spirits to avenge her. That set me thinking, and I began to wonder if they would let up on me if I abandoned Gilbert. The temptation was insidious, and I had to stiffen myself against it; but really, dear boy! he was too charming to be sacrificed to such demons. And so, after all, I never found out what they wanted . . .'

III

The fire crumbled, sending up a flash which threw into relief the narrator's gnarled face under its grey-black stubble. Pressed into the hollow of the chair-back, it stood out an instant like an intaglio of yellowish red-veined stone, with spots of enamel for the eyes; then the fire sank and it became once more a dim Rembrandtish blur.

Phil Frenham, sitting in a low chair on the opposite side of the hearth, one long arm propped on the table behind him, one hand supporting his thrown-back head, and his eyes fixed on his old friend's face, had not moved since the tale began. He continued to maintain his silent immobility after Culwin had ceased to speak, and it was I who, with a vague sense of disappointment at the sudden drop of the story, finally asked: 'But how long did you keep on seeing them?'

Culwin, so sunk into his chair that he seemed like a heap of his own empty clothes, stirred a little, as if in surprise at my question. He appeared to have half-forgotten what he had been telling us.

'How long? Oh, off and on all that winter. It was infernal. I never got used to them. I grew really ill.'

Frenham shifted his attitude, and as he did so his elbow struck against a small mirror in a bronze frame standing on the table behind him. He turned and changed its angle slightly; then he resumed his former attitude, his dark head thrown back on his lifted palm, his eyes intent on Culwin's face. Something in his silent gaze embarrassed me, and as if to divert attention from it I pressed on with another question:

'And you never tried sacrificing Noyes?'

'Oh, no. The fact is I didn't have to. He did it for me, poor boy!'

'Did it for you? How do you mean?'

'He wore me out – wore everybody out. He kept on pouring out his lamentable twaddle, and hawking it up and down the place till he became a thing of terror. I tried to wean him from writing – oh, ever so gently, you understand, by throwing him with agreeable people, giving him a chance to make himself felt, to come to a sense of what he *really* had to give. I'd foreseen this solution from the beginning – felt sure that, once the first ardour of authorship was quenched, he'd drop into his place as a charming parasitic thing, the kind of chronic Cherubino for whom, in old societies, there's always a seat at table, and a shelter behind the ladies' skirts. I saw him take his place as "the poet": the poet who doesn't write. One knows the type in every drawing-room. Living in that way doesn't cost much – I'd worked it all out in my mind, and felt sure that, with a little help, he could manage it for the next few years; and meanwhile he'd be sure to marry. I saw him married to a widow, rather older, with a good cook and a well-run house. And I actually had my eye on the widow . . . Meanwhile I did everything to help the transition – lent him money to ease his conscience, introduced him to pretty women to make him forget his vows. But nothing would do him: he had but one idea in his beautiful obstinate head. He wanted the laurel and not the rose, and he kept on repeating Gautier's axiom, and battering and filing at his limp prose till he'd spread it out over Lord knows how many hundred pages. Now and then he would send a barrelful to a publisher, and of course it would always come back.

'At first it didn't matter – he thought he was "misunderstood". He took the attitudes of genius, and whenever an opus came home he wrote another to keep it company. Then he had a reaction of despair, and accused me of deceiving him, and Lord knows what. I got angry at that, and told him it was he who had deceived himself He'd come to me determined to write, and I'd done my best to help him. That was the extent of my offence, and I'd done it for his cousin's sake, not his.

'That seemed to strike home, and he didn't answer for a minute. Then he said: "My time's up and my money's up. What do you think I'd better do?"

'"I think you'd better not be an ass," I said.

'"What do you mean by being an ass?" he asked.

'I took a letter from my desk and held it out to him.

'"I mean refusing this offer of Mrs Ellinger's: to be her secretary at a salary of five thousand dollars. There may be a lot more in it than that.'

'He flung out his hand with a violence that struck the letter from mine. "Oh, I know well enough what's in it!" he said, red to the roots of his hair.

'"And what's the answer, if you know?" I asked.

'He made none at the minute, but turned away slowly to the door. There, with his hand on the threshold, he stopped to say, almost under his breath: "Then you really think my stuff's no good?"

'I was tired and exasperated, and I laughed. I don't defend my laugh – it was in wretched taste. But I must plead in extenuation that the boy was a fool, and that I'd done my best for him – I really had.

'He went out of the room, shutting the door quietly after him. That afternoon I left for Frascati, where I'd promised to spend the Sunday with some friends. I was glad to escape from Gilbert, and by the same token, as I learned that night, I had also escaped from the eyes. I dropped into the same lethargic sleep that had come to me before when I left off seeing them; and when I woke the next morning, in my peaceful room above the ilexes, I felt the utter weariness and deep relief that always followed on that sleep. I put in two blessed nights at Frascati, and when I got back to my rooms in Rome I found that Gilbert had gone . . . Oh, nothing tragic had happened – the episode never rose to *that*. He'd simply packed his manuscripts and left for America – for his family and the Wall Street desk. He left a decent enough note to tell me of his decision, and behaved altogether, in the circumstances, as little like a fool as it's possible for a fool to behave . . .'

IV

Culwin paused again, and Frenham still sat motionless, the dusky contour of his young head reflected in the mirror at his back.

'And what became of Noyes afterward?' I finally asked, still disquieted by a sense of incompleteness, by the need of some connecting thread between parallel lines of the tale.

Culwin twitched his shoulders. 'Oh, nothing became of him – because he became nothing. There could be no question of "becoming" about it. He vegetated in an office, I believe, and finally got a clerkship in a consulate, and married drearily in China. I saw him once in Hong Kong, years afterward. He was fat and hadn't shaved. I was told he drank. He didn't recognize me.'

'And the eyes?' I asked, after another pause which Frenham's continued silence made oppressive.

Culwin, stroking his chin, blinked at me meditatively through the shadows. 'I never saw them after my last talk with Gilbert. Put two and two together if you can. For my part, I haven't found the link.'

He rose, his hands in his pockets, and walked stiffly over to the table on which reviving drinks had been set out.

'You must be parched – after this dry tale. Here, help yourself, my dear fellow. Here, Phil –' He turned back to the hearth.

Frenham made no response to his host's hospitable summons. He still sat in his low chair without moving, but, as Culwin advanced toward him, their eyes met in a long look; after which the young man, turning suddenly, flung his arms across the table behind him, and dropped his face upon them.

Culwin, at the unexpected gesture, stopped short, a flush on his face.

'Phil – what the deuce! Why, have the eyes scared *you*? My dear boy – my dear fellow – I never had such a tribute to my literary ability, never!'

He broke into a chuckle at the thought, and halted on the hearthrug, his hands still in his pockets, gazing down at the youth's bowed head. Then, as Frenham still made no answer, he moved a step or two nearer.

'Cheer up, my dear Phil! It's been years since I've seen them – apparently I've done nothing lately bad enough to call them out of chaos. Unless my present evocation of them has made *you* see them, which would be their worst stroke yet!'

His bantering appeal quivered off into an uneasy laugh, and he moved still nearer, bending over Frenham, and laying his gouty hands on the lad's shoulders.

'Phil, my dear boy, really – what's the matter? Why don't you answer? *Have* you seen the eyes?'

Frenham's face was still hidden, and from where I stood behind Culwin I saw the latter, as if under the rebuff of this unaccountable attitude, draw back slowly from his friend. As he did so, the light of the lamp on the table fell full on his congested face, and I caught its reflection in the mirror behind Frenham's head.

Culwin saw the reflection also. He paused, his face level with the mirror, as if scarcely recognizing the countenance in it as his own. But as he looked his expression gradually changed, and for an appreciable space of time he and the image in the glass confronted each other with a glare of slowly gathering hate. Then Culwin let go of Frenham's shoulders, and drew back a step . . .

Frenham, his face still hidden, did not stir.

MAY SINCLAIR

THE TOKEN

I

I have only known one absolutely adorable woman, and that was my brother's wife, Cicely Dunbar.

Sisters-in-law do not, I think, invariably adore each other, and I am aware that my chief merit in Cicely's eyes was that I am Donald's sister; but for me there was no question of extraneous quality – it was all pure Cicely.

And how Donald – But then, like all the Dunbars, Donald suffers from being Scottish, so that, if he has a feeling, he makes it a point of honour to pretend he hasn't it. I daresay he let himself go a bit during his courtship, when he was not, strictly speaking, himself; but after he had once married her I think he would have died rather than have told Cicely in so many words that he loved her. And Cicely wanted to be told. You say she ought to have known without telling? You don't know Donald. You can't conceive the perverse ingenuity he could put into hiding his affection. He has that peculiar temper – I think it's Scottish – that delights in snubbing and fault-finding and defeating expectation. If he knows you want him to do a thing, that alone is reason enough with Donald for not doing it. And my sister, who was as transparent as white crystal, was never able to conceal a want. So that Donald could, as we said, 'have' her at every turn.

And, then, I don't think my brother really knew how ill she was. He didn't want to know. Besides, he was so wrapt up in trying to finish his 'Development of Social Economics' (which, by the way, he hasn't finished yet) that he had no eyes to see what we all saw: that, the way her poor little heart was going, Cicely couldn't have very long to live.

Of course he understood that this was why, in those last months, they had to have separate rooms. And this in the first year of their marriage when he was still violently in love with her. I keep those two facts firmly in my mind when I try to excuse Donald; for it was the main cause of that unkindness and perversity which I find it so hard to forgive. Even now, when I think how he used to discharge it on the poor little thing, as if it had been her fault, I have to remind myself that the lamb's innocence made her a little trying.

She couldn't understand why Donald didn't want to have her with him in his library any more while he read or wrote. It seemed to her sheer cruelty to shut her out now when she was ill, seeing that, before she was ill, she had always had her chair by the fire-place, where she would sit over her book or her embroidery for hours without speaking, hardly daring to breathe lest she should interrupt him. Now was the time, she thought, when she might expect a little indulgence.

Do you suppose that Donald would give his feelings as an explanation? Not he. They were *his feelings*, and he wouldn't talk about them; and he never explained anything you didn't understand.

That – her wanting to sit with him in the library – was what they had the awful quarrel about, the day before she died; that and the paper-weight, the precious paper-weight that he wouldn't let any-body touch because George Meredith had given it him. It was a brass block, surmounted by a white alabaster Buddha painted and gilt. And it had an inscription: *To Donald Dunbar, from George Meredith. In Affectionate Regard.*

My brother was extremely attached to this paper-weight, partly,

I'm afraid, because it proclaimed his intimacy with the great man. For this reason it was known in the family ironically as the Token.

It stood on Donald's writing-table at his elbow, so near the ink-pot that the white Buddha had received a splash or two. And this evening Cicely had come in to us in the library, and had annoyed Donald by staying in it when he wanted her to go. She had taken up the Token, and was cleaning it to give herself a pretext.

She died after the quarrel they had then.

It began by Donald shouting at her.

'What are you doing with that paper-weight?'

'Only getting the ink off.'

I can see her now, the darling. She had wetted the corner of her handkerchief with her little pink tongue and was rubbing the Buddha. Her hands had begun to tremble when he shouted.

'Put it down, can't you? I've told you not to touch my things.'

'*You* inked him,' she said. She was giving one last rub as he rose, threatening.

'Put – it – down.'

And, poor child, she did put it down. Indeed, she dropped it at his feet.

'Oh!' she cried out, and stooped quickly and picked it up. Her large tear-glassed eyes glanced at him, frightened.

'He isn't broken.'

'No thanks to you,' he growled.

'You beast! You know I'd die rather than break anything you care about.'

'It'll be broken some day, if you *will* come meddling.'

I couldn't bear it. I said, 'You mustn't yell at her like that. You know she can't stand it. You'll make her ill again.'

That sobered him for a moment.

'I'm sorry,' he said; but he made it sound as if he wasn't.

'If you're sorry,' she persisted, 'you might let me stay with you. I'll be as quiet as a mouse.'

'No; I don't want you – I can't work with you in the room.'

'You can work with Helen.'

'You're not Helen.'

'He only means he's not in love with *me*, dear.'

'He means I'm no use to him. I know I'm not. I can't even sit on his manuscripts and keep them down. He cares more for that damned paper-weight that he does for me.'

'Well – George Meredith gave it me.'

'And nobody gave you me. I gave myself.'

That worked up his devil again. He *had* to torment her.

'It can't have cost you much,' he said. 'And I may remind you that the paper-weight has *some* intrinsic value.'

With that he left her.

'What's he gone out for?' she asked me.

'Because he's ashamed of himself, I suppose,' I said. 'Oh, Cicely, why *will* you answer him? You know what he is.'

'No!' she said passionately – 'that's what I don't know. I never have known.'

'At least you know he's in love with you.'

'He has a queer way of showing it, then. He never does anything but stamp and shout and find fault with me – all about an old paper-weight!'

She was caressing it as she spoke, stroking the alabaster Buddha as if it had been a live thing.

'His poor Buddha. Do you think it'll break if I stroke it? Better not . . . Honestly, Helen, I'd rather die than hurt anything he really cared for. Yet look how he hurts me.'

'Some men *must* hurt the things they care for.'

'I wouldn't mind his hurting, if only I knew he cared. Helen – I'd give anything to know.'

'I think you might know.'

'I don't! I don't!'

'Well, you'll know some day.'

'Never! He won't tell me.'

'He's Scotch, my dear. It would kill him to tell you.'

'Then how'm I to know! If I died tomorrow I should die not knowing.'

And that night, not knowing, she died.

She died because she had never really known.

II

We never talked about her. It was not my brother's way. Words hurt him, to speak or to hear them.

He had become more morose than ever, but less irritable, the source of his irritation being gone. Though he plunged into work as another man might have plunged into dissipation, to drown the thought of her, you could see that he had no longer any interest in it; he no longer loved it. He attacked it with a fury that had more hate in it than love. He would spend the greater part of the day and the long evenings shut up in his library, only going out for a short walk an hour before dinner. You could see that soon all spontaneous impulses would be checked in him and he would become the creature of habit and routine.

I tried to rouse him, to shake him up out of his deadly groove; but it was no use. The first effort – for he did make efforts – exhausted him, and he sank back into it again.

But he liked to have me with him; and all the time that I could spare from my housekeeping and gardening I spent in the library. I think he didn't like to be left alone there in the place where they had the quarrel that killed her; and I noticed that the cause of it, the Token, had disappeared from his table.

And all her things, everything that could remind him of her, had been put away. It was the dead burying its dead.

Only the chair she had loved remained in its place by the side of the hearth – *her* chair, if you could call it hers when she wasn't allowed to sit in it. It was always empty, for by tacit consent we both avoided it.

We would sit there for hours at a time without speaking, while he worked and I read or sewed. I never dared to ask him whether he sometimes had, as I had, the sense of Cicely's presence there, in that room which she had so longed to enter, from which she had been so cruelly shut out. You couldn't tell what he felt or didn't feel. My brother's face was a heavy, sombre mask; his back, bent over the writing-table, a wall behind which he hid himself.

You must know that twice in my life I have more than *felt* these presences; I have seen them. This may be because I am on both sides a Highland Celt, and my mother had the same uncanny gift. I have never spoken of these appearances to Donald because he would have put it all down to what he calls my hysterical fancy. And I am sure that if he ever felt or saw anything himself he would never own it.

I ought to explain that each time the vision was premonitory of a death (in Cicely's case I had no warning), and each time it only lasted for a second; also that, though I am certain I was wide awake each time, it is open to anybody to say I was asleep and dreamed it. The queer thing was that I was neither frightened nor surprised.

And so I was neither surprised nor frightened now, the first evening that I saw her.

It was in the early autumn twilight, about six o'clock. I was sitting in my place in front of the fireplace. Donald was in his armchair on my left, smoking a pipe, as usual, before the lamplight drove him out of doors into the dark.

I had had so strong a sense of Cicely's being there in the room that I felt nothing but a sudden sacred pang that was half joy when I looked up and saw her sitting in her chair on my right.

The phantasm was perfect and vivid, as if it had been flesh and blood. I should have thought that it was Cicely herself if I hadn't known that she was dead. She wasn't looking at me; her face was turned to Donald with that longing, wondering look it used to have, searching his face for the secret that he kept from her.

I looked at Donald. His chin was sunk a little, the pipe drooping from the corner of his mouth. He was heavy, absorbed in his smoking. It was clear that he did not see what I saw.

And whereas those other phantasms that I told you about disappeared at once, *this* lasted some little time, and always with its eyes fixed on Donald. It even lasted while Donald stirred, while he stooped forward, knocking the ashes out of his pipe against the hob, while he sighed, stretched himself, turned, and left the room. Then, as the door shut behind him, the whole figure went out suddenly – not flickering, but like a light you switch off.

I saw it again the next evening and the next, at the same time and in the same place, and with the same look turned towards Donald. And again I was sure that he did not see it. But I thought, from his uneasy sighing and stretching, that he had some sense of something there.

No; I was not frightened. I was glad. You see, I loved Cicely. I remember thinking, 'At last, at last, you poor darling, you've got in. And you can stay as long as you like now. He can't turn you away.'

The first few times I saw her just as I have said. I would look up and find the phantasm there, sitting in her chair. And it would disappear suddenly when Donald left the room. Then I knew I was alone.

But as I grew used to its presence, or perhaps as it grew used to mine and found out that I was not afraid of it, that indeed I loved to have it there, it came, I think, to trust me, so that I was made aware of all its movements. I would see it coming across the room from the doorway, making straight for its desired place, and settling in a little curled-up posture of satisfaction, appeased, as if it had expected opposition that it no longer found. Yet that it was not happy, I could still see by its look at Donald. *That* never changed. It was as uncertain of him now as she had been in her lifetime.

Up till now, the sixth or seventh time I had seen it, I had no clue to the secret of its appearance; and its movements seemed to me mysterious and without purpose. Only two things were clear: it was Donald that it came for – the instant he went it disappeared; and I never once saw it when I was alone. And always it chose this room and this hour before the lights came, when he sat doing nothing. It was clear also that he never saw it.

But that it was there with him sometimes when I was not I knew;

for, more than once, things on Donald's writing-table, books or papers, would be moved out of their places, though never beyond reach; and he would ask me whether I had touched them.

'Either you lie,' he would say, 'or I'm mistaken. I could have sworn I put those notes on the *left*-hand side; and they aren't there now.'

And once – that was wonderful – I saw, yes, I *saw* her come and push the lost thing under his hand. And all he said was, 'Well, I'm – I could have sworn—'

For whether it had gained a sense of security, or whether its purpose was now finally fixed, it began to move regularly about the room, and its movements had evidently a reason and an aim.

It was looking for something.

One evening we were all there in our places, Donald silent in his chair and I in mine, and it seated in its attitude of wonder and of waiting, when suddenly I saw Donald looking at me.

'Helen,' he said, 'what are you staring for like that?'

I started. I had forgotten that the direction of my eyes would be bound, sooner or later, to betray me.

I heard myself stammer: 'W – w – was I staring?'

'Yes. I wish you wouldn't.'

I knew what he meant. He didn't want me to keep on looking at that chair; he didn't want to know that I was thinking of her. I bent my head closer over my sewing, so that I no longer had the phantasm in sight.

It was then I was aware that it had risen and was crossing the hearthrug. It stopped at Donald's knees, and stood there, gazing at him with a look so intent and fixed that I could not doubt that this had some significance. I saw it put out its hand and touch him; and, though Donald sighed and shifted his position, I could tell that he had neither seen nor felt anything.

It turned to me then – and this was the first time it had given any sign that it was conscious of my presence – it turned on me a look of supplication, such supplication as I had seen on my sister's face in her lifetime, when she could do nothing with him and implored me to intercede. At the same time three words formed themselves in my brain with a sudden, quick impulsion, as if I had heard them cried:

'Speak to him – speak to him!'

I knew now what it wanted. It was trying to make itself seen by him, to make itself felt, and it was in anguish at finding that it could not. It knew then that I saw it, and the idea had come to it that it could make use of me to get through to him. I think I must have guessed even then what it had come for.

I said, 'You asked me what I was staring at, and I lied. I was looking at Cicely's chair.'

I saw him wince at the name.

'Because,' I went on, 'I don't know how *you* feel, but I always feel as if she were there.'

He said nothing; but he got up, as though to shake off the oppression of the memory I had evoked, and stood leaning on the chimneypiece with his back to me.

The phantasm retreated to its place, where it kept its eyes fixed on him as before.

I was determined to break down his defences, to make him say something it might hear, give some sign that it would understand.

'Donald, do you think it's a good thing, a *kind* thing, never to talk about her?'

'Kind? Kind to whom?'

'To yourself, first of all.'

'You can leave me out of it.'

'To me, then.'

'What's it got to do with you?' His voice was as hard and cutting as he could make it.

'Everything,' I said. 'You forget, I loved her.'

He was silent. He did at least respect my love for her.

'But that wasn't what she wanted.'

That hurt him. I could feel him stiffen under it.

'You see, Donald,' I persisted. '*I* like thinking about her.'

It was cruel of me; but I *had* to break him.

'You can think as much as you like,' he said, 'provided you stop talking.'

'All the same, it's as bad for you,' I said, 'as it is for me, not talking.'

'I don't care if it is bad for me. I *can't* talk about her, Helen. I don't want to.'

'How do you know,' I said, 'it isn't bad for *her*?'

'For *her*?'

I could see I had roused him.

'Yes. If she really is there, all the time.'

'How d'you mean, *there*?'

'Here – in this room. I tell you I can't get over that feeling that she's here.'

'Oh, feel, feel,' he said; 'but don't talk to me about it!'

And he left the room, flinging himself out in anger. And instantly her flame went out.

I thought, 'How he must have hurt her!' It was the old thing over again: I trying to break him down, to make him show her; he beating us both off, punishing us both. You see, I knew now what she had come back for: she had come back to find out whether he loved her. With a longing unquenched by death, she had come back for certainty. And now, as always, my clumsy interferences had only made him more hard, more obstinate. I thought, 'If only he could see her! But as long as he beats her off he never will.'

Still, if I could once get him to believe that she was there –

I made up my mind that the next time I saw the phantasm I would tell him.

The next evening and the next its chair was empty, and I judged that it was keeping away, hurt by what it had heard the last time.

But the third evening we were hardly seated before I saw it.

It was sitting up, alert and observant, not staring at Donald as it used to, but looking round the room, as if searching for something that it missed.

'Donald,' I said, 'if I told you that Cicely is in the room now, I suppose you wouldn't believe me?'

'Is it likely?'

'No. All the same, I see her as plainly as I see you.'

The phantasm rose and moved to his side.

'She's standing close beside you.'

And now it moved and went to the writing-table. I turned and followed its movements. It slid its open hands over the table, touching everything, unmistakably feeling for something it believed to be there.

I went on. 'She's at the writing-table now. She's looking for something.'

It stood back, baffled and distressed. Then suddenly it began opening and shutting the drawers, without a sound, searching each one in turn.

I said, 'Oh, she's trying the drawers now!'

Donald stood up. He was looking hard at me, in anxiety and a sort of fright. I suppose that was why he remained unaware of the opening and shutting of the drawers.

It continued its desperate searching.

The bottom drawer stuck fast. I saw it pull and shake it, and stand back again, baffled.

'It's locked,' I said.

'What's locked?'

'That bottom drawer.'

'Nonsense! It's nothing of the kind.'

'It is, I tell you. Give me the key. Oh, Donald, give it me!'

He shrugged his shoulders; but all the same he felt in his pockets for the key, which he gave me with a little teasing gesture, as if he humoured a child.

I unlocked the drawer, pulled it out to its full length, and there, thrust away at the back, out of sight, I found the Token.

I had not seen it since the day of Cicely's death.

'Who put it there?' I asked.

'I did.'

'Well, that's what she was looking for,' I said.

I held out the Token to him on the palm of my hand, as if it were the proof that I had seen her.

'Helen,' he said gravely, 'I think you must be ill.'

'You think so? I'm not so ill that I don't know what you put it away for,' I said. 'It was because she thought you cared for it more than you did for her.'

'You can remind me of that? There must be something very badly wrong with you, Helen,' he said.

'Perhaps. Perhaps I only want to know what *she* wanted . . . You *did* care for her, Donald?'

I couldn't see the phantasm now, but I could feel it, close, close, vibrating, palpitating, as I drove him.

'Care?' he cried. 'I was mad with caring for her! And she knew it.'

'She didn't. She wouldn't be here now if she knew.'

At that he turned from me to his station by the chimney-piece. I followed him there.

'What are you going to do about it?' I said.

'Do about it?'

'What are you going to do with this?'

I thrust the Token close towards him. He drew back, staring at it with a look of concentrated hate and loathing.

'Do with it?' he said. 'The damned thing killed her! This is what I'm going to do with it –'

He snatched it from my hand and hurled it with all his force against the bars of the grate. The Buddha fell, broken to bits, among the ashes.

Then I heard him give a short, groaning cry. He stepped forward, opening his arms, and I saw the phantasm slide between them. For a second it stood there, folded to his breast; then suddenly, before our eyes, it collapsed in a shining heap, a flicker of light on the floor, at his feet.

Then that went out too.

III

I never saw it again.

Neither did my brother. But I didn't know this till some time afterwards; for, somehow, we hadn't cared to speak about it. And in the end it was he who spoke first.

We were sitting together in that room, one evening in November, when he said, suddenly and irrelevantly:

'Helen – do you never see her now?'

'No,' I said – 'Never!'

'Do you think, then, she doesn't come?'

'Why should she?' I said. 'She found what she came for. She knows what she wanted to know.'

'And that – was what?'

'Why, that you loved her.'

His eyes had a queer, submissive, wistful look.

'You think that was why she came back?' he said.

RICHMAL CROMPTON

ROSALIND

I had known Rosalind long before Heath saw her. I don't know where she came from originally. I think she was serving in a shop before she became old Follett's model. If you remember old Follett's paintings, you'll remember what she was like – a girl about seventeen, with creamy skin, dewy grey-blue eyes, wonderful jet-black lashes, and a mop of short red-gold curls. I remember noticing that the upper outline of her lips was the perfect arc of a circle. Her nose was delicious – a hint of the *retroussé* about it and something childishly immature. She was small and graceful – not so much fairy-like as elfin-like . . . Of course, people talked when she went to Follett, but I happened to know that there was nothing in it. She was a perfect child, and old Follett treated her as though she were his daughter. He was a terrible old man, with a reputation like a piece of tissue paper, but Rosalind appealed to some hidden streak of fatherliness in him. I used to call at his studio a good deal and Rosalind was almost always there. When she was not posing for him, she was cooking his meals or mending his clothes or cleaning the studio. She made him change his underclothing. Periodically she cleaned his greasy old velvet jacket. Left to himself he was the most filthy old ruffian I have ever met. He had a villainous brown beard that reached almost to his waist, and that no amount of persuasion would induce him to have cut.

I think it was Follett who first made her dress in brown and gold. I never saw her wearing any other colours – apart from her models' costumes . . . always warm brown with a touch of golden yellow.

It was I who first took Heath at his own request to Follett's studio. And, curiously enough, it wasn't any of the Rosalind pictures that had attracted Heath. It was some sketches of Canterbury that he had seen in an exhibition that had attracted him and, hearing that I knew the artist, he had come round to ask me to introduce him. That was like Heath . . . He wasn't an artist and he wasn't particularly interested in art, but he was always darting off down side tracks – becoming suddenly interested in something, pursuing it madly for a time, then tiring of it as suddenly and wandering on aimlessly till some fresh interest attracted him. He was having an art phase just then . . .

I had known Heath from childhood. He seemed to have all the gifts that Fortune could bestow – good looks, money, charm, ability, position – yet he just missed being what he might have been. He wasn't quite reliable. You could never be quite sure of him. He could do things so easily that he generally seemed to put off doing them altogether. He could have been a successful poet or novelist but he had no patience for effort or disappointment. Even in athletics, in which he excelled, his 'off-days' were more numerous and erratic than other people's. When he promised to do anything for you, it was safer to assume that he'd forget. You must know the type. There are thousands of men like that, but Heath's good looks and charm seemed, somehow, to place him apart.

He fell in love with Rosalind at once. We sat in the studio and talked art, or rather old Follett held forth and we listened. Old Follett could always hold forth by the hour. Rosalind brought in sandwiches, and made coffee at a little machine on the table among the tubes of paint and palettes. I noticed that night for the first time how beautiful her hands were. She wore rather an absurd dress that Follett had designed for her – heavy brown silk made in a medieval style with a great Medici collar of gold lace. It didn't suit her a bit, but it made her look delicious and childish and – heartrending, somehow.

Anyway, I saw Heath watching her and knew that he'd fallen in love with her. I knew the signs of Heath's falling in love. I wasn't sure about Rosalind herself. She hardly looked at him, but with some women that's a bad sign.

Heath didn't mention her when we went home. I knew that he had had countless love-affairs but I had an idea even then that this had gone deeper than most.

I wasn't surprised when I heard that he was having lessons from Follett. He went there every evening. They must have been queer lessons. Follett had no more aptitude for teaching than Heath had for learning. But Follett could talk. Follett loved to talk . . . Follett, with his enormous expanse of brown beard and his greasy velvet jacket, a palette in one hand, a brush in the other, striding about the studio, talking, talking, talking. Heath sitting on the paint-stained table, his eyes fixed on Rosalind . . . and Rosalind moving about softly with her young graceful movements, her adorable mop of curls, her delicious nose and mouth, not looking at either of them. Follett never sketched Rosalind when Heath was there, and never allowed Heath to sketch her, so he may not have been as obtuse as he seemed. Of course, he could not resist the ridiculously high fee that Heath offered for his 'lessons'. I think Heath was tortured by the suspicion that Follett was her lover.

Then Follett died. I was out of England at the time, but I saw the news in the papers. I wondered what would become of the ramshackle studio with its broken-down chairs and tables – and Rosalind.

I went there the day after I returned to London. Heath opened the door. He was very voluble and excited. He'd bought the studio and all its motley furniture. He was an artist. He was working hard. He didn't mention Rosalind, but when she came into the studio with coffee and sandwiches it seemed quite natural. She had altered – glowed into radiant beauty without losing that rather poignant look of childishness. Her happiness was patent to anyone who looked at her. She was gloriously, recklessly happy. I think it was partly her ecstasy of happiness that gave her that curious look of pathos. Heath was the same. They were desperately in love with each other. And he was working hard. The strange thing was that he had a distinct talent for art (just as he seemed to have a distinct talent for anything he put his hand to), and was turning out stuff that was extraordinarily good in its way – bizarre, striking, and really original.

I went there every evening. Heath had, for the time being, quite dropped out of his old circle. He spent all his time in the shabby little studio tucked away in a corner of Chelsea, playing at being an artist and adoring Rosalind. I used to watch Rosalind curiously. I have never seen a woman so happy, so deeply in love, so regardless of past and future. Her eyes hardly ever left Heath. They worked together, laughed together, talked together, cooked together, washed up together. It was all a glorious game. They often forgot my presence; and Heath would take her in his arms and kiss her passionately on her lips as though I had not been there. I seem to see her now, leaning back in his arms in an anguish of ecstasy, her eyes closed, her face pale . . .

I sometimes wondered what went on in Rosalind's mind. Did she really think it could last, or had she decided that their present happiness was worth all the sorrow that was to come? Certainly she showed no apprehension, no foreboding. Yet no one could have seen them then, so young, so passionately in love, so handsome, without knowing that tragedy must be close on their heels. That sort of thing is too perfect to last in this life . . .

It had no more occurred to Heath to marry Rosalind than it had occurred to Rosalind that he should marry her. Heath would be Viscount Evesham when his father died, and there was a strong streak of racial pride in him. I had always known that when Heath married he would marry a woman of family and breeding and culture, a woman who could take her place in the world as Lady

Evesham. He would not necessarily love her, but he would deliberately choose such a woman.

The present Viscount Evesham was very old and feeble, and I thought that the end of the Rosalind idyll would come when he died and Heath became Viscount Evesham. But it came sooner than that. It came when Heath knew that Rosalind was going to have a baby. That pulled him up sharp – sobered him, took the carefree joy and happiness from the situation. Rosalind was so pleased herself that it was some time before she realized his attitude. At first, when she saw how he had changed towards her (he could no more hide his feelings than a child), she thought that he was ill. It was some time before she realized that her wonderful secret brought him only disgust, embarrassment and anxiety. The knowledge killed something in her, something that had been childishly joyous and trusting. It brought something very old and rather bitter into the lovely little face. I am not sure that she did not suffer more, then, than at anything that happened later. I remember a visit I paid them about this time. They were still in the studio. Heath was morose and silent. He avoided looking at her as though he found the sight of her distasteful (she had had about four months of her time and her boyish slenderness was gone). She was a white, unhappy ghost.

Of course, it wasn't like Heath to let any bonds hold him but those of his own inclination. He began to be seen again at his clubs and at his friends' houses. He visited Rosalind less and less frequently. Then one day he told me that he had sent her down to the country 'till afterwards'. 'She'll be better away from London,' he said. But I knew that the real reason was that he wanted her out of sight and, as far as possible, out of memory . . .

I'd met him several times at Frene Court before I realized what was in the wind. At first I hoped that it was Hope Cross, who was always staying there, but I soon discovered that it was Helen. He'd deliberately picked her out as the future Lady Evesham. She was everything he wanted his wife to be – of irreproachable birth and breeding, intelligent, cultured, dignified. In appearance she was the opposite of Rosalind. I've met people who called her colourless. She was ivory pale with soft waves of pale *cendré* hair, light-blue eyes, and calm sculptured lips. She looked like a princess lost in an enchanted forest. I'd been in love with her all my life, but I'd been waiting till I'd got a decent position to offer her. Now I knew I'd no earthly chance against Heath. To do Heath justice, he never knew that I loved Helen.

He came in one evening to tell me that Helen had accepted him. He was exuberant, excited, happy, almost the Heath of the Rosalind days. I could have hated him if it had been possible to hate him. But somehow you couldn't hate Heath. He was so infernally attractive . . .

'And Rosalind?' I said rather brutally.

His face darkened.

'I'll go down and tell her,' he said shortly.

'You'll provide for her and the child, of course?' I said.

He glared at me like a bad-tempered schoolboy.

'Of course,' he said.

I went down to see Rosalind the week after he'd told her. She was lying on a sofa very near her time. She still wore one of her brown and gold dresses. She was a ghost of her old self. Her face was sharpened and drained of its colour, her little mouth was set in lines of piteous suffering and bravery, her eyes were dull as though their brightness had been washed away by floods of salt tears . . . All her radiance was gone – and yet there still remained that poignant look of childishness that made her so pitiful.

'He told you?' I said.

She nodded, biting her pretty twisted lips.

'Rosalind,' I said, 'don't – don't take it so hard. You're young. You've all your life before you. You'll have the child.'

'I don't want the child,' she said in a dull little voice, 'now that he won't share it with me. I never thought it would be like this. I thought he'd be pleased.'

'Now look here, Rosalind,' I said with that abominable cheerfulness with which one tries to rally depressed invalids, 'you mustn't take it like this. You'll forget in time.'

'I shan't. I don't want to forget.' Then the colour crept into her pale cheeks and she clenched her fists. 'I can't *bear* to think of . . . her. I won't let her have him . . . Oh, she shan't . . . .they shan't . . .'

I was surprised. And I was frightened.

'Rosalind,' I said gently, 'don't do anything foolish.'

She was suddenly still and very quiet.

'What sort of thing do you mean?' she said

'I mean . . . don't tell Helen . . . or anything like that.'

'Oh, no,' she said in that strange little voice. 'I didn't mean anything that would make him angry with me . . . I don't think I shall live long, anyhow,' she ended.

I returned to my idiotic self-imposed task of 'cheering her up'. She watched me with a little smile as though she were amused.

The next week the baby was born dead and Rosalind died a day or two later.

I was with Heath when the news came. I guessed what it was from the sudden look of relief on his weak handsome face. He had been frightened. Helen was a deeply religious woman and an idealist, and he had been terrified of her finding out about Rosalind and the child. If it did not actually put an end to the engagement, it would bring him down with a pretty heavy bump from the pedestal on which she had set him. And now by an extraordinary stroke of luck both Rosalind and the child were dead . . .

'That's that,' he said as he handed me the telegram.

It was as if he said: 'A satisfactory end to an unsatisfactory business.'

At that moment I think I actually hated him.

I went abroad for two months after that and on my return I noticed that Heath was not looking well. He seemed to be developing 'nerves'. He started at every sound.

I stayed the weekend with him at his father's house in the country.

It was something of a strain. We kept so carefully to impersonal subjects, avoiding Helen and Rosalind and his approaching marriage. We rode in the woods on the Saturday afternoon. It was autumn, and the trees were turning to vivid reds and golds. As we were returning he reined his horse in suddenly with a quick jerky movement.

'Did you see her?' he whispered sharply.

I had seen before he spoke. We were passing an open grassy path at right angles to the one where we were riding. At the end was an enormous beech tree, a riot of browns and golds. As we passed and looked down the avenue, a gust of wind tossed a low branch that almost swept the ground, and just for a second in the shadowy distance it took the likeness of a girl dressed in brown and gold.

'It was the branch in the wind,' I said, 'a trick of the shadows.'

He bit his lip.

'It wasn't,' he said between his teeth, 'I'm always seeing her.'

Characteristically he had not entered the studio since he tired of Rosalind, neither had he taken any steps towards selling or letting it. I've forgotten how Helen came to know about it. I suppose that he or I mentioned it in some casual reference to old days. When he saw Helen's interest in it he quickly changed the subject, but Helen began eagerly to ask questions. Where was it? How big was it? Why hadn't she seen it before? He answered sulkily, but we were all used to his sulkiness. There was something rather attractive and boyish about it. Helen persisted. He must have a house-warming there. She must see it. Heath and I and she must have a picnic tea there the next day. She'd bring provisions and make tea for us . . . Heath objected. It would be damp. The place would be inches deep in dust. It was a barn of a place. He'd run her down to the coast instead and they'd have a decent picnic there . . . better than a mouldy old studio. But Helen persisted.

'Darling, I'd no idea you were an artist. I'm too thrilled for words. I must see it.'

She laughed as she spoke, her blue eyes alight, the sunshine turning the waves of her fair hair to silvery gold . . . I can see her now.

Heath gave in with a bad grace, then allowed himself to be teased back into good humour.

The picnic was foredoomed to failure from the start. The air of the studio struck strangely chill though there was bright sunshine outside. It seemed like a haunted place. I saw Helen shiver and draw her furs around her as she entered. Heath's face looked grey in the sudden gloom. The windows were filthy. The cord that drew back the blind from the skylight was broken and we could not reach it. The corners were full of cobwebs. Everything was covered with dust. The table was a medley of dirty paint tubes, paper, brushes, and palettes. A clay figure seemed to grin horribly from a dark corner. On a plate on the windowsill was a mouldy peach. There was a damp *dead* sort of smell over everything. And suddenly I had a vision of the place as it had been – bright and cosy and clean, full of love and light and laughter; Rosalind going to and fro with the inevitable coffee and sandwiches, Rosalind sitting on the hearthrug bobbing cherries, Rosalind laughing her hauntingly sweet little laugh, Rosalind in Heath's arms on the very spot where Helen now stood. No wonder the place was cold and grey and – heart-broken.

Helen gave a sudden little cry and we both turned to her.

'What's the matter?' I said quickly.

'Nothing,' said Helen. She looked startled, half-amused, half-ashamed. 'I'm so sorry. It was nothing. I – it must have been the sunshine on the dark oak. Just for a second it looked as if the door were open and a girl stood there dressed in brown and gold, then when I looked properly I saw that the door was closed and it was just the sunlight on the dark oak. I'm sorry I startled you.'

Of course, the thing was hopeless after that. Heath went white to the lips. He kept looking behind him into the dark corners of the room. When the door creaked as we were having tea he dropped his cup and saucer with a clatter. I could see perspiration on his brow. He kept moving his dry lips as he gazed fixedly at the closed door. Helen was splendid. She carried off the situation – made tea, laughed and chattered, and refused to notice the tenseness of the atmosphere.

After tea she opened a portfolio that lay on the table and began to look at his sketches. Of course, the first one she took up was one of Rosalind – Rosalind dressed as a page boy, her lips curved into a deliciously impudent smile, her mop of red-gold curls aflame in the sunshine. Rosalind – instinct – with life and laughter and roguery . . . Poor little dead, unhappy Rosalind . . .

'What an adorable child!' said Helen. 'Who is she?'

Heath had got himself in hand by this time.

'Oh, just a model,' he said almost casually.

Later, when Helen and I were looking at the view from the window, I saw him take out that sketch and slip it into his pocket.

There was another portfolio full of sketches of Rosalind which Helen never found. I saw Heath's eyes wander to it constantly as if afraid lest she should discover it, and once he carelessly pushed it still farther out of sight beneath some papers.

But Helen was genuinely surprised and impressed by the quality of Heath's paintings, and that gradually soothed him. He was always childishly susceptible to praise.

I didn't see Heath for some time after that. Our next meeting was a curious one. It occurred to me suddenly to go down to see Rosalind's grave. I hated to think of it untended and uncared for. I thought I might make some arrangements to have it looked after regularly. I took a train from Town to the village station and went to the little churchyard. When I found the grave I stood motionless with astonishment. It was February, but the grave was literally covered with roses and orchids freshly laid upon it – the most expensive roses and orchids it was possible to buy. Then I saw Heath coming round from behind the church to it. He'd brought armfuls of roses and orchids down from Bond Street and laid them on the grave with no means of keeping them fresh – no water or tins or anything like that, simply laid them in heaps on the grave of Rosalind and his child. He showed no embarrassment at being found there, no surprise at finding me there. He said, as casually as if we had met at the races: 'There's a train down in about fifteen minutes. Are you coming?'

We walked back to the station in silence. I looked at him curiously. He was thinner. His face was lined and – jerky, somehow. He looked on wires . . . and there was suffering in his face. When the station was in sight, he said suddenly:

'Did you see the baby?'

'No.'

'I didn't, either. I couldn't get down.' (That was Heath all over. He'd managed to persuade himself that he'd wanted to get down to Rosalind and the child and hadn't been able to.) 'But I'm glad it was a boy. She'd wanted a boy.'

Then I knew what had happened. His love for Rosalind was creeping back into his heart . . . the old, passionate, now torturing, love. I'd always known that Rosalind had gone deeper than any of his previous love-affairs. I'd suspected that it was Helen's suitability to fill the position of his wife that had attracted him rather than love for her. And now love for Rosalind, an aching, torturing, longing for Rosalind, stronger than any other passion he had ever known, was haunting him. Poor little unhappy ghost. She was amply avenged now.

We parted at the London terminus.

'You coming my way?' I said.

'No, I'm going to the studio.'

'Taking up painting again?'

'No.'

No, he wasn't taking up painting again. He was sitting alone in the haunted studio, longing for her, feeding his cheated love on memories of her every word and gesture, listening for the echoes of her silvery laughter, looking through the portfolio he had hidden from Helen . . .

His marriage day drew near. You will understand that, apart from my own feeling for Helen, I wasn't happy about the marriage. Yet I thought that once married to Helen he would forget Rosalind and learn to love Helen. No one could help it. And Helen would be an ideal wife for him. She was so wise. She would manage him so well.

I wanted him to be happy. With all his faults and weaknesses he was a likeable fellow ... And Helen – he could give her the sort of position she seemed born to fill.

I was to be best man, of course. Heath and I went down to stay at the inn at Craigford where Helen lived with her aunt Lady Frene. Lady Frene was deaf and very rheumaticky and doesn't come into the story. We arrived the day before the wedding and Helen insisted on our going to lunch with them. She said that she knew it was unconventional but it seemed so silly not to. We were all a bit on edge. Together we would be able to 'laugh it off'.

That lunch was a strange meal. The sunny panelled dining-room was very different from the dusty cobwebby studio, but that lunch with Helen reminded me of the never-to-be-forgotten 'picnic' in old Follett's studio. There was the same electric atmos-phere, the same sensation of standing on the crust of a volcano. Heath was unlike himself – feverishly gay at one minute and morosely glum the next. I thought again how white and drawn his handsome face looked. Helen was her usual self – charming, inter-esting, the perfect hostess.

After lunch Helen suggested that we should go for a walk. I believe she hoped that it would clear the air and restore Heath to his normal self. I think we all felt a heavy sense of apprehension, a dim foreboding of evil, all except Heath, who now seemed feverishly excited.

I want to tell what followed as accurately as I can, but it hap-pened so quickly that it is difficult.

We were walking along the road. On the side on which we were walking was a hedge, on the other the high wall that surrounded the grounds of Frene Court. A motorcar was coming towards us at a moderately slow rate. We all saw it for some time before it was abreast of us. Just as it came abreast of us Heath stepped forward sud-denly into its direct line. The driver had no chance to pull up. It simply knocked Heath down and went over him. Yet it was not as if Heath deliberately stepped in front of the car. He did not seem to see the car. It was as if he had started forward suddenly to cross to the other side of the road, car or no car. Nothing mattered except to reach the other side of the road. That was the impression I had as he stepped forward.

The driver was a good fellow. He took us all back to Frene Court and then drove like fury for a doctor. But Heath was dead when we picked him up from the road.

It was the day after the funeral. I felt that I'd got to have things out with Helen. It looked horribly as if Heath had deliberately committed suicide to avoid marrying her, but I was sure it wasn't that.

I found Helen in the garden. She looked very pale and very beautiful in her black dress.

'Helen,' I blurted out, 'he didn't do it on purpose.'

'I know,' she said, 'it was the girl on the other side of the road. She beckoned to him just as the car was passing.'

'What girl?'

'Didn't you see her? She wore a long brown dress with a gold Medici collar. She had a child in her arms and she held it out to him and beckoned.'

'I saw nothing.'

'He did. Didn't you hear?'

'Hear what?'

'He gave a little cry when he saw her, and then he ran to her . . .'

'There was no one there,' I said, 'the road was quite empty.'

'Who was she?' she said, as if she had not heard me.

'I saw nothing,' I repeated doggedly.

'Whose baby was it?'

I shrugged my shoulders. I felt horribly shaken.

'Hers, presumably, as she was holding it,' I said, trying to speak in the half-bantering tone in which one humours a romancing child.

She replied in a voice that was barely audible:

'And was it – his, too?'

'I can tell you nothing,' I said. 'I saw nothing.'

Helen had a bad breakdown after that and was ordered abroad for a year. We were married two years later and have been perfectly happy ever since. But we have never mentioned either Rosalind or Heath's death to each other. I think we feel that we owed him that much loyalty at least.

MARGERY LAWRENCE

THE HAUNTED SAUCEPAN

'Yes,' said the long lean man in the corner, 'I have had one odd experience that I suppose certainly comes under the heading of 'Spook' stories. Not that I ever *saw* the ghost – I never saw a real ghost in my life. But this was odd. Yes. Odd . . . tell you? Yes, of course, if you like, Saunderson! Ask that youngster by the drinks to pour me out another whisky-and-splash, if she will – thanks, Laurie! Now then. Here's the yarn, and don't interrupt . . .'

*

I was hunting for a flat in London say about three seasons ago – a furnished flat, as I didn't know how long I was going to stay in England, and it wasn't worth getting my furniture out of store. Rents were pretty high in the district I wanted – somewhere about St James's or thereabouts – and I didn't want to go out far, as it was essential that I kept in touch with my business interests. I had almost given up in despair and concluded that I should have to go either to a hotel or my Club, when an agent rang me up and said he had a flat for me, he thought. The owner, a woman, was abroad – he thought I might find it just the thing. The address was just what I wanted, the rent almost incredibly low – I jumped into a taxi and rushed round to see it, feeling sure there must be a catch somewhere, but it was a delightful flat, nicely furnished and as complete in every detail as you could wish. I was cautious and asked all sorts of questions – but as far as the agent knew it was a straightforward deal enough – the lady was staying abroad indefinitely, the previous tenants had gone . . . Why did they leave? I wanted to know . . . but the agent played with his pencil and assured me he didn't know. Illness in the family made them decide to leave very suddenly, he believed . . . Well, at any rate, a week's time saw me settled in, with my faithful man Strutt to do for me – you know Strutt, of course – one of the best fellows that ever lived? He plays an important part in the remarkable story I'm going to tell you.

The first evening I spent there seemed too delightful for words after the discomfort and inconvenience I had been enduring in various hotels for the last six months, and I drew a sigh of enjoyment as I stretched out my legs before the fire and sipped the excellent coffee at my elbow. Strutt had found me a woman of sorts to do the cooking – marvellous fellow Strutt! – and certainly she could cook, though the glimpse I had caught of her through the kitchen door as I went into the dining-room proved her a dour and in truth most ill-favoured looking old lady, with a chenille net, a thing I had thought as dead as the Dodo, holding up her back hair. I rang for some more coffee, and as usual, Strutt was at my elbow almost as my finger left the bell-push.

'More coffee, please Strutt – and, by the way, a very good dinner,' I said carelessly. 'Where did you find this cook – she seems an excellent one?' Strutt took up my empty cup as he replied in his usual even voice – is there anything quite so woodenly self-contained as the well-trained valet's voice, I wonder?

'She came one day to fetch something – day or so before you came in, sir, and I was here getting a few things ready for you. We got talking, sir, and I found she was servant to the lady who owns the flat, and caretaker when she left; she seemed a sensible useful sort of body, sir, and I engaged her – after trying to get references from the lady, sir, and failing, as nobody seemed to know her address, I took the liberty of exercising my own judgment, sir, and took her for a month on trial. I hope you think I did right, sir?'

'Oh, of course,' I said hastily – as indeed Strutt's judgment is invariably better than my own! 'I should say she's a find, if she can keep up this standard of cooking. All right – tell her I'm pleased . . .'

The door closed noiselessly and I sank into a brown study. The flat was very silent and the pleasant crackle of the flames sounded loud in the stillness, like little pistol-shots – the deep leather chair was comfortable, and beneath the red lampshade rested three books I particularly wanted to read. With a sigh of satisfaction I reached for one, and was in five minutes so deep in it that the entrance of Strutt with my second cup of coffee passed almost unnoticed, and I gulped it down heedlessly as I read. Buried civilisations have always been my hobby, though I've never had the money to go and explore in person – this book was a new and thrilling account of some recent diggings and discoveries, and I devoured the thing till I woke with a start to realise that it was after twelve and the fire out!

With a laugh and a shiver I struggled out of my chair, flipped on the full light and poured myself out a whisky – the syphon hissed as I pressed down the jet, and I cursed Strutt's forgetfulness (most unlike him it was, too!) as I saw it was empty. Perhaps there was another in the kitchen – I went along there to look, feeling rather peevish and very sleepy. The kitchen was flooded with moonlight and all the pots and pans and bottles and things struck little high lights of silver – it was quite a pretty effect; there were several things on the stove, and I remember now that one, a little saucepan, had its lid not quite on – not fitted on levelly, I mean – and it had the oddest look for a moment, just as if it had cocked up its lid to take a sly look at me! I found a fresh syphon on the dresser, had a drink and went to bed; my last thought as I curled luxuriously between the cool linen sheets was that the woman who had had this flat furnished and fitted it up so perfectly must have been a sybarite in her tastes, since I had yet to find the article in her flat that did not show the true lover of luxury. I wondered idly why she had left it, with all its contents, even to linen, plate, pots and pans . . . then sleep came, and I sank into unconsciousness, my query unanswered. I must have slept some two hours, I think, when I was awakened by a sudden attack of pain, of all extraordinary things! I awoke shaking and gasping, my hands alternately clutching my throat and stomach as the most awful griping agonies seized me, throwing me into convulsive writhings as the pain twisted me into knots and the sweat poured down my face, or fits of frantic coughing that I thought must surely split my lungs – I felt as though I had swallowed some ghastly acid that was burning my very vitals out! ... Feebly I reached for the bell, but before I touched it Strutt was in the room, awakened by my coughing, and bending anxiously over me.

'My God, sir, what's the matter? You waked me coughing! Wait a second, sir, and I'll get you a drop of brandy ...'

The spirit spilled against my chattering teeth, for I was shaking like a man with ague, and my staring eyes were glazed with pain – poor old Strutt's face was a study – he's always been very devoted to me. A few drops went down my throat, however, and after another dose of it I seemed to feel a shade better, and lay back against the pillows panting and shivering. My pyjamas were damp and streaked with perspiration, and now my perceptions were coming back to me and I began to wonder – why this attack, and what on earth had happened to cause it? Strutt bustled about my room getting out a fresh pair of pyjamas, his anxious eye flitting back to me every minute. No need to worry any further though, as I was rapidly returning to my normal healthy self – but this only made it stranger.

Strutt approached the bed.

'You feeling better now, sir? If you'll take my advice you'll change them damp things and let me rub you down before you go to sleep again.'

Feeling almost sound again, though still shaken from the memory of that ghastly ten minutes, I slipped out of bed and stood lost in speculation as Strutt rubbed me – certainly, back in bed in a few minutes in clean pyjamas, with a stiff brandy-and-soda inside me, I could not understand what on earth could have attacked me so terribly, yet passed away so entirely, leaving no trace – for I felt as well as before the attack.

'Strutt,' I said, 'Heaven only knows what was the matter with me – it can't have been anything I've eaten, since you've probably had the same, and you're all right. But it was the most damnable attack – fever's nothing to it. Besides, it *wasn't* fever; I've had too many bouts of that not to know it. Wonder if my heart's all right?'

'I should have said so, sir, but it might be as well to see the doctor tomorrow. What sort of pain was it? You'll forgive me saying so, sir, but you looked simply ghastly. Never seen fever make you look so – never, sir!' Strutt's voice held conviction – moreover, the fellow had seen me through enough fever to know. I knitted my brows:

'What did I have? Clear soup – a sole – piece of steak and vegetables. All well cooked – oh, and a savoury – mushrooms on toast. Mushrooms!'

I looked at Strutt triumphantly – for a minute I thought I'd hit it.

'Mushrooms – she must have got hold of some poisonous stuff, not real mushrooms. It's easily done—'

'Beg your pardon, sir,' said Strutt firmly, 'but that can't be it. Being rather partial to mushrooms myself, sir, I took a few – and Mrs Barker she did, too . . . so that can't be the reason. There's nothing else you had, sir, barring your coffee, which I made myself – the second lot at least, as Mrs Barker had gone home when you rang.'

I lay back on my pillows silenced, but more puzzled than ever – however, I was too thankful to feel well again to worry very much over the cause of my strange attack.

'Well, I can't worry any more over it, Strutt. Turn out the lights. I shall see the doctor in the morning.'

I did, and his report confirmed my own opinion and added not a little to my puzzlement – I was as sound as a bell in every respect; even the trace of occasional fever left by my long sojourn in the East seemed to have vanished. Old Macdonald punched me in the ribs as he said goodbye, and grinned.

'Don't you come flying to me next time you get a pain under your pinny from a whisky or two too many, young fellow-me-lad – go for a good long tramp and blow it away. You're as strong as a young horse, and as for heart – don't you try to pull any of that stuff on me. You've got a heart that'll work like a drayhorse, and never turn a hair . . .'

I walked up St James's more puzzled than ever – what on earth had happened to me last night? In the light of my present feeling of supreme health and well-being my last night's agonies seemed more inexplicable than ever – obviously old Mac thought I had been more or less tight and exaggerated a nightmare into this . . . It was very irritating – yet I still had the vivid memory of that terrible, choking, burning sensation, the torturing pains that had gripped my frame, tearing and wrenching me, it seemed, till my very bones groaned and quivered within me. Good Lord! – a dream? Still lost in thought about the whole curious affair I ran full tilt into an old chum of mine on the steps of the Club – George Trevanion, who seized me delightedly by the hand and poured forth questions. We dined together that night at the Club and spent a long time yarning over the fire afterwards – when we parted Trevanion had promised to dine with me the next night – I was, I admit, rather keen on showing him my new quarters. I had been so engrossed in talking shop – we're both engineers – and there had been so many things to say that I had forgotten to tell him, as I had meant, about my remarkable attack of pain, an omission that annoyed me a little, as having spent thirty years knocking about the world he might have been able to put his finger at once on the cause of it.

There were some letters lying on the table in the dark little hall of my flat as I let myself in. I picked them up; nothing interesting, only some bills and an invitation or two. I dropped them again and turned to hang up my coat. The kitchen door opened into the hall, and when I entered it had been shut – now I saw when I turned that it had swung noiselessly open, and I could see into the moon-lit kitchen, the usual little place one finds in these small flats. The gas stove was in line with the door, with various utensils upon it ready for use in the morning – I think there was a large kettle and two saucepans, a big one and a little enamel one. The open door made me jump for a second, but of course I said 'draughts' and thought so – I paused a second to light a cigarette – and the match dropped from my fingers and sputtered out upon the carpet. I held the unlighted cigarette between my fingers as I stared. As I am a living man, this is what I saw – or thought I saw. The saucepan – the little one on the stove, nearest the door – seemed to lift its lid a shade – it seemed to tilt, ever so slightly, cautiously, and from beneath its tilted lid, it looked at me! Yes, I suppose it doesn't sound as horrible as I want it to, but I swear to you that was the most eerie thing I ever saw, or want to see . . . For a second I stood cold and dumb, my mouth sticky with fright – somehow the utter banality of the thing made it more terrifying – then I swore at myself, strode into the kitchen and seized the saucepan, holding it to the light.

It was, of course, a mere trick of light – I remember noticing the previous night how brilliantly the moonlight streamed into the kitchen – but good heavens, it had shaken me for a minute, positively! That attack last night must have upset my nerves more than I knew – Lord, what a fool! I put the saucepan back, laughing heartily, and going into the hall, picked up my letters again, still grinning at my own folly. I glanced back at the kitchen as I went along to my room – I could still see the stove and the silent row of pans upon it. The lid of the little saucepan was still askew – it still had the absurd air of watching me stealthily from beneath it! There almost seemed a menace in its very stillness . . . I laughed again as I got into bed. It seemed so lunatic – fancy being scared of a saucepan . . . good Lord, a chunk of tin, an absurd piece of iron-mongery – it just shows you what light and a few jangled nerves can do for one! . . .

I slept splendidly, and awoke hungry as a hunter, and flung myself into work that day like a giant refreshed. Trevanion and I met at the Club about six-thirty for a cocktail, and had several cocktails – it was good to see the old man again; we'd been boon companions in all sorts of odd places, and I really didn't know how much I'd missed him till we met again. We walked back to the flat about seven fifteen and found a rattling good dinner awaiting us – I'd told Strutt to put Mrs Barker on her mettle, and, by Jove! she turned us out a feed fit for a king. Cream soup, oysters done with cheese – marvellous things they were – roast chicken and salad and a soufflé that melted in your mouth; we were too occupied appreciating flavours to talk much at first, but at last Trevanion sat back, regarding me with reverence, and drew a long breath of repletion.

'Man, you must be a perfect Croesus! Where on earth did you strike the cash to pay for this place, this feeding, and your *cordon bleu* in the kitchen, I should like to know?'

I grinned with triumph, sipping the last drops of my claret.

'Why, sheer luck, dear boy – the rent of this flat is a mere flea-bite – the cook fell into my hands with the flat, and being a bit of an epicure I feel justified in spreading myself a trifle in the feeding line – especially when an old companion in crime like you turns up!'

Trevanion's brow wrinkled.

'A flat in St James's – for a flea-bite rental? Are you sure you're not being done somehow, old man? It seems to me almost impossible.'

I shrugged as I rose and we sought our armchairs by the smoke-room fire; the reason why was still as obscure to me as ever, and after a while we dismissed the subject and began to talk of other things. Strutt brought in coffee and liqueurs, and the hours passed imperceptibly as we chewed our pipes and yarned over old times, adventures old and new. At last Trevanion looked at the clock and laughed, putting down his pipe.

'Good Lord, look at the time! Time I got along to my place, though I don't boast palatial quarters like these of yours, you lucky devil. Come and dine with me one night next week anyway, and I'll see if I can't raise a good drink or two for you, though I can't promise a dinner anywhere near your standard . . .' He was standing by the door, his hand on the handle, and I was on the hearthrug knocking out the dottle of my pipe; suddenly we both fell silent, and his sentence broke off short as we stood listening. In the silence, down the passage came the sound of something boiling – on the cold stove, black and silent since Mrs Barker left two hours ago! We looked at each other, our mouths open with astonishment, then Trevanion laughed.

'What an odd noise – just like a kettle or something boiling. Suppose your man's been making a drop of toddy for himself on the Q.T. and left the thing on . . .' For some reason we stared at each other, hard, as he spoke. I know that I, for one, knew somehow that Strutt had not left the gas burning – the kitchen door was open, but from where we stood we could not see into it: the smoke-room door was round an angle. The moonlight streamed into the dark passage through the invisible open door, and with the moonlight came the distant sound of bubbling and boiling – like water in a kettle – or saucepan . . . In the silence there seemed, however ridiculous it may sound, a sort of quiet menace in the sound – with a jerk I slewed round from the hearth and made towards the door.

'Probably it's only a draught – wind bubbling through a crevice or something of the sort. Come on, let's see at all events.'

Personally, the last thing I really wanted to do was to go into that kitchen – that beastly kitchen, as mentally I had already begun to call it; here was the door open again – Strutt assured me he had shut it when Mrs Barker left, and always did – there was something in the atmosphere of the whole flat now that I didn't like at all. But my funk was as yet not even definitely acknowledged even to myself, and I strode down the passage with my chin set, and round the angle into the kitchen. The bubbling sounds, clear and distinct till the second I turned the corner, ceased on the instant, and dead silence succeeded. In the moonlit kitchen Trevanion and I stared at each other blankly. The stove held only one utensil, the little enamel saucepan I had noticed before, but the gas beneath it was unlit; its lid was close down . . . Trevanion was rattling the window, examining the catch, a frown of bewilderment on his brow – I took up the saucepan, vaguely disturbed, and peered inside it; empty of course.

'Well, upon my soul, this is rum!' said Trevanion, scratching his head. 'There doesn't seem to be a chink anywhere that could let in a draught – air bubbling through a knot-hole *might* make a noise like that . . . I suppose there isn't another gas-jet left alight anywhere that might make a sound like water boiling – is the geyser on?'

The geyser was not on, nor was there any other gas-jet, the flat being lighted by electricity – at last we gave it up as a bad job, and gaped at each other, completely floored. Trevanion scratched his head again, then laughed and shrugged his shoulders as he reached for his hat.

'Well – it's the most extraordinary thing I ever knew – still, there's probably some perfectly simple reason for it. 'Phone me when you find out, Connor, old man; it's left me guessing for the present, and I'd really like to know what it is. Never heard anything so clearly – nor so odd, confound it! Think you must have some spook that boils water for its ghostly toddy! . . .'

Trevanion's cheery laugh died away down the street, and I slammed the door of the flat and stood for a minute, chin in hand, thinking. Damn it, something *had* been boiling, I'd take my oath – but what? As if in answer to my thought, a faint sound broke the stillness of the flat again – the bubbling of a boiling kettle – or saucepan? Why was it that somehow I always thought of a saucepan when that sound started? It was faint at first, but grew more distinct as I listened, every muscle taut with strain – now whatever the damned thing was, I *would* catch it!

The kitchen door stood ajar, of course – I had shut it when we went to look at the geyser, but it was open again when we came out of the bathroom – undoubtedly the sound came from the kitchen . . . cautious, I took a step forward, though my back crept unaccountably as I did so, and craning forward, I peered round the door. The little saucepan stood where I had put it, on the stove, still cold and unlit – but it was boiling! The lid was rakishly aslant, and tilted a shade every second or so as the liquid, whatever it was, bub-bled inside, and gusts of steam came out as I gaped, dumbfounded – somehow as I listened, the noise of the bubbling shaped itself into a devilish little song, almost as if the thing was singing to itself, secretly and abominably . . . chortling to itself in a disgusting sort of hidden way, if you know what I mean! I gave a half-gasp of sheer fright, and do you know, instantly the saucepan was . . . just an ordinary saucepan again, silent on the stove! I made myself go in, though I admit I was shaking with nerves – I took it up; cold and empty . . . Well, cursing myself for a fool, I took a stiff drink and despite a horrible little shivery feeling that there was more in this than I liked, told myself sternly that I must have had one whisky too many and mistaken light and the noise of a stray mouse might have made, for the whole thing. I knew, of course, inside me, that it wasn't so, and I *had* seen that abominable saucepan boiling some infernal brew – but I wouldn't admit it, and scrambled into bed with, I confess, considerable speed, and not a few glances over my shoulder into the dark.

However, I slept well again, and awoke laughing at myself not a little, but with sneaking thankfulness that Trevanion had also made a bit of an ass of himself over the mysterious noise! I lay for a few minutes blinking in the shaft of sunlight that filtered through my blinds, and reached for my watch – it was nine o'clock! Cursing Strutt for his laziness – I always had my bath at eight-thirty, confound him – I rang the bell. A shuffling step came along the passage, and the sullen lined face of Mrs Barker peeped in. I stared at her, then snapped:

'What on earth's the matter with Strutt? It's nine o'clock!'

The woman studied me in silence with her narrow, secret eyes for a few seconds – what an old hag she was, really, I thought impatiently – then jerked her thumb over her shoulder.

''E's took bad with summat – dunno what. Bin writhin' and cursin' like a good 'un . . .' Her lips wreathed themselves into a mirthless grin, and I eyed her with even less favour than before.

As she spoke I heard a faint moaning coming from poor old Strutt's room – curtly ordering Mrs Barker back to her kitchen I scrambled out of bed and went down the passage – poor Strutt was lying fully dressed on the bed, his lips blue and dry with pain, his limbs twitching convulsively – he was quite beyond speech, but his eyes implored help. I tore off his collar and shouted to Mrs Barker for brandy – the poor fellow's looks really frightened me to death. Bit by bit we pulled him round – though it struck me at the time that the woman's help was given none too willingly; and at last Strutt sat up, shaky, but himself. I sat on the bed staring at him, more concerned than I liked to say.

'What on earth happened, Sttutt? It seemed much the same sort of attack I had the other night – you'd better go and see my doctor, I can't have you cracking up like this. When did it come on?'

Strutt cleared his throat, his voice still husky and strained with pain.

'I got up about seven, sir, as usual, or perhaps a little before – Mrs Barker was late, so I made myself some tea and boiled an egg. I hadn't eaten it so very long, sir, before I began to feel as if something was on fire inside me, – awful the pain was, I couldn't move nor cry out – not a word. I dunno what it was, sir, but I'll take my oath it's the same sort of thing you was taken with the other night.'

I frowned and meditated.

'Well, you'd better see Macdonald. This is beyond me . . .'

Strutt was duly overhauled by the doctor and reported sound in wind and limb – this fresh puzzle made me feel almost as if there must be something in superstitions after all, and there must be a curse on my new flat. I was still lost in speculation about it when I met Trevanion in Bond Street, very spruce and dapper from lunching with the lady he happened to favour at the moment. He buttonholed me at once.

'Hullo, Connor, spotted the ghost yet?' I shook my head.

'Spotted it – I wish I could! Listen – there seems no end to the extraordinary things that are coming my way lately . . .' And I plunged into the story, beginning with my own attack of illness and winding up with what I had seen – or thought I had seen – in the kitchen after he had left, and Strutt's mysterious collapse this morning. Trevanion listened intently, not laughing as I half-expected . . . it seems a queer place to discuss a bogey-tale, the corner of Bond Street on a fine spring morning, but it struck neither of us at the time.

'It's certainly odd,' Trevanion said at last. 'It's the oddest yarn I've heard for a long time. Frankly, if it wasn't you – and if I hadn't heard that noise myself last night – I'd of course say it was too much whisky and you were seeing things – But . . . look here, I'll come up to your place tonight, say about eleven-thirty, and we'll try an experiment – I've got an idea slowly working its way out! So long, old man.'

I was relieved he had not laughed, and guessed, from his serious attitude towards the whole incomprehensible thing, that he must have been more impressed than I had thought with the episode of the mysterious bubbling – what connection had that, if any, with the equally mysterious attacks of pain that had seized both Strutt and myself? The whole thing obtruded itself upon my work, which did not go particularly well in consequence, and I was still cogitating when the bell rang that night, and Strutt let in Trevanion, accompanied by a dog, to my great astonishment. We shook hands warmly.

'Didn't know you'd got a dog,' I said, 'but while you were about it couldn't you have found a better specimen than this mouldy old semi-demi-collie?' Trevanion grinned at me mysteriously. When Strutt had gone out of the room he bent forward and whispered:

'This is the experiment!'

I gasped, and Trevanion went on, as the old beast settled himself down in front of the blazing fire.

'First and foremost, may I give this old beast a feed? – he's rather hungry, I'm afraid. It's the porter's dog from the Club. I borrowed him for tonight. Yes – as you say, he's a bit of a cheesehound, but not a bad old beast. What about that feed?'

'Of course,' I said, 'I daresay there are some bones in the kitchen – I'll tell Strutt.' Trevanion stopped my upraised hand on the way to the bell.

'I don't want Strutt, thanks old man. I want to give this myself – warm up some scraps for him; you know the sort of thing.' I stared rather, then shrugged my shoulders; I knew Trevanion too well to ask him too many questions at the start of a thing.

'Oh, all right, my dear fellow, though I really don't see why this fuss about warm stuff – you sound as if the beast was a Derby winner!'

'I'm not as cracked as I seem,' asserted Trevanion, going into the kitchen now brightly lighted and as cheerful as could well be imagined, 'You leave this to your Uncle Stalky – it's all part of the experiment!' I left him rummaging among pots and pans and betook myself to an armchair and my book on Egypt, till the entrance of my friend, the dog at his heels licking his lips after his feed, interrupted me. Throwing himself down in the opposite armchair, Trevanion reached for the whisky – I cocked an amused eyebrow at him.

'Finished your incantations over the kitchen stove, Trev?' I said, using my old abbreviation of his name. Trevanion laughed as he filled his pipe.

'You can pull my leg as much as you like, my dear chap, when we're through with this thing. It may be capable of an ordinary explanation – nine out of ten times it is – but there's always the faint possibility of the tenth time cropping up. D'you remember that case of the Box that Wouldn't keep Shut – when you and I were working on that road near Lahore? That was creepy if you like . . .' I nodded, silenced – for the moment I had forgotten that odd story, never fully explained. Trevanion went on:

'Well, I believe, from what I felt here the other night, and from various other little things – more than ever if the little experiment I've just tried on Ben here succeeds – I believe that we've got here one of the few cases of genuine "queerness." Something really uncanny, I mean.' I interrupted him, my back creeping uncomfortably.

'What have you tried on the dog, then?' Trevanion looked at me oddly.

'Fed him out of the saucepan – the saucepan that bubbled!' he said at last. My back crept again, though I did not quite get what he was driving at – I stared, puzzled.

'But what – I don't quite see your drift, Trev. What should that show you?'

'If I'm right we shall soon see,' Trevanion returned, 'but I don't want to tell you all my ideas entirely before we've got through the end of this sitting, as they might colour your impressions, and I want to leave your mind as open as possible tonight . . . Now about twelve I propose that you and I and old Ben shut ourselves up in the kitchen – and see if anything happens. I believe if we're right, and there is something more to this than the things of everyday life, the dog's behaviour will show it. Beasts are much more susceptible to psychic influence than we are, especially dogs and cats . . . At any rate, it's worth trying to see if he does seem to sense anything – if he does that will prove that you and I are not both slightly off our chumps' . . . A strangled gasp from Ben interrupted him, and like a flash we turned – the poor old dog was in convulsions of mortal agony, his eyes starting from his head, writhing and twisting, and snapping wildly at our hands as we tried to help him! I rushed for brandy and warm milk, and between us we got him round, and sat back staring at each other, our skins prickling faintly with a horrid little fright – at least mine was.

'I'm dead right in my first guess, I think,' Trevanion said soberly, stroking the head of the still panting and exhausted dog. 'Poor old Ben then! I boiled some scraps in that infernal saucepan – it was hard on Ben, but I had to find out somehow whether my idea was right, and by Jove it is! Everything cooked in that thing half-poisons people – or gives them an attack like poisoning . . .'

'D'you think there's something in the paint?' I hazarded. Trevanion was not sure – it was only an ordinary enamel saucepan – he didn't think so. Ben lay panting on the rug before the fire, still rather a wreck, but regaining his strength every minute – I stooped down and patted him.

'We shall have to give him another five minutes or so to recover,' said Trevanion, 'poor old brute – never mind, he'll be all right in a jiff. I don't mind telling you, though, that it will take us all our nerve to face that kitchen, and that infernal saucepan . . . that bubbling noise was quite the most unpleasant and disturbing thing I ever heard. The actual homeliness of it seeming to hide a sort of sinister meaning – and the purr of a boiling kettle is such a jolly thing as a

rule . . .' I nodded – I didn't want to think about it overmuch just
then to tell the truth, so I resolutely hunted out cards and we played
poker for half an hour or so, till Strutt came in with a fresh syphon,
and with his usual correct 'Anything more, sir? Good night, sir,'
went off to his own quarters.

Trevanion, with a glance at the clock – it marked just twelve, or
a few minutes before – got up and waked the old dog, who was
sleeping by this time with his chin on his paws. It was twelve
o'clock . . . in silence we turned the lights low and tiptoed along to
the kitchen. The door was open, of course, but otherwise the whole
place looked demure to a degree. We had brought cushions and
rugs with us, and threw them into a corner, the furthest away from
the stove, near the window, from where we could watch both door
and stove – and saucepan – without being too close. I felt, as usual,
a horrid little reluctance to enter the room, but Trevanion's large
presence went a long way towards scotching that – besides, I meant
to see what we might see, however I funked it. Settling ourselves
down, I rummaged in my pocket for my pipe, and realised the dog
was not with us. Trevanion craned out from his corner, calling
softly – the old beast's eyes gleamed from the shadows in the hall
beyond . . . he put a cautious nose across the threshold, and
retreated at once, ears flat. Trevanion looked at me and nodded.

'You see? There *is* a funny atmosphere here. Come on, Ben, old
man – come on . . .' By dint of much coaxing the dog crept into the
room, unwilling enough but obedient, and we made room for him
beside us. But he would not lie down, and kept raising his head and
sniffing the air, his eyes watchful, puzzled, and full of a vaguely stirring fear. The silence grew steadily as the minutes passed – even the
occasional low-toned remarks we exchanged to start with died into
the all enveloping silence, and we puffed our pipes solemnly, our
eyes glued to Ben's shaggy head. The air seemed to grow steadily
colder, too, as we sat there, despite the warmth of the spring night
air that stole through the slightly opened window. As the silence
deepened the cold seemed to intensify too – there seemed to come
a cold, dumb menace into the atmosphere, that fastened upon us so

gradually that we scarcely perceived its beginnings till we were surrounded, soaked in it. My hands were frozen, and my mind, too,
seemed to have grown cold and numbed: Trevanion told me later he
felt just the same. Ben's yellow hair was fluffed out into a ruff round
his head, his wary eyes, old, but alert, wandering ceaselessly round
and round the little kitchen. The moonlight, flooding the whole
place with eerie white light, helped the general uncanny effect – the
shadows lay sharp-edged, black, behind every piece of furniture –
the grandfather clock seemed to hide a long lean thing that peered
furtively at us with narrow horrible eyes . . . Trevanion moved his
leg and coughed – our eyes met and I read the same thought in his
mind – was the silence, helped by our vivid imagination, already
over-excited by the episode of poor old Ben, going to work on our
nerves till we made shapes and sounds out of mere shadows and the
silence of the night? At this moment, the dog suddenly decided for
us – with a faint wuff of uneasiness he sat up, his eyes on the open
door; I could hear nothing, but obviously his ears, more finely
attuned to degrees of sound, had caught something in the dark flat
that vaguely distressed him. Ordinarily any dog would have
promptly gone out to investigate, but Ben remained, stiff-poised, his
head held forwards, his paws braced against the floor – Trevanion
nudged me to watch him, but I did not need it – then suddenly the
dog flattened himself down between us, his head low, his eyes fixed
on the door, shivering in every limb. At the same moment it seemed
to me that I heard a faint movement in the darkness beyond the
door – very faint, but definite. The sound, it seemed to me, of a door
being shut with the most delicate care so as to avoid any possible
creaking or snap of the latch. The exquisite caution of the sound
made it peculiarly horrible – I felt my hair rise as I strained my ears,
wondering if the sound could possibly be my imagination? . . . The
pause of silence that followed was almost worse – it was like the
pause made by someone, having shut the door, waiting outside to be
certain they were not heard . . . I took a firm grip of myself, glanced
at Trevanion – his hand was cold too, but we were both steady
enough . . . we waited – as a matter of fact I doubt if we could either

of us have moved then, we were held in the fascination of fear. Suddenly Ben gave a terrified whimper and burrowed wildly into the rugs – another sound broke the awesome stillness. A faint movement in the passage, at the far end – on tiptoe, pausing for greater stealth, *Something* stole towards the kitchen door! The cold draught seemed to grow even colder, it lifted our hair and stirred Ben's rough coat . . . my flesh crept softly and horribly on my bones as I gripped Trev's clammy hand and stared at the door, setting my teeth as the Thing in the passage trailed softly nearer and nearer. I say trailed because that so neatly describes the sound – a faint footstep accompanied by a soft rustle like a trailing skirt. At this moment I became aware of another phenomenon – there grew a heavy scent in the air, like patchouli, I think . . . at any rate a definite perfume that seemed to herald Whatever approached. Our throats dry with fright, we shrank close to each other, staring at the dog as he moaned and whimpered – and the steps drew near, and paused outside the kitchen door, as if Whoever walked that night stood still to peer at us through the crack of the door . . . and laughed at us through the chink! For sheer terror, that beat all I had ever known, yet still the spell held us both motionless, staring, as Ben, shaking, his eyes bulging, slowly raised himself as if to face something. Dead silence – neither Trevanion nor I could see a thing – but the dog's eyes, fixed about five feet from the floor, followed – Someone – who entered. The moonlight lay white and sheer unbroken across the kitchen floor, yet Someone entered – paused – and walked towards the stove. As our terrified eyes followed Ben's, fixed on the Invisible, there came the faint click of a cautious hand moving among the pots and pans on the stove – and suddenly, upon the silence broke a sinister little sound – the clink of a saucepan lid, carefully lifted. My eyes bolting, dumb, I gaped – as I dreaded, the lid of the little saucepan was just raised, and from beneath it, there seemed to steal a faint curl of steam, thin and blue and horrible; it seems an absurd thing, but this just finished me – the spell of sheer terror that had held us both broke, and with a yell of mortal fear I flung aside the rugs and bolted past that horrible stove like a maniac, Trevanion at my heels, blundering madly over poor old Ben as he ran. We gained the smoke-room, and slamming the door upon the Horror that ruled that uncanny kitchen, we sank into two chairs, sweating with fright. I was white and clammy, and Trevanion's hand shook against the glasses as he poured us out each a stiff tot of whisky . . . even now in the silence there stole upon the air that vile sound of bubbling; there was almost a note of meditation in it now, as if the soul behind that hateful little purring noise was pleased, and sat grinning to itself, planning new evil – a mocking, threatening little note. Oh, it was beyond words vile and awful, that sound – and to know, as now we did know, that Something – Someone – did actually, *sans* human light, gas or anything of that sort, set a-boiling in that horrible little saucepan some devil's brew of some sort, every night of the Lord I'd spent in that flat! My skin crept again as I thought of it, and I took a hasty gulp of whisky. Trevanion's voice broke the silence, still rather shaky.

'Well! – I said you had a spook, Connor – and by Jove, you've got a beauty! I frankly admit I'm not going past the door of that kitchen again tonight – I'm claiming a shakedown on the floor if you can't sleep two in your bed!'

His laugh was rather harsh, but it served its purpose, and I shook myself together. Putting down my glass, I patted Ben, his rough hair now beginning to lie down and the light of terror fading from his eyes.

In the distance, but more faintly, still purred that infernal sound.

'What is it, in the name of the Lord?' I ejaculated. Trevanion's normal senses were rapidly returning – he lit a cigarette.

'I don't know, for certain, but we must interrogate your man Strutt. I think you'll find he knows more about this than you think – he passed the door of the kitchen when I was feeding Ben, and I saw him jump and look at the saucepan in a furtive sort of way – I pretended not to see him. Then he glanced at the shelf where it sometimes stands, and looked puzzled . . . I'm going to pump him. Obviously the whole thing centres round that infernal saucepan . . . Anyway, we're both too knocked up to do any more tonight – let's turn in, and we'll thrash the whole thing out tomorrow.'

We slept like logs, Trevanion on the couch in my room, buried in rugs and pillows. I woke to broad daylight and Strutt at my shoulder with a cup of tea. I always had a weakness for early tea, feminine though it sounds. Trevanion was already awake. As my man turned to hand him his tea, Trevanion looked up at him.

'Strutt,' he said, 'did you boil the water for the tea in the – saucepan?'

There was a pause, and Strutt's eyes, first blank, then full of a passionate relief, stared back at Trevanion's intent blue ones.

'You – know, sir? Then, thank God, I'm not mad . . .' I turned sharply.

'What, Strutt, you must have seen something, too!'

'Seen something, sir! . . . Well, gentlemen, if you knew what a relief it is to know you know, and don't think me crazy nor drunk – well, I can't tell you what it is. The last two days have been fair hell – beg your pardon, sir, but it's true – and I didn't dare tell you, sir, for fear you'd think I was mad or I'd bin drinking!' . . . Strutt's strained eyes, blue circled, told their own tale, and the passionate, almost tearful relief in his voice was nakedly real – I felt a very definite admiration for Strutt as I realised what terrors he must have fought down all alone during the past few days. Trevanion nodded, his eyes alert with interest.

'Go on, Strutt – this is most interesting. Now tell me; when you made the coffee for Mr Connor the first night he was here, did you use this saucepan for boiling the water – or a kettle?'

Strutt's eyes looked back unflinchingly at Trevanion's – I think we both knew his answer before he said it though.

'The saucepan, sir. The kettle was leaking. The little enamel saucepan – the – the – one that *boils*, sir.' Strutt's voice suddenly sank to a dreadful whisper, and although it was broad daylight, we involuntarily shuddered.

'And the day you were taken ill?' My man nodded.

'Yessir – I'd boiled an egg for my breakfast in it . . . I've . . . wanted to speak to you about all this before, sir, but it all seemed so crazy I didn't like . . . I was afraid if I told you all I seen and heard you'd think I'd taken to drink, sir . . .'

'Lord, not now!' I said fervently. 'After last night I'd believe anything of this infernal flat! Go on, Strutt, for goodness' sake. Tell us all you know about the thing – don't keep anything back.'

'Well, sir – the first night I come in here, the night you were taken ill, I left your room to see if everything was all right, and I heard something singing in the kitchen, like a kettle on the boil – bubbling and steaming like. I thought, well I must have left something on, or Mrs Barker, but I went in, and blest if everything wasn't quiet, and as cold and dark as Egypt! Not a sign . . . well, I was scared, but I thought I must have bin half asleep – but I got back to my room and left the door open, and in a few minutes the same noise come again. I tiptoed out then, sir, you may bet, to try and catch whatever made that noise – and round the corner I could see that little saucepan boiling away like fury . . . You don't think I'm drunk, sir?'

'By George, we don't – I don't. Go on – what did you do?'

'I went in, sir – don't mind saying it took a lot of doing – I'd a given a month's salary not to – but I didn't want to feel done, and I still thought I *must* be seeing things . . . Well, sir, the minute I stepped round that door that blamed thing stopped dead – as true as I'm standing here. Wasn't even warm – well, I bolted back to my room, and that's a fact. Well, in the morning I thought I *must* have been mad or seeing things – but I didn't like the look of that saucepan till I got to feel it was behaving silly to act so, and I boiled that egg in it to show I didn't care . . . Well, after I was took ill like you, sir, I said I wasn't going to meddle any more with the beastly thing, and I took and threw it into the dustbin – but last night it was back again – and begging your pardon, sirs, I wouldn't touch the . . . thing if I was you. There's something about it's not right – don't you touch it.'

Strutt's troubled voice ceased, and Trevanion's eyes met mine. He nodded.

You're right, Strutt. All you say goes to prove my theory. Obviously everything cooked in that thing produces acute symptoms of some sort of poisoning – arsenical, I should say, but we can find out the details later. Now what in the world is the story connected with this saucepan – I take it all the things here belonged to the woman who had this flat before?'

'Yessir – so I understand. Mrs Barker was with her a long time, and took care of the place when she left – I heard yesterday what we didn't know when you put in for this flat, sir; that three lots of tenants had had it and left very sudden. I did hear that one or two of them fell ill all of a sudden – I'm certain this saucepan'll be at the bottom of their going, sir – anyway they none of them stayed more than a month or so.'

'Mrs Barker – Mrs Barker—' mused Trevanion. 'Now I wonder whether that old soul knows anything . . .' As he spoke there seemed a faint shuffle outside the door, and bouncing out of bed, I flung it open; Mrs Barker herself was outside, her wrinkled, wicked old face alive with rage and fear, her knotted hands twisted in her apron. We all stared, then Trevanion seized her wrist as she tried to glide away.

'No, you don't, old lady! What were you listening for, I should like to know?' She eyed him sullenly and venomously, but vouchsafed no reply; dragging her into the room, Trevanion shut the door determinedly.

'Look here, there's something here I don't like, Connor. Do you suppose this is all a plant by this old hag, for reasons of her own?'

I shook my head, still blank – evil old woman as she looked now, her face all twisted with hate, I did not see how in the world she could have been responsible for all the strange things we had, the three of us, witnessed the last few days.

'You know – something!' Trevanion said sternly, 'now you tell us the whole truth about this beastly business and it'll be all right for you . . . if not—'

'I shan't tell you – besides, there ain't nothin' to tell,' the old woman answered sullenly – Strutt suddenly interrupted her.

'You're lying – beg your pardon, sir, but I seen her laugh when Mr Connor was took ill. Now, you wicked old sinner, you tell all you know about this, as you're told – or I'll make you eat something cooked in that saucepan . . .'

It was horrible – the hag crumpled like a shot rabbit at the threat, and put up her trembling, gnarled hands – her deadly terror was dreadfully sincere . . . I put up my hand.

'All right, Strutt – let her go, Trev. She'll tell us.'

Her voice shaky and strained, sullen, but vanquished, the old woman began her story. Shall I ever forget that scene, the untidy room, Trevanion and me in pyjamas, drinking it in, while Strutt, immovably correct as ever, with his back to the door as she talked? The story was incomplete; much had to be taken for granted, but it was a sufficiently grim picture that she conjured up before us of her late mistress. Young, beautiful, hard as marble; an old husband standing between her and her own ends . . . A lover – lovers – and riches to be gained by his death. One lover a doctor, a mysterious packet of powder seen to be given by him to the woman one day when the old woman was prying round – then the empty paper, found thrown away, with a few grains of white powder in the creases. Afterwards, gradually weakening health of the husband, only helped by the constant solicitude of his young wife, the apple of his eye . . . she was tireless in her goodness to him – how many times did she not rise in the middle of the night, to brew soup or tea or anything he fancied? At last he grew so that he would take nothing she had not prepared . . . his attacks of pain were terrible, folks said – seemed to twist him all to pieces – heart, the doctor said – the young doctor that was Madam's friend was attending him, and he and Madam used to laugh together on the stairs when he left the old man – then the death of the husband, and hasty burial . . . The doctor was crazy about Madam, and one night Mrs Barker heard them planning to be married very soon – she told him she was making her will in his favour and laughingly insisted he should return the compliment . . . He did, and Mrs Barker was called in to witness it; they were very merry together, and Madam insisted on making some of her special punch for him to drink to their happiness in . . . Madam came laughing into the kitchen, and seemed to talk and laugh even to the saucepan as she boiled the water for the punch. She sent Mrs Barker away then – but the doctor never got his honeymoon. Next day he was found dead in the flat, and Madam was away with another man, a Spaniard she was running an affair with at the same time . . . No – they said it was heart failure, but Mrs Barker – well, she thought a lot of things she didn't say. What was the use? and Madam left her instructions to take care of the place till it was let, and it was a good job; but she never fancied anything cooked in that saucepan somehow – put it up on a shelf till one day the new tenants used it and got sick and left . . . Same thing happened again with the next people, and they used to say they saw things and heard the kettle or something boiling when there was nothing there. Yes, Madam used a funny scent – began with 'p' but she couldn't say the word – all over the place it was some nights . . . Couldn't say she'd ever actually seen anything – she took good care to go to bed early when she was living in the flat, and, anyway, it never come further than the kitchen . . . Yes . . . (defiantly) she 'ad used the thing on purpose once or twice! She was a poor woman, and caretakin' was a good job when you got a post like this and no one to interfere; yes, she 'ad used it before to scare out tenants 'cos she wanted to stick to her job, and she didn't care. There were lots of other flats in London. No – She – It – never came unless that there saucepan was there on the stove as it used to be – yes, she'd missed it the day Strutt threw it into the dustbin, and looked about there till she had found and reinstated it. Of course she wanted us to go, like the rest – the agents were so sick of tenants leaving that they'd said if we went they shouldn't bother to let the place again . . . Sorry – why should she be? Nobody never died of it that she heard of – on'y got attacks like the old man used to get . . .

The door closed on her dismissed figure, and Trevanion's stare met mine.

Gingerly we went into the kitchen and picked up the saucepan, smooth and harmless-looking instrument of a ruthless woman's crimes. Gingerly I handed it to Strutt.

'For heaven's sake tie a stone to the vile thing, Strutt, and sink it in the Thames – or burn it – get rid of it somehow. We seem to have struck one of the most unpleasant stories I ever heard – however, once rid of this I don't think we shall be bothered any further, as obviously this horrible little thing is the 'germ' of the haunting . . .' which indeed was true, the ghostly bubbling and boiling never troubled the flat more, nor did the kitchen door persist in opening. The ghost was laid – but I often speculate on the fate probably in store for the unfortunate wretch now in love with the woman whose white hands once brewed death for her husband and lover in that uncanny saucepan.

Margaret Irwin

THE BOOK

On a foggy night in November, Mr Corbett, having guessed the murderer by the third chapter of his detective story, arose in disappointment from his bed and went downstairs in search of something more satisfactory to send him to sleep.

The fog had crept through the closed and curtained windows of the dining-room and hung thick on the air in a silence that seemed as heavy and breathless as the fog. The atmosphere was more choking than in his room, and very chill, although the remains of a large fire still burned in the grate.

The dining-room bookcase was the only considerable one in the house and held a careless unselected collection to suit all the tastes of the household, together with a few dull and obscure old theological books that had been left over from the sale of a learned uncle's library. Cheap red novels, bought on railway stalls by Mrs Corbett, who thought a journey the only time to read, were thrust in like pert, undersized intruders among the respectable nineteenth-century works of culture, chastely bound in dark blue or green, which Mr Corbett had considered the right thing to buy during his Oxford days; beside these there swaggered the children's large gaily bound story-books and collections of Fairy Tales in every colour.

From among this neat new cloth-bound crowd there towered

here and there a musty sepulchre of learning, brown with the colour of dust rather than leather, with no trace of gilded letters, however faded, on its crumbling back to tell what lay inside. A few of these moribund survivors from the Dean's library were inhospitably fastened with rusty clasps; all remained closed, and appeared impenetrable, their blank, forbidding backs uplifted above their frivolous surroundings with the air of scorn that belongs to a private and concealed knowledge. For only the worm of corruption now bored his way through their evil-smelling pages.

It was an unusual flight of fancy for Mr Corbett to imagine that the vaporous and fog-ridden air that seemed to hang more thickly about the bookcase was like a dank and poisonous breath exhaled by one or other of these slowly rotting volumes. Discomfort in this pervasive and impalpable presence came on him more acutely than at any time that day; in an attempt to clear his throat of it he choked most unpleasantly.

He hurriedly chose a Dickens from the second shelf as appropriate to a London fog, and had returned to the foot of the stairs when he decided that his reading tonight should by contrast be of blue Italian skies and white statues, in beautiful rhythmic sentences. He went back for a Walter Pater.

He found *Marius the Epicurean* tipped sideways across the gap left by his withdrawal of *The Old Curiosity Shop*. It was a very wide gap to have been left by a single volume, for the books on that shelf had been closely wedged together. He put the Dickens back into it and saw that there was still space for a large book. He said to himself in careful and precise words: 'This is nonsense. No one can possibly have gone into the dining-room and removed a book while I was crossing the hall. There must have been a gap before in the second shelf.' But another part of his mind kept saying in a hurried, tumbled torrent: 'There was no gap in the second shelf. There was no gap in the second shelf.'

He snatched at both the *Marius* and *The Old Curiosity Shop*, and went to his room in a haste that was unnecessary and absurd, since even if he believed in ghosts, which he did not, no one had the smallest reason for suspecting any in the modern Kensington house wherein he and his family had lived for the last fifteen years. Reading was the best thing to calm the nerves, and Dickens a pleasant, wholesome and robust author.

Tonight, however, Dickens struck him in a different light. Beneath the author's sentimental pity for the weak and helpless, he could discern a revolting pleasure in cruelty and suffering, while the grotesque figures of the people in Cruikshank's illustrations revealed too clearly the hideous distortions of their souls. What had seemed humorous now appeared diabolic, and in disgust at these two favourites he turned to Walter Pater for the repose and dignity of a classic spirit.

But presently he wondered if this spirit were not in itself of a marble quality, frigid and lifeless, contrary to the purpose of nature. 'I have often thought', he said to himself, 'that there is something evil in the austere worship of beauty for its own sake.' He had never thought so before, but he liked to think that this impulse of fancy was the result of mature consideration, and with this satisfaction he composed himself for sleep.

He woke two or three times in the night, an unusual occurrence, but he was glad of it, for each time he had been dreaming horribly of these blameless Victorian works. Sprightly devils in whiskers and peg-top trousers tortured a lovely maiden and leered in delight at her anguish; the gods and heroes of classic fable acted deeds whose naked crime and shame Mr Corbett had never appreciated in Latin and Greek Unseens. When he had woken in a cold sweat from the spectacle of the ravished Philomel's torn and bleeding tongue, he decided there was nothing for it but to go down and get another book that would turn his thoughts in some more pleasant direction. But his increasing reluctance to do this found a hundred excuses. The recollection of the gap in the shelf now occurred to him with a sense of unnatural importance; in the troubled dozes that followed, this gap between two books seemed the most hideous deformity, like a gap between the front teeth of some grinning monster.

But in the clear daylight of the morning Mr Corbett came down
to the pleasant dining-room, its sunny windows and smell of coffee
and toast, and ate an undiminished breakfast with a mind chiefly
occupied in self-congratulation that the wind had blown the fog
away in time for his Saturday game of golf. Whistling happily, he
was pouring out his final cup of coffee when his hand remained
arrested in the act as his glance, roving across the bookcase, noticed
that there was now no gap at all in the second shelf. He asked who
had been at the bookcase already, but neither of the girls had, nor
Dicky, and Mrs Corbett was not yet down. The maid never touched
the books. They wanted to know what book he missed in it, which
made him look foolish, as he could not say. The things that disturb
us at midnight are negligible at 9 a.m.

'I thought there was a gap in the second shelf,' he said, 'but it
doesn't matter.'

'There never is a gap in the second shelf,' said little Jean brightly.
'You can take out lots of books from it and when you go back the
gap's always filled up. Haven't you noticed that? I have.'

Nora, the middle one in age, said Jean was always being silly; she
had been found crying over the funny pictures in *The Rose and the
Ring* because she said all the people in them had such wicked faces,
and the picture of a black cat had upset her because she thought it
was a witch. Mr Corbett did not like to think of such fancies for his
Jeannie. She retaliated briskly by saying Dicky was just as bad, and
he was a big boy. He had kicked a book across the room and said,
'Filthy stuff,' just like that. Jean was a good mimic; her tone
expressed a venom of disgust, and she made the gesture of dropping
a book as though the very touch of it were loathsome. Dicky, who
had been making violent signs at her, now told her she was a beastly
little sneak and he would never again take her for rides on the step
of his bicycle. Mr Corbett was disturbed. Unpleasant housemaids
and bad schoolfriends passed through his head, as he gravely asked
his son how he had got hold of this book.

'Took it out of that bookcase of course,' said Dicky furiously.

It turned out to be the *Boy's Gulliver's Travels* that Granny had given him, and Dicky had at last to explain his rage with the devil who wrote it to show that men were worse than beasts and the human race a washout. A boy who never had good school reports had no right to be so morbidly sensitive as to penetrate to the under-lying cynicism of Swift's delightful fable, and that moreover in the bright and carefully expurgated edition they bring out nowadays. Mr Corbett could not say he had ever noticed the cynicism himself, though he knew from the critical books it must be there, and with some annoyance he advised his son to take out a nice bright modern boy's adventure story that could not depress anybody. It appeared, however, that Dicky was 'off reading just now', and the girls echoed this.

Mr Corbett soon found that he too was 'off reading'. Every new book seemed to him weak, tasteless and insipid; while his old and familiar books were depressing or even, in some obscure way, dis-gusting. Authors must all be filthy-minded; they probably wrote what they dared not express in their lives. Stevenson had said that literature was a morbid secretion; he read Stevenson again to dis-cover his peculiar morbidity, and detected in his essays a self-pity masquerading as courage, and in *Treasure Island* an invalid's sickly attraction to brutality.

This gave him a zest to find out what he disliked so much, and his taste for reading revived as he explored with relish the hidden infirmities of minds that had been valued by fools as great and noble. He saw Jane Austen and Charlotte Brontë as two unpleasant examples of spinsterhood; the one as a prying, sub-acid busybody in everyone else's flirtations, the other as a raving, craving maenad seeking self-immolation on the altar of her frustrated passions. He compared Wordsworth's love of nature to the monstrous egoism of an ancient bellwether, isolated from the flock.

These powers of penetration astonished him. With a mind so acute and original he should have achieved greatness, yet he was a mere solicitor and not prosperous at that. If he had but the money, he might do something with those ivory shares, but it would be a pure gamble, and he had no luck. His natural envy of his wealthier acquaintances now mingled with a contempt for their stupidity that approached loathing. The digestion of his lunch in the City was ruined by meeting sentimental yet successful dotards whom he had once regarded as pleasant fellows. The very sight of them spoiled his game of golf, so that he came to prefer reading alone in the dining-room even on sunny afternoons.

He discovered also and with a slight shock that Mrs Corbett had always bored him. Dicky he began actively to dislike as an impudent blockhead, and the two girls were as insipidly alike as white mice; it was a relief when he abolished their tiresome habit of coming in to say goodnight.

In the now unbroken silence and seclusion of the dining-room, he read with feverish haste as though he were seeking for some clue to knowledge, some secret key to existence which would quicken and inflame it, transform it from its present dull torpor to a life worthy of him and his powers.

He even explored the few decaying remains of his uncle's theological library. Bored and baffled, he yet persisted, and had the occasional relief of an ugly woodcut of Adam and Eve with figures like bolsters and hair like dahlias, or a map of the Cosmos with Hell-mouth in the corner, belching forth demons. One of these books had diagrams and symbols in the margin which he took to be mathematical formulae of a kind he did not know. He presently discovered that they were drawn, not printed, and that the book was in manuscript, in a very neat, crabbed black writing that resembled black-letter printing. It was moreover in Latin, a fact that gave Mr Corbett a shock of unreasoning disappointment. For while examining the signs in the margin, he had been filled with an extraordinary exultation as though he knew himself to be on the edge of a discovery that should alter his whole life. But he had forgotten his Latin.

With a secret and guilty air which would have looked absurd to anyone who knew his harmless purpose, he stole to the schoolroom for Dicky's Latin dictionary and grammar and hurried back to the dining-room, where he tried to discover what the book was about

with an anxious industry that surprised himself. There was no
name to it, nor of the author. Several blank pages had been left at
the end, and the writing ended at the bottom of a page, with no
flourish or superscription, as though the book had been left unfinished. From what sentences he could translate, it seemed to be a
work on theology rather than mathematics. There were constant
references to the Master, to his wishes and injunctions, which
appeared to be of a complicated kind. Mr Corbett began by skip-
ping these as mere accounts of ceremonial, but a word caught his
eye as one unlikely to occur in such an account. He read this passage attentively, looking up each word in the dictionary, and could
hardly believe the result of his translation. 'Clearly,' he decided,
'this book must be by some early missionary, and the passage I
have just read the account of some horrible rite practised by a
savage tribe of devil-worshippers.' Though he called it 'horrible',
he reflected on it, committing each detail to memory. He then
amused himself by copying the signs in the margin near it and
trying to discover their significance. But a sensation of sickly cold
came over him, his head swam, and he could hardly see the figures
before his eyes. He suspected a sudden attack of influenza, and
went to ask his wife for medicine.

They were all in the drawing-room, Mrs Corbett helping Nora
and Jean with a new game, Dicky playing the pianola, and Mike,
the Irish terrier, who had lately deserted his accustomed place on
the dining-room hearth-rug, stretched by the fire. Mr Corbett had
an instant's impression of this peaceful and cheerful scene, before
his family turned towards him and asked in scared tones what was
the matter. He thought how like sheep they looked and sounded;
nothing in his appearance in the mirror struck him as odd; it was
their gaping faces that were unfamiliar. He then noticed the
extraordinary behaviour of Mike, who had sprung from the hearthrug and was crouched in the furthest corner, uttering no sound, but
with his eyes distended and foam round his bared teeth. Under Mr
Corbett's glance, he slunk towards the door, whimpering in a faint
and abject manner, and then as his master called him, he snarled

horribly, and the hair bristled on the scruff of his neck. Dicky let him out, and they heard him scuffling at a frantic rate down the stairs to the kitchen, and then, again and again, a long-drawn howl.

'What *can* be the matter with Mike?' asked Mrs Corbett.

Her question broke a silence that seemed to have lasted a long time. Jean began to cry. Mr Corbett said irritably that he did not know what was the matter with any of them.

Then Nora asked, 'What is that red mark on your face?'

He looked again in the glass and could see nothing.

'It's quite clear from here,' said Dicky; 'I can see the lines in the fingerprint.'

'Yes, that's what it is,' said Mrs Corbett in her brisk staccato voice; 'the print of a finger on your forehead. Have you been writing in red ink?'

Mr Corbett precipitately left the room for his own, where he sent down a message that he was suffering from headache and would have his dinner in bed. He wanted no one fussing round him. By next morning he was amazed at his fancies of influenza, for he had never felt so well in his life.

No one commented on his looks at breakfast, so he concluded that the mark had disappeared. The old Latin book he had been translating on the previous night had been moved from the writing-bureau, although Dicky's grammar and dictionary were still there. The second shelf was, as always in the daytime, closely packed; the book had, he remembered, been in the second shelf. But this time he did not ask who had put it back.

That day he had an unexpected stroke of luck in a new client of the name of Crab, who entrusted him with large sums of money: nor was he irritated by the sight of his more prosperous acquaintances, but with difficulty refrained from grinning in their faces, so confident was he that his remarkable ability must soon place him higher than any of them. At dinner he chaffed his family with what he felt to be the gaiety of a schoolboy. But on them it had a contrary effect, for they stared, either at him in stupid astonishment, or at their

plates, depressed and nervous. Did they think him drunk? he wondered, and a fury came on him at their low and bestial suspicions
and heavy dullness of mind. Why, he was younger than any of them!

But in spite of this new alertness he could not attend to the letters
he should have written that evening and drifted to the bookcase for
a little light distraction, but found that for the first time there was
nothing he wished to read. He pulled out a book from above his head
at random, and saw that it was the old Latin book in manuscript. As
he turned over its stiff and yellow pages, he noticed with pleasure the
smell of corruption that had first repelled him in these decaying volumes, a smell, he now thought, of ancient and secret knowledge.

This idea of secrecy seemed to affect him personally, for on hearing a step in the hall he hastily closed the book and put it back in its
place. He went to the schoolroom where Dicky was doing his homework, and told him he required his Latin grammar and dictionary
again for an old law report. To his annoyance he stammered and put
his words awkwardly; he thought that the boy looked oddly at him
and he cursed him in his heart for a suspicious young devil, though
of what he should be suspicious he could not say. Nevertheless,
when back in the dining-room, he listened at the door and then
softly turned the lock before he opened the books on the writing-
bureau.

The script and Latin seemed much clearer than on the previous
evening, and he was able to read at random a passage relating to a
trial of a German midwife in 1620 for the murder and dissection of
783 children. Even allowing for the opportunities afforded by her
profession, the number appeared excessive, nor could he discover
any motive for the slaughter. He decided to translate the book from
the beginning.

It appeared to be an account of some secret society whose activities and ritual were of a nature so obscure, and when not, so vile
and terrible, that Mr Corbett would not at first believe that this
could be a record of any human mind, although his deep interest in
it should have convinced him that from his humanity at least it was
not altogether alien.

He read until far later than his usual hour for bed and when at last he rose, it was with the book in his hands. To defer his parting with it, he stood turning over the pages until he reached the end of the writing, and was struck by a new peculiarity.

The ink was much fresher and of a far poorer quality than the thick rusted ink in the bulk of the book; on close inspection he would have said that it was of modern manufacture and written quite recently were it not for the fact that it was in the same crabbed late-seventeenth-century handwriting.

This, however, did not explain the perplexity, even dismay and fear, he now felt as he stared at the last sentence. It ran: '*Contine te in perennibus studiis*', and he had at once recognized it as a Ciceronian tag that had been dinned into him at school. He could not understand how he had failed to notice it yesterday.

Then he remembered that the book had ended at the bottom of a page. But now, the last two sentences were written at the very top of a page. However long he looked at them, he could come to no other conclusion than that they had been added since the previous evening.

He now read the sentence before the last: '*Re imperfecta mortuus sum,*' and translated the whole as: 'I died with my purpose unachieved. Continue, thou, the never-ending studies.'

With his eyes still fixed upon it, Mr Corbett replaced the book on the writing-bureau and stepped back from it to the door, his hand outstretched behind him, groping and then tugging at the door handle. As the door failed to open, his breath came in a faint, hardly articulate scream. Then he remembered that he had himself locked it, and he fumbled with the key in frantic ineffectual movements until at last he opened it and banged it after him as he plunged backwards into the hall.

For a moment he stood there looking at the door handle; then with a stealthy, sneaking movement, his hand crept out towards it, touched it, began to turn it, when suddenly he pulled his hand away and went up to his bedroom, three steps at a time.

There he behaved in a manner only comparable with the way

he had lost his head after losing his innocence when a schoolboy of sixteen. He hid his face in the pillow, he cried, he raved in meaningless words, repeating: 'Never, never, never. I will never do it again. Help me never to do it again.' With the words, 'Help me', he noticed what he was saying, they reminded him of other words, and he began to pray aloud. But the words sounded jumbled, they persisted in coming into his head in a reverse order so that he found he was saying his prayers backwards, and at this final absurdity he suddenly began to laugh very loud. He sat up on the bed, delighted at this return to sanity, common sense and humour, when the door leading into Mrs Corbett's room opened, and he saw his wife staring at him with a strange, grey, drawn face that made her seem like the terror-stricken ghost of her usually smug and placid self.

'It's not burglars,' he said irritably. 'I've come to bed late, that is all, and must have waked you.'

'Henry,' said Mrs Corbett, and he noticed that she had not heard him, 'Henry, didn't you hear it?'

'What?'

'That laugh.'

He was silent, an instinctive caution warning him to wait until she spoke again. And this she did, imploring him with her eyes to reassure her.

'It was not a human laugh. It was like the laugh of a devil.'

He checked his violent inclination to laugh again. It was wiser not to let her know that it was only his laughter she had heard. He told her to stop being fanciful, and Mrs Corbett, gradually recovering her docility, returned to obey an impossible command, since she could not stop being what she had never been.

The next morning, Mr Corbett rose before any of the servants and crept down to the dining-room. As before, the dictionary and grammar alone remained on the writing-bureau; the book was back in the second shelf. He opened it at the end. Two more lines had been added, carrying the writing down to the middle of the page. They ran:

Ex auro canceris
In dentem elephantis.

which he translated as:

> Out of the money of the crab
> Into the tooth of the elephant.

From this time on, his acquaintances in the City noticed a change in the mediocre, rather flabby and unenterprising 'old Corbett'. His recent sour depression dropped from him: he seemed to have grown twenty years younger, strong, brisk and cheerful, and with a self-confidence in business that struck them as lunacy. They waited with a not unpleasant excitement for the inevitable crash, but his every speculation, however wild and hare-brained, turned out successful. He no longer avoided them, but went out of his way to display his consciousness of luck, daring and vigour, and to chaff them in a manner that began to make him actively disliked. This he welcomed with delight as a sign of others' envy and his superiority.

He never stayed in town for dinners or theatres, for he was always now in a hurry to get home, where, as soon as he was sure of being undisturbed, he would take down the manuscript book from the second shelf of the dining-room and turn to the last pages.

Every morning he found that a few words had been added since the evening before, and always they formed, as he considered, injunctions to himself. These were at first only with regard to his money transactions, giving assurance to his boldest fancies, and since the brilliant and unforeseen success that had attended his gamble with Mr Crab's money in African ivory, he followed all such advice unhesitatingly.

But presently, interspersed with these commands, were others of a meaningless, childish, yet revolting character such as might be invented by a decadent imbecile, or, it must be admitted, by the idle fancies of any ordinary man who permits his imagination to wander unbridled. Mr Corbett was startled to recognize one or two such fancies of his own, which had occurred to him during his frequent boredom in church, and which he had not thought any other mind could conceive.

He at first paid no attention to these directions, but found that his new speculations declined so rapidly that he became terrified not merely for his fortune but for his reputation and even safety, since the money of various of his clients was involved. It was made clear to him that he must follow the commands in the book altogether or not at all, and he began to carry out their puerile and grotesque blasphemies with a contemptuous amusement, which, however, gradually changed to a sense of their monstrous significance. They became more capricious and difficult of execution, but he now never hesitated to obey blindly, urged by a fear that he could not understand, but knew only that it was not of mere financial failure.

By now he understood the effect of this book on the others near it, and the reason that had impelled its mysterious agent to move the books into the second shelf so that all in turn should come under the influence of that ancient and secret knowledge.

In respect to it, he encouraged his children, with jeers at their stupidity, to read more, but he could not observe that they ever now took a book from the dining-room bookcase. He himself no longer needed to read, but went to bed early and slept sound. The things that all his life he had longed to do when he should have enough money now seemed to him insipid. His most exciting pleasure was the smell and touch of these mouldering pages as he turned them to find the last message inscribed to him.

One evening it was in two words only: 'Canem occide.'

He laughed at this simple and pleasant request to kill the dog, for he bore Mike a grudge for his change from devotion to slinking aversion. Moreover, it could not have come more opportunely, since in turning out an old desk he had just discovered some packets of rat poison bought years ago and forgotten. No one therefore knew of its existence and it would be easy to poison Mike without any further suspicion than that of a neighbour's carelessness. He whistled light-heartedly as he ran upstairs to rummage for the packets, and returned to empty one in the dog's dish of water in the hall.

That night the household was awakened by terrified screams proceeding from the stairs. Mr Corbett was the first to hasten there, prompted by the instinctive caution that was always with him these days. He saw Jean, in her nightdress, scrambling up on to the landing on her hands and knees, clutching at anything that afforded support and screaming in a choking, tearless, unnatural manner. He carried her to the room she shared with Nora, where they were quickly followed by Mrs Corbett.

Nothing coherent could be got from Jean. Nora said that she must have been having her old dream again; when her father demanded what this was, she said that Jean sometimes woke in the night, crying, because she had dreamed of a hand passing backwards and forwards over the dining-room bookcase, until it found a certain book and took it out of the shelf. At this point she was always so frightened that she woke up.

On hearing this, Jean broke into fresh screams, and Mrs Corbett would have no more explanations. Mr Corbett went out on to the stairs to find what had brought the child there from her bed. On looking down into the lighted hall, he saw Mike's dish overturned. He went down to examine it and saw that the water he had poisoned must have been upset and absorbed by the rough doormat, which was quite wet.

He went back to the little girls' room, told his wife that she was tired and must go to bed, and he would take his turn at comforting Jean. She was now much quieter. He took her on his knee where at first she shrank from him. Mr Corbett remembered with an angry sense of injury that she never now sat on his knee, and would have liked to pay her out for it by mocking and frightening her. But he had to coax her into telling him what he wanted, and with this object he soothed her, calling her by pet names that he thought he had forgotten, telling her that nothing could hurt her now he was with her.

At first his cleverness amused him; he chuckled softly when Jean buried her head in his dressing-gown. But presently an uncomfortable sensation came over him, he gripped at Jean as though for her protection, while he was so smoothly assuring her of his. With difficulty, he listened to what he had at last induced her to tell him.

She and Nora had kept Mike with them all the evening and taken him to sleep in their room for a treat. He had lain at the foot of Jean's bed and they had all gone to sleep. Then Jean began her old dream of the hand moving over the books in the dining-room bookcase; but instead of taking out a book, it came across the dining-room and out on to the stairs. It came up over the banisters and to the door of their room, and turned their door handle very softly and opened it. At this point she jumped up wide awake and turned on the light, calling to Nora. The door, which had been shut when they went to sleep, was wide open, and Mike was gone.

She told Nora that she was sure something dreadful would happen to him if she did not go and bring him back, and ran down into the hall where she saw him just about to drink from his dish. She called to him and he looked up, but did not come, so she ran to him, and began to pull him along with her, when her nightdress was clutched from behind and then she felt a hand seize her arm.

She fell down, and then clambered upstairs as fast as she could, screaming all the way.

It was now clear to Mr Corbett that Mike's dish must have been upset in the scuffle. She was again crying, but this time he felt himself unable to comfort her. He retired to his room, where he walked up and down in an agitation he could not understand, for he found his thoughts perpetually arguing on a point that had never troubled him before.

'I am not a bad man,' he kept saying to himself. 'I have never done anything actually wrong. My clients are none the worse for my speculations, only the better. Nor have I spent my new wealth on gross and sensual pleasures; these now have even no attraction for me.'

Presently he added: 'It is not wrong to try and kill a dog, an ill-tempered brute. It turned against me. It might have bitten Jeannie.'

He noticed that he had thought of her as Jeannie, which he had not done for some time; it must have been because he had called her that tonight. He must forbid her ever to leave her room at night, he could not have her meddling. It would be safer for him if she were not there at all.

Again that sick and cold sensation of fear swept over him: he seized the bedpost as though he were falling, and held on to it for some minutes. 'I was thinking of a boarding-school,' he told himself, and then, 'I must go down and find out – find out—' He would not think what it was he must find out.

He opened his door and listened. The house was quiet. He crept on to the landing and along to Nora's and Jean's door where again he stood, listening. There was no sound, and at that he was again overcome with unreasonable terror. He imagined Jean lying very still in her bed, too still. He hastened away from the door, shuffling in his bedroom slippers along the passage and down the stairs.

A bright fire still burned in the dining-room grate. A glance at the clock told him it was not yet twelve. He stared at the bookcase. In the second shelf was a gap which had not been there when he had left. On the writing-bureau lay a large open book. He knew that he must cross the room and see what was written in it. Then, as before, words that he did not intend came sobbing and crying to his lips, muttering, 'No, no, not that. Never, never, never.' But he crossed the room and looked down at the book. As last time, the message was in only two words: '*Infantem occide.*'

He slipped and fell forward against the bureau. His hands clutched at the book, lifted it as he recovered himself and with his finger he traced out the words that had been written. The smell of corruption crept into his nostrils. He told himself that he was not a snivelling dotard, but a man stronger and wiser than his fellows, superior to the common emotions of humanity, who held in his hands the sources of ancient and secret power.

He had known what the message would be. It was after all the only safe and logical thing to do. Jean had acquired dangerous knowledge. She was a spy, an antagonist. That she was so unconsciously, that she was eight years old, his youngest and favourite child, were sentimental appeals that could make no difference to a man of sane reasoning power such as his own. Jean had sided with Mike against him. 'All that are not with me are against me,' he repeated softly. He would kill both dog and child with the white powder that no one knew to be in his possession. It would be quite safe.

He laid down the book and went to the door. What he had to do, he would do quickly, for again that sensation of deadly cold was sweeping over him. He wished he had not to do it tonight; last night it would have been easier, but tonight she had sat on his knee and made him afraid. He imagined her lying very still in her bed, too still. But it would be she who would lie there, not he, so why should he be afraid? He was protected by ancient and secret powers. He held on to the door handle, but his fingers seemed to have grown numb, for he could not turn it. He clung to it, crouched and shivering, bending over it until he knelt on the ground, his head beneath the handle which he still clutched with upraised hands. Suddenly the hands were loosened and flung outwards with the frantic gesture of a man falling from a great height, and he stumbled to his feet. He seized the book and threw it on the fire. A violent sensation of choking overcame him, he felt he was being strangled, as in a nightmare he tried again and again to shriek aloud, but his breath would make no sound. His breath would not come at all. He fell backwards heavily, down on the floor, where he lay very still.

In the morning, the maid who came to open the dining-room windows found her master dead. The sensation caused by this was scarcely so great in the City as that given by the simultaneous collapse of all Mr Corbett's recent speculations. It was instantly assumed that he must have had previous knowledge of this and so committed suicide.

The stumbling-block to this theory was that the medical report defined the cause of Mr Corbett's death as strangulation of the windpipe by the pressure of a hand which had left the marks of its fingers on his throat.

F.M. MAYOR

MISS DE MANNERING OF ASHAM

Oct. 9

My dear Evelyn,

   As you say you really are interested in this experience of mine, I am doing what you asked, and writing you an account of it. You can accept it as a token of friendship for, to tell you the truth, I had been trying to forget it, whatever it was. I hope in the end to bring myself to the belief that I never had it, but at present my remembrance is more vivid than I care for.

Yours affectionately

MARGARET LATIMER

You remember my friend, Kate Ware? She had been ill, and she asked me to stay in lodgings with her at an East Coast resort. 'It is simply Brixton-by-the-Sea, with a dash of Kensington,' Kate wrote; 'but I ought to go, because my aunt lives there, and likes to see me. So come, if you can bear it.'

   'I think we might take a day off,' said Kate one morning, after we had been there a week. 'Too much front makes me think there really is no England but this. Let's have some sandwiches, and bicycle out as far away as we can.'

   We came to a wayside inn, so quiet, so undisturbed, so cheerful in its quietness, that we felt at last we had found the soothing and rest we were in need of. Yes, I suppose our nerves were a little unstrung; at any rate, being high school mistresses, we knew what nerves were. But hitherto I have felt capable of controlling mine, only, as Hamlet says, I have had dreams. And Kate is rather strange by nature; I do not think her nerves make her any stranger.

'Now,' said Kate, when we had finished our meal – she always settles everything – 'I propose we borrow the pony here, and have a drive. I don't like desecrating these solitary lanes, which have existed for generations and generations before bicycles, with anything more modern than Tommy.'

Kate generally wants to have a map, and know exactly where she is going, but today we agreed to take the first turn to the left, and see where it led to. It was a sleepy afternoon, and Tommy trotted so gently that we were all three dozing, before we had gone a mile or two. Then we came to what had been magnificent wrought iron gates with stone pillars on either side. The pillars were now ruined, and the wall beyond was falling down. Kate said, 'Let's go in.' I said it was private, but we did go in.

We came into an avenue of laurels, resembling the sepulchral shrubberies with which our fathers and our fathers' fathers loved to surround their residences, only those were generally more serpentine. It must have been there many years, and had had time to grow so high as to block out almost all the sky. It was very narrow, and the dankness, the closeness, the black ground that never gets dry, which have always oppressed me in such places, seemed almost intolerable here. I thought we should never get out to the small piece of white light we saw at the end of it. At the same time I dreaded what I expected to find there; one of those great, lugubrious, black mausoleums of a mansion, which so often are the complement of the shrubbery. But this avenue seemed to have been planted at haphazard, for it led only to another gate, and that opened on a neglected park. We saw before us an expanse of unfertile-looking grass, and then the horizon was completely hidden by ridges of very heavy greenish-black trees. There were other trees scattered about; they

looked very old, and some had been struck by lightning. I felt sorry
for their wounds; it seemed as if no one cared whether they lived or
died.

There was a small church standing at the left-hand corner of the
park, so small that it must have been a chapel for the private worship of the owners of the park; but we thought they could not have
valued their church, for there was actually no path to it, nothing but
grass, long, rank and damp.

I do not know when it was that I became so certain that I
abhorred parks, but I remember it came over me very strongly all of
a sudden. I was extremely anxious that Kate should not know what
I felt. However, I said to her that grandeur was oppressive, and that
after all I preferred small gardens.

'Yes,' said Kate, 'one might feel too much enclosed, if one lived in
a park, as if one could never get out, and as if other things . . .'

Here Kate stopped. I asked her to go on, and she said that was all
she had to say. I don't know if you want to hear these minute
details, but nearly everything I have to tell you is merely a succession of minute details. I remember looking up at the sky, because I
wanted to keep my eyes away from the distant trees. I did not like
to see them – it seems a very poor reason for a woman of thirty-
eight – because they were so black. When I was six years old, I was
afraid of black, and also, though I loved the country, I used to feel
a sense of fear and isolation, if the sun was not shining, and I was
alone in a large field; but then a child's mind is open to every
terror, or rather it creates a terror out of everything. I thought I had
as much forgotten that condition as if I had never known it. I
should have supposed the weight of my many grown-up years would
have defended me, but I assure you that I felt all at once that I
was – what after all we are – as much at the mercy of the universe
as an insect.

I remember when I looked up at the sky I observed that it had
changed. As we were coming it had had the ordinary pale no-colour
aspect, which it bears for quite half the days in the year. Some
people grumble at it, but it is very English, and if you do not like it,

or more than like it, relish it, you cannot really relish England. The sky had now that strange appearance to which days in the north are liable; I do not think they know anything about it in Italy or the south of France. It is a fancy of mine that the sudden strangeness and wildness one finds in our literature is due to these days; it is something to compensate us for them.

If I said the day was dying, you would think of beautiful sunsets, and certainly the day could not be dying, for it was only three o'clock in the afternoon, but it looked ill; and the grey of the atmosphere was not that silvery grey, which I think the sweetest of all the skies in the year, but an unwholesome grey, which made the trees look blacker still. I should have felt it a relief if only it had begun to rain, then there would have been a noise; it was so utterly silent.

Just as I was wondering where I should turn my eyes next, Tommy came to a sudden stop, and nearly jerked us out of the cart. 'Clever,' said Kate, 'you're letting Tommy stumble.'

But it was simply that Tommy would not go on. He was such a mild little pony too, anxious, as Kate said, to do everything one asked, before one asked him.

'Tommy's frightened,' said Kate. 'He's all trembling and sweating.'

Kate got out, and tried to soothe him, but for some time it was very little good.

'It's another snub for the men of science,' said Kate. 'Tommy sees an angel in the way. Animals are very odd you know. Haven't you noticed dogs scurrying past ghosts in the twilight? I am so glad we haven't got their faculties.'

Then Tommy all at once surprised us by going on as quietly as before.

We drove a little further, and we came to the hall. It was built 150 years before the mausoleum period, but it could not well have been drearier, though it must formerly have been a noble Jacobean mansion. It was not that it looked out of repair; a house can be very cheerful, in fact rather more cheerful, if it is shabby. And here there was a terrace with greenhouse plants in stucco vases placed at intervals, and also a clean-shaven lawn, so that man must have been there recently; nevertheless it seemed as if it had been abandoned for years.

I cannot tell you how relieved I was when a respectable young man in shirt sleeves made his appearance. It is Kate generally who talks to strangers, but the moment he was in sight I felt I must cling to him, as a protection. I felt Tommy and Kate no protection.

I apologized for trespassing in private grounds.

'No trespassing at all, miss, I'm sure.' He went on to say he wished it happened oftener, Colonel Winterton, the owner, being hardly ever there, only liking to keep the place up with servants, and 'if there wasn't a number of us to make it lively, one room being shut up and all,' he really did not know—

It did not seem right to encourage him on the subject of a shut-up room; we changed the conversation, and asked him about the church.

He said it was a very ancient church, and there were tombs and that, people came a wonderful way to see. Not that he cared much about them himself.

Kate, who is fond of sight-seeing, declared she would visit the church.

I would not go, though I should like to have seen the tombs. I said I must hold the pony. The young man said he was a groom, and would hold the pony for us. Then I said I was tired: Kate said she would go alone. She started.

'Don't go down there, miss,' said the groom, 'the grass is so wet. Round by the right it's better.'

His way looked the same as hers to me, but Kate followed his advice.

I talked to the groom while Kate was away, and I was glad to hear that he liked the pictures in reason, and that his father was a saddler, living in the High Street of some small town. This was cheerful and distracting to my thoughts, and I had managed to become so much interested that it was the young man who said, 'There's the lady coming back.'

'Well,' I said, 'what was the church like?'

'It was locked,' Kate answered, 'however, it was nice outside.'

'But Kate,' I said, 'how pale you are!'

'Of course I am,' said Kate. 'I always am.'

The young man hastened to ask if he should get Kate a glass of water.

'Oh dear no, thank you,' said Kate. 'But I think we might be going now. Is there any other road out? I don't want to drive exactly the same way back.'

There was, and we set off. As soon as we had said good-bye to the young man, Kate began: 'About Grace Martin; what do you think of her chances for the Certificate?' and we talked about the Certificate until we got back to the inn. As to that oppressed feeling, I could hardly imagine now what it was. It had passed, and the world seemed its usual dear, safe self, irritating and comfortable. It was clearing up, and the trees and hedges looked as they generally look at the end of August. They were dusty and a little shabby, showing here and there a red leaf, occasional bits of toadflax, and all those little yellow flowers whose names one forgets, but to which one turns tenderly in recollection, when seeing the beauty of foreign lands. My thoughts broke away from our conversation now and then to wonder what I could possibly have been afraid of.

They gave us tea at Tommy's home, and the innkeeper's wife was glad to have some conversation.

'Yes, the poor old Hall, it seems a pity the Colonel coming down so seldom. He only bought it seven years ago, and he seems tired of it already, and then only bringing gentlemen. Gentlemen spend more, but I always think there's more life with ladies. It's changed hands so often. Yes, there's a shut-up room. They say it was something about a housemaid many years ago and a baby, if you'll excuse my mentioning it, but I'm sure I couldn't say. If you listen to all the tales in a village like this, in a little place you know, one says one thing and one another. I come from Norwich myself.'

'The church looks rather dismal,' said Kate. 'The churchyard is so overgrown.'

'Yes, poor Mr Fuller, he's a nice gentleman, though he is so high.

First when he come there was great goings on, services and antics. He says to me, "Tell me, Mrs Gage, is that why the people don't come?" "Oh," I says, "well, of course, I've been about, and seen life, so whether it's high or low, I just take no notice." I said that to put him off, poor gentleman, because it wasn't that. They won't come at all hardly after dark, particularly November; December it's better again; and for his communion service, what he sets his heart on so, we have such a small party, sometimes hardly more than two or three, and then he gets so downhearted. He seems to have lost all his spirit now.'

'But why is it better in December?'

'I'm sure I couldn't tell you, miss, but they always say those things is worse in November. I always heard my grandfather say that.'

I had rather expected that what I had forgotten in the day would come back at night, and about two, when I was reading *Framley Parsonage* with all possible resolution, I heard a knock at the door, and Kate came in.

'I saw your light,' said she. 'I can't sleep either. I think you felt uncomfortable in the park too, didn't you? Your face betrays you rather easily, you know. Going to the church, at least not going first of all, but as I got near the church, and the churchyard – ugh! However, I am *not* going to be conquered by a thought, and I mean to go there tomorrow. Still, I think, if you don't very much mind, I should like to sleep in here.'

I asked her to get into my bed.

'Thank you, I will,' said she. 'It's very good of you, Margaret, for I'm sure you loathe sharing somebody's bed as much as I do, but things being as they are—'

The next morning Kate was studying the guidebook at breakfast.

'Here we are,' said she. '"Asham Hall is a fine Jacobean mansion. The church, which is situated in the park, was originally the private chapel of the de Mannerings. Many members of the family are buried there, and their tombs are well worth a visit. The inscriptions in Norman French are of particular interest. The keys can be obtained from the sexton." Nothing about the shut-up room; I suppose we could hardly hope for it. We must see the tombs, don't you think so?'

Kate was one who very rarely showed her feelings, and I knew better than to refer to last night.

We bicycled to the Hall. It was a very sweet, bright windy morning, such a morning as would have pleased Wordsworth, I think, and may have brought forth many a poem from him.

'Now,' said Kate, 'when we get into the park, we'll walk our bicycles over the grass to the church.'

I began: then exactly the same feeling came over me as before, only this time there could be nothing in calm, beautiful nature to have produced it. The trees, though dark, did not look at all sinister, but stately and benignant, as they often do in late August, and early September. Whatever it was, it was within me. I felt I could not go to the church.

'You go on alone,' I said.

'You'd better come,' said Kate. 'I know just what you feel, but it will be worse here by yourself.'

'I think perhaps I won't,' I said.

'Very well,' said Kate. 'Bicycle on and meet me at the other gate.'

I said I was a coward, and Kate said she did not think it mattered being a coward. I meant to start at once, but I found something wrong with the bicycle. It took quite half an hour to repair, but as I was repairing it all my oppression passed, and I felt light and at ease. By the time I was ready, Kate had visited the tombs, and was coming out of the church door. I looked at her going down the path, and saw there was another woman in the churchyard. She was walking rather slowly. She came up behind Kate, then passed quite close to Kate on her left side. I was too far off to see her face. I felt thankful Kate had someone with her. I mounted; when I looked again the woman was gone.

I met Kate outside the church. She always had odd eyes; now they had a glittering look, half scared and half excited, which made me very uncomfortable. I asked her if she had spoken to the woman about the church.

'What woman? Where?' said Kate.

'The one in the churchyard just now.'

'I didn't see anyone.'

'You must have. She passed quite close to you.'

'Did she?' said Kate. 'She passed on my left side then?'

'Yes, she did. How did you know?'

'Oh, I don't know. We give the keys in here, and let's bicycle home fast, it's turned so cold.'

I always think Kate rather manlike, and she was manlike in her extreme moodiness. If anything of any sort went wrong, she clothed herself in a mood, and became impenetrable. Such a mood came on her now.

'I don't know why I never will tell things at the time,' said Kate next day. It was raining, and we were sitting over a nice little fire after tea. 'It's a sign of great feebleness of mind, I think. However, if you like to hear about Asham Church, you shall. I saw the tombs, and they are all that they should be. I hope the de Mannerings were worthy of them. But the church; perhaps being a clergyman's daughter made me take it so much to heart, but there was a filthy old carpet rolled up on the altar, all the draperies are full of holes, the paint is coming off, part of the chancel rail is broken, and it seems an abode of insects. I did not know there were such forsaken churches in England. That rather spoilt the tombs for me, also an uncomfortable idea that I did not want to look behind me; I don't know what I thought I was going to see. However, I gave every tomb its due. Then, when I was in the churchyard, I had the same feeling as last time; I could not get it out of my head that something I did not like was going to happen the next minute. Then I had that sensation, which books call the blood running chill; that really means, I think, a catch in one's heart as if one cannot breathe; and at the same time I had such an acute consciousness of someone standing at my left side that I almost felt I was being pushed, no one being there at all, you understand. That lasted a second, I should think, but after that I felt as if I were an intruder in the churchyard, and had better go.'

*

One afternoon a week later, the great-aunt of the smart townlike landlady at our lodgings came to clear away tea. First of all she was deferential and overwhelmed, but I have never known anyone have such a way with old ladies and gentlemen of the agricultural classes as Kate. In a few moments Mrs Croucher was sitting on the sofa with Kate beside her.

'Asham Hall,' said she. 'Why, my dear mother was sewing maid there, when she was a girl. Oh dear me, yes, the times she's told me about it all. Oh, it's a beautiful place, and them lovely laurels in the avenue, where Miss de Mannering was so fond of walking. It was the old gentleman, Mr de Mannering, he planted them; they was to have gone right up to the Hall, so they say. There was to be wonderful improvements, he was to have pulled down the old Hall and built something better, and then he hadn't the money. Yes, even then it was going down, for Mr William, that was the only son, that lived abroad, he was so wild. Yes, my mother was there in the family's time, not with them things which hev a-took it since.'

'You don't think much of Colonel Winterton, then?'

'Oh, I daresay he's a kind sort of gentleman, they say he's very free at Christmas with coals and that, but them new people they comes and goes, it stands to reason they can't be like the family. In the village we calls them jumped-up bit-of-a-things, but I'm sure I've nothing to say against Colonel Winterton.'

'Are there any of the family still here?'

'Oh no, mum. They've all gone. Some says there's a Mr de Mannering still in America, but he's never been near the place.'

'It's very sad when the old families go,' said Kate sympathetically.

'Oh, it is, mum. Poor old Mr de Mannering; but the place wasn't sold till after his death. My mother, she did feel it.'

'Was there a room shut up in your mother's time, Mrs Croucher?'

'Not when she first went there, mum.'

'It was a housemaid, wasn't it?'

'Not a housemaid,' with a look of important mystery. 'That's what they say, and it's better it *should* be said; I shouldn't tell it to everybody, but I don't mind telling a lady like you; it wasn't a housemaid at all.'

'Not a housemaid?'

'No; my mother's often told me. Miss de Mannering, she was a very high lady, well, she was a lady that *was* a lady, if you catch my meaning, and she must have been six or seven and forty, when she was took with her last illness. And the night before she died, my mother she was sitting sewing in Mrs Packe's room (she was the lady's maid, my mother was sewing maid, you know) and she heard Doctor Mason say, "Don't take any notice of what Miss de Mannering says, Mrs Packe. People get very odd fancies, when they're ill," he says. And she says, "No, sir, I won't," and she comes straight to my mother, and she says, "If you could hear the way she's a-going on. 'Oh, my baby,' she says, 'if I could have seen him smile. Oh, if he had lived just one day, one hour, even one moment.' I says to her, says Mrs Packe to my mother, 'Your baby, ma'am, whatever are you talking about?' It was such a peculiar thing for her to say," says Mrs Packe. "Don't you think so, Bessie?" Bessie was my mother. "I'm sure I don't know," says my mother; she never liked Mrs Packe. "Miss de Mannering didn't take no notice," Mrs Packe went on, "then she says, 'If only I'd buried him in the churchyard.' So I says to her, 'But where did you bury him then, ma'am?' and fancy! she turns round, and looks at me, and she says, 'I burnt him.'" Well, that's the truth, that's what my mother told me, and she always said, my mother did, Mrs Packe had no call to repeat such a thing.'

'I think your mother was quite right,' said Kate. 'Burnt! Poor Miss de Mannering must have been delirious. It is such a frightful . . .'

'No, my mother didn't like carrying tales about the family,' said Mrs Croucher, engaged on quite a different line of thought. And whether it was that she had heard the story so often, or whether it was that they are still more inured to horrors in the country – I have observed far stranger things happen in the country than in the town – Mrs Croucher did not seem to have any idea that she was relating what was terrible. On the contrary, I think she found it homely, recalling a happy part of her childhood.

'Then,' went on Mrs Croucher, 'Mrs Packe, she says to my mother, "You come and hear her," she says, and my mother says, "I don't like to, whatever would she say?" "Oh," says Mrs Packe, "she don't take any notice of anything, you come and peep in at the door." "So I went," my mother says, "and I just peeped in, but I couldn't see anything, only just Miss de Mannering lying in bed, for there was no candle, only the firelight. Only I heard Miss de Mannering give a terrible sigh, and say very faint, but you could hear her quite plain, 'Oh, if only I'd buried him in the churchyard.' I wouldn't stay any longer," says my mother, "and Miss de Mannering died at seven in the evening next day." Whenever my mother spoke of it to me, she always said, "I only regretted going into her room once, and that was all my life. It was taking a liberty, which never should have been took."'

'But,' said Kate, framing the question with difficulty, 'did anybody—? Had anybody had a suspicion that Miss de Mannering—?'

'No, mum. Miss de Mannering was always very reserved, she was not a lady that was at all free in her ways like some ladies; not like you are, if you'll excuse me, mum. Not that I mean she would have said anything to anyone of course, and she had no relations, no sisters, and they never had no company at the Hall, and the old gentleman, he'd married very late in life, so he was what you might call aged, and the servants was terrible afraid of him, his temper was so bad; even Miss de Mannering had a wonderful dread of him, they said.

'There was a deal of talk among the servants after what Mrs Packe said, and there was a housemaid, she'd been in the family a long time, and she remembered one winter years before, I daresay eighteen or twenty years before, Miss de Mannering was ailing, and she sent away her maid, and then she didn't sleep in her own room, but in a room in another part of the house not near anyone, that's the room they shut up, mum. And they remembered once she was ill for months and months, and her nurse that lived at Selby, when she was very old, she got a-talking as sometimes old people will, she died years after Miss de Mannering, and she let out what she would have done better to keep to herself.

'It wasn't long after Miss de Mannering's death they began to say you could see her come out of that there room, walk down the stairs, out at the front door, down through the park, along the avenue, and back again to the house, and then across the park to the churchyard. And of course they say she's trying to find a place for her baby. Then there's some as says Mr Northfield, what lived at Asham before Colonel Winterton came, he saw her. They say that's why he sold it. Mr Fuller they say he's spoke to her; they say that's why he's turned so quiet.

'Then there's some say, Miss Jarvis – she kept The Blue Boar in the village, when I was a girl – she used to say, that Miss Emily Robinson, the daughter of Sir Thomas Robinson, who bought the place from Mr Seaton, who bought it after Mr de Mannering's death – he wasn't much of a "Sir" to my mind, just kept a draper's shop in London, the saying was – she was took very sudden with the heart disease, and was found dead, flat on her face in the avenue. Of course the tale was, she met Miss de Mannering and she laid a hand on her. The footman that was attending Miss Robinson – she was regular pomped up with pride *she* was, and always would have a footman after her – he says he *see* a woman quite plain come up behind her, and then she fell. He told Mr Jarvis. Poor Mrs Dicey – they was at the Hall before the Northfields – she went off sudden too at the end, but she was always sickly, and I don't hold with all those tales myself.

'But people will believe anything. Why, not long ago, well, perhaps twenty years ago, in Northfield's time, there was a footman got one of the housemaids into trouble, and of course there's new people about in the village since the family went, and they say the room was shut up along of *her*. It's really ridickerlous.'

'Did you ever see her, Mrs Croucher?'

'Not to say see her, mum, but more than once as I've been walking in the park, I've *heard* her quite plain behind me. That was in November. November is the month, as you very well know, mum,' – I could see Kate was gratified that it was supposed she should know – 'and you could hear the leaves a-rustling as she walked. There's no need to be frightened, if you don't take no notice, and just walk straight on. They won't never harm you; they only gives you a chill.'

'Did your mother ever see her?'

'If she did, she never would say so. My mother wouldn't have any tales against Miss de Mannering. She said she never had any complaints to make. There was a young man treated my mother badly, and one day she was crying, and Miss de Mannering heard her, and she comes into the sewing-room, and she says, "What is it?" and my mother told her, and Miss de Mannering spoke very feeling, and said, "It's very sad, Bessie, but life is very sad." In general Miss de Mannering never spoke to anybody.

'My mother bought a picture of Miss de Mannering, if you young ladies would like to see it. Everything was in great confusion when Mr de Mannering died. Nothing had been touched for years, and there were all Miss de Mannering's dresses and her private things. No one had looked through them since her death. So what my mother could afford to buy she did, and she left them to me, and charged me to see they should never fall into hands that would not take care of them. There's a lot of writing I know, but I'm not much of a scholar myself, though my dear mother was, and I can't tell you what it's all about, not that my mother had read Miss de Mannering's papers, for she said that would never have been her place.'

Mrs Croucher went to her bedroom and brought us the papers and the portrait. It was a water-colour drawing dated Bath, 1805. The artist had done his best for Miss de Mannering with the blue sash to match the bit of blue sky, and the coral necklace to match her coral lips. The likeness presented to us was that of a young woman, dark, pale, thin, elegant, lady-like, long-nosed and plain. One gathers from pictures that such a type was not uncommon at that period. I should have been afraid of Miss de Mannering from her mouth and the turn of the head, they were so proud and aristocratic, but I loved her sad, timid eyes, which seemed appealing for kindness and protection.

Mrs Croucher was anxious to give Kate the portrait, 'for none of 'em don't care for my old things.' Kate refused. 'But after you are gone,' she said, for she knows that all such as Mrs Croucher are ready to discuss their deaths openly, 'if your niece will send her to me, I should like to have Miss de Mannering; I shall prize her very much.'

Then Mrs Croucher withdrew, 'for I shall be tiring you two young ladies with my talk.' It is rather touching how poor people, however old and feeble, think that everything will tire 'a lady,' however young and robust.

We turned to Miss de Mannering's papers. It was strange to look at something, written over a century ago, so long put by and never read. I had a terrible sensation of intruding, but Kate said she thought, if we were going to be as fastidious as all that, life would never get on at all. So I have copied out the narrative for you. I am sure, if Mrs Croucher knew you, she would feel you worthy to share the signal honour she conferred on us.

MISS DE MANNERING'S NARRATIVE

It is now twenty-two years since, yet the events of the year 1805 are engraved upon my memory with greater accuracy than those of any other in my life. It is to escape their pressing so heavily upon my brain that I commit them to paper, confiding to the pages of a book what may never be related to a human friend.

Had my lot been one more in accordance with that of other young women of my position, I might have been preserved from the calamity which befell me. But we are in the hands of a merciful Creator, who appoints to each his course. I sinned of my own free will, nor do I seek to mitigate my sin. My mother, Lady Jane de Mannering, daughter of the Earl of Poveril, died when I was five years old. She entrusted me to the care of a faithful governess and nurse, and owing to their affectionate solicitude in childhood and girlhood I hardly missed a mother's care. Of my father I saw but little. He was violent and moody. My brother, fourteen years older than I, was already causing him the greatest anxiety by his dissipation. Some words of my father's, and a chance remark, lightly spoken in my hearing, made an ineffaceable impression on me. In the unusual solitude of my existence I had ample, too ample, leisure to brood over recollections which had best be forgotten. Cheerful thoughts, natural to my age, should have left them no room in my heart. When I was thirteen years old, my father said to me one day, 'I don't want you skulking here, you're too much of a Poveril. Everyone knows that a Poveril once, for all their pride, stooped to marry a French waiting-maid. That's why every man Jack of them is black and sallow, as you are.' I fled from the room in terror.

Another day Miss Fanshawe was talking with the governess of a young lady who had come to spend the afternoon with me. They were walking behind us, and I heard their conversation.

'Is not Miss Maynard beautiful?' said Miss Adams. 'I believe that golden hair and brilliant eye will make a sensation even in London. What a pity Miss de Mannering is so black! Fair beauties are all the rage they say, and her eyes are too small.'

'Beauty is a very desirable possession for a young woman,' said Miss Fanshawe, 'but one which is perhaps too highly valued. Anyone may have beauty; a milkmaid may have beauty; but there is an air of rank and breeding which outlasts beauty, and is, I believe, more prized by a man of fastidious taste. Such an air is possessed by Miss de Mannering in a remarkable degree.'

My kind, beloved Fan! but at fifteen how much rather would I have shared the gift possessed by milkmaids! From henceforth I was certain I should not please.

Miss Fanshawe, who never failed to give me the encouragement and confidence I lacked, died when I was seventeen and had reached the age which, above all others in a woman's life, requires the comfort and protection of a female friend. My father, more and more engrossed with money difficulties, made no arrangement for my introduction to the world. He had no relations, but my mother's sisters had several times invited me to visit them. My father however, who was on bad terms with the family, would not permit me to go. The most rigid economy was necessary. He would allow no guests to be invited, and therefore no invitations to be accepted. The Hall was situated in a very solitary part of the country, and it was rare indeed for any visitor to find his way thither. My brother was forbidden the house. Months, nay years passed, and I saw no one.

Suddenly my father said to me one day, 'You are twenty-five, so that cursed lawyer of the Poverils tells me; twenty-five, and not yet married. I have no money to leave you after my death. Write and tell your aunt at Bath that you will visit her, and she must find you a husband.'

Secluded from society as I had been, the prospect of leaving the Hall and being plunged into the world of fashion filled me with the utmost apprehension. 'I entreat you, sir, to excuse me,' I cried. 'Let me stay here. I ask nothing from you, but I cannot go to Bath.'

I fell on my knees before him, but he would take no denial, and a few weeks after I found myself at Bath.

My aunt, Lady Theresa Lindsay, a widow, was one of the gayest in that gay city, and especially this season, for she was introducing her daughter Miss Leonora.

My father had given me ten pounds to buy myself clothes for my visit, but, entirely inexperienced as I was, I acquitted myself ill.

'My dear creature,' said my cousin in a coaxing manner that could not wound. 'Poor Nancy in the scullery would blush to see herself like you. You must hide yourself completely from the world for the next few days like the monks of La Trappe, and put yourself in Mamma's hands and mine. After that time I doubt not Miss Sophia de Mannering will rival the fashionable toast Lady Charlotte Harper.'

My dear Leonora did all in her power to set me off to the best advantage, to praise and encourage me, and my formidable aunt was kind for my mother's sake. But my terror at the crowd of gentlemen, that filled my aunt's drawing-room, was not easily allayed.

'I tremble at their approach,' I said to Leonora.

'Tremble at their approach?' said Leonora. 'But it is their part to tremble at ours, my little cousin, to tremble with hopes that we shall be kind, or with fears that we shall not. I say my little cousin, because I am a giantess,' she was very tall and exquisitely beautiful, 'and also I am very old and experienced, and you are to look up to me in everything.'

I wished to have remained retired at the assemblies, but Leonora always sought me out, and presented her partners to me. But my awkwardness and embarrassment soon wearied them, and after such attentions as courtesy required they left me for more congenial company. Certainly I could not blame them; it was what I had anticipated. Yet the mortification wounded me and I said to my cousin, 'It is of no use, Leonora. I can never, never hope to please.'

'Those who fish diligently,' she replied, 'shall not go unrewarded. A gentleman said to me this evening, "Your cousin attracts me; she has so much countenance." Captain Phillimore is accounted a connoisseur in our sex. That is a large fish, and I congratulate you with all my heart.'

Captain Phillimore came constantly to my aunt's house. Once he entered into conversation with me. Afterwards he sought me out; at first I could not believe it possible, but again he sought me out, and yet again.

'Captain Phillimore is a connexion not to be despised by the ancient house of de Mannering,' said my aunt. 'There are tales of his extravagance it is true, and other matters; but the family is wealthy, and of what man of fashion are not such tales related? Marriage will steady him.'

Weeks passed by. It was now April. My aunt was to leave Bath in a few days, and I was to return home; the season was drawing to its close. My aunt was giving a farewell reception to her friends. Captain Phillimore drew me into an anteroom adjoining one of the drawing-rooms. He told me that he loved me, that he had loved me from the moment he first saw me. He kissed me. Never, never can I forget the bliss of that moment. 'There are,' he said, 'important reasons why our engagement must at present be known only to ourselves. As soon as it is possible I will apprise my father, and hasten to Asham to obtain Mr de Mannering's consent. Till then not a word to your aunt. It will be safest not even to correspond.' He told me that he had been summoned suddenly to join his regiment in Ireland and must leave Bath the following day. 'I must therefore see you once more before I go. The night is as warm as summer. Have you the resolution to meet me in an hour's time in the garden? We must enjoy a few minutes' solitude away from the teasing crowd.'

I, who was usually timid, had now no fears. I easily escaped unnoticed. The whole household was occupied with the reception. At the end of a long terrace there was an arbour. Here we met. He urged me to give myself entirely to him, using the wicked sophistries which had been circulated by the infidel philosophers of France; that marriage is a superstitious form with no value for the more enlightened of mankind. But alas, there was no need of sophistries. Whatever he had proposed, had he bidden me throw myself over a precipice, I should have obeyed. I loved him as no weak mortal should be loved. When his bright blue eye gazed into mine, and his hand caressed me, I sank before him as a worshipper before a shrine. With my eyes fully open I yielded to him.

I returned to the house. My absence had not been observed. My cousin came to my room, and said with her arch smile, 'I ask no question, I am too proud to beg for confidences. But I know what I know. Kiss me, and receive my blessing.'

I retired to rest, and could not sleep all night for feverish exaltation. It was not till the next day that I recognized my guilt. I hardly dared look my aunt and cousin in the face, but my demeanour passed unnoticed; for during the morning a Russian nobleman attached to the Imperial court, who had been paying Leonora great attentions, solicited her hand and was accepted. In the ensuing agitation I was forgotten, and my proposal that I should return to Asham a day or two earlier was welcomed. My aunt was anxious to go to London without delay to begin preparations for the wedding.

She made me a cordial farewell, engaging me to accompany her to Bath next year. 'But, Mamma,' said Leonora, 'I think Captain Phillimore will have something to say to that. All I stipulate is that Captain and Mrs Phillimore shall be my first visitors at St Petersburgh.'

Their kindness went through me like a knife, and I returned to Asham with a heavy heart.

'Where is your husband?' was my father's greeting.

'I have none, sir,' said I.

'The more fool you,' he answered, and asked no further particulars of my visit.

Time passed on. Every day I hoped for the appearance of Captain Phillimore. In vain; he came not. Certainty was succeeded by hope, hope by doubt, doubt by dread. I would not, I could not despair. Ere long it was evident that I was to become a mother. The horror of this discovery, with my total ignorance of Captain Phillimore's whereabouts, caused me the most miserable perturbation. I walked continually with the fever of madness along the laurel avenue and in the Park. I went to the Church, hoping that there I might find consolation, but the memorials of former de Mannerings reminded me too painfully that I alone of all the women of the family had brought dishonour on our name.

I longed to pour out my misery to some human ear, even though I exposed my disgrace. There was but one in my solitude whom I could trust; my old nurse, who lived at Selby three miles off. I walked thither one summer evening, and with many tears I told her all. She mingled her tears with mine. I was her nursling, she did not shrink from me. All in her power she would do for me. She knew a discreet woman in Ipswich, whither she might arrange for me to go as my time approached, who would later take charge of the infant.

She suggested all that could be done to allay suspicion in the household and village.

At first my aunt and cousin wrote constantly, and even after Leonora's marriage I continued to hear from Russia. My letters were short and cold. When I knew that I was to be a mother, I could not bear to have further communication with them. My aunt wrote to me kindly and reproachfully. I did not answer, and gradually all correspondence ceased. Yet their affectionate letters were all I had to cheer the misery of those ensuing months. I shall never forget them. Although it was now summer, the weather was almost continuously gloomy and tempestuous. There were many thunderstorms, which wrought havoc among our elm trees in the Park. The rushing of the wind at night through the heavy branches and the falling of the rain against my window gave me an indescribable feeling of apprehension, so that I hid my head under the bedclothes that I might hear nothing. Yet more terrible to me were the long days of August, when the leaden sky oppressed my spirit, and it seemed as if I and the world alike were dead. I struggled against the domination of such fancies, fancies perhaps not uncommon in my condition, and in general soothed by the tenderness of an indulgent husband. I could imagine such tenderness. Night and day Captain Phillimore was in my thoughts. No female pride came to my aid; I loved him more passionately than ever.

On the 20th November some ladies visited us at the Hall. We had a common bond in two cousins of theirs I had met frequently in Bath. They talked of our mutual acquaintance. At length Captain Phillimore's name was mentioned. Shall I ever forget those words? 'Have you heard the tale of Captain Phillimore, the all-conquering Captain Phillimore? Major Richardson, who was an intimate of his at Bath, told my brother that he said to him at the beginning of the season, "What do you bet me that in one season I shall successfully assault the virtue of the three most innocent and immaculate maids, old or young, in Bath? Easy virtue has no charms for me, I prefer the difficult, but my passion is for the impregnable," and Major

Richardson assures my brother that Captain Phillimore won his bet. Mr de Mannering, we are telling very shocking scandals; three ladies of strict virtue fallen in one season at Bath. What is the world coming to?'

My father had appeared to pay little heed to their chatter, but he now burst forth, 'If any woman lets her virtue be assaulted by a rake, she's a rake herself. Should such a fate befall a daughter of mine, I should first horsewhip her, and then turn her from my doors.'

During this conversation I felt a stab at the heart, so that I could neither speak nor breathe. How it was my companions noticed nothing I cannot say. I dared not move, I dared not leave my seat to get a glass of water to relieve me. Yet I believe I remained outwardly at ease, and as soon as speech returned, I forced myself to say with tolerable composure, 'Major Richardson was paying great attention to Miss Burdett. Does your brother say anything of that affair?'

Shortly afterwards the ladies took their leave.

I retired to my room. I had moved to one in the most solitary part of the house, far from either my father or the servants. I tried in vain to calm myself, but each moment my fever became more uncontrollable. I dispatched a messenger to my nurse, begging her to come to me without delay. I longed to sob my sorrows out to her with her kind arms round me. The destruction of all my hopes was as nothing to the shattering of my idol. My love was dead, but though I might despise him, I could not, could not hate him.

Later in the day I was taken ill, and in the night my baby was born. My room was so isolated that I need have little fear of discovery. An unnatural strength seemed to be given me, so that I was able to do what was necessary for my little one. He opened his eyes; the look on his innocent face exactly recalled my mother. My joy who shall describe? I was comforted with the fancy that in my hour of trial my mother was with me. I lay with my sweet babe in my arms, and kissed him a hundred times. The little tender cries were the most melodious music to my ears. But short-lived was my joy;

my precious treasure was granted me but three brief hours. It was long ere I could bring myself to believe he had ceased to breathe. What could I do with the lovely waxen body? The horror that my privacy would be invaded, that some intruder should find my baby, and desecrate the sweet lifeless frame by questions and reproaches, was unendurable. I would have carried him to the churchyard, and dug the little grave with my own hands. But the first snow of the winter had been falling for some hours; it would be useless to venture forth.

The fire was still burning; I piled wood and coal upon it. I wrapped him in a cashmere handkerchief of my mother's; I repeated what I could remember of the funeral service, comforting and tranquillizing myself with its promises. I could not watch the flames destroy him. I fled to the other end of the room, and hid my face on the floor. Afterwards I remember a confused feeling that I myself was burning and must escape the flames. I knew no more, till I opened my eyes and found myself lying on my bed, with my nurse near me, and our attached old Brooks, the village apothecary, sitting by my side.

'How do you feel yourself, Miss de Mannering?' said he.

'Have I been ill?'

'Very ill for many weeks,' said he, 'but I think we shall do very well now.'

My nurse told me that, as soon as my message had reached her, she had set out to walk to Asham, but the snow had impeded her progress, and she was forced to stop the night at an inn not far from Selby. She was up before dawn, and reached the Hall, as the servants were unbarring the shutters. She hastened to my room, and found me lying on the floor, overcome by a dangerous attack of fever. She tended me all the many weeks of my illness, and would allow none to come near me but the doctor, for throughout my delirium I spoke constantly of my child.

The doctor visited me daily. At first I was so weak that I hardly noticed him, but my strength increased, and with strength came remembrance. He said to me one morning, 'You have been brought from the brink of the grave, Miss de Mannering. I did not think it possible that we should have saved you.'

In the anguish of my spirit I could not refrain from crying out, 'Would God that I had died.'

'Nay,' said he, 'since your life has been spared, should you reject the gift from the hands of the Almighty?'

'Ah,' I said in bitterness. 'You do not know—'

'Yes, madam,' said he, looking earnestly upon me, 'I know all.'

I turned from him trembling.

'Do not fear,' he said. 'The knowledge will never be revealed.'

I remained with my face against the wall.

'My dear Madam,' he said with the utmost kindness. 'Do not turn from an old man, who has attended you since babyhood and your mother also. My father and my father before me doctored the de Mannerings, and I wish to do all in my power to serve you. A physician may sometimes give his humble aid to the soul as well as to the body. Let me recall to your suffering soul that all of us sinners are promised mercy through our Redeemer. I entreat you not to lose heart. Now for my proper domain, the body. You must not spend your period of convalescence in this inclement native county of ours. You must seek sun and warmth, and change of scene to cheer your mind.'

His benevolence touched me, and my tears fell fast. Amid tears I answered him, 'Alas, I am without friends; I have nowhere to go.'

'Do not let that discourage us,' he said with a smile, 'we shall devise a plan. Let me sit by my own fireside with my own glass of whisky, and I shall certainly devise a plan.'

By his generous exertions I went on a visit to his sister at Worthing. She watched over me with a mother's care, and I returned to Asham with my health restored. Peace came to my soul; I learnt to forgive him. The years passed in outward tranquillity, but in each succeeding November, or whenever the winds were high or the sky leaden, I would suffer, as I had suffered in the months preceding the birth of my child. My mind was filled with baseless fears, above all that I should not meet my baby in Heaven, because his

body did not lie in consecrated ground. Nor were the assurances of
my Reason and my Faith able to conjure the delusion: yet I had –

Here the writing stopped.

'Wait, though,' said Kate, 'there's a letter.' She read the following:

> 3 Hen and Chicken Court,
> Clerkenwell.
> March 7, 1810.

Madam,

I have been told that my days are numbered. Standing as
I do on the confines of eternity, I venture to address you.
Long have I desired to implore your forgiveness, but have
not presumed so far. I entreat you not to spurn my letter.
God knows you have cause to hate the name of him who
betrayed you. Yes, Madam, my vows were false, but even at
the time I faltered, as I encountered your trusting and
affectionate gaze, and often during my subsequent career of
debauchery has that vision appealed before me. Had I
embraced the opportunity offered me by Destiny to link my
happiness with one as innocent and confiding as yourself, I
might have been spared the wretchedness which has been
my portion.

I am Madam, your obedient servant,

Frederic Phillimore.

I could not speak for a minute; I was so engrossed with thinking
what Miss de Mannering must have felt when she got that letter.

Kate said, 'I wonder what she wrote back to him. How often it
has been folded and refolded, read and re-read, and do you see
where words have got all smudged? I believe those are her tears,
tears for that skunk!'

But I felt I could imagine better than Kate all that letter, with its
stilted old-fashioned style, which makes it hard for us to believe the
writer was in earnest, would have meant to Miss de Mannering.

'Tomorrow is our last afternoon,' said Kate. 'What do you think,' coaxingly, 'of making a farewell visit to Asham?'

But though Miss de Mannering is a gentle ghost, I do not like ghosts; besides, now I know her secret, I *could* not intrude upon her. So we did not go to Asham again. Now we are back at school, and that is the end of my story.

Ann Bridge

THE STATION ROAD

There was a little pause when the last speaker finished. We sat round the fire, each occupied with his own thoughts; the mind of each seeking its own solution of the problems raised by the uncanny story to which we had just listened. It was Tredgold who broke the silence.

'That was a good story – very,' he said, meditatively filling a fresh pipe. 'I always wish the psychologists could get us a little nearer to understanding these happenings, or appearances, or whatever you like to call them. Sometimes they look like communications, and sometimes they don't.' He lit a pipe carefully, and then turned round in his chair towards his immediate neighbour. 'I always think that business of your wife's, Doctor, was one of the oddest I ever heard in that line.'

'The train story, eh?' said Dr Freeland. 'Yes, that was a queer business.'

Of course we were urgent with the Doctor to let us have it.

'Very well,' he said, 'you shall.' He also made preparations for a fresh pipe, pushing his chair back a little from the fire.

'It happened when we were living in the country,' began the Doctor, stuffing his tobacco well down into the bowl. 'I had no practice then, but a mixed sort of job – doing hospital work in London two or three days a week, and relieving a man at that big private place at Westlea over the weekends. It was rather an up-and-down sort of life, but it suited him and it suited me.

'One day – it was early in the week, a Tuesday, I think – I got a letter in town from a man I used to know well, saying that he was returning to England by a certain boat, and wished to see me at once when he arrived. I had – well, looked after him to some extent in old days, and he had got into the habit of coming to me for advice and so on; but he had been in Canada for several years, and I had seen very little of him. I had not seen him since my marriage, and he had never seen my wife. He was urgent about the necessity for seeing me immediately, but he did not say what the trouble was.

'Well, I looked up the boat in the paper, and then rang up the London office of the line, and I found that she was due to arrive at Plymouth two days later. In those days the boat trains used to slip a coach at Westbury, and from there a fast train up the other line slipped a couple of coaches at Hedworth Junction, about seven miles from us. There was an hour's wait at Westbury, but it was far quicker than going right up to town by the boat train and down again.

'So I sent off a wire to this man, to meet him at Plymouth, telling him to come to Hedworth in this way, and I wrote a letter too, bidding him welcome. Also I sent a line to my wife, and told her to meet the 7.11 at Hedworth to fetch off this man. I explained who he was, for I couldn't be sure of getting down myself that night; but my wife is quite accustomed to having casual strangers shot on to her, and I knew she would deal with him well enough till I got home.'

The Doctor paused, lit another match, and puffed at his pipe.

'I must say I thought it a little odd', he went on, 'that he should want so urgently to see me, right off the boat, as it were. But I supposed he was in some trouble, and he had got into the habit, as I said, of coming to me for help. Ah well, it is generally the wrong thing that one thinks odd.

'Well, my wife, like a good sensible creature as she is, thought nothing odd at all. She prepared a room, and a dinner, and then set off in the car to meet the stranger at the Junction. I always rode my old motorbike in and out, so that she did not have to worry about meeting me.

'It was early winter, November, and by the time she started it was black dark. Of course we both knew the station road painfully well – there wasn't a bump in the whole seven miles that we weren't perfectly familiar with. It's a very ordinary bit of south-country road; first a straight stretch between pastures – clay, with oaks in the hedgerows, for about three miles – then a patch of thick woodland; and after that the road climbs over the open downs before it drops to the valley, where the river, the main road, and the railway all run together. It was a cold, dry, cloudy night, with no moon; my wife told me how she noticed, perhaps for the hundredth time, as she drove along, how white the dry road looked, except where the fallen leaves had moistened and stained it; and how the light from her lamps picked out the trunks of the oak trees as she passed them one after another. She was keeping rather a sharp lookout on the foot-passengers, because she half expected that a young brother of hers might be turning up that evening – he used to come, very casually, by any train, and walk out from the Junction with a knapsack.

'So she was, as I say, keeping a particularly sharp lookout, and somewhere about the middle of the first flat straight stretch I spoke of, she saw a man on foot coming towards her, walking on the right-hand side of the road. She slowed down, she said, the least little bit, to have time to see him. It wasn't Jim, her brother; it was a medium-tall man, in a very pale raincoat, which looked almost white in the strong light. She observed him, even when she had seen that it wasn't Jim, with the sort of involuntary precision with which one sometimes takes in unimportant details, and she noticed that there was a dark stain or mark showing up very clearly on the left side of this white trench-coat of his, and that he had a very noticeable cast or twist of his right eye and eyebrow. Of course she paid no attention to this at the time, but just registered the impression automatically, as it were.

'Well, she drove on perhaps another couple of miles, and was well into the stretch of wood – young beeches, planted thick, so that the trunks look like rain in a dim light – when she saw ahead another man walking towards her, again on the right-hand side of the road. She had met one or two cars and cyclists in between – it wasn't a particularly lonely road by any means; but nothing had passed her. She began to look carefully at this man, as before, as soon as she saw him; and as she got nearer, and could see him in increasing detail, she noticed, first, that he too had a very pale raincoat, and then that it had a dark stain on the left side – and then, as she actually passed him, and could see his face clearly, she saw that he had the same cast of the right eye and eyebrow as the man she had passed a couple of miles further back. *It was the same man.*

'She said that the full strangeness of it didn't strike her instantly – she was puzzled, for a few seconds, as to where she had seen him before. Then, as she remembered, she had a pronouncedly disagreeable sensation. She wasted a few moments more trying to make some hypothesis to account for the disquieting facts – it is the way we all treat disquieting facts. But it wouldn't do. She knew she had seen him, she knew where she had seen him; she remembered distinctly that nothing had passed her, going the same way as herself. She could not cheat herself into the belief that it wasn't the same man; her involuntary and spontaneous attention, in both cases, had registered too clear and sharp an impression for that.

'She began to feel very uncomfortable indeed. It was then that she looked back. But in the woods the road was no longer straight – it curved a good deal, and quick as her thoughts had passed, she had covered a good stretch; the man would anyhow, as she realized, have been out of sight. The road behind her was, of course, empty, between the chalky banks and grey walls of trees – what she could see of it, for the road behind your lights is very black.

'She drove on. But she was now perceptibly glad to meet another car or two, and she had a strong desire not to see any more foot-passengers. Nor, after that first pause, had she any further wish to look back – somehow the blackness of the road behind her, in that one glance, had begun to let something like horror in on her.

'She pushed on at a good pace, shoving the car up the long hill on to the down. Right at the top there is a signpost at four cross-roads. Her light picked up the white post at a good distance, and she was glad to see it, for it meant that her drive was nearly over – there remained only the drop down to the valley and the station. But the next moment she saw that there was a man under the sign-post. She stood on the accelerator, determined, in a panic-stricken way, not to look at him. But she had to look – she couldn't help her-self; and she saw, as she rushed past, in the pitiless light, again the white raincoat, the dark stain on the left side, the twisted eyebrow, and the cast eye.

'This time she was terrified. For a little while, she said, she quite lost control of herself, and raced along blindly, her one idea to get to lights and faces and human speech. She found herself descending the hill at a perfectly reckless pace, and the sense of actual physical danger pulled her together. There is a bad turn at the pitch of the hill; she managed to slow down for that, and drove on, more rea-sonably, to the station.

'She left the car outside, and fairly ran in. It was ten minutes past seven by the station clock. The lobby was warm and brightly lit, pas-sengers and porters were moving about, and the whole place was so *normal* that it steadied her. The old station-master, who was a great ally of ours, came up and began to talk to her, and his fatherly chat added to her comfort. He asked whom she had come to meet, and she told him; the reflection that she would have a companion on the drive home made her almost at ease. They went out together on to the platform and stood waiting for the express. It was fairly late, but at 7.32 – the station-master took out his watch and checked the fact aloud – it came roaring through, and the slipped coaches, grind-ing and groaning on the metals, came to a stop well up the platform. "Now we'll find your gentleman for you, ma'am," said the old boy.

'Well, they didn't find him. The coaches emptied themselves, and people collected their luggage and began to leave the station in the waiting cars, or afoot; but no one appeared to be hanging about in the inquiring way, so easy to spot, of the total stranger who hopes to be met. They were puzzled. The station-master consulted the guard who took charge of the slip coaches from Westbury to Hedworth, and stopped with them at the latter place. "This lady's come to meet a gentleman off the boat train – should have taken this train at Westbury." What was the name, the guard wanted to know? "Macmurdo," says my wife. Oh, yes, he was there all right; the guard had his stuff in the van. They went to look, and there, sure enough, were three boxes with his name, and the steamer labels. But there was by this time no one on the platform but themselves and the porters. "Well, that's a puzzle," said the guard, lifting his hat and rubbing his head. "I saw him at Westbury, took 'is stuff and talked to him. An American gentleman, isn't he? Talked like one, anyway." Then the blow fell, as it were. My wife was up to now merely rather annoyed and bored by the man's not turning up; she was standing quite at ease, under the lamps, when the guard called out to the porter who had been collecting tickets as the passengers went out: "George, seen a gentleman go out in a white mackintosh, with a twitch in 'is right eye?"

"*What* do you say?" she said to the guard – so sharply that she saw his surprise. But she was too agitated to care. "*What* do you say he was like?" she repeated.

"'Why, he's a tallish gentleman, isn't 'e?" said the guard. "And he had on a whitish coat, and this twitch in 'is eye; sort of affliction – I noticed 'im particular. That's right, isn't it?"

'Of course it was – the horror lay just in the guard having seen so precisely what she had seen. She was on the point of asking if the white mackintosh had a dark stain on the left side, when she remembered that for the purposes of a sane world, a world of guards and porters, she hadn't seen the man at all. She couldn't have, you see. The guard had seen him at Westbury, and no earthly power could have got him on to the station road, where she had seen him, before seven o'clock. For the second time that night she pulled herself together, and asked the proper, rational questions. Was he sure he had seen him get into the train? How did he know his name, that it was the man? The guard was quite positive and clear. The express was late in leaving Westbury, and this gentleman come fidgeting up to him and asked when the train would start. " 'E gave me 'is luggage for the van, so I saw the name; and 'e asked for the refreshment room, and I showed 'im. We had quite a chat – he was very free, like most American gentlemen, in his talk. I *should* remember him," said the guard, "for he gave me half a Bradbury for that. A great roll of notes he had on him."

'Well, there was no doubt about it – Macmurdo she had clearly seen; but you can guess that my wife took no very active part in the search of the empty carriages that followed. They found nothing, though one carriage was a litter of papers which the guard tossed over a little, carelessly. Of Macmurdo there was no trace, nor did my wife expect to find him. She guessed him to be in another world. Poor soul, he was, sure enough. Next morning when the slipped coaches were cleaned, blood-stains were found on the seat and floor of the carriage which had been full of scattered newspapers, and before twenty-four hours were out a gang of plate-layers, making their daily round of that section, came on the corpse of a man lying halfway down the embankment of the line, between Westbury and Armlea. He had fallen with violence, but the fall was not the cause of death; a great stain of blood on the left side of his pale raincoat marked where he had been cruelly stabbed – murdered, there could be little doubt, for the sake of the "great roll of notes" which the guard had noticed when he got his tip. His watch, ring, and so on had not been touched, nor anything but his money; and among the papers which easily identified him was my letter of welcome, telling him his train.'

The Doctor paused, and knocked out his pipe against the grate.

'That letter took me to the inquest,' he went on, 'so I heard all that the police could put together. He was stabbed and thrown out at some time between 6.40, when the train left Westbury – late, as you remember – and when it reached Armlea about 7.17. Armlea was the one stop between Westbury and Hedworth; and my wife had been at the Junction for some time when the train left that place.'

'That is where the murderer must have got out, of course,' some-one put in.

'That was the supposition,' said the Doctor, 'but it was confirmed afterwards.'

'How?' asked five voices at once.

'That's the most curious part of all,' said the Doctor. 'Over a year later my wife was at the Junction again, in the evening, to meet me, this time. She's a courageous creature, and she did not let her distaste for the station road after dark keep her off it for long. "Poor soul," she said more than once, "he wanted help, and he was coming to you for it, as usual – that was all. I wish I *could* have helped him." Well, there she was at the station, and this time the down train was late. She was sitting in the waiting-room, looking at the paper, just under the lamp, when a man came in. She looked up, as one does, when she heard him, so that the light fell, I suppose, on her face. There was no one else in the room. Well, when this man saw her she said that his whole face changed – "went ghastly" was her expression – he almost staggered back a step or two, and then turned and went out like a man who had received a blow. She was rather upset, as you may suppose, at producing this effect on a total stranger, and actually went and tried to look at herself in one of those faded pictures of ocean liners which always hang in waiting-rooms. She could find nothing odd in her appearance, so she went on reading the paper. Presently something made her look up, and there was the man again, peering in through the window which gave on to the platform. He went on hanging about for a bit, and at last came in, looking shockingly disordered, and said that he must speak to her. She made him sit down, for he was shaking in every limb, and there and then he made a full confession of the murder of my poor friend. My wife thought at first that he was raving, but there could be no mistake: he gave the name, the date, and the time of the train. He had been desperate for money, had seen the notes when Macmurdo tipped the guard at Westbury, and on a sudden impulse had committed the murder. He got out at Armlea, as the police had surmised, and got clear away.'

'But why in the world—' someone began.

'Did he tell my wife?' said the Doctor.

'Exactly. She asked him that, and you must make what you can of his answer. "You should tell this to the police," she said. "Why have you told me?"

'"Because *you were there!*" he said.

'"How do you mean, 'there'?" says my wife, startled.

'"You came and looked at me," said the poor wretch, trembling like a leaf. "Three times, while I was putting the papers about, before I got to Armlea, you stood at the door and looked in at me. You don't suppose I could forget your face?" he almost shrieked. "I knew that one day I should see you again, and then I should have to tell you."'

The Doctor paused again, but this time nobody said anything.

'There,' he said after a few moments, 'make what you like of that.'

We asked what became of the murderer.

'Oh, we handed him over to the police,' said the Doctor. 'One could do nothing else, and he wished it. But before he could be tried he went completely insane, and he's in the asylum now, I believe.'

'And what do you make of it yourself, Doctor?' Tredgold asked, after another pause.

The Doctor leaned forward and knocked out his pipe for the last time against the grate.

'God knows!' he said.

STELLA GIBBONS

ROARING TOWER

My father bent his head to kiss me, but I turned my face away and his lips brushed the edge of my veil instead. Over his shoulder I met my mother's grieved eyes, and my own filled with tears.

I lowered my veil, with trembling fingers, murmured some words which I have now forgotten, and stepped into the compartment, my father holding open the door for me. On the seat in the corner lay a bunch of white roses, a copy of a ladies' journal, and a basket packed with my refreshment for the journey.

My heart was like stone. The roses, picked from the garden of our house in Islington, softened it not a whit. I moved them aside carefully and sank into my corner seat. I said not a word; and my father and mother stood in silence too; how I wished they would go away!

'You will write tomorrow, my child, and tell us what your journey was like and how your Aunt Julia is?' said my mother.

'Yes, Mamma.' My lips felt stiff and cold.

'Remember, Clara, we shall expect you to take full advantage of the Cornish air, and to return to us in a very different frame of mind and quite restored to health.' My father's voice was a warning.

'Yes, Papa.'

I folded my black-gloved hands on my lap, and stared out of the window, avoiding my mother's eyes.

The passions which invade a heart at nineteen, like a beautiful menacing army, seem faded and small enough if one looks back on them after a lapse of fifty years, as I am doing now, but on the late summer morning I describe, as I waited with my parents under the dome of the railway station, no heart could have been fiercer, and yet colder, than mine. One voice, which I should never hear again, sounded in my ears, and one face, which I had promised to forget, filled my eyes.

'All else' (as that German philosopher wrote) 'was folly.'

Well, my parents had parted us; and my heart was broken; and there was no more to be said. I wished the train would start, so that I could be alone.

The journey was uneventful. My Aunt Julia was not wealthy enough to afford a carriage, and when, on the evening of the same day, I got out of the train at the Cornish town of N— I found that I must take a fly to the village two miles hence where she lived, which was near the sea.

I found an ancient carriage, driven by a surly-looking old man in a great cape, and the porter, with this old fellow's help, hoisted my trunk into the driver's seat, gave me a gallant arm into the carriage with a wink at the cabby, and we were off.

We left the town behind; and at last, in twilight, we came to the end of the last lane, and faced a little sandy bay in which broke the waves of the open sea. On the other side of the bay stood the village where my aunt lived.

The horse slackened his pace almost to a walk and the wheels slid in the fine sand as we crossed the bay; the soft sound of the falling waves and the lights shining in the village windows were balm to me.

Suddenly I saw something which – even then – startled and impressed me so much that I leaned forward and plucked at the driver's cape.

'What is that – what are those ruins there, on the left?' I asked, pointing.

He did not turn his head in the direction in which I pointed and

I had some difficulty in hearing his surly, indistinct reply, which came after a pause:

'That be the Roaring Tower,' he said at last, curling his whip round his horse's ribs.

I looked, with a livelier interest than I had looked at any object for months past, at the indistinct outline of the ruined circular tower, which faced the breaking waves, and which was almost covered by a fine bush of wild roses. It was no more than a circular rim of stone, higher at some points than at others, but the circle was unbroken. It stood by itself, in the lowest curve of the low cliff encircling the bay.

I remember that I sat upright in the swaying carriage, as we drew nearer to the village, and eagerly studied the tower until a curve in the cliff hid it from sight; and even when it had disappeared, I saw it plainly in my mind's eye, like the dazzling memory of a light after it has gone out.

My Aunt Julia's greeting was kindly but reserved, as befitted a welcome to a troublesome and headstrong niece who had been so imprudent as to bestow her affections on an unsuitable wooer. I was given to understand that my month's stay with her was not to be a time of idle repining – 'mooning,' I remember she called my listless air. I was to help her with hemming sheets, with her fowls, and with her garden.

But after I had made my bed in the mornings, tidied my room, and helped Bessie to feed the fowls my time was my own until midday dinner; and this was the time I liked best of all – as much, that is, as I liked any 'time' in those unhappy days.

I clambered from rock to rock, waded through pools in a bitter dream, and saw with unseeing, unhappy eyes the conservatories and hothouses of the sea, green fronds and purple and red, swaying below me in innocent beauty.

But I only grieved the more to see them. Was I not alone in the midst of beauty, and would be so for ever? And my heart grew harder, my tongue less apt to exclaim or praise, and my thoughts turned every day more and more inward upon myself.

The Roaring Tower, which, you may be sure, was the first place I visited on the first day of my stay, became my favourite haunt. Its rose-bush was in fullest flower, and no matter at what time of the day I visited it, the first sound I heard as I flung myself down on the parching grass, breathless with my climb up the cliffside, was the sustained, slumberous drone of the wild bees, ravaging the open chalices of the roses.

I have written 'the first sound I heard.'

But there was another sound.

I learned, before I had been staying with Aunt Julia a week, whence the Tower got its strange name.

It was the noon of a burning and cloudless day. I was returning languidly along the cliff-edge from a walk to a village which lay inland, swinging my hat in my hand, my eyes half closed against the waving glitter of the grass and the smiting glitter of the sea.

I was not thinking of anything in particular, not even of my sorrow; my mind lay like a black marsh under the sun – flowerless, stagnant. If there was a thought hovering at the back of my head (I can write it now with a smile) it was a hopeful surmise that there might be fresh fish for dinner. But had I been taxed with this I should have denied it with anger. I hugged my grief; it was all I had. Nothing could heal it; it was a deathless wound.

Alas! the bitterest lesson I have since learned is how gently and remorselessly Time steals even our dearest wounds from us.

As I drew near the Tower I glanced, as usual, in its direction. A little group of village people stood about it, the women clustering together at some distance, the men scattered round it in a broken circle, like a doubtful advance guard.

As I drew near I heard an indescribable sound which seemed to come from no particular spot but from the whole surrounding air, which I thought at first (for lack of better knowledge) to be the drone of bees in swarm.

It was a soft, hollow, furious roaring, such a sound as a giant distant waterfall might make; the sound I have heard that great hunter, my Uncle Max, describe when he told us how his heart would shake in his body to hear, in the dead of night, the solemn far-off voices of lions at their wooing and hunting in the starlit desert.

The sound rose and fell in waves, exactly as the roaring of an animal rises and falls.

As I advanced over the grass, intending to ask one of the women what was amiss, I saw my own inward uneasiness reflected in the sly, downward glances of the village people.

'What is it? What's the matter?' I asked sharply of a woman near me. 'What is that strange noise?'

She hesitated, glancing appealingly at the man by her side, but he avoided her eyes. I repeated my question imperiously.

'It's only the Roaring Tower,' she said at last, reluctantly. 'When the rose-bush is all out, and on sweltering hot days, miss, the Tower roars, like you can hear.'

'But what is it? What makes that awful sound?'

Again there was silence. The other villagers were looking curiously at me; a few of them drew slowly near to our little group, but no one attempted to answer me.

At length, from the back of the group, a man's doubtful voice volunteered:

'They say it's the water under the Tower, miss. There's a great cave under the Tower, so they say, and when the tide gets into it it makes that noise.'

There were one or two half-hearted assents to this.

But I was not satisfied; the explanation was plausible and yet unconvincing. But the uneasy manner of the villagers and their inquisitive eyes repelled me, and I hastened to leave the spot.

I had been with Aunt Julia a week when one morning I went out into the kitchen to give Bessie some linen which she had promised to wash for me.

She was not there, but at a corner of the kitchen table sat a little fair-haired girl, busy with paper and pencils, which she used from a painted box at her elbow. This was Jennie, Bessie's niece, whom my aunt allowed to play in the kitchen as she was a good, quiet child.

'Good morning, Miss Clara,' she whispered, looking shyly at me.

'Where is your aunt, Jennie?' I asked, impatiently; I wanted to be off to the seashore. 'She must wash these ruffles for me today, I shall need them for church tomorrow.'

'She's gone to market, Miss Clara, and won't be back for an hour or more.'

'Then it's very forgetful and careless of her. They will never be dry and pressed in time for tomorrow. Give them to her as soon as she comes in, Jennie, and say I must have them by this evening.'

But just as I was flouncing out of the kitchen, my annoyance increased by Jennie's solemn, timid stare, I stopped suddenly and picked up her pencil-box from the table.

'Why – there's the Roaring Tower!' I said, half to myself in a new voice, full of the pleasure I felt at the sight of the picture painted on the lid of the box. 'Where did you get this, Jennie? Who painted it? And what's this queer creature with the snout, close to the Tower?'

'Davy gave me that,' drawled Jennie. 'Daft Davy, they call him. He's not right in the head. He painted the box for me with that queer beast. And Davy said he's seen it.'

I stared at her, and back at the box, wondering where the weak-minded old man could have found his model for the gross, long-snouted monster with four brown paws which he had painted squatting close to the Tower.

'You mustn't tell lies, Jennie. It's wicked,' I said, primly.

'But Davy *has* seen it, Miss Clara,' Jennie persisted. 'Long ago, when he was a little boy. That's the noise we hears, coming out of the Tower, when the rose-bush is all out. That's why it's called the Roaring Tower. It's that poor bear-thing, shut up in there, and he can't get away, Davy says.'

I continued to stare at her. She did not seem at all frightened; one little hand was posed over her drawing, as though she was about to go on with her game.

'Well—' I said at last, drawing a deep breath, 'you are a very wicked little girl to repeat Davy's lies, Jennie. You ought to be ashamed of yourself.' But my voice did not sound so severe as I should have liked.

'Yes, Miss Clara. I'm sorry,' whispered Jennie, anxiously, and then I went towards the door. But at the door I paused, and called back to her, curiously:

'Weren't you frightened, Jennie, when Davy told you about it?'

'Oh, no, Miss Clara,' she replied, sedately. 'He don't hurt people, that bear-thing don't. Everyone's afeard of him round here, and no one's sorry for him a bit, but he don't hurt people. He only wants to get away home, Davy says.'

Well, after such a talk between us, where should my steps go but towards the Tower, that afternoon, when my aunt was taking her nap in the garden?

I crossed the sands, and climbed the gentle slope towards it. There it was, half-mantled with its rose-bush, its very stones steeped in quivering heat and silence. Bees droned in the flowers and butterflies reeled above the higher branches.

I crossed the grass and mounted the fallen stone which I always used as a step whenever I wanted to look down on to the circle of grass inside the Tower.

In the early morning the rose-bush and the wall cast a lop-sided shadow half-way across the grass, and at sunset the shadow reappeared on the other side, but now, at high noon, when I looked down on the grass, it was shadowless, clear and deep as emeralds.

I leaned my elbows on the broken stone rim and stared downwards. My thoughts were vague. Certainly, I was not afraid, and this now seems strange to me, for Daft Davy's drawing depicted a beast that was enough to put queer thoughts into the mind of a better-balanced girl than I was.

But all I felt, idling there in the heat and drowsy silence, was a kind of mischievous curiosity, and a return of the inexplicable pity I had experienced when I heard the Tower at its roaring.

As I lingered, more asleep than awake, an infinitely soft tremor began to jar in the air, scarce distinguishable from the far-off rumour of the sea, and it grew in volume, rising above the sound of the waves and the bees until it dominated them entirely, and I realised that the Tower was roaring, and that I stood, like a swimmer on a sea-girt spit of sand, in the full tide of its sound.

Then, indeed, my heart began to beat a little faster. I glanced quickly over my shoulder, and took my elbows from the wall, and prepared for flight.

But I did not go – I stayed, and no one was more surprised than myself. For pity had come back into my heart; that astonishing, irrational pity for a mere sound which I had felt before.

I hesitated on my stone pedestal, gripping the wall with one hand, and peering down into the silent pit of green. There was nothing there, of course. The grass burned coolly in the sunlight, the bees hung among the roses. And the soft, piteous sound roared about me in waves, abandoned, despairing.

Frightened and moved as I was, I did a strange thing. I hung over that empty pit, calling softly: 'Can you hear me? Poor soul! Poor tormented creature! Can I help you? I would if I could.'

The foolish words, banal and human, faltered back from the airy but impassable wall of beauty presented by rose-bush and glimmering grass. I called again, over the ominous hollow:

'Listen! I am here. I would pray for you, if prayers would help you. You poor, lost thing, you! You have a friend left on earth, if you care to have her. I will do what I can . . .'

My eyes streamed with the first unselfish tears I had shed for months. Scarce knowing what I did, I put my hands firmly on the wall, and vaulted the low drop into the hollow. Heaven alone knows what purpose I thought that would serve!

I landed with a jarring shock, staggered forward, and fell on my hands and knees in the grass. I was conscious that all I could see of the familiar world I had left was a rough circle of bluest sky, against which the rose-bush moved in the wind.

All about me, stunning the ears with soft reiteration, rose and fell the voice of Roaring Tower.

'Well!' I said aloud, shakily, scrambling to my feet, and standing with my back almost touching the wall as though I were at bay.

'Here I am, in the middle of things, with a vengeance. I must go through with it now.'

But the words were unnecessarily bold. Nothing happened, not even the catastrophe expected. These feelings, relieved by my shower of tears, slowly grew calmer. The roaring seemed to be dying down in long exhausted peals of sound, or else my ears were growing used to it.

'Of course. The tide is going out,' I murmured, walking slowly round the circle of grass, brushing the wall with the tips of my fingers. 'How silly of me.' I blushed for my tears and pity of a few moments ago.

My prison was not really a prison. I knew I could get out the moment I wanted to by scrambling up the six feet or so of rough wall, which provided more footholds than I needed. But I liked to linger there, shut away from the world in the sunshine and silence. I sat down on the grass, under the overhanging mass of the rose-bush, and leaned back against the wall with a tired sigh.

How deep the quiet was! For now the roaring had ceased. Not a bee droned, not a butterfly stirred. The air of summer, cooled in this pit of silence, smelled sweet.

It would be easy for me to write at this point, 'I must have fallen asleep.'

But I know, as I know that my body must soon die, that I did not sleep, even for a few seconds. I was awake, wide awake. And I saw what I saw.

A shadow rose from the emerald grass.

It was brown, and large, larger by many times than I was, and at first it seemed like a thickening of the air immediately above the grass, and I blinked my eyes once or twice, thinking they were still dim from my recent tears. But the shadow persisted. It grew darker and thicker, and began to take shape. It was squat, obese, crouching, with a small head sunk between its shoulders, a long snout, and four paws drawn up ratlike against its furred sides.

I bent forward, blinking my eyes again; I even rubbed them with my fists, but the shadow did not move. And as I watched it, the faint sound jarred again on the still air, rose to a rumour of noise, fell to a whisper, and rose again.

The Tower was roaring, and the sound came from the throat of the monster before me, with its head flung back. The creature – vision, spectre, whatever it may have been – turned its head from side to side as it roared, as though in extremity of anguish; I caught the glint of its oblique eyes as the head swayed.

Did the monster look at me? Strange question, with more than a hint of ludicrousness! How can one speak, in sober earnest, of looks exchanged between a dweller in this world and a visitor from some world at which I cannot even guess? But it seems to me, remembering, that the beast recognized my presence there, for soon it made a blundering, circular movement and turned its head towards me, still roaring piteously, as though entreating my help.

So we faced each other, I and the Voice of Roaring Tower, and as I looked, every feeling driven from my heart suddenly flooded back in a huge wave of pity.

I held out my hands, I spoke to the monstrosity before me as though it could understand: 'Is there anything I can do?' I whispered. 'Shall I fetch a clergyman?'

But even as the foolish words left my dry lips the brown shadow changed.

I cannot describe what followed. I am only a human being; the pen of one of Milton's archangels would be needed for that.

The shadow streamed upwards, melting as it streamed. It seemed to be drawn straight into the zenith, sucked by some invisible strength.

I had, for a terrifying flash of time, a glimpse of huge wings, feathered with copper plumes from tip to tip, of a face crowned with hair like springing rays of gold, a wild face, smiling down on me in ecstasy, of a sexless body, veined again with gold as a leaf is veined. A blinding shock passed through my frame, which may have been (may the creature's God forgive me if I blaspheme) an embrace of gratitude.

Then it had gone. It had gone as though I had never seen it.

There was nothing left. The Roaring Tower was empty as a sun-dried bone; I could feel that, as I sat with my eyes now closed. Virtue had gone out of the very roses; they were mysterious only with the mystery of all growing things.

Presently I roused myself, and after several attempts climbed out of the Roaring Tower.

Weak as a kitten, I sauntered home by the sea's margin. The crisping foam ran to my feet; I could trace its snow under my tired, lowered lids. The slow, strong sea wind, blowing along the evening clouds, smoothed my cheeks. I thought of nothing. My mind was calm as the sands stretched before me.

I was not unhappy any more. I looked at the great sky, the sand, the darkening sea, the flower-fringed cliffs, and thought, with tired pleasure, how rich I was in having many, many years before me in which to love their beauty.

For now they belonged to me, as all beauty did. This was the gift of that terrible spirit I had pitied in the Tower. My pity, I believed, had released it, and in return it had swept personal sorrow out of my heart, and made me free of all beauty.

I felt strangely impersonal, as (with our human limitations) we imagine a grain of sand or a clover-flower must feel. Light-footed, unthinking, calm, I idled homewards with the homing light.

That was fifty years ago.

During the rest of the time I stayed there, I asked cautious questions of my aunt, Daft Davy, and in the village, but never a shred of a legend could I find that might explain (if explanation were possible) what had happened in Roaring Tower. Davy was terrified, and refused to answer me; and my aunt stared at me as though I had gone mad.

But the gift of Roaring Tower has never left me throughout my long life filled to the brim with sorrow and happiness. Part of me is untouchable; part of me can always escape into the watching, surrounding beauty of the natural world, and be free.

Is it to be wondered at, now I am too old a woman to make con-
cessions to those who believe that this world is the only world we
shall ever inhabit, that I am not afraid to die?

Unhaunted, voiceless, a mere ruin of stones, the Roaring Tower
may stand to this day. But I have never returned there to see.

ELIZABETH BOWEN

THE HAPPY AUTUMN FIELDS

The family walking party, though it comprised so many, did not deploy or straggle over the stubble but kept in a procession of threes and twos. Papa, who carried his Alpine stick, led, flanked by Constance and little Arthur. Robert and Cousin Theodore, locked in studious talk, had Emily attached but not quite abreast. Next came Digby and Lucius, taking, to left and right, imaginary aim at rooks. Henrietta and Sarah brought up the rear.

It was Sarah who saw the others ahead on the blond stubble, who knew them, knew what they were to each other, knew their names and knew her own. It was she who felt the stubble under her feet, and who heard it give beneath the tread of the others a continuous different more distant soft stiff scrunch. The field and all these out-lying fields in view knew as Sarah knew that they were Papa's. The harvest had been good and was now in: he was satisfied – for this afternoon he had made the instinctive choice of his most womanly daughter, most nearly infant son. Arthur, whose hand Papa was holding, took an anxious hop, a skip and a jump to every stride of the great man's. As for Constance – Sarah could often see the flash of her hat-feather as she turned her head, the curve of her close bodice as she turned her torso. Constance gave Papa her attention but not her thoughts, for she had already been sought in marriage.

The landowners' daughters, from Constance down, walked with

their beetle-green, mole or maroon skirts gathered up and carried clear of the ground, but for Henrietta, who was still ankle-free. They walked inside a continuous stuffy sound, but left silence behind them. Behind them, rooks that had risen and circled, sun striking blue from their blue-black wings, planed one by one to the earth and settled to peck again. Papa and the boys were dark-clad as the rooks but with no sheen, but for their white collars.

It was Sarah who located the thoughts of Constance, knew what a twisting prisoner was Arthur's hand, felt to the depths of Emily's pique at Cousin Theodore's inattention, rejoiced with Digby and Lucius at the imaginary fall of so many rooks. She fell back, however, as from a rocky range, from the converse of Robert and Cousin Theodore. Most she knew that she swam with love at the nearness of Henrietta's young and alert face and eyes which shone with the sky and queried the afternoon.

She recognized the colour of valediction, tasted sweet sadness, while from the cottage inside the screen of trees wood-smoke rose melting pungent and blue. This was the eve of the brothers' return to school. It was like a Sunday; Papa had kept the late afternoon free; all (all but one) encircling Robert, Digby and Lucius, they walked the estate the brothers would not see again for so long. Robert, it could be felt, was not unwilling to return to his books; next year he would go to college like Theodore; besides, to all this they saw he was not the heir. But in Digby and Lucius aiming and popping hid a bodily grief, the repugnance of victims, though these two were further from being heirs than Robert.

Sarah said to Henrietta: 'To think they will not be here tomorrow!'

'*Is* that what you are thinking about?' Henrietta asked, with her subtle taste for the truth.

'More, I was thinking that you and I will be back again by one another at table . . .'

'You know we are always sad when the boys are going, but we are never sad when the boys have gone.' The sweet reciprocal guilty smile that started on Henrietta's lips finished on those of Sarah.

'Also,' the young sister said, 'we know this is only something happening again. It happened last year, and it will happen next. But oh how should I feel, and how should you feel, if it were something that had not happened before?'

'For instance, when Constance goes to be married?'

'Oh, I don't mean *Constance*!' said Henrietta.

'So long,' said Sarah, considering, 'as, whatever it is, it happens to both of us?' She must never have to wake in the early morning except to the birdlike stirrings of Henrietta, or have her cheek brushed in the dark by the frill of another pillow in whose hollow did not repose Henrietta's cheek. Rather than they should cease to lie in the same bed she prayed they might lie in the same grave. 'You and I will stay as we are,' she said, 'then nothing can touch one without touching the other.'

'So you say; so I hear you say!' exclaimed Henrietta, who then, lips apart, sent Sarah her most tormenting look. 'But I cannot forget that you chose to be born without me; that you would not wait—' But here she broke off, laughed outright and said: 'Oh, *see*!'

Ahead of them there had been a dislocation. Emily took advantage of having gained the ridge to kneel down to tie her bootlace so abruptly that Digby all but fell over her, with an exclamation. Cousin Theodore had been civil enough to pause beside Emily, but Robert, lost to all but what he was saying, strode on, head down, only just not colliding into Papa and Constance, who had turned to look back. Papa, astounded, let go of Arthur's hand, whereupon Arthur fell flat on the stubble.

'Dear me,' said the affronted Constance to Robert.

Papa said: 'What is the matter there? May I ask, Robert, where you are going, sir? Digby, remember that is your sister Emily.'

'Cousin Emily is in trouble,' said Cousin Theodore.

Poor Emily, telescoped in her skirts and by now scarlet under her hatbrim, said in a muffled voice: 'It is just my bootlace, Papa.'

'Your bootlace, Emily?'

'I was just tying it.'

'Then you had better tie it. – Am I to think,' said Papa, looking round them all, 'that you must all go down like a pack of ninepins because Emily has occasion to stoop?'

At this Henrietta uttered a little whoop, flung her arms round Sarah, buried her face in her sister and fairly suffered with laughter. She could contain this no longer; she shook all over. Papa, who found Henrietta so hopelessly out of order that he took no notice of her except at table, took no notice, simply giving the signal for the others to collect themselves and move on. Cousin Theodore, helping Emily to her feet, could be seen to see how her heightened colour became her, but she dispensed with his hand chillily, looked elsewhere, touched the brooch at her throat and said: 'Thank you, I have not sustained an accident.' Digby apologized to Emily, Robert to Papa and Constance. Constance righted Arthur, flicking his breeches over with her handkerchief. All fell into their different steps and resumed their way.

Sarah, with no idea how to console laughter, coaxed, 'Come, come, come,' into Henrietta's ear. Between the girls and the others the distance widened; it began to seem that they would be left alone.

'And why not?' said Henrietta, lifting her head in answer to Sarah's thought.

They looked around them with the same eyes. The shorn uplands seemed to float on the distance, which extended dazzling to tiny blue glassy hills. There was no end to the afternoon, whose light went on ripening now they had scythed the corn. Light filled the silence which, now Papa and the others were out of hearing, was complete. Only screens of trees intersected and knolls made islands in the vast fields. The mansion and the home farm had sunk for ever below them in the expanse of woods, so that hardly a ripple showed where the girls dwelled.

The shadow of the same rook circling passed over Sarah then over Henrietta, who in their turn cast one shadow across the stubble. 'But, Henrietta, we cannot stay here for ever.'

Henrietta immediately turned her eyes to the only lonely plume of smoke, from the cottage. 'Then let us go and visit the poor old man. He is dying and the others are happy. One day we shall pass and see no more smoke; then soon his roof will fall in, and we shall always be sorry we did not go today.'

'But he no longer remembers us any longer.'

'All the same, he will feel us there in the door.'

'But can we forget this is Robert's and Digby's and Lucius's good-bye walk? It would be heartless of both of us to neglect them.'

'Then how heartless Fitzgeorge is!' smiled Henrietta.

'Fitzgeorge is himself, the eldest and in the Army. Fitzgeorge I'm afraid is not an excuse for us.'

A resigned sigh, or perhaps the pretence of one, heaved up Henrietta's still narrow bosom. To delay matters for just a moment more she shaded her eyes with one hand, to search the distance like a sailor looking for a sail. She gazed with hope and zeal in every direction but that in which she and Sarah were bound to go. Then – 'Oh, but Sarah, here *they* are, coming – they are!' she cried. She brought out her handkerchief and began to fly it, drawing it to and fro through the windless air.

In the glass of the distance, two horsemen came into view, can-tering on a grass track between the fields. When the track dropped into a hollow they dropped with it, but by now the drumming of hoofs was heard. The reverberation filled the land, the silence and Sarah's being; not watching for the riders to reappear she instead fixed her eyes on her sister's handkerchief which, let hang limp while its owner intently waited, showed a bitten corner as well as a damson stain. Again it became a flag, in furious motion – 'Wave too, Sarah, wave too! Make your bracelet flash!'

'They must have seen us if they will ever see us,' said Sarah, standing still as a stone.

Henrietta's waving at once ceased. Facing her sister she crunched up her handkerchief, as though to stop it acting a lie. 'I can see you are shy,' she said in a dead voice. 'So shy you won't even wave to *Fitzgeorge?*'

Her way of not speaking the *other* name had a hundred meanings; she drove them all in by the way she did not look at Sarah's face. The impulsive breath she had caught stole silently out again, while her eyes – till now at their brightest, their most speaking – dulled with uncomprehending solitary alarm. The ordeal of awaiting Eugene's approach thus became for Sarah, from moment to moment, torture.

Fitzgeorge, Papa's heir, and his friend Eugene, the young neighbouring squire, struck off the track and rode up at a trot with their hats doffed. Sun striking low turned Fitzgeorge's flesh to coral and made Eugene blink his dark eyes. The young men reined in; the girls looked up at the horses. 'And my father, Constance, the others?' Fitzgeorge demanded, as though the stubble had swallowed them.

'Ahead, on the way to the quarry, the other side of the hill.'

'We heard you were all walking together,' Fitzgeorge said, seeming dissatisfied.

'We are following.'

'What, alone?' said Eugene, speaking for the first time.

'Forlorn!' glittered Henrietta, raising two mocking hands.

Fitzgeorge considered, said 'Good' severely, and signified to Eugene that they would ride on. But too late: Eugene had dismounted. Fitzgeorge saw, shrugged and flicked his horse to a trot; but Eugene led his slowly between the sisters. Or rather, Sarah walked on his left hand, the horse on his right and Henrietta the other side of the horse. Henrietta, acting like somebody quite alone, looked up at the sky, idly holding one of the empty stirrups. Sarah, however, looked at the ground, with Eugene inclined as though to speak but not speaking. Enfolded, dizzied, blinded as though inside a wave, she could feel his features carved in brightness above her. Alongside the slender stepping of his horse, Eugene matched his naturally long free step to hers. His elbow was through the reins; with his fingers he brushed back the lock that his bending to her had sent falling over his forehead. She recorded the sublime act and knew what smile shaped his lips. So each without looking trembled before an image, while slow colour burned up the curves of her cheeks. The consummation would be when their eyes met.

At the other side of the horse, Henrietta began to sing. At once her pain, like a scientific ray, passed through the horse and Eugene to penetrate Sarah's heart.

We surmount the skyline: the family come into our view, we into theirs. They are halted, waiting, on the decline to the quarry. The handsome statufied group in strong yellow sunshine, aligned by Papa and crowned by Fitzgeorge, turn their judging eyes on the laggards, waiting to close their ranks round Henrietta and Sarah and Eugene. One more moment and it will be too late; no further communication will be possible. Stop oh stop Henrietta's heartbreaking singing! Embrace her close again! Speak the only possible word! Say – oh, say what? Oh, the word is lost!

'Henrietta . . .'

A shock of striking pain in the knuckles of the outflung hand – Sarah's? The eyes, opening, saw that the hand had struck, not been struck: there was a corner of a table. Dust, whitish and gritty, lay on the top of the table and on the telephone. Dull but piercing white light filled the room and what was left of the ceiling; her first thought was that it must have snowed. If so, it was winter now.

Through the calico stretched and tacked over the window came the sound of a piano: someone was playing Tchaikowsky badly in a room without windows or doors. From somewhere else in the hollowness came a cascade of hammering. Close up, a voice: 'Oh, *awake*, Mary?' It came from the other side of the open door, which jutted out between herself and the speaker – he on the threshold, she lying on the uncovered mattress of a bed. The speaker added: 'I had been going away.'

Summoning words from somewhere she said: 'Why? I didn't know you were here.'

'Evidently – Say, who is "Henrietta"?'

Despairing tears filled her eyes. She drew back her hurt hand, began to suck at the knuckle and whimpered, 'I've hurt myself'.

A man she knew to be 'Travis', but failed to focus, came round the door saying: 'Really I don't wonder.' Sitting down on the edge of the mattress he drew her hand away from her lips and held it:

the act, in itself gentle, was accompanied by an almost hostile stare of concern. 'Do listen, Mary,' he said. 'While you've slept I've been all over the house again, and I'm less than ever satisfied that it's safe. In your normal sense you'd never attempt to stay here. There've been alerts, and more than alerts, all day; one more bang anywhere near, which may happen at any moment, could bring the rest of this down. You keep telling me that you have things to see to – but do you know what chaos the rooms are in? Till they've gone ahead with more clearing, where can you hope to start? And if there *were* anything you could do, you couldn't do it. Your own nerves know that, if you don't: it was almost frightening, when I looked in just now, to see the way you were sleeping – you've shut up shop.'

She lay staring over his shoulder at the calico window. He went on: 'You don't like it here. Your self doesn't like it. Your will keeps driving your self, but it can't be driven the whole way – it makes its own get-out: sleep. Well, I want you to sleep as much as you (really) do. But *not* here. So I've taken a room for you in a hotel; I'm going now for a taxi; you can practically make the move without waking up.'

'No, I can't get into a taxi without waking.'

'Do you realize you're the last soul left in the terrace?'

'Then who is that playing the piano?'

'Oh, one of the furniture-movers in Number Six. I didn't count the jaquerie; of course *they're* in possession – unsupervised, teeming, having a high old time. While I looked in on you in here ten minutes ago they were smashing out that conservatory at the other end. Glass being done in in cold blood – it was brutalizing. You never batted an eyelid; in fact, I thought you smiled.' He listened. 'Yes, the piano – they are highbrow all right. You know there's a workman downstairs lying on your blue sofa looking for pictures in one of your French books?'

'No,' she said, 'I've no idea who is there.'

'Obviously. With the lock blown off your front door anyone who likes can get in and out.'

'Including you.'

'Yes. I've had a word with a chap about getting that lock back before tonight. As for you, you don't know what is happening.'

'I did,' she said, locking her fingers before her eyes.

The unreality of this room and of Travis's presence preyed on her as figments of dreams that one knows to be dreams can do. This environment's being in semi-ruin struck her less than its being some sort of device or trap; and she rejoiced, if anything, in its decrepitude. As for Travis, he had his own part in the conspiracy to keep her from the beloved two. She felt he began to feel he was now unmeaning. She was struggling not to condemn him, scorn him for his ignorance of Henrietta, Eugene, her loss. His possessive angry fondness was part, of course, of the story of him and Mary, which like a book once read she remembered clearly but with indifference. Frantic at being delayed here, while the moment awaited her in the cornfield, she all but afforded a smile at the grotesquerie of being saddled with Mary's body and lover. Rearing up her head from the bare pillow, she looked, as far as the crossed feet, along the form inside which she found herself trapped: the irrelevant body of Mary, weighted down to the bed, wore a short black modern dress, flaked with plaster. The toes of the black suède shoes by their sickly whiteness showed Mary must have climbed over fallen ceilings; dirt engraved the fate-lines in Mary's palms.

This inspired her to say: 'But I've made a start; I've been pulling out things of value or things I want.'

For answer Travis turned to look down, expressively, at some object out of her sight, on the floor close by the bed. '*I see*,' he said, 'a musty old leather box gaping open with God knows what – junk, illegible letters, diaries, yellow photographs, chiefly plaster and dust. Of all things, Mary! – after a missing will?'

'Everything one unburies seems the same age.'

'Then what are these, where do they come from – family stuff?'

'No idea,' she yawned into Mary's hand. 'They may not even be mine. Having a house like this that had empty rooms must have made me store more than I knew, for years. I came on these, so I wondered. Look if you like.'

He bent and began to go through the box – it seemed to her, not unsuspiciously. While he blew grit off packets and fumbled with tapes she lay staring at the exposed laths of the ceiling, calculating. She then said: 'Sorry if I've been cranky, about the hotel and all. Go away just for two hours, then come back with a taxi, and I'll go quiet. Will that do?'

'Fine – except why not now?'

'Travis . . .'

'Sorry. It shall be as you say . . . You've got some good morbid stuff in this box, Mary – so far as I can see at a glance. The photographs seem more your sort of thing. Comic but lyrical. All of one set of people – a beard, a gun and a pot hat, a schoolboy with a moustache, a phaeton drawn up in front of mansion, a group on steps, a *carte de visite* of two young ladies hand-in-hand in front of a painted field—'

'*Give that to me!*'

She instinctively tried, and failed, to unbutton the bosom of Mary's dress: it offered no hospitality to the photograph. So she could only fling herself over on the mattress, away from Travis, covering the two faces with her body. Racked by that oblique look of Henrietta's she recorded, too, a sort of personal shock at having seen Sarah for the first time.

Travis's hand came over her, and she shuddered. Wounded, he said: 'Mary . . .'

'Can't you leave *me* alone?'

She did not move or look till he had gone out saying: 'Then, in two hours.' She did not therefore see him pick up the dangerous box, which he took away under his arm, out of her reach.

They were back. Now the sun was setting behind the trees, but its rays passed dazzling between the branches into the beautiful warm red room. The tips of the ferns in the jardiniere curled gold, and Sarah, standing by the jardiniere, pinched at a leaf of scented geranium. The carpet had a great centre wreath of pomegranates, on which no tables or chairs stood, and its whole circle was between herself and the others.

No fire was lit yet, but where they were grouped was a hearth. Henrietta sat on a low stool, resting her elbow above her head on the arm of Mamma's chair, looking away intently as though into a fire, idle. Mamma embroidered, her needle slowed down by her thoughts; the length of tatting with roses she had already done overflowed stiffly over her supple skirts. Stretched on the rug at Mamma's feet, Arthur looked through an album of Swiss views, not liking them but vowed to be very quiet. Sarah, from where she stood, saw fuming cataracts and null eternal snows as poor Arthur kept turning over the pages, which had tissue paper between.

Against the white marble mantelpiece stood Eugene. The dark red shadows gathering in the drawing-room as the trees drowned more and more of the sun would reach him last, perhaps never: it seemed to Sarah that a lamp was lighted behind his face. He was the only gentleman with the ladies: Fitzgeorge had gone to the stables, Papa to give an order; Cousin Theodore was consulting a dictionary; in the gunroom Robert, Lucius and Digby went through the sad rites, putting away their guns. All this was known to go on but none of it could be heard.

This particular hour of subtle light – not to be fixed by the clock, for it was early in winter and late in summer and in spring and autumn now, about Arthur's bedtime – had always, for Sarah, been Henrietta's. To be with her indoors or out, upstairs or down, was to share the same crepitation. Her spirit ran on past yours with a laughing shiver into an element of its own. Leaves and branches and mirrors in empty rooms became animate. The sisters rustled and scampered and concealed themselves where nobody else was in play that was full of fear, fear that was full of play. Till, by dint of making each other's hearts beat violently, Henrietta so wholly and Sarah so nearly lost all human reason that Mamma had been known to look at them searchingly as she sat instated for evening among the calm amber lamps.

But now Henrietta had locked the hour inside her breast. By spending it seated beside Mamma, in young imitation of Constance the Society daughter, she disclaimed for ever anything else. It had always been she who with one fierce act destroyed any toy that might be outgrown. She sat with straight back, poising her cheek remotely against her finger. Only by never looking at Sarah did she admit their eternal loss.

Eugene, not long returned from a foreign tour, spoke of travel, addressing himself to Mamma, who thought but did not speak of her wedding journey. But every now and then she had to ask Henrietta to pass the scissors or tray of carded wools, and Eugene seized every such moment to look at Sarah. Into eyes always brilliant with melancholy he dared begin to allow no other expression. But this in itself declared the conspiracy of still undeclared love. For her part she looked at him as though he, transfigured by the strange light, were indeed a picture, a picture who could not see her. The wallpaper now flamed scarlet behind his shoulder. Mamma, Henrietta, even unknowing Arthur were in no hurry to raise their heads.

Henrietta said: 'If I were a man I should take my bride to Italy.'

'There are mules in Switzerland,' said Arthur.

'Sarah,' said Mamma, who turned in her chair mildly, 'where are you, my love; do you never mean to sit down?'

'To Naples,' said Henrietta.

'Are you not thinking of Venice?' said Eugene.

'No,' returned Henrietta, 'why should I be? I should like to climb the volcano. But then I am not a man, and am still less likely ever to be a bride.'

'Arthur . . .' Mamma said.

'Mamma?'

'Look at the clock.'

Arthur sighed politely, got up and replaced the album on the circular table, balanced upon the rest. He offered his hand to Eugene, his cheek to Henrietta and to Mamma; then he started towards Sarah, who came to meet him. 'Tell me, Arthur,' she said, embracing him, 'what did you do today?'

Arthur only stared with his button blue eyes. 'You were there too: we went for a walk in the cornfield, with Fitzgeorge on his horse, and I fell down.' He pulled out of her arms and said: 'I must go back to my beetle.' He had difficulty, as always, in turning the handle of the mahogany door. Mamma waited till he had left the room, then said: 'Arthur is quite a man now; he no longer comes running to me when he has hurt himself. Why, I did not even know he had fallen down. Before we know, he will be going away to school too.' She sighed and lifted her eyes to Eugene. 'Tomorrow is to be a sad day.'

Eugene with a gesture signified his own sorrow. The sentiments of Mamma could have been uttered only here in the drawing-room, which for all its size and formality was lyrical and almost exotic. There was a look like velvet in darker parts of the air; sombre window draperies let out gushes of lace; the music on the pianoforte bore tender titles, and the harp though unplayed gleamed in a corner, beyond sofas, whatnots, armchairs, occasional tables that all stood on tottering little feet. At any moment a tinkle might have been struck from the lustres' drops of the brighter day, a vibration from the musical instruments, or a quiver from the fringes and ferns. But the towering vases upon the consoles, the albums piled on the tables, the shells and figurines on the flights of brackets, all had, like the alabaster Leaning Tower of Pisa, an equilibrium of their own. Nothing would fall or change. And everything in the drawing-room was muted, weighted, pivoted by Mamma. When she added: 'We shall not feel quite the same,' it was to be understood that she would not have spoken thus from her place at the opposite end of Papa's table.

'Sarah,' said Henrietta curiously, 'what made you ask Arthur what he had been doing? Surely you have not forgotten today?'

The sisters were seldom known to address or question one another in public; it was taken that they knew each other's minds. Mamma, though untroubled, looked from one to the other. Henrietta continued: 'No day, least of all today, is like any other – surely that must be true?' she said to Eugene. 'You will never forget my waving my handkerchief?'

Before Eugene had composed an answer, she turned to Sarah: 'Or *you*, them riding across the fields?'

Eugene also slowly turned his eyes on Sarah, as though awaiting with something like dread her answer to the question he had not asked. She drew a light little gold chair into the middle of the wreath of the carpet, where no one ever sat, and sat down. She said: 'But since then I think I have been asleep.'

'Charles the First walked and talked half an hour after his head was cut off,' said Henrietta mockingly. Sarah in anguish pressed the palms of her hands together upon a shred of geranium leaf.

'How else,' she said, 'could I have had such a bad dream?'

'That must be the explanation!' said Henrietta.

'A trifle fanciful,' said Mamma.

However rash it might be to speak at all, Sarah wished she knew how to speak more clearly. The obscurity and loneliness of her trouble was not to be borne. How could she put into words the feeling of dislocation, the formless dread that had been with her since she found herself in the drawing-room? The source of both had been what she must call her dream. How could she tell the others with what vehemence she tried to attach her being to each second, not because each was singular in itself, each a drop condensed from the mist of love in the room, but because she apprehended that the seconds were numbered? Her hope was that the others at least half knew. Were Henrietta and Eugene able to understand how completely, how nearly for ever, she had been swept from them, would they not without fail each grasp one of her hands? – She went so far as to throw her hands out, as though alarmed by a wasp. The shred of geranium fell to the carpet.

Mamma, tracing this behaviour of Sarah's to only one cause, could not but think reproachfully of Eugene. Delightful as his conversation had been, he would have done better had he paid this call with the object of interviewing Papa. Turning to Henrietta she asked her to ring for the lamps, as the sun had set.

Eugene, no longer where he had stood, was able to make no gesture towards the bell-rope. His dark head was under the tide of dusk; for, down on one knee on the edge of the wreath, he was feeling over the carpet for what had fallen from Sarah's hand. In the inevitable silence rooks on the return from the fields could be heard streaming over the house; their sound filled the sky and even the room, and it appeared so useless to ring the bell that Henrietta stayed quivering by Mamma's chair. Eugene rose, brought out his fine white handkerchief and, while they watched, enfolded carefully in it what he had just found, then returning the handkerchief to his breast pocket. This was done so deep in the reverie that accompanies any final act that Mamma instinctively murmured to Henrietta: 'But you will be my child when Arthur has gone.'

The door opened for Constance to appear on the threshold. Behind her queenly figure globes approached, swimming in their own light: these were the lamps for which Henrietta had not rung, but these first were put on the hall tables. 'Why, Mamma,' exclaimed Constance, 'I cannot see who is with you!'

'Eugene is with us,' said Henrietta, 'but on the point of asking if he may send for his horse.'

'Indeed?' said Constance to Eugene. 'Fitzgeorge has been asking for you, but I cannot tell where he is now.'

The figures of Emily, Lucius and Cousin Theodore criss-crossed the lamplight there in the hall, to mass behind Constance's in the drawing-room door. Emily, over her sister's shoulder, said: 'Mamma, Lucius wishes to ask you whether for once he may take his guitar to school.' – 'One objection, however,' said Cousin Theodore, 'is that Lucius's trunk is already locked and strapped.' 'Since Robert is taking his box of inks,' said Lucius, 'I do not see why I should not take my guitar.' – 'But Robert,' said Constance, 'will soon be going to college.'

Lucius squeezed past the others into the drawing-room in order to look anxiously at Mamma, who said: 'You have thought of this late; we must go and see.' The others parted to let Mamma, followed by Lucius, out. Then Constance, Emily and Cousin Theodore deployed and sat down in different parts of the drawing-room, to await the lamps.

'I am glad the rooks have done passing over,' said Emily, 'they make me nervous.' – 'Why?' yawned Constance haughtily, 'what do you think could happen?' Robert and Digby silently came in.

Eugene said to Sarah: 'I shall be back tomorrow.'

'But, oh—' she began. She turned to cry: 'Henrietta!'

'Why, what is the matter?' said Henrietta, unseen at the back of the gold chair. 'What could be sooner than tomorrow?'

'But something terrible may be going to happen.'

'There cannot fail to be tomorrow,' said Eugene gravely.

'I will see that there is tomorrow,' said Henrietta.

'You will never let me out of your sight?'

Eugene, addressing himself to Henrietta, said: 'Yes, promise her what she asks.'

Henrietta cried: 'She *is* never out of my sight. Who are you to ask me that, you Eugene? Whatever tries to come between me and Sarah becomes nothing. Yes, come tomorrow, come sooner, come – when you like, but no one will ever be quite alone with Sarah. You do not even know what you are trying to do. It is *you* who are making something terrible happen – Sarah, tell him that that is true! Sarah—'

The others, in the dark in the chairs and sofas, could be felt to turn their judging eyes upon Sarah, who, as once before, could not speak –

– The house rocked: simultaneously the calico window split and more ceiling fell, though not on the bed. The enormous dull sound of the explosion died, leaving a minor trickle of dissolution still to be heard in parts of the house. Until the choking stinging plaster dust had had time to settle, she lay with lips pressed close, nostrils not breathing and eyes shut. Remembering the box, Mary wondered if it had been again buried. No, she found, looking over the edge of the bed: that had been unable to happen because the box was missing. Travis, who must have taken it, would when he came back no doubt explain why. She looked at her watch, which had stopped, which was not surprising; she did not remember winding it for the last two days, but then she could not remember much. Through the torn window appeared the timelessness of an impermeably clouded late summer afternoon.

There being nothing left, she wished he would come to take her to the hotel. The one way back to the fields was barred by Mary's surviving the fall of ceiling. Sarah was right in doubting that there would be tomorrow: Eugene, Henrietta were lost in time to the woman weeping there on the bed, no longer reckoning who she was.

At last she heard the taxi, then Travis hurrying up the littered stairs. 'Mary, you're all right, Mary – *another*?' Such a helpless white face came round the door that she could only hold out her arms and say: 'Yes, but where have *you* been?'

'You said two hours. But I wish—'

'I have missed you.'

'Have you? Do you know you are crying?'

'Yes. How are we to live without natures? We only know inconvenience now, not sorrow. Everything pulverizes so easily because it is rot-dry; one can only wonder that it makes so much noise. The source, the sap must have dried up, or the pulse must have stopped, before you and I were conceived. So much flowed through people; so little flows through us. All we can do is imitate love or sorrow. – Why did you take away my box?'

He only said: 'It is in my office.'

She continued: 'What has happened is cruel: I am left with a fragment torn out of a day, a day I don't even know where or when; and now how am I to help laying that like a pattern against the poor stuff of everything else? – Alternatively, I am a person drained by a dream. I cannot forget the climate of those hours. Or life at that pitch, eventful – not happy, no, but strung like a harp. I have had a sister called Henrietta.'

'And I have been looking inside your box. What else can you expect? – I have had to write off this day, from the work point of view, thanks to you. So could I sit and do nothing for the last two hours? I just glanced through this and that – still, I know the family.'

'You said it was morbid stuff.'

'Did I? I still say it gives off something.'

She said: 'And then there was Eugene.'

'Probably. I don't think I came on much of his except some notes he must have made for Fitzgeorge from some book on scientific farming. Well, there it is: I have sorted everything out and put it back again, all but a lock of hair that tumbled out of a letter I could not trace. So I've got the hair in my pocket.'

'What colour is it?'

'Ash-brown. Of course, it is a bit – desiccated. Do you want it?'

'No,' she said with a shudder. 'Really, Travis, what revenges you take!'

'I didn't look at it that way,' he said puzzled.

'Is the taxi waiting?' Mary got off the bed and, picking her way across the room, began to look about for things she ought to take with her, now and then stopping to brush her dress. She took the mirror out of her bag to see how dirty her face was. 'Travis –' she said suddenly.

'Mary?'

'Only, I –'

'That's all right. Don't let us imitate anything just at present.'

In the taxi, looking out of the window, she said: 'I suppose, then, that I am descended from Sarah?'

'No,' he said, 'that would be impossible. There must be some reason why you should have those papers, but that is not the one. From all negative evidence Sarah, like Henrietta, remained unmarried. I found no mention of either, after a certain date, in the letters of Constance, Robert or Emily, which makes it seem likely both died young. Fitzgeorge refers, in a letter to Robert written in his old age, to some friend of their youth who was thrown from his horse and killed, riding back after a visit to their home. The young man, whose name doesn't appear, was alone; and the evening, which was in autumn, was fine though late. Fitzgeorge wonders, and says he will always wonder, what made the horse shy in those empty fields.'

ROSEMARY TIMPERLEY

THE MISTRESS IN BLACK

The school was deathly quiet and seemed to be deserted. Nervously I approached it from the road, followed a path round the side of the building and came to the main entrance. I tried the door but it was locked, so I rang the bell.

Footsteps approached. The door opened. A tall, pleasant-faced man with a grey moustache stood there.

'Good morning,' I said. 'I'm Miss Anderson. I have an appointment with the Headmistress at ten o'clock.'

'Oh, yes. Come in, Miss. I'm the caretaker.' He stood aside for me to pass and closed the door again. 'If you'll wait here, I'll see if Miss Leonard is ready for you.'

He went along the corridor in front of me, turned to the right and vanished.

With my back to the front door, I looked round the hall. On the wall to my left was a green baize notice-board with a few notices neatly arranged and secured with drawing-pins. I wondered whether that board would still be so tidy when the vacation was over and the children were back. Past the notice-board were swing doors opening on to an empty gymnasium, its equipment idle, its floor shining with polish. The paintwork was fresh and the place looked as if it had just been redecorated. To my right were a number of other doors, closed and mysterious – for everything in an unfamiliar building seems mysterious. And ahead of me, to the left of the corridor and alongside it, was a flight of stairs leading upwards.

My nervousness increased. Interviews always panic me and I really needed this job. Trembling a little, I waited. The silence itself seemed to make a noise in my ears. I listened for the caretaker's returning footsteps.

Suddenly a woman appeared at the top of the stairs and began to descend. She startled me as she had made no sound in her approach, and I was reminded of one of my previous headmistresses whose habit of wearing soft-soled shoes had given her an uncanny ability to turn up silently when she was least expected. This woman on the stairs was pale, dark, very thin, and wearing a black dress unrelieved by any sort of ornament. Unsmiling, she looked at me with beautiful but very unhappy dark eyes.

'Miss Leonard?' I said.

She didn't reply or even pause, merely moved towards the doors of the gymnasium. At the same moment I heard the caretaker's returning footsteps and turned to see him re-enter the corridor.

'This way, dear,' he called. 'Miss Leonard will see you now.'

As I went towards him, I thought I smelt something burning, so hesitated. Again I looked through the glass at the top half of the gymnasium doors. The woman in black was out of sight.

'What's the matter?' The caretaker came up to me. 'Feeling nervous?'

'Yes, I am – but it's not that – I thought I smelt burning.'

He looked at me sharply. 'No, not now,' he said. 'That's all over, and I should know. But I've got a bonfire going in the grounds. Maybe the smoke is blowing this way.'

'That'll be it. Anyway, I can't smell it any more. Was that Miss Leonard I saw a second ago?'

'Where?' he asked.

'On the stairs, then she went into the gymnasium –'

'You're in a proper state of nerves, you are,' he said, as I followed him along the corridor. 'There's no one in the building today except you, me and Miss Leonard, and she's in her office waiting for you. Coming on the staff, are you?'

'I hope so. I've applied for the job of English teacher.'

'Good luck, then,' he said.

We stopped outside a door.

'This is Miss Leonard's room, Miss.' He knocked on the door. A voice called: 'Come in!'

And I went into the Headmistress's room.

Miss Leonard was at her desk, the window behind her. She rose immediately, a plump yet dignified figure with neat white hair and a pink suit which heightened the colour in her cheeks. She was utterly unlike the woman in black.

She smiled. 'Do come right in and sit down, Miss Anderson. I'm glad to see you. It's not easy to find staff at a moment's notice at the end of the autumn term.'

'It's not easy to find a job at this time either,' I said. 'Most schools are fixed up for the whole of the school year.'

'We were too – then suddenly there was a vacancy. Now, you're twenty-five, you have a B.A. degree in English, and two years' teaching experience.' She was looking at my letter of application which lay on her desk.

'That's right, Miss Leonard.'

'You haven't been teaching for the past twelve months. May I ask why?'

'My mother and I went to live in Rome with my sister and her husband, who is Italian. Mother was ill and she wanted to see my sister again before – well, Mother's dead now so I decided to come back to England.'

'And do you know anything about this school?'

'No. I simply answered your advertisement.'

'I'm glad you did.' She picked up a folder of papers and handed it to me. 'In here I've enclosed your timetable for next term and details of syllabus and set books. So you can "do your homework" before you arrive.'

'You mean I've got the job?'

'Yes. Why not?'

'That's marvellous. Thank you.'

We talked for a while then, as she took me back to the main door, she said: 'You'll find the rest of the staff very nice and friendly.'

'I think I've seen one of them already,' I said.

'Really? Which one?'

'I don't know. It was just that she came down the stairs while I was waiting in the hall. She was wearing a black dress.'

Miss Leonard said casually: 'Staff do come back during the vacation sometimes, to collect forgotten property or whatever. Goodbye for the present, Miss Anderson. When you arrive on the first day of term, come to my office and I'll show you the staff room then take you to your first class.'

And the interview was over.

Christmas passed, January began, diligently I studied my folder of information and then, on the night before first day of term, snow fell. My lodgings were a train journey away from the school and on the very morning when I wanted to be punctual, my train stuck. Ice on the points. By the time I reached the school, I was late, and distraught.

Added to this, the school itself looked different under snow. I couldn't even find the path to the main door. I took a wrong path, lost myself wandering round the building, then peered through a classroom window.

Lights were on inside. About thirty-five little girls in white blouses and dark tunics were sitting at their desks and listening to the teacher. That teacher was the dark, thin woman in the black dress whom I had seen before. Fascinated, I stood and gazed. It was like watching a silent play, myself in the outside dark, the actors in the light, playing their parts.

In the front row of the class was a little girl with golden hair falling like bright rain over her shoulders. Next to her was a dark child, her black hair cropped close as a boy's. And next to this one was a child with a mop of red curls.

All the pupils were attentive, but this red-haired child was gazing at the teacher with an expression of adoration. It was touching, yet a little alarming. No human being deserves that much young worship . . .

I retraced my steps along the wrong path in the snow, found the right one and finally reached the entrance door. It was not locked this time. I let myself in and hurried to Miss Leonard's room.

'Come in!' she called in answer to my knock.

As I went in I blurted out: 'I'm so sorry I'm late. It was my train – the snow—'

'Never mind, Miss Anderson. I guessed as much. I'll take you to the staff room.'

She led me up the stairs from the hall, along a first floor corridor, into a room. It was an ordinary staff room – notice-board, lockers, tables, hard chairs, easy chairs, electric fire. The light was on but the room was empty – at least, I thought it was empty at first, then realized that someone was sitting in one of the chairs. I saw her only out of the corner of my eye, and she was in a chair in the far corner of the room, away from the fire; so although I recognized her as the woman in black, I didn't turn to look at her. If I thought anything, it was just that she had a bit of a nerve to leave her class, which I'd seen her teaching a few minutes ago, and come to sit in the staff room – and now she'd been caught out by the entrance of the Headmistress.

Miss Leonard, however, took no notice of her. She said: 'This will be your locker, Miss Anderson. The bell will ring any minute now for the end of first period, then I'll take you to your first class. It's a double-period of English – you'll have seen that from your timetable. Mrs Gage is looking after them at the moment – she's our biology teacher – and she'll be glad to see you as by rights these first two periods should be her free ones. That's why the staffroom is empty.'

But the staff room was not empty. There was the woman in black, looking at me seriously, with those beautiful sad dark eyes . . .

Miss Leonard led the way to my first class. The teacher there looked quickly round as we entered. She was a lively, dark, fairly young woman with eagerly bent shoulders and black-rimmed spectacles. She wore a red sweater and brown skirt.

'Here we are, Mrs Gage,' said Miss Leonard. 'Now you'll get your second free period all right.' She faced the class. 'Now, girls, this is Miss Anderson, your new English teacher. Help her as much as you can, won't you?'

And I too stood facing the class. It was the same class which I had seen through the window only fifteen minutes earlier. There was the child with fair hair in the front row, and the dark one next to her – and . . .

No. It was different. The child with curly red hair was not there. Her desk was empty. And, of course, the teacher was different . . .

Miss Leonard and Mrs Gage left the room. I was on my own with this familiar, unfamiliar class. I spent the next forty minutes or so in trying to get to know them, checking on their set books, and so on, then the bell rang for morning break and I returned to the staffroom.

The chair where the woman in black had been sitting was empty now but other chairs were occupied. The staff had gathered for elevenses. I heard someone say, above the noise of the many voices: 'How does that damned chair get over into the corner like that? Who puts it there?'

'Night cleaners have strange ways,' said another voice.

'Extraordinary about night cleaners,' said the first. 'They work here for years, and so do we – and which of us are the ghosts? We co-exist, but never meet.'

A woman in an overall came in with a tray bearing a pot of coffee and cups and saucers. Mrs Gage came over to me. 'Coffee, Miss Anderson?'

'Oh – thank you.'

'How do you like it?'

'Black. No sugar.'

'Same here.' She collected coffee for us both.

'Sorry you missed a free period because of me,' I said. 'My train got held up in the snow.'

'That's all right.'

Sipping my coffee, I studied the other women around me.

'Doesn't everyone come here for coffee at break?' I asked Mrs Gage.

'Everyone! It's only our elevenses that keep us going.'

'Then where is – well – one of the teachers? She was taking your class – my class – this morning – I saw her through the window –'

'Not that class,' said Mrs Gage. 'I started with them immediately after morning assembly.'

'But it *was* that class. I recognized some of the girls. And the one with red hair wasn't there.'

Mrs Gage looked at me sympathetically. 'You're all upset over being late, aren't you? And maybe you're upset for other reasons too. I don't blame you. It's not easy to be taking Miss Carey's place.'

'Miss Carey? Who –' But as I tried to ask more, the woman in the overall came to collect our dirty cups and the bell rang for third period. We all went off to our classes.

I still had one more period with the same class I'd taken before – or so I thought, until I reached the room. Then I saw that the teacher's chair was already occupied.

The woman in black sat there.

And the child with red hair was in the third desk in the front row.

'Sorry,' I murmured, withdrew again, and stood in the corridor to re-examine my timetable. Surely I hadn't made a mistake – no – I was right – this was my class. So I went back. And the teacher's chair was empty now. So was the third desk in the front row . . .

That was when I began to be afraid. So afraid that a sick shiver travelled down my spine, sweat sprang out on my skin, and I needed all my self-control to face the class and give a lesson.

At the end of the lesson, when the bell rang for next period, I asked the class in general: 'Where's the girl who sits there?' I indicated the third desk in the front row.

No one answered. The children became unnaturally quiet and stared at me.

'Well?' I said.

Then the fair-haired child said: 'No one sits there, Miss.' And the dark child next to her added: 'That was Joan's desk.'

'But where is Joan?'

Silence again.

Then Mrs Gage walked in. 'Hello, Miss Anderson. We seem to be playing Box and Cox this morning. Do you know which class to go to for last period?'

'Yes, thank you. I've got my timetable.' I hurried away.

Busyness is the best panacea for fear, and I was very busy getting to know a different class until the bell rang for lunch. Back to the staff room again – and it was full again – and there was Mrs Gage, kindly taking me under her wing.

'Miss Leonard asked me to look after you until you find your way around,' she said. 'The staff dining-room is on the second floor. Would you like to come up with me?'

I was glad of the offer.

The staff, all female, sat at three long tables in the dining-room, and the place was as noisy as a classroom before the teacher arrives! Two overalled women, one of whom I had seen at break, served our meal. Conversation was mostly 'shop' – the besetting sin of female teachers. As the newcomer, I kept quiet, but I looked at those women one by one, trying to identify the woman in black.

She wasn't there.

Unhungry, I did my best with the meat pie and carrots, then when rice pudding and prunes arrived (for teachers have children's diet) I murmured to Mrs Gage: 'Who is the member of staff who wears a black dress?'

She looked round. 'No one, as far as I can see.'

'No – she's not here – but I've seen her.'

'Really? But I think everyone's here today. We do go out for lunch sometimes, but when the weather is like this it's easier to have it on the premises. What was she like?'

'Dark, pale, thin, not very young – with lovely eyes –'

'And wearing a black dress, you said?'

'Yes.'

Mrs Gage gave a small, unamused laugh. 'Sounds like Miss Carey, but you can't possibly have seen her.'

'The one who's left – whose place I've taken—'

'No one could take Joanna's place.'

'Oh – I didn't mean—'

'Miss Anderson, I'm sorry. I didn't mean anything either.' She didn't look at me, but she had stopped eating her prunes.

'Did something bad happen to her?' I asked.

'She tried to burn down the school.'

The words were whispered and the noise of voices around us was so loud that I thought I must have misheard, so I said: 'What?'

'She tried to burn down the school,' Mrs Gage repeated. Others at our table heard her this time. Conversation faded, ceased. Heads turned towards Mrs Gage.

'Don't all look at me like that,' said Mrs Gage. 'I'm only telling Miss Anderson what happened last term. She has a right to know.' Leaving her sweet unfinished, she pushed back her chair with a scraping noise and left the room. I sat petrified. Murmurs of conversation began again, but no one spoke to me, so I pretended to eat a little more, then rose and left.

I found my way back to the staff room.

Mrs Gage, cigarette in hand, was sitting by the electric fire. 'Sorry about that,' she said. 'Until you asked, I presumed you knew. It was in the newspapers.'

'I've been living in Italy. I only came back just before Christmas. Could you tell me what happened, before the others return from lunch?'

'Sure. Have a fag. Rotten first day for you.' She passed me a cigarette and lit it for me.

'This smell of burning,' I said. 'I've noticed it before.'

'It's only our cigarettes, Miss Anderson. And we'd better get them smoked before the rest of the staff come back. Some of them abhor cigarette smoke. These spinsters!'

'I'm one too.'

'Not really. You're still young. So you want to know about Joanna Carey?'

'Of course I do. After all, I've seen her. Did she get the sack, and now she comes back uninvited – or what?'

'My dear child, you can't have seen her. She's dead.'

'Then whom did I see?'

Mrs Gage ignored this question. She said: 'Miss Carey, Joanna, had been a teacher here for twenty years. She was excellent at her job and the kids adored her. Then, about a year ago, she changed.'

'In what way?'

'Not in the way she taught. Her teaching was always brilliant. But in her attitude. After being most understanding and sympathetic with the young, she gradually became more and more cynical, to the point of cruelty. She made it clear to all of us, staff and pupils, that she now hated her job and only went on doing it because she had to earn a living somehow.'

'But why did this happen?'

'Why? Who knows why anything? But in fact I do know more about her than most of the staff. Joanna and I were friends, before she changed. She often visited my husband and me, in the old days. She and I had occasional heart-to-hearts over the washing-up. So I learned something of her private life. She was the mistress of a married man, for about ten years. That *was* her private life. Then he ditched her – decided to "be a good boy" again. When it happened, she told me, and she laughed, and didn't seem to care very much. But it was from that moment that she began to change, grow bitter, disillusioned. The world went stale for her. The salt had lost its savour. She began to take revenge, not against the man, but against everyone else with whom she came into contact. That meant us – staff and kids. She was filled with hate, and hate breeds hate. Even I, who had been her friend, began to avoid her. She was left alone.'

'You said she tried to burn down the school.'

'She did. She failed in that. But while she was trying, she burned herself to death. And one of the children.'

'One of the children? Oh, no!'

'It's true, Miss Anderson. I wouldn't say it if it weren't. I, of all people, once so friendly with Joanna – I'd be the last person to admit it, if it weren't true. But it happened.'

'What exactly did happen?'

'One Friday evening, towards the end of last term, she came back to school. This is what the police found out when they investigated afterwards. Everyone except Mr Brown, the caretaker, had gone. She soaked the base of the long curtains in the gymnasium with paraffin and set fire to them. Imagine the flare-up that would make – all those curtains in that big room. Why she didn't get away afterwards, no one knows. Maybe she fainted. Maybe she deliberately let herself be burned – like that Czech student – you know. People do these things. When they're desperate. Mr Brown saw the flames, sent for the fire service, and after they'd come and put out the fire, her body was found among the ashes of the curtains.'

'And the child? You said –'

'Yes. Little Joan Hanley. A dear little girl with red curly hair. She adored Joanna. She was found there too, burned to death, among the ashes of the curtains.'

'But how did she come to be there in the first place?'

'Once again, no one knows. She was one of Joanna's worshippers. There were several in the school. Girls' schools are diabolical in this respect. Rather all-female wards in hospitals. Unnatural passions are aroused. Joan Hanley would have done anything in the world for Joanna Carey. So did Joanna invite the child to the "party"? I don't know. But it looks like it.'

'Didn't the police find out anything about why Joan Hanley was there?'

'They tried. She had told her parents that she was going to the cinema, which she often did on Friday nights. When she didn't come home at her usual time, her parents wondered – and the next thing they knew, the police were on their doorstep, telling them that their daughter had been burned to death at the school. That's all I know, Miss Anderson – all any of us knows. Since it happened, workmen have put the gymnasium to rights, hence all the fresh

paint and the pretty new curtains. These tragedies are happening all
the time, all over the world – I know that – but when I think of
Joanna, in her hatred and bitterness, drawing a child into such a
burning – Oh God!' She put her hands over her face.

The staff room became deathly quiet. Only the two of us there,
Mrs Gage and me, crouching over the electric fire, our cigarettes
burning down, the silent snow covering the world outside – and
God knows why I suddenly looked behind me.

I looked at that chair in the far corner of the room. It was no
longer empty. The woman in black sat there. She looked straight at
me, with those tragic eyes.

Then the staff room door burst open and the other women
poured in, filling the quietness with noise, filling the empty chairs
with bodies, talking 'shop' – and I thought: No wonder Joanna
Carey took a hate against all this. And yet – to burn a child – along
with oneself – No!

'I didn't!' The sound came over, clearly, loudly, as if it filled the
world. Yet no one seemed to hear it. It had spoken into my head
only.

'I'll prove it,' said the loud voice in my head. 'Come!'

Mrs Gage was leaning back in the chair by the fire. She had lit
another cigarette and closed her eyes. She looked tired out, and no
wonder. I got up and left the room, that room full of talking
women.

I walked, blindly, yet guided, along the unfamiliar corridors.
Outside, in the snow, the children were having snowball battles.
They were having a lovely lunch-hour! Heaven was outside. Hell
was within.

I walked, without knowing why, into the classroom which I had
seen through the window, the classroom where I had taught during
the second and third periods of the school morning.

I walked up to the third desk in the front row.

I sat down in that desk, as if I were the little girl, Joan Hanley,
who had, day after day, sat down in that desk . . .

I opened the desk lid. There was nothing inside.

I looked at the scratchings and carved initials on the top of the desk lid.

I found: 'J.H. LOVES J.C.' And, over it, an unsymmetrical heart pierced by a rather wonky arrow.

But I knew already that J.H. had loved J.C. I had seen the child's face through the window, only this morning – I had seen what did not exist – yet which did exist –

What to do now?

My hand, guided, by God knows whom or what, put its fingers into the empty inkwell-socket. The fingers found a closely folded piece of paper.

I unfolded it, carefully, and read:

'Dear Mum and Dad, I do not love you. I love Miss Carey. Where she goes, I go. I follow her everywhere. Tonight I have followed her to the school. She has gone to the gymnasium. I shall follow her there. Something is going to happen. That is why I am writing. Whatever she does, I shall do too. Because I love her. I must hurry now, to be with her. Funny really – as she does not even know I follow her! I'll put this under my inkwell. I don't expect you'll ever read it, but you never know. Yours sincerely – Your daughter, Joan.'

'I didn't know she was there!' cried that voice in my head, loud with its silence. 'I didn't know she was there!'

'Of course you didn't!' I answered aloud, loudly. 'It's all right! I'll tell them!'

The classroom door opened and Miss Leonard walked in.

'Miss Anderson, what on earth are you doing?'

What on earth was I doing? I was sitting at a dead child's desk, a scrap of paper in my hand, and 'talking to myself'.

'I've found something, Miss Leonard.' I passed her the letter. She read it. 'So that's what happened,' she said. 'Miss Carey didn't take the child there with her at all. The little girl secretly imitated her goddess, even to the point of suicide. Where did you find the letter?'

'In the inkwell-socket. I'm surprised it hasn't been found before, maybe by one of the children.'

'No. I cleared that desk myself, removed the inkwell and didn't think to look underneath it. And the children never touch this desk. I did think of removing it, but that's too much like giving in to superstition. What made *you* look there, Miss Anderson?'

'She – she led me here – she spoke in my head – I don't understand it – but it happened—'

'You're psychic, aren't you? Did you know that already?'

'Not until I came to this school.'

'You saw her on the day of your interview, didn't you?'

'Yes. On the stairs.'

'I remember. And I fobbed you off with a practical explanation.'

'Did you ever see her, Miss Leonard?'

'No. But Mr Brown did, more than once. And one of the children, last term, after the fire, insisted that Miss Carey wasn't dead as she'd seen her in the corridor. Neither of them was lying. Some individuals see and hear more than others. Have you been very frightened?'

'At first I wasn't, because I thought she was real. Later, I did feel frightened.'

'And now?'

'Now I just feel desperately sorry for her. Her eyes, Miss Leonard. If you could have seen the sadness in her eyes!'

'Mr Brown mentioned that. You may talk to him if you like, but please no talk of ghosts to anyone else.'

'Of course not. Anyway, I think she'll go away now. She'll be free of the place. She's been punished so dreadfully. Maybe ghosts are people in purgatory and we see them around us all the time without realizing that they are ghosts.'

'Maybe *you* do,' said Miss Leonard, smiling a little.

The bell rang for the beginning of afternoon school. A wail of disappointment rose from outside. I looked out of the window, saw the children cease their snowballing and move obediently towards the building.

Only one figure moved away from the building, moved through the oncoming crowd of girls, who took no notice of her at all. She walked farther away, on and on, past the playground, across the snow-covered playing-field. A pale sun was shining and the snow dazzled, accentuating the thin, dark outline of the woman in black. She looked so utterly alone. Then a small figure began to follow her, running quickly and eagerly, and the sun turned the little figure's mop of red curls into a flame shaped like a rose.

The child overtook the woman in black and walked beside her, lightly, dancingly. And the two retreating figures cast no shadows on the snow, and left no footprints.

CELIA FREMLIN

DON'T TELL CISSIE

'Friday, then. The six-ten from Liverpool Street,' said Rosemary, gathering up her gloves and bag. 'And don't tell Cissie!' she added, 'You *will* be careful about that, won't you, Lois?'

I nodded. People are always talking like this about Cissie, she's that kind of person. She was like that at school, and now, when we're all coming up towards retirement, she's like it still.

You know the kind of person I mean? Friendly, good-hearted, and desperately anxious to be in on everything, and yet with this mysterious knack of ruining things – of bringing every project grinding to a halt, simply by being there.

Because it wasn't ever her fault. Not really. 'Let me come! Oh, *please* let me come too!' she'd beg, when three or four of us from the Lower Fourth had schemed up an illicit trip to the shops on Saturday afternoon. And, because she was our friend (well, sort of – anyway, it was *our* set that she hovered on the fringe of all the time, not anyone else's) – because of this, we usually let her come; and always it ended in disaster. *She'd* be the one to slip on the edge of the kerb outside Woolworth's, and cut her knee so that the blood ran, and a little crowd collected, and a kind lady rang up the school to have us fetched home. *She'd* be the one to get lost . . . to miss the bus . . . to arrive back at school bedraggled and tear-stained and late for evening preparation, hopelessly giving the game away for all of us.

You'd think, wouldn't you, that after a few such episodes she'd have given up, or at least have learned caution. But no. Her persistence (perhaps one would have called it courage if only it hadn't been so annoying) – well, her persistence, then, was indomitable. Neither school punishments nor the reproaches of her companions ever kept her under for long. 'Oh, *please* let me come!' she'd be pleading again, barely a week after the last débâcle. 'Oh, plee-ee-ease! Oh, don't be so *mean!*'

And so there, once again, she'd inexorably be, back in action once more. Throwing-up in the middle of the dormitory feast. Crying with blisters as we trudged back from a ramble out of bounds. Soaked, and shivering, and starting pneumonia from having fallen through the ice of the pond we'd been forbidden to skate on.

So you can understand, can't you, why Rosemary and I didn't want Cissie with us when we went to investigate the ghost at Rosemary's new weekend cottage. Small as our chances might be of pinning down the ghost in any case, Cissie could have been counted on to reduce them to zero. Dropping a tray of tea-things just as the rapping began . . . Calling out, 'What? *I* can't hear anything!' as we held our breaths trying to locate the ghostly sobbing . . . Falling over a tombstone as we tiptoed through the moonlit churchyard . . . No, Cissie must at all costs be kept out of our little adventure; and by now, after nearly half a century, we knew that the only way of keeping Cissie out of anything was to make sure that she knew nothing about it, right from the beginning.

But let me get back to Rosemary's new cottage. I say 'new', because Rosemary has only recently bought it – not because the cottage itself is new. Far from it. It is early eighteenth-century, and damp, and dark, and built of the local stone, and Rosemary loves it (*did* love it, rather – but let me not get ahead of myself). Anyway, as I was saying, Rosemary loved the place, loved it on sight, and bought it almost on impulse with the best part of her life's savings. *Their* life's savings, I suppose I should say, because she and Norman are still married to each other, and it must have been his money just as

much as hers. But Norman never seems to have much to do with
these sort of decisions – indeed, he doesn't seem to have much to do
with Rosemary's life at all, these days – certainly, he never comes
down to the cottage. I think that was part of the idea, really – that
they should be able to get away from each other at weekends.
During the week, of course, it's all right, as they are both working
full-time, and they both bring plenty of work home in the evenings.
Rosemary sits in one room correcting history essays, while Norman
sits in another working out Export Quotas, or something; and the
mutual non-communication must be almost companionable, in an
arid sort of a way. But the crunch will come, of course, when they
both retire in a year or so's time. I think Rosemary was thinking of
this when she bought the cottage; it would become a real port in a
storm then – a bolt-hole from what she refers to as 'the last and
worst lap of married life'.

At one time, we used to be sorry for Cissie, the only one of our
set who never married. But now, when the slow revolving of the
decades has left me a widow and Rosemary stranded among the
flotsam of a dead marriage – now, lately I have begun wondering
whether Cissie hasn't done just as well for herself as any of us, in the
long run. Certainly, she has had plenty of fun on the fringes of
other people's lives, over the years. She wangles invitations to silver-
wedding parties; worms her way into other people's family holidays –
and even if it ends up with the whole lot of them in quarantine at
the airport because of Cissie coming out in spots – well, at least she's
usually had a good run for her money first.

And, to be fair to her, it's not just the pleasures and luxuries of
our lives that she tries to share; it's the problems and crises, too.
I remember she managed to be present at the birth of my younger
son, and if only she hadn't dropped the boiling kettle on her
foot just as I went into the second stage of labour, her presence
would have been a real help. As it was, the doctor and midwife
were both busy treating her for shock in the kitchen, and binding
up her scalded leg, while upstairs my son arrived unattended,
and mercifully without fuss. Perhaps even the unborn are sensi-

tive to atmosphere? Perhaps he sensed, even then, that, with Cissie around, it's just *no use* anyone else making a fuss about anything?

But let me get back to Rosemary's haunted cottage (or not haunted, as the case may be – let me not prejudge the issue before I have given you all the facts). Of course, to begin with, we were half playing a game, Rosemary and I. The tension tends to go out of life as you come up towards your sixties. Whatever problems once tore at you, and kept you fighting, and alive, and gasping for breath – they are solved now, or else have died, quietly, while you weren't noticing. Anyway, what with one thing and another, life can become a bit dull and flavourless when you get to our age; and, to be honest, a ghost was just what Rosemary and I were needing. A spice of danger; a spark of the unknown to reactivate these waterlogged minds of ours, weighed down as they are by such a lifetime's accumulation of the known.

I am telling you this because I want to be absolutely honest. In evaluating the events I am to describe, you must remember, and allow for, the fact that Rosemary and I *wanted* there to be a ghost. Well, no, perhaps that's putting it too strongly; we wanted there to *might* be a ghost – if you see what I so ungrammatically mean. We wanted our weekend to bring us at least a small tingling of the blood; a tiny prickling of the scalp. We wanted our journey to reach a little way into the delicious outskirts of fear, even if it *did* have to start from Liverpool Street.

We felt marvellously superior, Rosemary and I, as we stood jam-packed in the corridor, rocking through the rainy December night. We glanced with secret pity at all those blank, commuter faces, trundling towards the security of their homes. *We* were different. *We* were travelling into the Unknown.

Our first problems, of course, were nothing to do with ghosts. They were to do with milk, and bread, and damp firewood, and why Mrs Thorpe from the village hadn't come in to air the beds as she'd promised. She hadn't filled the lamps, either, or brought in the paraffin . . . how did she think Rosemary was going to get it from the shed in all this rain and dark? And where were all those tins she'd stocked up with in the summer? They couldn't *all* have been eaten . . .?

I'm afraid I left it all to Rosemary. I know visitors are supposed to trot around at the heels of their hostesses, yapping helpfully, like terriers; but I just won't. After all, I know how little help it is to *me*, when I am a hostess, so why should I suppose that everyone else is different? Besides, by this time I was half-frozen, what with the black, sodden fields and marshlands without, and the damp stone within; and so I decided to concentrate my meagre store of obligingness on getting a fire going.

What a job it was, though! It was as if some demon was working against me, spitting and sighing down the cavernous chimney, whistling wickedly along the icy, stone-flagged floor, blowing out each feeble flicker of flame as fast as I coaxed it from the damp balls of newspaper piled under the damper wood.

Fortunately there were plenty of matches, and gradually, as each of my abortive efforts left the materials a tiny bit drier than before, hope of success came nearer. Or maybe it was that the mischievous demon grew tired of his dance of obstruction – the awful sameness of frustrating me time and time again – anyway, for whatever reason, I at last got a few splinters of wood feebly smouldering. Bending close, and cupping my hands around the precious whorls to protect them from the sudden damp gusts and sputters of rain down the chimney, I watched, enchanted, while first one tiny speck of gold and then another glimmered on the charred wood. Another . . . and yet another . . . until suddenly, like the very dawn of creation, a flame licked upwards.

It was the first time in years and years that I had had anything to do with an open fire. I have lived in centrally heated flats for almost all of my adult life, and I had forgotten this apocalyptic moment when fire comes into being under your hands. Like God on the morning of creation, I sat there, all-powerful, tending the spark I had created. A sliver more of wood here . . . a knob of coal there . . .

soon my little fire was bright, and growing, and needing me no more.

But still I tended it – or pretended to – leaning over it, spreading my icy hands to the beginnings of warmth. Vaguely, in the background, I was aware of Rosemary blundering around the place, clutching in her left hand the only oil-lamp that worked, peering disconsolately into drawers and cupboards, and muttering under her breath at each new evidence of disorder and depletion.

Honestly, it was no use trying to help. We'd have to manage, somehow, for tonight, and then tomorrow, with the coming of the blessed daylight, we'd be able to get everything to rights. Fill the lamps. Fetch food from the village. Get the place properly warm . . .

Warm! I shivered, and huddled closer into the wide chimney-alcove. Although the fire was burning up nicely now, it had as yet made little impact on the icy chill of the room. It was cold as only these ancient, little-used cottages *can* be cold. The cold of centuries seems to be stored up in their old stones, and the idea that you can warm it away with a single brisk weekend of paraffin heaters and hastily lit fires has always seemed to me laughable.

Not to Rosemary, though. She is an impatient sort of person, and it always seems to her that heaters *must* produce heat. That's what the word *means*! So she was first angered, then puzzled, and finally half-scared by the fact that she just *couldn't* get the cottage warm. Even in late August, when the air outside was still soft, and the warmth of summer lingered over the fields and marshes – even then, the cottage was like an ice-box inside. I remember remarking on it during my first visit – 'Marvellously cool!' was how I put it at the time, for we had just returned, hot and exhausted, from a long tramp through the hazy, windless countryside; and that was the first time (I think) that Rosemary mentioned to me that the place was supposed to be haunted.

'One of those tragic, wailing ladies that the Past specializes in,' she explained, rather facetiously. 'She's supposed to have drowned herself away on the marsh somewhere – for love, I suppose; it always was, wasn't it? My God, though, what a thing to drown oneself for! – if only she'd *known* . . .!'

This set us off giggling, of course; and by the time we'd finished our wry reminiscences, and our speculations about the less-than-ecstatic love-lives of our various friends – by this time, of course, the end of the ghost story had rather got lost. Something about the woman's ghost moaning around the cottage on stormy nights (or was it moonlight ones?), and about the permanent, icy chill that had settled upon the cottage, and particularly upon the upstairs back bedroom, into which they'd carried her body, all dripping wet from the marsh.

'As good a tale as any, for when your tenants start demanding proper heating,' I remember remarking cheerfully (for Rosemary, at that time, had vague and grandiose plans for making a fortune by letting the place for part of the year) and we had both laughed, and that, it had seemed, was the end of it.

But when late summer became autumn, and autumn deepened into winter, and the north-east wind, straight from Siberia, howled in over the marshes, then Rosemary began to get both annoyed and perturbed.

'I just *can't* get the place warm,' she grumbled. 'I can't understand it! And as for that back room – the one that looks out over the marsh – it's uncanny how cold it is! Two oil-heaters, burning day and night, and it's *still* . . .!'

I couldn't pretend to be surprised: as I say, I *expect* my friends' weekend cottages to be like this. But I tried to be sympathetic; and when, late in November, Rosemary confessed, half-laughing, that she really *did* think the place was haunted, it was I who suggested that we should go down together and see if we could lay the ghost.

She welcomed the suggestion with both pleasure and relief.

'If it was just the cold, I wouldn't be bothering,' she explained. 'But there seems to be something eerie about the place – there really does, Lois! It's like being in the presence of the dead.' (Rosemary never has been in the presence of the dead, or she'd know it's not like that at all, but I let it pass.) 'I'm getting to hate being there on my own. Sometimes – I know it sounds crazy, but sometimes I really *do* seem to hear voices!' She laughed, uncomfortably. 'I must be in a bad way, mustn't I? *Hearing voices . . .! Me . . .!'*

To this day, I don't know how much she was really scared, and how much she was just trying to work a bit of drama into her lonely – and probably unexpectedly boring – trips down to her dream cottage. I don't suppose she even knows herself. All I can say for certain is that her mood of slightly factitious trepidation touched exactly on some deep need of my own, and at once we knew that we would go. And that it would be fun. And that Cissie must at all costs be kept out of it. Once *her* deep needs get involved, you've had it.

A little cry from somewhere in the shadows, beyond the circle of firelight, jerked me from my reverie, and for a moment I felt my heart pounding. Then, a moment later, I was laughing, for the cry came again:

'Spaghetti! Spaghetti Bolognese! Four whole tins of it, all stacked up under the sink! Now, *who* could have . . .?'

And who could care, anyway? Food, real food, was now within our grasp! Unless . . . Oh dear . . .!

'I bet you've lost the tin-opener!' I hazarded, with a sinking heart – for at the words 'Spaghetti Bolognese' I had realized just how hungry I was – and it was with corresponding relief that, in the flickering firelight, I saw a smug smile overspreading her face.

'See?' She held up the vital implement; it flickered through the shadows like a shining minnow as she gesticulated her triumph. '*See?* Though of course, if *Cissie* had been here . . .!'

We both began to giggle; and later, as we sat over the fire scooping spaghetti bolognese from pottery bowls, and drinking the red wine which Rosemary had managed to unearth – as we sat there, revelling in creature comforts, we amused ourselves by speculating on the disasters which would have befallen us by now had Cissie been one of the party. How she would have dropped the last of the

matches into a puddle, looking for a lost glove . . . would have left
the front door swinging open in the wind, blowing out our only oil-
lamp. And the tin-opener, of course, would have been a write-off
from the word go; if she hadn't lost it in some dark corner, it would
certainly have collapsed into two useless pieces under her big, willing hands . . . By now, we would have been without light, heat or
food . . .

This depressing picture seemed, somehow, to be the funniest
thing imaginable as we sat there, with our stomachs comfortably full
and with our third helping of red wine gleaming jewel-like in the
firelight.

'To absent friends!' we giggled, raising our glasses. 'And let's hope
they *remain* absent,' I added, wickedly, thinking of Cissie; and while
we were both still laughing over this cynical toast, I saw Rosemary
suddenly go rigid, her glass an inch from her lips, and I watched the
laughter freeze on her face.

'Listen!' she hissed. 'Listen, Lois! Do you *hear*?'

For long seconds, we sat absolutely still, and the noises of the
night impinged, for the first time, on my consciousness. The wind,
rising now, was groaning and sighing around the cottage, moaning
in the chimney and among the old beams. The rain spattered in
little gusts against the windows, which creaked and rattled on their
old hinges. Beyond them, in the dark, overgrown garden, you could
hear the stir and rustle of bare twigs and sodden leaves . . . and
beyond that again there was the faint, endless sighing of the marsh,
mile upon mile of it, half-hidden under the dry, winter reeds.

'No . . .' I began, in a whisper; but Rosemary made a sharp little
movement, commanding silence. '*Listen!*' she whispered once more;
and this time – or was it my imagination? – I did begin to hear
something.

'Ee . . . ee . . . ee . . .!' came the sound, faint and weird upon the
wind. 'Ee . . . ee . . . ee . . .!' – and for a moment it sounded so
human, and so imploring, that I, too, caught my breath. It must be
a trick of the wind, of course; it *must* – and as we sat there, tensed
almost beyond bearing by the intentness of our listening, another

sound impinged upon our preternaturally sharpened senses – a sound just as faint, and just as far away, but this time very far from ghostly.

'Pr-rr-rr! Ch-ch-ch . . .!' – the sound grew nearer . . . unmistakable . . . The prosaic sound of a car, bouncing and crunching up the rough track to the cottage.

Rosemary and I looked at each other.

'Norman?' she hazarded, scrambling worriedly to her feet. 'But it *can't* be Norman, he *never* comes! And at this time of night, too! Oh dear, I wonder what can have happened . . .?' By this time she had reached the window, and she parted the curtains just as the mysterious vehicle screeched to a halt outside the gate. All I could see, from where I sat, was the triangle of darkness between the parted curtains, and Rosemary's broad back, rigid with disbelief and dismay.

Then, she turned on me.

'Lois!' she hissed. 'How *could you* . . .!'

I didn't ask her what she meant. Not after all these years.

'I didn't! Of course I didn't! What do you take me for?' I retorted, and I don't doubt that by now my face was almost as white as hers.

For, of course, she did not need to tell me who it was who had arrived. Not after nearly half a century of this sort of thing. Besides, who else was there who slammed a car door as if slapping down an invasion from Mars? Who else would announce her arrival by yelling 'Yoo-hoo!' into the midnight air and bashing open the garden gate with a hat-box, so that latch and socket hurtled together into the night?

'Oops – sorry!' said Cissie, for perhaps the fifty-thousandth time in our joint lives; and she blundered forward towards the light, like an untidy grey moth. For by now we had got the front door open, and lamplight was pouring down the garden path, lighting up her round, radiant face and her halo of wild grey curls, all a-glitter with drops of rain.

'You naughty things! Fancy not *telling* me!' she reproached us, as she surged through the lighted doorway, dumping her luggage to left and right. It was, as always, like a one-man army of occupation.

Always, she manages to fill any situation so totally with herself, and her belongings, and her eagerness, that there simply isn't *room* for anyone else's point of view. It's not selfishness, exactly; it's more like being a walking takeover bid, with no control over one's operations.

'A real, live ghost! Isn't it thrilling!' she babbled, as we edged her into the firelit room. 'Oh, but you *should* have told me! You *know* how I love this sort of thing . . .!'

On and on she chattered, in her loud, eager, unstoppable voice . . . and this, too, we recognized as part of her technique of infiltration. By the time her victims have managed to get a word in edgeways, their first fine fury has already begun to wilt . . . the cutting-edge of their protests has been blunted . . . their sense of outrage has become blurred. And anyway, by that time she is *there*. Inescapably, irreversibly, *there*!

Well, what can you do? By the time Rosemary and I got a chance to put a word in, Cissie already had her coat off, her luggage spilling on to the floor, and a glass of red wine in her hand. There she was, reclining in the big easy chair (mine), the firelight playing on her face, exactly as if she had lived in the place for years.

'But, Cissie, how did you find *out*?' was the nearest, somehow, that we could get to a reproof; and she laughed her big, merry laugh, and the bright wine sloshed perilously in her raised glass.

'Simple, you poor Watsons!' she declared. 'You see, I happened to be phoning Josie, and Josie happened to mention that Mary had said that Phyllis had told her that she'd heard from Ruth, and . . .'

See what I mean? You can't win. You might as well try to dodge the Recording Angel himself.

'And when I heard about the ghost, then of course I just *had* to come!' she went on. 'It sounded just *too* fascinating! You see, it just happens that at the moment I know a good deal about ghosts, because . . .'

Well, of course she did. It was her knowing a good deal about Classical Greek architecture last spring that had kept her arguing with the guide on the Parthenon for so long that the coach went off without us. And it was precisely because she'd boned-up so assiduously on rare Alpine plants that she'd broken her leg trying to reach one of them a couple of years ago, and we had to call out the Mountain Rescue for her. The rest of us had thought it was just a daisy.

'Yes, well, we don't even know yet that there *is* a ghost,' said Rosemary, dampingly; but not dampingly enough, evidently, for we spent the rest of the evening – and indeed far into the small hours – trying to dissuade Cissie from putting into practice, then and there, various uncomfortable and hazardous methods of ghost-hunting of which she had recently informed herself – methods which ranged from fixing a tape-recorder on the thatched roof, to ourselves lying all night in the churchyard, keeping our minds a blank.

By two o'clock, our minds were blank anyway – well, Rosemary's and mine were – and we could think about nothing but bed. Here, though, there were new obstacles to be overcome, for not only was Cissie's arrival unexpected and unprepared-for, but she insisted on being put in the Haunted Room. If it *was* haunted – anyway, the room that was coldest, dampest, and most uncomfortable, and therefore entitled her (well, what can you do?) to the only functioning oil-heater, and more than her share of the blankets.

'Of course, I shan't *sleep!*' she promised (as if this was some sort of special treat for me and Rosemary). 'I shall be keeping vigil all night long! And tomorrow night, darlings, as soon as the moon rises, we must each take a white willow-twig, and pace in silent procession through the garden . . .'

We nodded, simply because we were too sleepy to argue; but beyond the circle of lamplight, Rosemary and I exchanged glances of undiluted negativism. I mean, apart from anything else, you'd have to be crazy to embark on any project which depended for its success on Cissie's not falling over something.

But we did agree, without too much reluctance, to her further suggestion that tomorrow morning we should call on the Vicar and ask him if we might look through the Parish archives. Even Cissie, we guardedly surmised, could hardly wreck a call on a vicar.

But the next morning, guess what? Cissie was laid up with lumbago, stiff as a board, and unable even to get out of bed, let alone go visiting.

'Oh dear – Oh, please don't bother!' she kept saying, as we ran around with hot-water bottles and extra pillows. 'Oh dear, I do so hate to be a nuisance!'

We hated her to be a nuisance, too, but we just managed not to say so; and after a bit our efforts, combined with her own determination not to miss the fun (yes, she was still counting it fun) – after a bit, all this succeeded in loosening her up sufficiently to let her get out of bed and on to her feet; and at once her spirits rocketed sky-high. She decided, gleefully, that her affliction was a supernatural one, consequent on sleeping in the haunted room.

'Damp sheets, more likely!' said Rosemary, witheringly. 'If people will turn up unexpectedly like this . . .'

But Cissie is unsquashable. *Damp sheets?* When the alternative was the ghost of a lady who'd died two hundred years ago? Cissie has never been one to rest content with a likely explanation if there is an *un*likely one to hand.

'I know what I'm talking about!' she retorted. 'I know more about this sort of thing than either of you. I'm a Sensitive, you see. I only discovered it just recently, but it seems I'm one of those people with a sort of sixth sense when it comes to the supernatural. It makes me more *vulnerable*, of course, to this sort of thing – look at my bad back – but it also makes me more *aware*. I can *sense* things. Do you know, the moment I walked into this room last night, I could tell that it was haunted! I could feel the . . . Ouch!'

Her back had caught her again; all that gesticulating while she talked had been a mistake. However, between us we got her straightened up once more, and even managed to help her down the stairs – though I must say it wasn't long before we were both wishing we'd left well alone – if I may put it so uncharitably. For Cissie, up, was far, far more nuisance than Cissie in bed. In bed, her good intentions could harm no one; but once up and about, there seemed no limit to the trouble she could cause in the name of 'helping'. Trying to lift pans from shelves above her head; trying to rake out cinders without bending, and setting the hearth-brush on fire in the process; trying to fetch paraffin in cans too heavy for her to lift, and slopping it all over the floor. Rosemary and I seemed to be forever clearing up after her, or trying to un-crick her from some position she'd got stuck in for some maddening, altruistic reason.

Disturbingly, she seemed to get worse as the day went on, not better. The stiffness increased, and by afternoon she looked blue with cold, and was scarcely able to move. But nothing would induce her to let us call a doctor, or put her to bed.

'What, and miss all the fun?' she protested, through numbed lips. 'Don't you realize that this freezing cold is *significant*? It's the chilling of the air that you always get before the coming of an apparition . . .!'

By now, it was quite hard to make out what she was saying, so hoarse had her voice become, and so stiff her lips; but you could still hear the excitement and triumph in her croaked exhortations:

'Isn't it thrilling! This is the Chill of Death, you know, darlings! It's the warning that the dead person is now about to appear! Oh, I'm so thrilled! Any moment now, and we're going to know the truth . . .!'

We did, too. A loud knocking sounded on the cottage door, and Rosemary ran to answer it. From where I stood, in the living-room doorway, I could see her framed against the winter twilight – already the short December afternoon was nearly at an end. Beyond her, I glimpsed the uniforms of policemen, heard their solemn voices.

'"Miss Cecily Curtis?" – Cissie? Yes, of course we know her!' I heard Rosemary saying, in a frightened voice; and then came the two deeper voices, grave and sympathetic.

I could hardly hear their words from where I was standing, yet somehow the story wasn't difficult to follow. It was almost as if, in some queer way, I'd known all along. How last night, at about 10.30 p.m., a Miss Cecily Curtis had skidded while driving – too fast –

along the dyke road, and had plunged, car and all, into deep water. The body had only been recovered and identified this morning.

As I say, I did not really need to hear the men's actual words. Already the picture was in my mind, the picture which has never left it: the picture of Cissie, all lit up with curiosity and excitement, belting through the rain and dark to be in on the fun. Nothing would keep her away, not even death itself . . .

A little sound in the room behind me roused me from my state of shock, and I turned to see Cissie smiling that annoying smile of hers, for the very last time. It's maddened us for years, the plucky way she smiles in the face of whatever adversity she's got us all into.

'You see?' she said, a trifle smugly, 'I've been dead ever since last night – it's no wonder I've been feeling so awful!' – and with a triumphant little toss of her head she turned, fell over her dressing-gown cord, and was gone.

Yes, gone. We never saw her again. The object they carried in, wet and dripping from the marsh, seemed to be nothing to do with her at all.

We never discovered whether the cottage had been haunted all along; but it's haunted now, all right. I don't suppose Rosemary will go down there much any more – certainly, we will never go ghost-hunting there again. Apart from anything else, we are too scared. There is so much that might go wrong. It was different in the old days, when we could play just any wild escapade we liked, confident that whatever went wrong would merely be the fault of our idiotic, infuriating, impossible, irreplaceable friend.

ANTONIA FRASER

WHO'S BEEN SITTING
IN MY CAR?

'Who's been sitting in my car?' said Jacobine. She said it in a stern gruff voice, like a bear. In fact Jacobine looked more like Goldilocks with her pale fair hair pulled back from her round forehead. The style betokened haste and worry, the worry of a girl late for school. But it was Jacobine's children who were late, and she was supposed to be driving them.

'Someone's been smoking in my car,' Jacobine added, pointing to the ashtray crammed with butts.

'Someone's been driving your car, you mean.' It was Gavin, contradictory as usual. 'People don't just sit in cars. They drive them.' He elaborated. 'Someone's been driving my car, said the little bear—'

'People do sit in cars. We're sitting in a car now.' Tessa, because she was twelve months older, could never let that sort of remark from Gavin pass.

'Be quiet, darlings,' said Jacobine automatically. She continued to sit looking at the ashtray in front of her. It certainly looked quite horrible with all its mess of ash and brown stubs. And there was a sort of violence about the way it had been stuffed: you wondered that the smoker had not bothered to throw at least a few of them out of the window. Instead he had remorselessly gone on pressing them into the little chromium tray, hard, harder, into the stale pyre.

Jacobine did not smoke. Rory, her ex-husband, had been a heavy smoker. And for one moment she supposed that Rory might have used an old key to get into the Mini, and then sat endlessly smoking outside the house . . . It was a mad thought and almost instantly Jacobine recognized it as such. For one thing she had bought the Mini second-hand after the divorce. Since ferrying the children had become her main activity these days, she had spent a little money on making it as convenient as possible. More to the point, Jacobine and Rory were on perfectly good terms.

'Married too young' was the general verdict. Jacobine agreed. She still felt rather too young for marriage, as a matter of fact: in an upside-down sort of way, two children seemed to be all she could cope with. She really quite liked Rory's new wife, Fiona, for her evident competence in dealing with the problem of living with him.

It was only that the mucky filled ashtray had reminded Jacobine of the household details of life with Rory. But if not Rory, who? And why did she feel, on top of disgust, a very strong sensation of physical fear? Jacobine, habitually timid, did not remember feeling fear before in quite such an alarmingly physical manner. Her terrors were generally projections into the future, possible worries concerned with the children. She was suddenly convinced that the smoker had an ugly streak of cruelty in his nature – as well as being of course a potential thief. She had a nasty new image of him sitting there in her car outside her house. Waiting for her. Watching the house. She dismissed it.

'Tessa, Gavin, stay where you are.' Jacobine jumped out of the driver's seat and examined the locks of the car.

'Mummy, we are going to be late,' whined Tessa. That decided Jacobine. Back to the car, key in lock and away. They had reached the corner of Melville Street when the next odd thing happened. The engine died and the little Mini gradually and rather feebly came to a halt.

'No petrol!' shouted Gavin from the back.

'Oh darling, do be quiet,' began Jacobine. Then her eye fell on the gauge. He was right. The Mini was out of petrol. Jacobine felt completely jolted as if she had been hit in the face. It was as uncharacteristic of her carefully ordered existence to run out of petrol as, for example, to run out of milk for the children's breakfast – a thing which had happened once and still gave Jacobine shivers of self-reproach. In any case, another unpleasantly dawning realization, she had only filled up two days ago . . .

'Someone's definitely been driving this car,' she exclaimed before she could stop herself.

'That's what I said!' crowed Gavin. 'Someone's been driving my car, said the little bear.'

'Oh Mummy, we are going to be awfully late,' pleaded Tessa. 'Miss Hamilton doesn't like us to be late. She says Mummies should be more thoughtful.'

The best thing to do was to take them both to school in a taxi and sort out the car's problems later. One way and another, it was lunch-time before Jacobine was able to consider the intruding driver again. And then, sturdily, she dismissed the thought. So that, curiously enough, finding the Mini once more empty of petrol and the ashtray packed with stubs the following morning was even more of a shock. Nor was it possible to escape the sharp eyes of the children, or gloss over the significance of the rapid visit to the petrol station. In any case, Tessa had been agonizing on the subject of lateness due to petrol failure since breakfast.

'I shall go to the police,' said Jacobine firmly. She said it as much to reassure herself as to shut up the children. In fact the visit was more irritating than reassuring. Although Jacobine began her complaint with the statement that she had locked her car, and the lock had not been tampered with, she was left with the strong impression that the police did not believe any part of her story. They did not seem to accept either that the doors had been locked or that the petrol was missing, let alone appreciate the significance of the used ashtray. All the same, they viewed her tale quite indulgently, and were positively gallant when Jacobine revealed that she lived, as they put it, 'with no man to look after you'.

'Of course you worry about the car, madam, it's natural. I expect your husband did all that when you were married,' said the man behind the broad desk. 'Tell you what, I know where you live, I'll tell the policeman on the beat to keep a special watch on it, shall I? Set your mind at rest. That's what we're here for. Prevention is better than cure.'

Jacobine trailed doubtfully out of the station. Prevention is better than cure. It was this parting homily which gave her the inspiration to park the Mini for the night directly under the street light, which again lay under the children's window. If the police did not altogether believe her, she did not altogether believe them in their kindly promises. Anyway, the light would make their task easier, if they did choose to patrol the tree-shaded square.

That evening Jacobine paid an unusually large number of visits to the children's room after they went to sleep. Each time she looked cautiously out of the window. The Mini, small and green, looked like a prize car at the motor show, in its new spotlight. You could hardly believe it had an engine inside it. It might have been a newly painted dummy. The shock of seeing the Mini gone on her fifth visit of inspection was therefore enormous. At the same time, Jacobine did feel a tiny pang of satisfaction. Now let the police treat her as a hysterical female she thought, as she dialled 999 with slightly shaking fingers. Her lips trembled too as she dictated the number of the car: 'AST 5690. A bright green Mini. Stolen not more than ten minutes ago. I warned you it might happen.'

'Don't worry, madam, we'll put out a general call for it.' Why did everyone tell her not to worry?

'No, it's my car, not my husband's. I haven't got a husband.'

Jacobine tried to sleep after that, but her mind raced, half in rage at the impudence of the intruder, half in imagined triumph that he would be hauled before her, cigarette hanging from his lips, those telltale polluting cigarettes . . . It was the door bell weaving in and out of these hazy dreams which finally ended them. At first she assumed they were bringing round the thief, even at this time of night.

It was a policeman, a new one from the morning's encounter. But he was alone.

'Mrs Esk? Sorry to call so late. About your stolen Mini—'

'Have you found it? Who took it?'

'Well that's the point, madam. A green Mini, number AST 5690, reported stolen twenty minutes ago at Ferry Road police station, is now outside your door.'

Jacobine stared. It was true. The Mini was back.

'He must have known you were looking for him.' She blurted out the remark and then regretted it. Silently, Jacobine in her quilted dressing-gown and slippers, and the policeman in his thick night-black uniform, examined the Mini from every angle. The locks were pristine, and the car itself was locked. They examined the dashboard. It was untouched.

'Perhaps there was some mistake?' suggested the policeman in the gentle tone Jacobine had come to associate with his colleagues. 'You only looked out of the window, you said. In the lamplight, you know . . . Well, I'd better be getting back to the station and report that all is well. You don't want to be arrested for driving your own Mini tomorrow, do you?' He sounded quite paternal.

'Look, he only had time for two cigarettes,' said Jacobine suddenly. At least she had curtailed the nocturnal pleasures of her adversary. On the other hand there was a new and rather horrible development. The car positively *smelt*. It did. She did not like to point that out to the policeman, since he had not mentioned it. Perhaps he was embarrassed. It was a strong, pungent, human smell which had nothing to do with Jacobine or the children or even cigarettes. As Jacobine had envisaged someone cruel and even violent when she first saw the ashtray, she now conjured up involuntarily someone coarse and even brutal.

Jacobine had not thought much about sex since the end of her marriage. Now she found herself thinking of it, in spite of herself. It was the unmistakable animal smell of sex which overpoweringly filled her nostrils.

The next night she put the children to bed early. Still fully dressed, with a new large torch beside her, she took up her vigil in the lobby next to the front door. A little after eleven o'clock, with apprehension but also with excitement, she heard the noise of an engine running. It was close to the house. It was the peculiar coughing start of her own car.

Without considering what she was doing, Jacobine flung open the front door, ran towards the kerb and shouted: 'Stop it, stop it, stop, thief!' The engine stopped running instantly. It was as though it had been cut short in mid-sentence. She wrenched upon the handle of the passenger seat, her fingers trembling so much that she fumbled with the familiar door. It did not open. Even locked against her: her own car! In her passion, Jacobine rapped hard on the window.

Nothing happened. Very slowly, she realized that the driver's seat, and indeed the whole of the tiny car, was empty. In the ashtray, illuminated by the street lamp like a detail in a moonlight picture, lay one cigarette, still alight. Jacobine was now suddenly aware of her thumping heart as the anger which had driven her on drained away. For the first time she had no idea what to do. After a pause, during which she stood gazing at the locked Mini and the gradually disintegrating cigarette, she walked back into the house. She picked up the car keys. Even more slowly, she returned to the car and unlocked it. Deliberately, but very gingerly she climbed into the front seat and touched the cigarette. Yes, warm. The car smelt fearfully.

'Sweetheart,' said a voice very close to her ear. 'You shouldn't have told the police, you know. You shouldn't have done that. You have to be punished for that, don't you?'

Jacobine felt herself grasped roughly and horribly. What happened next was so unexpected in its outrageous nature that she tried to scream out her revulsion. But at the same time a pair of lips, thick hard rubbery lips, were pressed on to her own. The car was still, to her staring frantic eyes above her muted mouth, palpably empty.

'Oh God, I've been taken,' she thought, as she choked and struggled.

'But you like it, don't you, Sweetheart?' as though she had managed to speak aloud. It was not true.

'I'm going to be sick, I think,' said Jacobine. This time she did manage to say it out loud.

'But you'll come back for more tomorrow night, won't you, Sweetheart,' said the voice. 'And we'll go for a drive together.' She was released. Jacobine fumbled with the door once more and, half-retching, fled towards the house.

She did not dare leave it again that night but lay in her bed, trembling and shaking. Even a bath did not help to wash away her body's memories of the assault. The next morning, as soon as the children were at school, Jacobine went to the police station. From the start, the man behind the desk was altogether more wary of her, she thought. He listened to her new story with rather a different expression, no less kind, but somewhat more speculative. At the end, without commenting on Jacobine's nocturnal experience, he asked her abruptly if she had ever seen a doctor since the break-up of her marriage.

'I need the police, not a doctor, for something like this,' said Jacobine desperately. 'I need protection.'

'I'm not quite so sure, Mrs Esk,' said the policeman. 'Now look here, why don't you have a word first of all with your GP? It's not very pleasant being a woman on your own, is it, and maybe a few pills, a few tranquillizers . . .'

When Jacobine left the station, it was with a sinking feeling that he had not believed her at all. The rest of the day she agonized over what to do. Ring Rory? That was ridiculous. But Jacobine had no other figure of authority in her life. A lawyer might help, she thought vaguely, remembering the sweet young man who had helped her over the divorce. Yet even a lawyer would ask for more proof, if the police had proved so sceptical. With dread, Jacobine realized that it was up to her to provide it.

About eleven o'clock that night, therefore, she took up her position in the driver's seat. She was not quite sure what to expect, except that there would be a moment's wait while she settled herself.

'I'm glad you're early, Sweetheart,' said the voice conversationally. 'Because we'll be able to go for a really long drive. We've got so much to talk about, haven't we? The children, for example. I don't really like your children. You'll have to get rid of them, you know.'

'Don't you dare touch my children,' gasped Jacobine.

'Oh, rather you than me,' said the voice. 'My methods aren't as pretty as yours. A car crash on the way to school, for example, which would leave you uninjured . . .'

Jacobine gave a little sick cry. She envisaged those precious tender bodies . . . the recurring nightmare of motherhood.

'I know all about crashes and children, their precious bodies,' went on the voice. He seemed to read her thoughts, her ghastly images. 'Poor little mangled things.'

Jacobine could no longer bear it. The smell combined with terror overwhelmed her. And the police station was so near. Jumping out of the car, abandoning her persecutor, she ran along the road in the general direction of the station. A few minutes later she heard the engine start up. The car was following her. Her heart banged in her chest. She had time to think that it was more frightening being pursued by a car, an empty car, than by anything in the world human and alive, when she gained the safety of the steps. The car stopped, neatly, and remained still.

'He's threatening the children now. He says he's going to kill them,' Jacobine began her story. It seemed that she had hardly gulped it out before a policewoman was taking her back – on foot – to her house. The policewoman concentrated on the fact that Jacobine had left her children alone in the house while she went out to the car. Indeed, although it had not occurred to Jacobine at the time, it was very much outside her usual character. The car was driven back by a policeman. It looked very chic and small and harmless when it came to rest once more outside her front door.

It was two days later that Rory rang up. In between Jacobine had not dared to leave the intruder alone in the car at night in case he carried out his threat against the children during the day. On Saturday he performed the same act of possession which had initiated their relationship. On Sunday he brought up the subject of the children again. First he made Jacobine drive as far as Arthur's Seat, then round through silent Edinburgh. Jacobine was tired when she got back, and the Mini was allowed to park beside her house once more. A policeman noted her sitting there, a smouldering cigarette propped above the dashboard, and he heard her cry out. In answer to his questions, she would only point to the cigarette. She was wearing, he saw, a nightdress under her coat. At the time, the policeman was not quite sure whether Jacobine was crying out in terror or delight.

Actually what had forced that strange hoarse sound out of Jacobine was neither fear nor pleasure. It was, in its weird way, a sort of cry of discovery, a confirmation of a dread, but also bringing relief from the unknown.

She had got to know, perforce, the voice a little better during their long night drive. It was some chance remark of his about the car, some piece of mechanical knowledge, which gave her the clue. Proceeding warily – because the voice could often, but not always, read her thoughts – Jacobine followed up her suspicions. In any case, she preferred talking about the car to listening to the voice on the subject of her children. She tried to shut her mind to his gibes and sometimes quite surprisingly petty digs against Tessa and Gavin. He seemed to be out to belittle the children as well as eliminate them from Jacobine's life.

'Fancy Gavin not being able to read – at seven,' he would say. 'I heard him stumbling over the smallest words the other day. What a baby!' And again: 'Tessa makes an awful fuss about being punctual for one so young, doesn't she? I can just see her when she grows up. A proper little spinster. If she grows up, that is . . .'

Jacobine interrupted this by wondering aloud how she had got such a bargain in the shape of a second-hand Mini which had hardly done a thousand miles.

'Oh yes, Sweetheart,' exclaimed the voice, 'you certainly did get a bargain when you bought this car. All things considered. It had always been very well looked after, I can tell you—'

'Then it was your car,' Jacobine tried to stop her own voice shaking as she burst out with her discovery. 'This was your car once, wasn't it?'

'There was an accident,' replied the voice. He spoke in quite a different tone, she noticed, dully, flatly, nothing like his usual accents which varied from a horrid predatory kind of lustfulness to the near frenzy of his dislike for the children.

'Tell me.'

'It was her children. On the way to school. There was an accident.' It was still quite a different tone, so much so that Jacobine almost thought – it was a ridiculous word to use under the circumstances – that he sounded quite human. The smell in the car lessened and even the grip which he habitually kept on her knee, that odious grip, seemed to become softer, more beseeching than possessing.

'She worked so hard. She always had so many things to do for them. I was just trying to help her, taking them to school for her. It was an accident. A mistake. Otherwise why didn't I save myself? An accident, I tell you. And she won't forgive me. Oh, why won't she forgive me? I can't rest till she forgives me.' It was piteous now and Jacobine heard a harsh, racking sobbing, a man's sobbing which hurts the listener. She yielded to some strange new impulse and tentatively put out her hand towards the passenger seat. The next moment she was grasped again, more firmly than before; the assault began again, the smell intensified.

'I've got you now, Sweetheart, haven't I?' said the voice. 'It doesn't matter about her any more. Let her curse me all she likes. We've got each other. Once we get rid of your children, that is. And I'm awfully good at getting rid of children.'

When Rory rang on Monday he was uneasy and embarrassed.

'It's all so unlike Jacobine,' he complained later to Fiona. 'She's really not the type. And you should have heard some of the things she told the policeman this fellow in the car had done to her.'

'Oh those quiet types,' exclaimed Fiona. Without knowing Jacobine intimately, she had always thought it odd that she should have surrendered such an attractive man as Rory, virtually without a struggle. 'Still waters,' Fiona added brightly.

Rory suggested a visit to the doctor. He also wondered whether the strain of running a car ... Jacobine felt the tears coming into her eyes. Why hadn't she thought of that? Get rid of him. Get rid of the car. Free herself.

'Oh, Rory,' she begged. 'Would you take Tessa and Gavin for a few days? I know it's not your time, and I appreciate that Fiona's job—'

'I'll have them at the weekend,' suggested Rory, always as placating as possible, out of guilt that Jacobine, unlike him, had not married again. 'Fiona's got a marketing conference this week and I'll be in Aberdeen.'

'No, please, Rory, today, I implore you. I tell you what, I'll send them round in a taxi. I won't come too. I'll just put them in a taxi this afternoon.'

But Rory was adamant. It would have to be the weekend.

That afternoon, picking up Tessa and Gavin from school, Jacobine very nearly hit an old woman on a zebra crossing. She had simply not seen her. She could not understand it. She always slowed down before zebra crossings and yet she had been almost speeding across this one. Both children bumped themselves badly and Gavin in the front seat who was not wearing his safety belt (another odd factor, since Jacobine could have sworn she fastened it herself), cut himself on the driving mirror.

'That's your warning,' he said that night. 'The children must go. You spend too much time thinking about them and bothering about them. Tiresome little creatures. I'm glad they hurt themselves this afternoon. Crybabies, both of them. Besides, I don't want you having any other calls on your time.'

And Jacobine was wrenched very violently to and fro, shaken like a bag of shopping. The next moment was worse. A cigarette was stubbed, hard, on her wrist, just where the veins ran.

Even at the instant of torture, Jacobine thought:

'Now they'll have to believe me.'

But it seemed that they didn't. In spite of the mark and in spite of the fact that surely everyone knew Jacobine did not smoke. A doctor came. And Rory came. Jacobine got her wish in the sense that Tessa and Gavin were taken away by Rory. Fiona had to break off halfway through her marketing conference, although you would never have guessed it from the cheery way she saluted the children.

'Just because their mother's gone nuts,' Fiona said sensibly to Rory afterwards, 'it doesn't mean that I can't give them a jolly good tea. And supper too. I have no idea what happened about their meals with all that jazzing about at night, and running around in her nightie, and screaming.'

Then Rory took Jacobine down to a really pleasant countrified place not far from Edinburgh, recommended by the doctor. It had to be Rory: there was no one else to do it. Jacobine was very quiet all the way. Rory wondered whether it was because he was driving her car – the car. But Fiona needed the Cortina to fetch the children from school. Once or twice he almost thought Jacobine was listening to something in her own head. It gave him a creepy feeling. Rory put on the radio.

'Don't do that,' said Jacobine, quite sharply for her. 'He doesn't like it.' Rory thought it prudent to say nothing. But he made a mental note to report back to Fiona when he got home. For it was Fiona who felt some concern about despatching Jacobine in this way.

'It's really rather awful, darling,' she argued, 'taking her children away from her. They're all she had in her life. Poor dotty girl.'

'They are my children too,' said Rory humbly. But he knew just what Fiona meant. He admired her more than ever for being so resolutely kind-hearted: it was wonderful how well she got on with both Tessa and Gavin as a result. Fiona also took her turn visiting Jacobine when Rory was too busy. There were really no limits to her practical good nature. And so it was Fiona who brought back the news.

'She wants the car.'

'The car!' cried Rory. 'I should have thought that was the very last thing she should have under the circumstances.'

'Not to drive. She doesn't even want the keys. Just the car. She says she likes the idea of sitting in it. It makes her feel safe to know the car's there and not free to go about wherever it likes. I promise you, those were her very words.'

'What did Dr Mackie say? It seems very rum to me.'

'Oh, he seemed quite airy about it. Talked about womb transference – can that be right? – anyway that sort of thing. He said it could stay in the grounds. Like a sort of Wendy house, I suppose. She hasn't been making very good progress. She cries so much, you see. It's pathetic. Poor thing, let her have the car. She has so little,' ended Fiona generously.

So Jacobine got her car back. Dr Mackie had it parked as promised in a secluded corner of the gardens. He was encouraged to find that Jacobine cried much less now. She spent a great deal of time sitting alone in the driver's seat, talking to herself. She was clearly happier.

'It's much better like this,' said the voice. 'I'm glad we got rid of your children the *nice* way. You won't ever see them again, you know.' Jacobine did not answer. She was getting quite practised at pleasing him. He was generally waiting for her when she arrived at the Mini in its shady corner.

'Who's been sitting in my car?' she would say in a mock gruff voice, pointing to the heap of butts in the ashtray. But in spite of everything Jacobine still looked more like Goldilocks than a bear. Indeed, her face had come to look even younger since she lost the responsibility of the children – or so Fiona told Rory.

Jacobine had to be specially charming on the days when Fiona came down to see her, in case He got into her car and went back to find the children after all. She thought about them all the time. But she no longer cried in front of Him. Because that made Him angry and then He would leave her. She had to keep Him sitting beside her. That way the children would be safe. From Him.

RUTH RENDELL

THE HAUNTING OF
SHAWLEY RECTORY

I don't believe in the supernatural, but just the same I wouldn't live in Shawley Rectory.

That was what I had been thinking and what Gordon Scott said to me when we heard we were to have a new rector at St Mary's. Our wives gave us quizzical looks.

'Not very logical,' said Eleanor, my wife.

'What I mean is,' said Gordon, 'that however certain you might be that ghosts don't exist, if you lived in a place that was reputedly haunted you wouldn't be able to help wondering every time you heard a stair creak. All the normal sounds of an old house would take on a different significance.'

I agreed with him. It wouldn't be very pleasant feeling uneasy every time one was alone in one's own home at night.

'Personally,' said Patsy Scott, 'I've always believed there are no ghosts in the Rectory that a good central-heating system wouldn't get rid of.'

We laughed at that, but Eleanor said, 'You can't just dismiss it like that. The Cobworths heard and felt things even if they didn't actually see anything. And so did the Bucklands before them. And you won't find anyone more level-headed than Kate Cobworth.'

Patsy shrugged. 'The Loys didn't even hear or feel anything. They'd heard the stories, they *expected* to hear the footsteps and the carriage wheels. Diana Loy told me. And Diana was quite a nervy highly strung sort of person. But absolutely nothing happened while they were there.'

'Well, maybe the Church of England or whoever's responsible will install central heating for the new person,' I said, 'and we'll see if your theory's right, Patsy.'

Eleanor and I went home after that. We went on foot because our house is only about a quarter of a mile up Shawley Lane. On the way we stopped in front of the Rectory, which is about a hundred yards along. We stood and looked over the gate.

I may as well describe the Rectory to you before I get on with this story. The date of it is around 1760 and it's built of pale dun-coloured brick with plain classical windows and a front door in the middle with a pediment over it. It's a big house with three reception rooms, six bedrooms, two kitchens and two staircases – and one poky little bathroom made by having converted a linen closet. The house is a bit stark to look at, a bit forbidding; it seems to stare straight back at you, but the trees round it are pretty enough and so are the stables on the left-hand side with a clock in their gable and a weathervane on top. Tom Cobworth, the last Rector, kept his old Morris in there. The garden is huge, a wilderness that no one could keep tidy these days – eight acres of it including the glebe.

It was years since I had been inside the Rectory. I remember wondering if the interior was as shabby and in need of paint as the outside. The windows had that black, blank, hazy look of windows at which no curtains hang and which no one has cleaned for months or even years.

'Who exactly does it *belong* to?' said Eleanor.

'Lazarus College, Oxford,' I said. 'Tom was a Fellow of Lazarus.'

'And what about this new man?'

'I don't know,' I said. 'I think all that system of livings has changed but I'm pretty vague about it.'

I'm not a churchgoer, not religious at all really. Perhaps that was why I hadn't got to know the Cobworths all that well. I used to feel a bit uneasy in Tom's company, I used to have the feeling he might suddenly round on me and demand to know why he never saw me in church. Eleanor had no such inhibitions with Kate. They were friends, close friends, and Eleanor had missed her after Tom died suddenly of a heart attack and she had had to leave the Rectory. She had gone back to her people up north, taking her fifteen-year-old daughter Louise with her.

Kate is a practical down-to-earth Yorkshirewoman. She had been a nurse – a ward sister, I believe – before her marriage. When Tom got the living of Shawley she several times met Mrs Buckland, the wife of the retiring incumbent, and from her learned to expect what Mrs Buckland called 'manifestations'.

'I couldn't believe she was actually saying it,' Kate had said to Eleanor. 'I thought I was dreaming and then I thought she was mad. I mean really psychotic, mentally ill. Ghosts! I ask you – people believing things like that in this day and age. And then we moved in and I heard them too.'

The crunch of carriage wheels on the gravel drive when there was no carriage or any kind of vehicle to be seen. Doors closing softly when no doors had been left open. Footsteps crossing the landing and going downstairs, crossing the hall, then the front door opening softly and closing softly.

'But how could you bear it?' Eleanor said. 'Weren't you afraid? Weren't you terrified?'

'We got used to it. We had to, you see. It wasn't as if we could sell the house and buy another. Besides, I love Shawley – I loved it from the first moment I set foot in the village. After the harshness of the north, Dorset is so gentle and mild and pretty. The doors clos-ing and the footsteps and the wheels on the drive – they didn't do us any harm. And we had each other, we weren't alone. You can get used to anything – to ghosts as much as to damp and woodworm and dry rot. There's all that in the Rectory too and I found it much more trying!'

The Bucklands, apparently, had got used to it too. Thirty years he had been Rector of the parish, thirty years they had lived there with the wheels and the footsteps, and had brought up their son and daughter there. No harm had come to them; they slept soundly, and their grown-up children used to joke about their haunted house.

'Nobody ever seems to *see* anything,' I said to Eleanor as we walked home. 'And no one ever comes up with a story, a sort of background to all this walking about and banging and crunching. Is there supposed to have been a murder there or some other sort of violent death?'

She said she didn't know, Kate had never said. The sound of the wheels, the closing of the doors, always took place at about nine in the evening, followed by the footsteps and the opening and closing of the front door. After that there was silence, and it hadn't happened every evening by any means. The only other thing was that Kate had never cared to use the big drawing-room in the evenings. She and Tom and Louise had always stayed in the dining-room or the morning-room.

They did use the drawing-room in the daytime – it was just that in the evenings the room felt strange to her, chilly even in summer, and indefinably hostile. Once she had had to go in there at ten-thirty. She needed her reading glasses which she had left in the drawing-room during the afternoon. She ran into the room and ran out again. She hadn't looked about her, just rushed in, keeping her eyes fixed on the eyeglass case on the mantelpiece. The icy hostility in that room had really frightened her, and that had been the only time she had felt dislike and fear of Shawley Rectory.

Of course one doesn't have to find explanations for an icy hostility. It's much more easily understood as being the product of tension and fear than aural phenomena are. I didn't have much faith in Kate's feelings about the drawing-room. I thought with a kind of admiration of Jack and Diana Loy, that elderly couple who had rented the Rectory for a year after Kate's departure, had been primed with stories of hauntings by Kate, yet had neither heard nor felt a thing. As far as I know, they had used that drawing-room constantly. Often, when I had passed the gate in their time, I had seen lights in the drawing-room windows, at nine, at ten-thirty, and even at midnight.

The Loys had been gone three months. When Lazarus had first offered the Rectory for rent, the idea had been that Shawley should do without a clergyman of its own. I think this must have been the Church economizing – nothing to do certainly with ghosts. The services at St Mary's were to be undertaken by the Vicar of the next parish, Mr Hartley. Whether he found this too much for him in conjunction with the duties of his own parish or whether the powers-that-be in affairs Anglican had second thoughts, I can't say; but on the departure of the Loys it was decided there should be an incumbent to replace Tom.

The first hint of this we had from local gossip; next the facts appeared in our monthly news sheet, the *Shawley Post*. Couched in its customary parish magazine journalese it said: 'Shawley residents all extend a hearty welcome to their new Rector, the Reverend Stephen Galton, whose coming to the parish with his charming wife will fill a long-felt need.'

'He's very young,' said Eleanor a few days after our discussion of haunting with the Scotts. 'Under thirty.'

'That won't bother me,' I said. 'I don't intend to be preached at by him. Anyway, why not? Out of the mouths of babes and sucklings,' I said, 'hast Thou ordained strength.'

'Hark at the devil quoting scripture,' said Eleanor. 'They say his wife's only twenty-three.'

I thought she must have met them, she knew so much. But no.

'It's just what's being said. Patsy got it from Judy Lawrence. Judy said they're moving in next month and her mother's coming with them.'

'Who, Judy's?' I said.

'Don't be silly,' said my wife. 'Mrs Galton's mother, the Rector's mother-in-law. She's coming to live with them.'

Move in they did. And out again two days later.

*

The first we knew that something had gone very wrong for the Galtons was when I was out for my usual evening walk with our Irish setter Liam. We were coming back past the cottage that belongs to Charlie Lawrence (who is by way of being Shawley's squire) and which he keeps for the occupation of his gardener when he is lucky enough to have a gardener. At that time, last June, he hadn't had a gardener for at least six months, and the cottage should have been empty. As I approached, however, I saw a woman's face, young, fair, very pretty, at one of the upstairs windows.

I rounded the hedge and Liam began an insane barking, for just inside the cottage gate, on the drive, peering in under the hood of an aged Wolseley, was a tall young man wearing a tweed sports jacket over one of those black-top things the clergy wear, and a clerical collar.

'Good evening,' I said. 'Shut up, Liam, will you?'

'Good evening,' he said in a quiet, abstracted sort of way.

I told Eleanor. She couldn't account for the Galtons occupying Charlie Lawrence's gardener's cottage instead of Shawley Rectory, their proper abode. But Patsy Scott could. She came round on the following morning with a punnet of strawberries for us. The Scotts grow the best strawberries for miles around.

'They've been driven out by the ghosts,' she said. 'Can you credit it? A clergyman of the Church of England! An educated man! They were in that place not forty-eight hours before they were screaming to Charlie Lawrence to find them somewhere else to go.'

I asked her if she was sure it wasn't just the damp and the dry rot.

'Look, you know me. I don't believe the Rectory's haunted or anywhere can be haunted, come to that. I'm telling you what Mrs Galton told me. She came in to us on Thursday morning and said did I think there was anyone in Shawley had a house or a cottage to rent because they couldn't stick the Rectory another night. I asked her what was wrong. And she said she knew it sounded crazy – it did too, she was right there – she knew it sounded mad, but they'd been terrified out of their lives by what they'd heard and seen since they moved in.'

'*Seen?*' I said. 'She actually claims to have seen something?'

'She said her mother did. She said her mother saw something in the drawing-room the first evening they were there. They'd already heard the carriage wheels and the doors closing and the footsteps and all that. The second evening no one dared go in the drawing-room. They heard all the sounds again and Mrs Grainger – that's the mother – heard voices in the drawing-room, and it was then that they decided they couldn't stand it, they'd have to get out.'

'I don't believe it!' I said. 'I don't believe any of it. The woman's a psychopath, she's playing some sort of ghastly joke.'

'Just as Kate was and the Bucklands,' said Eleanor quietly.

Patsy ignored her and turned to me. 'I feel just like you. It's awful, but what can you do? These stories grow and they sort of infect people and the more suggestible the people are, the worse the infection. Charlie and Judy are furious, they don't want it getting in the papers that Shawley Rectory is haunted. Think of all the people we shall get coming in cars on Sundays and gawping over the gates. But they had to let them have the cottage in common humanity. Mrs Grainger was hysterical and poor little Mrs Galton wasn't much better. Who told them to expect all those horrors? That's what I'd like to know.'

'What does Gordon say?' I said.

'He's keeping an open mind, but he says he'd like to spend an evening there.'

In spite of the Lawrences' fury, the haunting of Shawley Rectory did get quite a lot of publicity. There was a sensational story about it in one of the popular Sundays and then Stephen Galton's mother-in-law went on television. Western TV interviewed her on a local news programme. I hadn't ever seen Mrs Grainger in the flesh and her youthful appearance rather surprised me. She looked no more than thirty-five, though she must be into her forties.

The interviewer asked her if she had ever heard any stories of ghosts at Shawley Rectory before she went there and she said she hadn't. Did she believe in ghosts? Now she did. What had happened, asked the interviewer, after they had moved in?

It had started at nine o'clock, she said, at nine on their first evening. She and her daughter were sitting in the bigger of the two kitchens, having a cup of coffee. They had been moving in all day, unpacking, putting things away. They heard two doors close upstairs, then footsteps coming down the main staircase. She had thought it was her son-in-law, except that it couldn't have been because as the footsteps died away he came in through the door from the back kitchen. They couldn't understand what it had been, but they weren't frightened. Not then.

'We were planning on going to bed early,' said Mrs Grainger. She was very articulate, very much at ease in front of the cameras. 'Just about half-past ten I had to go into the big room they call the drawing-room. The removal men had put some of our boxes in there and my radio was in one of them. I wanted to listen to my radio in bed. I opened the drawing-room door and put my hand to the light switch. I didn't put the light on. The moon was quite bright that night and it was shining into the room.

'There were two people, two figures, I don't know what to call them, between the windows. One of them, the girl, was lying huddled on the floor. The other figure, an older woman, was bending over her. She stood up when I opened the door and looked at me. I knew I wasn't seeing real people, I don't know how but I knew that. I remember I couldn't move my hand to switch the light on. I was frozen, just staring at that pale tragic face while it stared back at me. I did manage at last to back out and close the door, and I got back to my daughter and my son-in-law in the kitchen and I – well, I collapsed. It was the most terrifying experience of my life.'

Yet you stayed a night and a day and another night in the Rectory? said the interviewer. Yes, well, her daughter and her son-in-law had persuaded her it had been some sort of hallucination, the consequence of being overtired. Not that she had ever really believed that. The night had been quiet and so had the next day until nine in the evening when they were all this time in the morning-room and they heard a car drive up to the front door. They had all heard it, wheels crunching on the gravel, the sound of

the engine, the brakes going on. Then had followed the closing of
the doors upstairs and the footsteps, the opening and closing of the
front door.

Yes, they had been very frightened, or she and her daughter had.
Her son-in-law had made a thorough search of the whole house
but found nothing, seen or heard no one. At ten-thirty they had all
gone into the hall and listened outside the drawing-room door and
she and her daughter had heard voices from inside the room,
women's voices. Stephen had wanted to go in, but they had stopped
him, they had been so frightened.

Now the interesting thing was that there had been something in
the *Sunday Express* account about the Rectory being haunted by the
ghosts of two women. The story quoted someone it described as a
'local antiquarian', a man named Joseph Lamb, whom I had heard of
but never met. Lamb had told the *Express* there was an old tradition
that the ghosts were of a mother and her daughter and that the
mother had killed the daughter in the drawing-room.

'I never heard any of that before,' I said to Gordon Scott, 'and I'm
sure Kate Cobworth hadn't. Who is this Joseph Lamb?'

'He's a nice chap,' said Gordon. 'And he's supposed to know
more of local history than anyone else around. I'll ask him over and
you can come and meet him if you like.'

Joseph Lamb lives in a rather fine Jacobean house in a hamlet –
you could hardly call it a village – about a mile to the north of
Shawley. I had often admired it without knowing who had lived
there. The Scotts asked him and his wife to dinner shortly after Mrs
Grainger's appearance on television, and after dinner we got him on
to the subject of the hauntings. Lamb wasn't at all unwilling to
enlighten us. He's a man of about sixty and he said he first heard the
story of the two women from his nurse when he was a little boy. Not
a very suitable subject with which to regale a seven-year-old, he said.

'These two are supposed to have lived in the Rectory at one time,'
he said. 'The story is that the mother had a lover or a man friend or
whatever, and the daughter took him away from her. When the
daughter confessed it, the mother killed her in a jealous rage.'

It was Eleanor who objected to this. 'But surely if they lived in the Rectory they must have been the wife and daughter of a Rector. I don't really see how in those circumstances the mother could have had a lover or the daughter could steal him away.'

'No, it doesn't sound much like what we've come to think of as the domestic life of the English country parson, does it?' said Lamb. 'And the strange thing is, although my nanny used to swear by the story and I heard it later from someone who worked at the Rectory, I haven't been able to find any trace of these women in the Rectory's history. It's not hard to research, you see, because only the Rectors of Shawley had ever lived there until the Loys rented it, and the Rectors' names are all up on that plaque in the church from 1380 onwards. There was another house on the site before this present one, of course, and parts of the older building are incorporated in the newer.

'My nanny used to say that the elder lady hadn't got a husband, he had presumably died. She was supposed to be forty years old and the girl nineteen. Well, I tracked back through the families of the various Rectors and I found a good many cases where the Rectors had predeceased their wives. But none of them fitted my nanny's story. They were either too old – one was much too young – or their daughters were too old or they had no daughters.'

'It's a pity Mrs Grainger didn't tell us what kind of clothes her ghosts were wearing,' said Patsy with sarcasm. 'You could have pinpointed the date then, couldn't you?'

'You mean that if the lady had had a steeple hat on she'd be medieval or around 1850 if she was wearing a crinoline?'

'Something like that,' said Patsy.

At this point Gordon repeated his wish to spend an evening in the Rectory. 'I think I'll write to the Master of Lazarus and ask permission,' he said.

Very soon after we heard that the Rectory was to be sold. Notice boards appeared by the front gate and at the corner where the glebe abutted Shawley Lane, announcing that the house would go up for auction on October the 30th. Patsy, who always seems to know everything, told us that a reserve price of £60,000 had been put on it.

'Not as much as I'd have expected,' she said. 'It must be the ghosts keeping the price down.'

'Whoever buys it will have to spend another ten thousand on it,' said Eleanor.

'And central heating will be a priority.'

Whatever was keeping the price down – ghosts, cold, or dry rot – there were plenty of people anxious to view the house and land with, I supposed, an idea of buying it. I could hardly be at work in my garden or out with Liam without a car stopping and the driver asking me the way to the Rectory. Gordon and Patsy got quite irritable about what they described as 'crowds milling about' in the lane and trippers everywhere, waving orders to view.

The estate agents handling the sale were a firm called Curlew, Pond and Co. Gordon didn't bother with the Master of Lazarus but managed to get the key from Graham Curlew, whom he knew quite well, and permission to spend an evening in the Rectory. Curlew didn't like the idea of anyone staying the night, but Gordon didn't want to do that anyway; no one had ever heard or seen anything after ten-thirty. He asked me if I'd go with him. Patsy wouldn't – she thought it was all too adolescent and stupid.

'Of course I will,' I said. 'As long as you'll agree to our taking some sort of heating arrangement with us and brandy in case of need.'

By then it was the beginning of October and the evenings were turning cool. The day on which we decided to have our vigil happened also to be the one on which Stephen Galton and his wife moved out of Charlie Lawrence's cottage and left Shawley for good. According to the *Shawley Post*, he had got a living in Manchester. Mrs Grainger had gone back to her own home in London from where she had written an article about the Rectory for *Psychic News*.

Patsy shrieked with laughter to see the two of us setting forth with our oil-stove, a dozen candles, two torches, and half a bottle of Courvoisier. She did well to laugh, her amusement wasn't misplaced. We crossed the lane and opened the Rectory gate and went up the gravel drive on which those spirit wheels had so often been heard to crunch. It was seven o'clock in the evening and still light. The day had been fine and the sky was red with the aftermath of a spectacular sunset.

I unlocked the front door and in we went.

The first thing I did was put a match to one of the candles because it wasn't at all light inside. We walked down the passage to the kitchens, I carrying the candle and Gordon shining one of the torches across the walls. The place was a mess. I suppose it hadn't had anything done to it, not even a cleaning, since the Loys moved out. It smelled damp and there was even fungus growing in patches on the kitchen walls. And it was extremely cold. There was a kind of deathly chill in the air, far more of a chill than one would have expected on a warm day in October. That kitchen had the feel you get when you open the door of a refrigerator that hasn't been kept too clean and is in need of defrosting.

We put our stuff down on a kitchen table someone had left behind and made our way up the back stairs. All the bedroom doors were open and we closed them. The upstairs had a neglected, dreary feel but it was less cold. We went down the main staircase, a rather fine curving affair with elegant banisters and carved newel posts, and entered the drawing-room. It was empty, palely lit by the evening light from two windows. On the mantelpiece was a glass jar with greenish water in it, a half-burnt candle in a saucer, and a screwed-up paper table napkin. We had decided not to remain in this room but to open the door and look in at ten-thirty; so accordingly we returned to the kitchen, fetched out candles and torches and brandy, and settled down in the morning-room, which was at the front of the house, on the other side of the front door.

Curlew had told Gordon there were a couple of deckchairs in this room. We found them resting against the wall and we put them up. We lit our oil-stove and a second candle, and we set one candle on the window sill and one on the floor between us. It was still and silent and cold. The dark closed in fairly rapidly, the red fading from the sky, which became a deep hard blue, then indigo.

We sat and talked. It was about the haunting that we talked, collating the various pieces of evidence, assessing the times this or that was supposed to happen and making sure we both knew the sequence in which things happened. We were both wearing watches and I remember that we constantly checked the time. At half-past eight we again opened the drawing-room door and looked inside. The moon had come up and was shining through the windows as it had shone for Mrs Grainger.

Gordon went upstairs with a torch and checked that all the doors remained closed and then we both looked into the other large downstairs room, the dining-room, I suppose. Here a fanlight in one of the windows was open. That accounted for some of the feeling of cold and damp, Gordon said. The window must have been opened by some prospective buyer, viewing the place. We closed it and went back into the morning-room to wait.

The silence was absolute. We didn't talk any more. We waited, watching the candles and the glow of the stove, which had taken some of the chill from the air. Outside it was pitch-dark. The hands of our watches slowly approached nine.

At three minutes to nine we heard the noise.

Not wheels or doors closing or a tread on the stairs but a faint, dainty, pattering sound. It was very faint, it was distant, it was on the ground floor. It was as if made by something less than human, lighter than that, tiptoeing. I had never thought about this moment beyond telling myself that if anything did happen, if there was a manifestation, it would be enormously interesting. It had never occurred to me even once that I should be so dreadfully, so hideously, afraid.

I didn't look at Gordon, I couldn't. I couldn't move either. The pattering feet were less faint now, were coming closer. I felt myself go white, the blood all drawn in from the surface of my skin, as I was gripped by that awful primitive terror that has nothing to do with reason or with knowing what you believe in and what you don't.

Gordon got to his feet, and stood there looking at the door. And then I couldn't stand it any more. I jumped up and threw open the door, holding the candle aloft – and looked into a pair of brilliant golden-green eyes, staring steadily back at me about a foot from the ground.

'My God,' said Gordon. 'My God, it's Lawrence's cat. It must have got in through the window.'

He bent down and picked up the cat, a soft, stout, marmalade-coloured creature. I felt sick at the anticlimax. The time was exactly nine o'clock. With the cat draped over his arm, Gordon went back into the morning-room and I followed him. We didn't sit down. We stood waiting for the wheels and the closing of the doors.

Nothing happened.

I have no business to keep you in suspense any longer for the fact is that after the business with the cat nothing happened at all. At nine-fifteen we sat down in our deckchairs. The cat lay on the floor beside the oil-stove and went to sleep. Twice we heard a car pass along Shawley Lane, a remotely distant sound, but we heard nothing else.

'Feel like a spot of brandy?' said Gordon.

'Why not?' I said.

So we each had a nip of brandy and at ten we had another look in the drawing-room. By then we were both feeling bored and quite sure that since nothing had happened at nine nothing would happen at ten-thirty either. Of course we stayed till ten-thirty and for half an hour after that, and then we decamped. We put the cat over the wall into Lawrence's grounds and went back to Gordon's house where Patsy awaited us, smiling cynically.

I had had quite enough of the Rectory but that wasn't true of Gordon. He said it was well known that the phenomena didn't take place every night; we had simply struck an off-night, and he was going back on his own. He did too, half a dozen times between then and the 30th, even going so far as to have (rather unethically) a key cut from the one Curlew had lent him. Patsy would never go with him, though he tried hard to persuade her.

But in all those visits he never saw or heard anything. And the effect on him was to make him as great a sceptic as Patsy.

'I've a good mind to make an offer for the Rectory myself,' he said. 'It's a fine house and I've got quite attached to it.'

'You're not serious,' I said.

'I'm perfectly serious. I'll go to the auction with a view to buying it if I can get Patsy to agree.'

But Patsy preferred her own house and, very reluctantly, Gordon had to give up the idea. The Rectory was sold for £62,000 to an American woman, a friend of Judy Lawrence. About a month after the sale the builders moved in. Eleanor used to get progress reports from Patsy, how they had rewired and treated the whole place for woodworm and painted and relaid floors. The central-heating engineers came too, much to Patsy's satisfaction.

We met Carol Marcus, the Rectory's new owner, when we were asked round to the Hall for drinks one Sunday morning. She was staying there with the Lawrences until such time as the improvements and decorations to the Rectory were complete. We were introduced by Judy to a very pretty, well-dressed woman in young middle age. I asked her when she expected to move in. April, she hoped, as soon as the builders had finished the two extra bathrooms. She had heard rumours that the Rectory was supposed to be haunted and these had amused her very much. A haunted house in the English countryside! It was too good to be true.

'It's all nonsense, you know,' said Gordon, who had joined us. 'It's all purely imaginary.' And he went on to tell her of his own experiences in the house during October – or his non-experiences, I should say.

'Well, for goodness' sake, I didn't *believe* it!' she said, and she laughed and went on to say how much she loved the house and wanted to make it a real home for her children to come to. She had three, she said, all in their teens, two boys away at school and a girl a bit older.

That was the only time I ever talked to her and I remember thinking she would be a welcome addition to the neighbourhood. A nice woman. Serene is the word that best described her. There was a man friend of hers there too. I didn't catch his surname but she called him Guy. He was staying at one of the local hotels, to be near her presumably.

'I should think those two would get married, wouldn't you?' said Eleanor on the way home. 'Judy told me she's waiting to get her divorce.'

Later that day I took Liam for a walk along Shawley Lane and when I came to the Rectory I found the gate open. So I walked up the gravel drive and looked through the drawing-room window at the new woodblock floor and ivory-painted walls and radiators. The place was swiftly being transformed. It was no longer sinister or grim. I walked round the back and peered in at the splendidly fitted kitchens, one a laundry now, and wondered what on earth had made sensible women like Mrs Buckland and Kate spread such vulgar tales and the Galtons panic. What had come over them? I could only imagine that they felt a need to attract attention to themselves which they perhaps could do in no other way.

 I whistled for Liam and strolled down to the gate and looked back at the Rectory It stared back at me. Is it hindsight that makes me say this or did I really feel it then? I think I did feel it, that the house stared at me with a kind of steady insolence.

Carol Marcus moved in three weeks ago, on a sunny day in the middle of April. Two nights later, just before eleven, there came a sustained ringing at Gordon's front door as if someone were leaning on the bell. Gordon went to the door. Carol Marcus stood outside, absolutely calm but deathly white.

She said to him, 'May I use your phone, please? Mine isn't in yet and I have to call the police. I just shot my daughter.'

She took a step forward and crumpled in a heap on the threshold.

Gordon picked her up and carried her into the house and Patsy gave her brandy, and then he went across the road to the Rectory. There were lights on all over the house; the front door was open and light was streaming out on to the drive and the little Citroën Diane that was parked there.

He went into the house. The drawing-room door was open and he walked in there and saw a young girl lying on the carpet between the windows. She was dead. There was blood from a bullet wound on the front of her dress, and on a low round table lay the small automatic that Carol Marcus had used.

In the meantime Patsy had been the unwilling listener to a confession. Carol Marcus told her that the girl, who was nineteen, had unexpectedly driven down from London, arriving at the Rectory at nine o'clock. She had had a drink and something to eat and then said she had something to tell her mother, that was why she had come down. While in London she had been seeing a lot of the man called Guy and now they found that they were in love with each other. She knew it would hurt her mother, but she wanted to tell her at once, she wanted to be honest about it.

Carol Marcus told Patsy she felt nothing, no shock, no hatred or resentment, no jealousy. It was as if she were impelled by some external force to do what she did – take the gun she always kept with her from a drawer in the writing-desk and kill her daughter.

At this point Gordon came back and they phoned the police. Within a quarter of an hour the police were at the house. They arrested Carol Marcus and took her away and now she is on remand, awaiting trial on a charge of murder.

So what is the explanation of all this? Or does there, in fact, have to be an explanation? Eleanor and I were so shocked by what had happened, and awed too, that for a while we were somehow wary of talking about it even to each other. Then Eleanor said, 'It's as if all this time the coming event cast its shadow before it.'

I nodded, yet it didn't seem quite that to me. It was more that the Rectory was waiting for the right people to come along, the people who would *fit* its still unplayed scenario, the woman of forty, the daughter of nineteen, the lover. And only to those who approximated these characters could it show shadows and whispers of the drama; the closer the approximation, the clearer the sounds and signs.

The Loys were old and childless, so they saw nothing. Nor did Gordon and I – we were of the wrong sex. But the Bucklands, who had a daughter, heard and felt things, and so did Kate, though she was too old for the tragic leading role and her adolescent girl too young for victim. The Galtons had been nearly right – had Mrs Grainger once hoped the young Rector would marry her before he showed his preference for her daughter? – but the women had been a few years too senior for the parts. Even so, they had come closer to participation than those before them.

All this is very fanciful and I haven't mentioned a word of it to Gordon and Patsy. They wouldn't listen if I did. They persist in seeing the events of three weeks ago as no more than a sordid murder, a crime of jealousy committed by someone whose mind was disturbed.

But I haven't been able to keep from asking myself what would have happened if Gordon had bought the Rectory when he talked of doing so. Patsy will be forty this year. I don't think I've mentioned that she has a daughter by her first marriage who is away at the university and going on nineteen now, a girl that they say is extravagantly fond of Gordon.

He is talking once more of buying, since Carol Marcus, whatever may become of her, will hardly keep the place now. The play is played out, but need that mean there will never be a repeat performance . . .?

A.S. BYATT

THE JULY GHOST

'I think I must move out of where I'm living,' he said. 'I have this problem with my landlady.'

He picked a long, bright hair off the back of her dress, so deftly that the act seemed simply considerate. He had been skilful at balancing glass, plate and cutlery, too. He had a look of dignified misery, like a dejected hawk. She was interested.

'What sort of problem? Amatory, financial, or domestic?'

'None of those, really. Well, not financial.'

He turned the hair on his finger, examining it intently, not meeting her eye.

'Not financial. Can you tell me? I might know somewhere you could stay. I know a lot of people.'

'You would.' He smiled shyly. 'It's not an easy problem to describe. There's just the two of us. I occupy the attics. Mostly.'

He came to a stop. He was obviously reserved and secretive. But he was telling her something. This is usually attractive.

'Mostly?' Encouraging him.

'Oh, it's not like *that*. Well, not . . . Shall we sit down?'

They moved across the party, which was a big party, on a hot day. He stopped and found a bottle and filled her glass. He had not needed to ask what she was drinking. They sat side by side on a sofa: he admired the brilliant poppies bold on her emerald dress, and her pretty sandals. She had come to London for the summer to work in the British Museum. She could really have managed with microfilm in Tucson for what little manuscript research was needed, but there was a dragging love affair to end. There is an age at which, however desperately happy one is in stolen moments, days, or weekends with one's married professor, one either prises him loose or cuts and runs. She had had a stab at both, and now considered she had successfully cut and run. So it was nice to be immediately appreciated. Problems are capable of solution. She said as much to him, turning her soft face to his ravaged one, swinging the long bright hair. It had begun a year ago, he told her in a rush, at another party actually; he had met this woman, the landlady in question, and had made, not immediately, a kind of *faux pas*, he now saw, and she had been very decent, all things considered, and so . . .

He had said, 'I think I must move out of where I'm living.' He had been quite wild, had nearly not come to the party, but could not go on drinking alone. The woman had considered him coolly and asked, 'Why?' One could not, he said, go on in a place where one had once been blissfully happy, and was now miserable, however convenient the place. Convenient, that was, for work, and friends, and things that seemed, as he mentioned them, ashy and insubstantial compared to the memory and the hope of opening the door and finding Anne outside it, laughing and breathless, waiting to be told what he had read, or thought, or eaten, or felt that day. Someone I loved left, he told the woman. Reticent on that occasion too, he bit back the flurry of sentences about the total unexpectedness of it, the arriving back and finding only an envelope on a clean table, and spaces in the bookshelves, the record stack, the kitchen cupboard. It must have been planned for weeks, she must have been thinking it out while he rolled on her, while she poured wine for him, while . . . No, no. Vituperation is undignified and in this case what he felt was lower and worse than rage: just pure, childlike loss. 'One ought not to mind places,' he said to the woman. 'But one does,' she had said. 'I know.'

She had suggested to him that he could come and be her lodger, then; she had, she said, a lot of spare space going to waste, and her husband wasn't there much. 'We've not had a lot to say to each other, lately.' He could be quite self-contained, there was a kitchen and bathroom in the attics; she wouldn't bother him. There was a large garden. It was possibly this that decided him: it was very hot, central London, the time of year when a man feels he would give anything to live in a room opening on to grass and trees, not a high flat in a dusty street. And if Anne came back, the door would be locked and mortice-locked. He could stop thinking about Anne coming back. That was a decisive move: Anne thought he wasn't decisive. He would live without Anne.

For some weeks after he moved in he had seen very little of the woman. They met on the stairs, and once she came up, on a hot Sunday, to tell him he must feel free to use the garden. He had offered to do some weeding and mowing, and she had accepted. That was the weekend her husband came back, driving furiously up to the front door, running in, and calling in the empty hall, 'Imogen, Imogen!' To which she had replied, uncharacteristically, by screaming hysterically. There was nothing in her husband, Noel's, appearance to warrant this reaction; their lodger, peering over the banister at the sound, had seen their upturned faces in the stairwell and watched hers settle into its usual prim and placid expression as he did so. Seeing Noel, a balding, fluffy-templed, stooping thirty-five or so, shabby corduroy suit, cotton polo neck, he realized he was now able to guess her age, as he had not been. She was a very neat woman, faded blonde, her hair in a knot on the back of her head, her legs long and slender, her eyes downcast. Mild was not quite the right word for her, though. She explained then that she had screamed because Noel had come home unexpectedly and startled her: she was sorry. It seemed a reasonable explanation. The extraordinary vehemence of the screaming was probably an echo in the stairwell. Noel seemed wholly downcast by it, all the same.

He had kept out of the way, that weekend, taking the stairs two at a time and lightly, feeling a little aggrieved, looking out of his kitchen window into the lovely, overgrown garden, that they were lurking indoors, wasting all the summer sun. At Sunday lunch-time he had heard the husband, Noel, shouting on the stairs.

'I can't go on, if you go on like that. I've done my best, I've tried to get through. Nothing will shift you, will it, you won't *try*, will you, you just go on and on. Well, I have my life to live, you can't throw a life away . . . can you?'

He had crept out again on to the dark upper landing and seen her standing, halfway down the stairs, quite still, watching Noel wave his arms and roar, or almost roar, with a look of impassive patience, as though this nuisance must pass off. Noel swallowed and gasped; he turned his face up to her and said plaintively,

'You do see I can't stand it? I'll be in touch, shall I? You must want . . . you must need . . . you must . . .'

She didn't speak.

'If you need anything, you know where to get me.'

'Yes.'

'Oh, well . . .' said Noel, and went to the door. She watched him, from the stairs, until it was shut, and then came up again, step by step, as though it was an effort, a little, and went on coming past her bedroom, to his landing, to come in and ask him, entirely naturally, please to use the garden if he wanted to, and please not to mind marital rows. She was sure he understood . . . things were difficult . . . Noel wouldn't be back for some time. He was a journalist: his work took him away a lot. Just as well. She committed herself to the 'just as well'. She was a very economical speaker.

So he took to sitting in the garden. It was a lovely place: a huge, hidden, walled south London garden, with old fruit trees at the end, a wildly waving disorderly buddleia, curving beds full of old roses, and a lawn of overgrown, dense rye-grass. Over the wall at the foot was the Common, with a footpath running behind all the gardens. She came out to the shed and helped him to assemble and oil the lawnmower, standing on the little path under the apple branches while he cut an experimental serpentine across her hay. Over the wall came the high sound of children's voices, and the thunk and thud of a football. He asked her how to raise the blades: he was not mechanically minded.

'The children get quite noisy,' she said. 'And dogs. I hope they don't bother you . There aren't many safe places for children, round here.'

He replied truthfully that he never heard sounds that didn't concern him, when he was concentrating. When he'd got the lawn into shape, he was going to sit on it and do a lot of reading, try to get his mind in trim again, to write a paper on Hardy's poems, on their curiously archaic vocabulary.

'It isn't very far to the road on the other side, really,' she said. 'It just seems to be. The Common is an illusion of space, really. Just a spur of brambles and gorse-bushes and bits of football pitch between two fast four-laned main roads. I hate London commons.'

'There's a lovely smell, though, from the gorse and the wet grass. It's a pleasant illusion.'

'No illusions are pleasant,' she said, decisively, and went in. He wondered what she did with her time: apart from little shopping expeditions she seemed to be always in the house. He was sure that when he'd met her she'd been introduced as having some profession: vaguely literary, vaguely academic, like everyone else he knew. Perhaps she wrote poetry in her north-facing living-room. He had no idea what it would be like. Women generally wrote emotional poetry, much nicer than men, as Kingsley Amis has stated, but she seemed, despite her placid stillness, too spare and too fierce – grim? – for that. He remembered the screaming. Perhaps she wrote Plath-like chants of violence. He didn't think that quite fitted the bill, either. Perhaps she was a freelance radio journalist. He didn't bother to ask anyone who might be a common acquaintance. During the whole year, he explained to the American at the party, he hadn't actually *discussed* her with anyone. Of course he wouldn't, she agreed vaguely and warmly. She knew he wouldn't. He didn't see why he shouldn't, in fact, but went on, for the time, with his narrative.

They had got to know each other a little better over the next few weeks, at least on the level of borrowing tea, or even sharing pots of it. The weather had got hotter. He had found an old-fashioned deckchair, with faded striped canvas, in the shed, and had brushed it over and brought it out on to his mown lawn, where he sat writing a little, reading a little, getting up and pulling up a tuft of couch grass. He had been wrong about the children not bothering him: there was a succession of incursions by all sizes of children looking for all sizes of balls, which bounced to his feet, or crashed in the shrubs, or vanished in the herbaceous border, black and white footballs, beach-balls with concentric circles of primary colours, acid yellow tennis balls. The children came over the wall: black faces, brown faces, floppy long hair, shaven heads, respectable dotted sun-hats and camouflaged cotton army hats from Milletts. They came over easily, as though they were used to it, sandals, training shoes, a few bare toes, grubby sunburned legs, cotton skirts, jeans, football shorts. Sometimes, perched on the top, they saw him and gestured at the balls; one or two asked permission. Sometimes he threw a ball back, but was apt to knock down a few knobby little unripe apples or pears. There was a gate in the wall, under the fringing trees, which he once tried to open, spending time on rusty bolts only to discover that the lock was new and secure, and the key not in it.

The boy sitting in the tree did not seem to be looking for a ball. He was in a fork of the tree nearest the gate, swinging his legs, doing something to a knot in a frayed end of rope that was attached to the branch he sat on. He wore blue jeans and training shoes, and a brilliant tee shirt, striped in the colours of the spectrum, arranged in the right order, which the man on the grass found visually pleasing. He had rather long blond hair, falling over his eyes, so that his face was obscured.

'Hey, you. Do you think you ought to be up there? It might not be safe.'

The boy looked up, grinned, and vanished monkey-like over the wall. He had a nice, frank grin, friendly, not cheeky.

He was there again, the next day, leaning back in the crook of the tree, arms crossed. He had on the same shirt and jeans. The man watched him, expecting him to move again, but he sat, immobile, smiling down pleasantly, and then staring up at the sky. The man read a little, looked up, saw him still there and said:

'Have you lost anything?'

The child did not reply: after a moment he climbed down a little, swung along the branch hand over hand, dropped to the ground, raised an arm in salute, and was up over the usual route over the wall.

Two days later he was lying on his stomach on the edge of the lawn, out of the shade, this time in a white tee shirt with a pattern of blue ships and water-lines on it, his bare feet and legs stretched in the sun. He was chewing a grass stem, and studying the earth, as though watching for insects. The man said 'Hi, there,' and the boy looked up, met his look with intensely blue eyes under long lashes, smiled with the same complete warmth and openness, and returned his look to the earth.

He felt reluctant to inform on the boy, who seemed so harmless and considerate: but when he met him walking out of the kitchen door, spoke to him, and got no answer but the gentle smile before the boy ran off towards the wall, he wondered if he should speak to his landlady. So he asked her, did she mind the children coming in the garden. She said no, children must look for balls, that was part of being children. He persisted – they sat there, too, and he had met one coming out of the house. He hadn't seemed to be doing any harm, the boy, but you couldn't tell. He thought she should know.

He was probably a friend of her son's, she said. She looked at him kindly and explained. Her son had run off the Common with some other children, two years ago, in the summer, in July, and had been killed on the road. More or less instantly, she had added drily, as though calculating that just *enough* information would preclude the need for further questions. He said he was sorry, very sorry, feeling to blame, which was ridiculous, and a little injured, because he had not known about her son, and might inadvertently have made a fool of himself with some casual reference whose ignorance would be embarrassing.

What was the boy like, she said. The one in the house? 'I don't – talk to his friends. I find it painful. It could be Timmy, or Martin. They might have lost something, or want . . .'

He described the boy. Blond, about ten at a guess, he was not very good at children's ages, very blue eyes, slightly built, with a rainbow-striped tee shirt and jeans, mostly though not always – oh, and those football practice shoes black and green. And the other tee shirt, with the ships and wavy lines. And an extraordinarily nice smile. A really *warm* smile. A nice-looking boy.

He was used to her being silent. But this silence went on and on and on. She was just staring into the garden. After a time, she said, in her precise conversational tone,

'The only thing I want, the only thing I want at all in this world, is to see that boy.'

She stared at the garden and he stared with her, until the grass began to dance with empty light, and the edges of the shrubbery wavered. For a brief moment he shared the strain of not seeing the boy. Then she gave a little sigh, sat down, neatly, as always, and passed out at his feet.

After this she became, for her, voluble. He didn't move after she fainted but sat patiently by her, until she stirred and sat up; then he fetched her some water, and would have gone away, but she talked.

'I'm too rational to see ghosts, I'm not someone who would see anything there was to see, I don't believe in an after-life. I don't see how anyone can, I always found a kind of satisfaction for myself in the idea that one just came to an end, to a sliced-off stop. But that was myself; I didn't think he – not he – I thought ghosts were what people *wanted* to see, or were afraid to see . . . and after he died, and the best hope I had, it sounds silly, was that I would go mad enough so that instead of waiting every day for him to come home from school and rattle the letter-box I might actually have the illusion of seeing or hearing him come in. Because I can't stop my body and mind waiting, every day, every day, I can't let go. And his bedroom, sometimes at night I go in, I think I might just for a moment forget he *wasn't* in there sleeping, I think I would pay almost anything – anything at all – for a moment of seeing him like I used to. In his pyjamas, with his – his – his hair . . . ruffled, and, his . . . you said, his . . . that *smile*.

'When it happened, they got Noel, and Noel came in and shouted my name, like he did the other day, that's why I screamed, because it – seemed the same – and then they said, he is dead, and I thought coolly, *is* dead, that will go on and on and on till the end of time, it's a continuous present tense, one thinks the most ridiculous things, there I was thinking about grammar, the verb to be, when it ends to be dead . . . And then I came out into the garden, and I half saw, in my mind's eye, a kind of ghost of his face, just the eyes and hair, coming towards me – like every day waiting for him to come home, the way you think of your son, with such pleasure, when he's – not there – and I – I thought – no, I won't *see* him, because he is dead, and I won't dream about him because he is dead, I'll be rational and practical and continue to live because one must, and there was Noel . . .

'I got it wrong, you see, I was so *sensible*, and then I was so shocked because I couldn't get to want anything – I couldn't *talk* to Noel – I – I – made Noel take away, destroy, all the photos, I – didn't dream, you can will not to dream, I didn't . . . visit a grave, flowers, there isn't any point. I was so sensible. Only my body wouldn't stop waiting and all it wants is to – see that boy. *That* boy. That boy you – saw.'

*

He did not say that he might have seen another boy, maybe even a boy who had been given the tee shirts and jeans afterwards. He did not say, though the idea crossed his mind, that maybe what he had seen was some kind of impression from her terrible desire to see a boy where nothing was. The boy had had nothing terrible, no aura of pain about him: he had been, his memory insisted, such a pleasant, courteous, self-contained boy, with his own purposes. And in fact the woman herself almost immediately raised the possibility that what he had seen was what she desired to see, a kind of mix-up of radio waves, like when you overheard police messages on the radio, or got BBC1 on a switch that said ITV. She was thinking fast, and went on almost immediately to say that perhaps his sense of loss, his loss of Anne, which was what had led her to feel she could bear his presence in her house, was what had brought them – dare she say – near enough, for their wavelengths, to mingle, perhaps, had made him susceptible . . . You mean, he had said, we are a kind of emotional vacuum, between us, that must be filled. Something like that, she had said, and had added, 'But I don't believe in ghosts.'

Anne, he thought, could not be a ghost, because she was elsewhere, with someone else, doing for someone else those little things she had done so gaily for him, tasty little suppers, bits of research, a sudden vase of unusual flowers, a new bold shirt, unlike his own cautious taste, but suiting him. In a sense, Anne was worse lost because voluntarily absent, an absence that could not be loved because love was at an end, for Anne.

'I don't suppose you will, now,' the woman was saying. 'I think talking would probably stop any – mixing of messages, if that's what it is, don't you? But – if – *if* he comes again' – and here for the first time her eyes were full of tears – 'if – you must promise, you will *tell* me, you must promise.'

He had promised, easily enough, because he was fairly sure she was right, the boy would not be seen again. But the next day he was on the lawn, nearer than ever, sitting on the grass beside the deckchair, his arms clasping his bent, warm brown knees, the thick, pale hair glittering in the sun. He was wearing a football shirt, this time, Chelsea's colours. Sitting down in the deckchair, the man could have put out a hand and touched him, but he did not: it was not, it seemed, a possible gesture to make. But the boy looked up and smiled, with a pleasant complicity, as though they now understood each other very well. The man tried speech: he said, 'It's nice to see you again,' and the boy nodded acknowledgement of this remark, without speaking himself. This was the beginning of communication between them, or what the man supposed to be communication. He did not think of fetching the woman. He became aware that he was in some strange way *enjoying the boy's company*. His pleasant stillness – and he sat there all morning, occasionally lying back on the grass, occasionally staring thoughtfully at the house – was calming and comfortable. The man did quite a lot of work – wrote about three reasonable pages on Hardy's original air-blue gown – and looked up now and then to make sure the boy was still there and happy.

He went to report to the woman – as he had after all promised to do – that evening. She had obviously been waiting and hoping – her unnatural calm had given way to agitated pacing, and her eyes were dark and deeper in. At this point in the story he found in himself a necessity to bowdlerize for the sympathetic American, as he had indeed already begun to do. He had mentioned only a child who had 'seemed like' the woman's lost son, and he now ceased to mention the child at all, as an actor in the story, with the result that what the American woman heard was a tale of how he, the man, had become increasingly involved in the woman's solitary grief, how their two losses had become a kind of *folie à deux* from which he could not extricate himself. What follows is not what he told the American girl, though it may be clear at which points the bowdlerized version coincided with what he really believed to have happened. There was a sense he could not at first analyse that it was improper to talk about the boy – not because he might not be believed; that did not come into it; but because something dreadful might happen.

'He sat on the lawn all morning. In a football shirt.'

'Chelsea?'

'Chelsea.'

'What did he do? Does he look happy? Did he speak?' Her desire to know was terrible.

'He doesn't speak. He didn't move much. He seemed – very calm. He stayed a long time.'

'This is terrible. This is ludicrous. There is *no boy*.'

'No. But I saw him.'

'Why you?'

'I don't know.' A pause. 'I do *like* him.'

'He is – was – a most likeable boy.'

Some days later he saw the boy running along the landing in the evening, wearing what might have been pyjamas, in peacock towelling, or might have been a track suit. Pyjamas, the woman stated confidently, when he told her: his new pyjamas. With white ribbed cuffs, weren't they? and a white polo neck? He corroborated this, watching her cry – she cried more easily now – finding her anxiety and disturbance very hard to bear. But it never occurred to him that it was possible to break his promise to tell her when he saw the boy. That was another curious imperative from some undefined authority.

They discussed clothes. If there were ghosts, how could they appear in clothes long burned, or rotted, or worn away by other people? You could imagine, they agreed, that something of a person might linger – as the Tibetans and others believe the soul lingers near the body before setting out on its lone journey. But clothes? And in this case so many clothes? I must be seeing your memories, he told her, and she nodded fiercely, compressing her lips, agreeing that this was likely, adding, 'I am too rational to go mad, so I seem to be putting it on you.'

He tried a joke. 'That isn't very kind to me, to infer that madness comes more easily to me.'

'No, sensitivity. I am insensible. I was always a bit like that, and this made it worse. I am the *last* person to see any ghost that was trying to haunt me.'

'We agreed it was your memories I saw.'

'Yes. We agreed. That's rational. As rational as we can be, considering.'

All the same, the brilliance of the boy's blue regard, his gravely smiling salutation in the garden next morning, did not seem like anyone's tortured memories of earlier happiness. The man spoke to him directly then:

'Is there anything I can *do* for you? Anything you want? Can I help you?'

The boy seemed to puzzle about this for a while, inclining his head as though hearing was difficult. Then he nodded quickly and perhaps urgently turned, and ran into the house, looking back to make sure he was followed. The man entered the living-room through the French windows, behind the running boy, who stopped for a moment in the centre of the room, with the man blinking behind him at the sudden transition from sunlight to comparative dark. The woman was sitting in an armchair, looking at nothing there. She often sat like that. She looked up, across the boy, at the man, and the boy, his face for the first time anxious, met the man's eyes again, asking, before he went out into the house.

'What is it? What is it? Have you seen him again? Why are you . . .?'

'He came in here. He went – out through the door.'

'I didn't see him.'

'No.'

'Did he – oh, this is so *silly* – did he see me?'

He could not remember. He told the only truth he knew.

'He brought me in here.'

'Oh, what can I do, what am I going to *do*? If I killed myself – I have thought of that – but the idea that I should be with him is an illusion I . . . this silly situation is the nearest I shall ever get. To him. He was *in here with me?*'

'Yes.'

And she was crying again. Out in the garden he could see the boy, swinging agile on the apple branch.

He was not quite sure, looking back, when he had thought he had realized what the boy had wanted him to do. This was also at the party, his worst piece of what he called bowdlerization, though in some sense it was clearly the opposite of bowdlerization. He told the American girl that he had come to the conclusion that it was the woman herself who had wanted it, though there was in fact, throughout, no sign of her wanting anything except to see the boy, as she said. The boy, bolder and more frequent, had appeared several nights running on the landing, wandering in and out of bathrooms and bedrooms, restlessly, a little agitated, questing almost, until it had 'come to' the man that what he required was to be re-engendered, for him, the man, to give to his mother another child, into which he could peacefully vanish. The idea was so clear that it was like another imperative, though he did not have the courage to ask the child to confirm it. Possibly this was out of delicacy – the child was too young to be talked to about sex. Possibly there were other reasons. Possibly he was mistaken: the situation was making him hysterical, he felt action of some kind was required and must be possible. He could not spend the rest of the summer, the rest of his life, describing non-existent tee shirts and blond smiles.

He could think of no sensible way of embarking on his venture, so in the end simply walked into her bedroom one night. She was lying there, reading; when she saw him her instinctive gesture was to hide, not her bare arms and throat, but her book. She seemed, in fact, quite unsurprised to see his pyjamaed figure, and, after she had recovered her coolness, brought out the book definitely and laid it on the bedspread.

'My new taste in illegitimate literature. I keep them in a box under the bed.'

Ena Twigg, Medium. The Infinite Hive. The Spirit World. Is There Life After Death?

'Pathetic,' she proffered.

He sat down delicately on the bed.

'Please, don't grieve so. Please, let yourself be comforted. Please . . .'

He put an arm round her. She shuddered. He pulled her closer. He asked why she had had only the one son, and she seemed to understand the purport of his question, for she tried, angular and chilly, to lean on him a little, she became apparently compliant. 'No real reason,' she assured him, no material reason. Just her husband's profession and lack of inclination: that covered it.

'Perhaps,' he suggested, 'if she would be comforted a little, perhaps she could hope, perhaps . . .'

For comfort then, she said, dolefully, and lay back, pushing Ena Twigg off the bed with one fierce gesture, then lying placidly. He got in beside her, put his arms round her, kissed her cold cheek, thought of Anne, of what was never to be again. Come on, he said to the woman, you must live, you must try to live, let us hold each other for comfort.

She hissed at him 'Don't *talk*' between clenched teeth, so he stroked her lightly, over her nightdress, breasts and buttocks and long stiff legs, composed like an effigy on an Elizabethan tomb. She allowed this, trembling slightly, and then trembling violently: he took this to be a sign of some mixture of pleasure and pain, of the return of life to stone. He put a hand between her legs and she moved them heavily apart; he heaved himself over her and pushed, unsuccessfully. She was contorted and locked tight: frigid, he thought grimly, was not the word. *Rigor mortis*, his mind said to him, before she began to scream.

He was ridiculously cross about this. He jumped away and said quite rudely 'Shut up,' and then ungraciously 'I'm sorry.' She stopped screaming as suddenly as she had begun and made one of her painstaking economical explanations.

'Sex and death don't go. I can't afford to let go of my grip on myself. I hoped. What you hoped. It was a bad idea. I apologize.'

'Oh, never mind,' he said and rushed out again on to the landing, feeling foolish and almost in tears for warm, lovely Anne.

The child was on the landing, waiting. When the man saw him, he looked questioning, and then turned his face against the wall and leant there, rigid, his shoulders hunched, his hair hiding his expression. There was a similarity between woman and child. The man felt, for the first time, almost uncharitable towards the boy, and then felt something else.

'Look, I'm sorry. I tried. I did try. Please turn round.'

Uncompromising, rigid, clenched back view.

'Oh well,' said the man, and went into his bedroom.

So now, he said to the American woman at the party, I feel a fool, I feel embarrassed, I feel we are hurting, not helping each other, I feel it isn't a refuge. Of course you feel that, she said, of course you're right – it was temporarily necessary, it helped both of you, but you've got to live your life. Yes, he said, I've done my best, I've tried to get through, I have my life to live. Look, she said, I want to help, I really do, I have these wonderful friends I'm renting this flat from, why don't you come, just for a few days, just for a break, why don't you? They're real sympathetic people, you'd like them, I like them, you could get your emotions kind of straightened out. She'd probably be glad to see the back of you, she must feel as bad as you do, she's got to relate to her situation in her own way in the end. We all have.

He said he would think about it. He knew he had elected to tell the sympathetic American because he had sensed she would be – would offer – a way out. He had to get out. He took her home from the party and went back to his house and landlady without seeing her into her flat. They both knew that this reticence was

promising – that he hadn't come in then, because he meant to
come later. Her warmth and readiness were like sunshine, she was
open. He did not know what to say to the woman.

In fact, she made it easy for him: she asked, briskly, if he now found
it perhaps uncomfortable to stay, and he replied that he had felt he
should move on, he was of so little use . . . Very well, she had agreed,
and had added crisply that it had to be better for everyone if 'all this'
came to an end. He remembered the firmness with which she had
told him that no illusions were pleasant. She was strong: too strong
for her own good. It would take years to wear away that stony,
closed, simply surviving insensibility. It was not his job. He would
go. All the same, he felt bad.

He got out his suitcases and put some things in them. He went
down to the garden, nervously and put away the deckchair. The
garden was empty. There were no voices over the wall. The
silence was thick and deadening. He wondered, knowing he
would not see the boy again, if anyone else would do so, or if, now
he was gone, no one would describe a tee shirt, a sandal, a smile,
seen, remembered, or desired. He went slowly up to his room
again.

The boy was sitting on his suitcase, arms crossed, face frowning and
serious. He held the man's look for a long moment, and then the
man went and sat on his bed. The boy continued to sit. The man
found himself speaking.

'You do see I have to go? I've tried to get through. I can't get
through. I'm no use to you, am I?'

The boy remained immobile, his head on one side, considering.
The man stood up and walked towards him.

'Please. Let me go. What are we, in this house? A man and a
woman and a child, and none of us can get through. You can't want
that?'

He went as close as he dared. He had, he thought, the intention of putting his hand on or through the child. But could not bring himself to feel there was no boy. So he stood, and repeated,

'I can't get through. Do you want me to stay?'

Upon which, as he stood helplessly there, the boy turned on him again the brilliant, open, confiding, beautiful desired smile.

A.L. BARKER

THE DREAM OF FAIR WOMEN

'Is it really called that?'

'Why not?'

'Couldn't you have found somewhere else!'

'You asked me to suggest somewhere Janine wouldn't find you and you could rest up. This is it. The landlord owes me a favour. Are you going to quibble about a name?'

'I can't stand women. I've done with them.'

'You? You won't be done till you're in your wooden overcoat.'

'I mean it. So far as I'm concerned it's not a dream, it's a bloody nightmare.'

'It's a poem by Tennyson.'

'So it's a poem by Tennyson! But if Janine tracks me down—'

'Beach – he's the landlord – will see her off.'

'I tell you she's sworn to kill me. And she'll do it.'

'It beats me how you get into these situations.'

Selwyn grinned. 'That's because you don't know the power of love.'

He made Miller take his key and go to the flat and check that Janine was out. Then he went in and got his things together. She had locked the wardrobe but he had no qualms about breaking it open. He took the whisky and gin, he liked whisky and she liked gin and he reckoned she deserved to suffer for illegally impounding his clothes. He frisked the mattress, felt in the space under the Sleepeezie label. It was empty, as half expected, seeing that he had removed some cash from there only the day before. But it was worth a look, she was such a creature of habit. He could say that twice, he could say anything boring about Janine twice.

'She's mentally unbalanced,' he called to Miller, who was keeping watch from the front window. 'If she's crossed she goes bananas.'

'Find yourself a nice homely girl with money.'

'All women are crazy, I've definitely done with them. Come on, let's get out of here, I don't feel safe.'

In the car on the way to the pub Miller said, 'Beach isn't exactly mild-tempered either. He's an ex-Commando, so don't start anything unless you want your neck squeezed.'

'Is he married?'

Miller nodded and grinned, showing his eye-teeth. 'I'd be surprised if you started anything there.'

It turned out to be a Victorian-style red-brick hostelry in a mini-minor road, not much more than a lay-by, off the motorway. Miller could be right, Janine wouldn't come looking for him here. Selwyn, observing the thick carpets, claret-shaded lamps and claw-footed chairs, guessed that it was pricey. He needn't mind, he had the money Janine had been putting by for a new cooker, it would see him through the week and he was entitled to a spell of comfort – morning tea and newspapers in bed, full English breakfasts, three-tiered lunches and brandy after dinner.

Beach, the mine host, looked out of character with the place. He was beetle-browed, no longer young, but big in hams and fists, with a hot hard eye and hairy nostrils. Miller introduced Selwyn as 'this friend who's having trouble with his life-style and needs peace and quiet to sort it out'. Beach finished what he was doing, wiping the bar counter with a piece of mutton cloth before he shook hands. It was like being saluted by something cold, damp and powerful: a boa constrictor. Miller said, 'If anyone comes asking for him, he's not here, you've never seen him, or anyone like him.'

Selwyn, who was wiping his shaken hand on the seat of his trousers, put in, 'Especially if it's a woman asking.'

'What sort of woman?'

Miller said, 'Tall, slender, thirtyish, foreign-looking.'

'Blonde or brunette?'

'Dark brunette.'

'That goes for a lot of women that come in here.'

'Home-dyed,' said Selwyn. 'And built like a race-horse, she's got the same twitchy skin.'

'Money?'

'Excuse me?'

'Do you owe her money?'

'Certainly not.' Selwyn had perfected the art of clearing his face and retracting his ears with a boyish openness which most people – women, anyway – found irresistible. Beach found it totally resistible and gave him a non-complicit stare. 'It's an emotional entanglement, you know what I mean. She'll get over it. But she's liable to say and do things she'll be sorry for later on.'

'I'll put you at the back,' said Beach. 'If you see her coming you can get away down the fire-escape.' He wasn't smiling and there was no twinkle in his eye.

Selwyn thought it politic to laugh, so did Miller. 'You'll be OK, Sel. Call me if there's anything else I can do.'

'You've done enough,' said Selwyn. Later he might need to borrow Miller's car, but as of now Miller was welcome to go. Selwyn clapped him across the shoulders. 'I won't forget it, sport.'

He was probably doing Miller a favour. The inn, tucked away as it was, couldn't be much patronized and whatever Miller owed the landlord would be covered by the introduction of a paying guest. At present, anyway, Selwyn was prepared to pay. If he became unprepared by force of circumstance there might have to be a reappraisal.

A little old man with legs like a jockey and wearing button gaiters carried his bag upstairs. He opened a door on the first landing.

'Here we are, sir, I hope you'll be comfortable.'

'If I'm not you'll soon hear about it.'

But he approved of the room. It was dignified, full of solid, well-polished furniture and good old Turkey carpet, not Janine's plastic wrought-iron chairs and skid-mats on bare parquet. The bed was double, well-sprung, noiseless, the pillows plump, the eiderdown billowy and pink satin.

He lay down, closed his eyes and summoned a few erotic memories. When, sighing, even soulful, he got up, the short winter dusk had set in and the room was full of substantial shadows.

He was not, and never had been, a fanciful type. His school reports complained 'lacks imagination', but in the one and only important respect that was not true. He had plenty of imagination when it came to the little old three-letter word that made the world go round. One of those shadows looked uncommonly like a woman. Wishful thinking, of course.

He switched on the light and the shadows vanished. There was a sort of tallboy with a vase on top which could have looked like a figure, a woman's if he was sufficiently wishful. Whistling, he unpacked his clothes and hung them in the closet; he was of a sanguine disposition and Fate, or Nature, or the law of averages would provide.

He filled the bath and tipped into it half a bottle of Janine's bath oil which he had taken more to annoy her than because he liked it. It made the gloomy old hotel bathroom smell like a sauna and streaked the bath bright green. Afterwards he put on his dressing-gown and drank Janine's gin. This was the life and he was grateful to her for putting him up to it.

While he shaved he took a good look at himself. He had not been born with money but he had the remote next best, a thoroughly prepossessing exterior. In fact women were too damn prepossessed and couldn't wait for the property to become vacant.

Which was how the trouble with Janine had started, over some wretched girl who thought she owned him.

He stroked his nose. Roman, Janine called it. It wasn't, it was Greek. And his skin, olive and warm, with greenish shadows after his shave, had positively obsessed her. He watched his smile light up his face and he couldn't wonder, he honestly couldn't, at the damage he inflicted. He couldn't be blamed for it either.

He dressed and went down to dinner. The tables in the dining-room were all set, white cloths and sparkling glasses, cutlery for three courses, bread baskets and napkins folded into bishops' mitres.

But company, though expected, did not arrive. He ate with a thousand of his selves reflected to infinity in the mirrors that lined the walls. The food was above average, country pâté and toast, followed by veal cutlets, creamed potatoes and button sprouts, then a nice apple charlotte with clotted cream, cheese and biscuits.

The woman who waited at table was as black as the ace of spades. He asked her what her name was.

'Rosanna.'

'That's two names, Rose and Anna.'

'Just the one. Like glory.'

'Glory?'

She drew the cork from his bottle of wine with a report like a gun shot. 'Hosanna in the highest.'

He watched her take her big hips away between the tables. She was majestical, even stately. In her own country she would rate as a beauty. But looking at her was like looking at a newly black-leaded grate.

When she brought his veal chops he raised his glass to her. 'Bottoms up.'

She inclined her head and smiled, not the melon grin of her kind, no more than a quirk of her lips. 'I hope you enjoy your meal.'

He saw her afterwards serving behind the bar. He didn't stay long. There was nothing to interest him, executive types talking about 'demand-promotion', elderly housewives, and a man with a smelly dog.

Anyway, he had demands of his own to promote. He was thinking of getting away somewhere warm for the winter. It would need organization to stretch Janine's cooker money to pay for his bed and board here and buy him an air ticket to Cyprus or Benidorm or wherever. He needed to think – and take a look at the fire-escape.

On the way up to his room he met a woman. He was deep in thought and didn't see her until they came face to face, or rather, knee to knee. It gave them both a surprise – wholly pleasant for him. As she stood on the stair above he was close enough to follow the blush that ran swiftly and softly from her neck to her temples. He did not stand aside, his hand went out to the banister rail and his arm barred her way. He smiled deep into her eyes and that again was a wholly pleasant experience.

She was young, but not too young, mid-thirties perhaps, he could see tiny scarlet threads under her skin. He could also see that she was a natural pure blonde. But she had raven black brows and lashes which, contrasting with her corngold hair, stopped his heart as well as his eye. Over her blue silk dress she wore a frilly apron, decorative rather than menial.

'I do beg your pardon,' he said warmly.

She lowered her eyes and made a movement, not quite a curt-sey, nor yet a bob, but it acknowledged his status as a paying guest – and a promising male. All without a trace of coquetry or coyness.

He would have handed her down the stair but she drew back and stood against the wall so that he could pass.

'Mrs Beach?' She lifted her chin, smiling. 'My name's Selwyn.'

She nodded and next minute was gone, slipping away down the stairs and along the passage to the bar. Whistling, he went up to his room.

But he couldn't settle to his own affairs. He kept thinking about the woman. It was the old story, he was about to start something. Only this time he had a feeling that a start had already been made. Who by? Mrs Beach? He had only seen her for a couple of minutes but he could see she wasn't bold like Janine, nor forward. She had class, something he tended to forget women could have. It was in the way she looked at him, sure of her quality and expecting his to be up to the same standard. Well, he wouldn't disappoint her, there was a best in him, let her bring it out and see how good it was.

'Mrs Beach, you're a peach.' He went to the window and looked at the fire-escape. His plans had changed, he might be staying longer than first budgeted for, and there were other emergencies besides fire that he might want to escape from.

He decided to go back to the bar and have another look at Mrs Beach. But she wasn't there. Beach and the black woman were getting ready to close. She was rinsing glasses, Beach was re-arranging chairs. He stood, a chair in each hand, and stared at Selwyn, eyes as hard as bullets. Selwyn did not ask him where his wife was; he disliked the idea of talking to Beach about her.

Hopefully, he thought, he might find her upstairs. He hung about outside his room and when he went in, left the door ajar. The dress she wore made a whispering sound when she moved and he would certainly hear if she passed by.

All he heard was Beach's heavy tread going along the passage and up the next flight of stairs. Selwyn shut his door and went to bed.

Next morning he was wakened with tea and newspaper, brought not by Mrs Beach, as he had confidently expected, but by the old fellow with elliptical legs.

'I hope you slept well, sir.'

'Where's Mrs Beach?'

'Gone shopping.' The old fellow drew back the heavy curtains and let in a blaze of light.

Selwyn flinched. 'Hey, I ordered the *Sun* newspaper, not the bloody solar system. Leave the curtains.'

'I beg your pardon, sir.'

'Another thing, Barney, I want a pot of tea in the morning, and biscuits, not one cup going cold.'

'My name's Harold, sir. I'll see about the tea.'

'Ridden many winners, Barney?'

'Harold, sir. Winners, sir?'

Selwyn pointed to his legs and the old fellow put his hands over his kneecaps with the gesture of a girl covering her modesty. 'That's the arthritis, sir.'

Selwyn burst out laughing. There was no point in getting up right away, so he ordered breakfast in bed.

He looked through his newspaper. News didn't interest him, girlie pictures did. He had once gone so far as to cut out the best ones and stick them on the wall in the bathroom at the flat, but Janine and the steam between them soon curtailed that little show.

It was after eleven when he strolled downstairs. He left the inn and walked along the road, thinking he might meet Mrs Beach coming back from shopping.

The sun had gone in, the clouds were building up for rain or snow. This was marginal country, the fields still spattered with clay from the excavations for the motorway, the hedges broken down and a dredger like a dead dinosaur rusting in the ditch. He could hear the roar of traffic on the M-road, but the only traffic in this lane was an orange Mini, driven by Rosanna. She lifted her hand to him as she passed. They had it made over here, he thought. A car to come to work in! In her own country she'd be walking barefoot with a bundle on her head.

Chilled to the bone – he hadn't put on a top coat – he turned back. The name of the inn still irked him. 'The Dream of Fair Women'. Whose dream? Not Beach's, that ape wouldn't have the delicacy to dream. Though he did have one of the fair women. Selwyn found that he actively objected to the notion that he and Beach had the same tastes.

He was the only one for lunch and again he was served by old Barney, creaking across the dining-room with his thumb in the soup. Selwyn sent it back. 'When I want a taste of horse in my Brown Windsor I'll say so.'

'Sir?'

'Is Mrs B back from shopping?'

Barney picked up the plate and his thumb went under the soup to the base of his nail. 'Mrs Beach is in the kitchen.'

Selwyn went to the lounge after lunch. He kicked the fire into a blaze and stretched himself on the Knole settee. It was sleeting outside, the room was twilit and warm and he fell asleep.

A sound wakened him, a sort of remote whispering. He knew what it was before he opened his eyes. It deeply and deliciously disturbed him. He sat up and saw her walking slowly to and fro in the firelight.

'Hallo there,' he said, sounding surprised, though he was not. He believed his luck, he was lucky in love, only when he was out of it did his troubles begin.

She stopped, turned to him, and now that the whisper of her dress had ceased he was left with the astonishing contrast between her black winged eyebrows and golden hair. It could have been a mistake, but Nature did not make that kind of mistake and it was an unqualified triumph. The skin of her lips was so fine and so full of warm blood that again there was a contrast, almost fierce, between the redness of her mouth and the pallor of her face.

'I waited for you,' he said, and another voice, not the one he used every day but one which he reserved for private and primary communications, said, 'I've been waiting all my life.'

And he knew that if he never spoke another, he had just spoken something which was a whole truth.

Standing before him, head bowed, her hands clasped in front of her, she too seemed to be waiting, for his wishes – his pleasure. He felt himself go hot, then cold, then hot again, and put up his hand to her. But his reach wasn't long enough, or his arm wasn't right, or his timing, and he did not quite touch her. 'I don't even know your name.'

She raised her head, and with that slight movement her dress whispered. He had not yet heard her speak. Perhaps she was dumb? Was that what Miller had been getting at when he said he would be surprised if Selwyn started anything?

Selwyn could have laughed out loud. Words he could very well dispense with when he started anything – words and clothes. Smiling broadly, he stood up to look deep into the neck of her dress to the beautiful shadow between her breasts.

'I'm called Alice.' She glanced up from under her lashes and as quickly lowered her eyes.

'In your Alice-blue-gown.' He made a move towards her, but she bent away from him like a flame in a draught. 'You're not scared of me, are you?'

'No. It's my husband I'm scared of – he is so terribly jealous.'

'I don't blame him.'

'So terribly jealous,' she said again. 'It is terrible to kill someone out of jealousy.'

'Kill?'

She drew herself together, clasped her arms about herself, suddenly cold perhaps, or fearful, or in pain. 'A young man, a student, he was just a boy. Years ago. He came here to work in his vacation and my husband murdered him.'

'For God's sake!' said Selwyn. 'Why?'

'He thought he was my lover.'

'Was he?'

'I never had a lover.' She raised her face to his, opened her eyes wide, violet eyes – the only colour he had ever seen to match it was in one of those old-fashioned carboys in a chemist's window. 'I only had my husband.'

Selwyn felt quite dizzy. 'How could he – I mean, how did he get away with murder?'

'He strangled him and hanged him from a beam in the cellar. He made it look as though the boy had killed himself, you see.'

Selwyn, who did not see, said, 'Why should he kill himself?'

'Because of unrequited love. That's what everyone thought. But my husband thought I requited it.'

'How can you go on living with someone like that?'

She smiled. Selwyn sensed an awful lot in that smile, but was unable then to appreciate just how much, and how awful. 'Next time I shall make sure there's a witness.'

'Next time?'

'Next time he kills someone.'

He flung out his hands with the impulsive gesture which had endeared him to so many women. 'There's no reason why it should happen again! Don't be scared on my account. I'm not a boy, I'm a man of the world, I can take care of myself.'

'Ah, you—' She uttered a sigh. It said plainer than words that she knew the difference – and all the other differences there would be between a man and a boy.

But instead of taking his hands, her own flew to her throat. She murmured, 'Tonight.' Any of the women he knew who still remembered how to colour up went blotting-paper pink and puffy. Alice Beach blushed the tenderest shade of rose.

'Where?' he said eagerly. 'What time?'

A sudden gust of wind hurled heavy rain, or hail, against the window. He had turned his head to look, and in that moment she slipped away. When he turned back the room was empty.

'Damn and blast!'

'I beg your pardon, sir?'

That was Barney, bringing in an armful of logs.

'Where did Mrs Beach go?'

'I came in the back way, ain't seen nobody.'

Selwyn was joined in the dining-room that evening by a gang of commercials. They were having a reunion and kept Rosanna busy fetching wines from the cellar and chasers from the bar. He wanted to ask where Mrs Beach was, but decided not to prejudice anything. For all he knew she had made arrangements which would not bear inquiring into at this stage.

He sat at his meal, scarcely aware of what he ate, going over in some detail his expectations for later on. He was able, because of many past encounters, to vary the opening gambits. He couldn't make up his mind which he would prefer. One thing was certain, Alice Beach was intended for him. And he for her. The mutuality was going to make it a memorable experience. His bones, as well as his flesh, melted at some of his expectations.

When the salesmen started singing a smutty song to the tune of 'Annie Laurie' – it wasn't even original, just the same old smut from his schooldays – he got up and went into the bar.

It was still sleeting outside, there weren't many drinkers in the 'Dream' that night – the man with the smelly dog which was wet-through and smellier than ever, and some girls and boys getting stoned on vodka and Cokes. They looked under age, Beach probably couldn't afford to turn them away. He was leaning on the counter reading a newspaper.

Selwyn got himself a double whisky. He sat quietly taking it between his teeth and his tongue and turning over in his mind the question of whether Beach could have done murder. He had been wondering – not all that often, having better things to think about – since Alice had told him. The man was certainly an ugly customer and had plenty of bad coming to him. But on the whole Selwyn was inclined to think she had exaggerated, kidded herself. A woman, any woman, loved the idea of murder being committed on her account.

The salesmen came in from the dining-room and at once the bar was in an uproar. They had had a skinful, they were all in the same hairy skin together, jolly old pals, auld acquaintance never to be forgot, buddies, all for one and one big headache for all. They were singing another worn-out classic, about the nun and the undertaker. Beach was kept busy as they ordered and counter-ordered and forgot to pay, and spilled their drinks. Selwyn had to laugh, watching him run to and fro, wild-eyed and sweating, trying to cope. A beerpull jammed and he lost his nerve and started bellowing.

Barney appeared, none too readily. 'I told you to fix this bloody thing!' shouted Beach. 'Get Rosanna. Where is she?'

'Got a headache.'

Selwyn wasn't surprised to hear that. He strolled over to the bar and watched Beach wrestling with the beerpull. 'Give me another whisky.'

Beach looked up with hatred. 'You'll have to wait. Can't you see I'm single-handed?'

'So was Rosanna.' Selwyn winked. 'It's your turn now, sport.'

He went upstairs after his third whisky. He knew when to stop. Alcohol was good, was practically medicinal at such times. It was a guarantor. But only up to a point, beyond that point was no return, only rapid deterioration. He meant to acquit himself perfectly tonight, for her sake as well as his own. 'I never had a lover,' she had said. He was filled with the pure and uplifting spirit of self-lessness.

It was also reasonable to suppose that the first place she would look for him would be in his room.

He undressed, put on his pyjamas and dressing gown, tucked a silk cravat over his pyjama-collar. She was a creature of refinement and delicacy. There would be no time to waste, but she would require a little dalliance and – he rinsed his glass and put it ready beside the remains of Janine's gin – a little of the guarantor.

An hour passed. He had left his door ajar and a dozen times went out into the passage to look for her. He heard the salesmen go, packing into their cars, engines roaring and tyres screeching as they belted along the lane. They'd be lucky if they ran into nothing worse than a squad-car and breathalyzers. Afterwards, all was quiet downstairs. He looked at his watch and saw that it wanted but half an hour to closing time.

She wasn't coming. Either she had been prevented or she had been teasing him. Even ladies could be teases. Especially ladies. He cursed her aloud.

'Damn and blast you, Alice Beach!'

'No – please!'

He swung round. She was there in her Alice-blue, holding out her arms to him, her golden hair ablaze, her cheeks shining with tears.

'My dear – I didn't mean it!'

He started towards her, but she put her finger to her lips. 'Shhhh—'

'I thought you weren't coming!'

'Oh, nothing could stop me now!'

'Why did you leave it so late?'

'Late? If you knew how long I have waited!'

It was more of a wail than an exclamation. He went cold, and did not immediately go hot again. 'What about Beach? Won't he be coming up soon?'

'Not yet, not just yet.'

It occurred to Selwyn that she didn't even know how long a love-making would take, how long it *could* take.

'We don't want to hurry anything,' he said, and went to close the door, 'but I've been waiting too.'

She flung up her hands in a quaint, old-fashioned gesture of protest. 'Not here – it cannot be in this room.'

'Why not? It's the safest place. I'll lock the door.'

'He has a pass-key, he'll come looking for me. We must go somewhere else.'

'Where?'

'Come—' She slipped out of the room and was gone. When he went into the passage she was standing at the point where the stairs went up to the second floor.

'Not up there,' said Selwyn. 'He sleeps up there.'

'You must trust me.'

He was close enough to see how her eyes shone and her parted lips. She was breathing fast, and so was he, but her breasts moved in perfect rhythm as if there was a soft little motor under them. And the Alice-blue dress whispered to him.

He said hoarsely, 'I don't care where we go so long as it's now!'

'It is now – I promise.' She ran up the stairs and opened a door. He followed, found they were in a room, in darkness. He could just make out the shape of a bed, the clothes tumbled, a mound of eiderdown. It looked promising.

The time for delicacy was past. He threw off his dressing-gown and cravat, stood in his pyjamas. There was a movement on the bed, she was waiting for him.

'Alice—' he groped among the bedclothes.

At once several things happened. A light was switched on. Selwyn blinked, dazzled and disbelieving. A black face was looking up at him from the pillow. At the same moment he heard Beach's voice in the passage below. There was no one else in the room, no Alice, just himself and Rosanna. She raised herself on her elbow, her eyes rolling white with alarm.

'What are you doing here?'

He might have asked her that, but Beach's footsteps were on the stairs. He cried, 'Where's Alice? Where is she?'

'Alice?'

'Alice Beach – Mrs Beach—'

It wasn't possible, yet Rosanna's skin seemed to darken. The shine went out of it. She said, 'That Mrs Beach has been dead a long time.'

'Dead?'

'Killed in a car accident four, maybe five, years ago.'

'Goddamit!' cried Selwyn, 'That's crazy, up the creek! She was here a minute ago. She's framing me, why I don't know, but it doesn't matter now—' It was a matter, now, of self-preservation. 'Beach is coming—'

'He is coming here.'

'You've got to help me – Rosanna, I'll make it worth your while – I'll have to brazen it out – he can't object – it won't look – I mean it's not as if you're his wife, is it?'

'I am his wife.'

'What?'

'His second wife.'

Selwyn's jaw dropped. His mouth fell open and dried. Then Beach came into the room, and there was a moment of crammed and unpeaceful silence. Beach took in the scene – Selwyn in his pyjamas, Rosanna in the tumbled bed. A moment was enough, even for Beach, a man of not especially quick intelligence. He was also a plain man, and in that moment became downright ugly.

He made for Selwyn, unstoppable as a tank making for an enemy trench. Selwyn ran round the bed, shouted with all the strength of his lungs. He found he was trapped, his back to the wall, but, desperate, kept shouting. For help, for understanding – for a little more time. Beach's hands gripping his throat stopped him at last.

He didn't see Barney come running as fast as his crooked legs would bring him. Barney arrived in the doorway, stood and gaped. It was really all he was required to do. Had Selwyn been the fanciful type, and had the opportunity – which, naturally, he had not – he might have recalled at least one promise Alice Beach had kept: 'Next time I'll make sure there's a witness.'

PENELOPE LIVELY

BLACK DOG

John Case came home one summer evening to find his wife huddled in the corner of the sofa with the sitting-room curtains
drawn. She said there was a black dog in the garden, looking at her
through the window. Her husband put his briefcase in the hall and
went outside. There was no dog; a blackbird fled shrieking across the
lawn and next door someone was using a mower. He did not see how
any dog could get into the garden: the fences at either side were five
feet high and there was a wall at the far end. He returned to the
house and pointed this out to his wife, who shrugged and continued
to sit hunched in the corner of the sofa. He found her there again
the next evening and at the weekend she refused to go outside and
sat for much of the time watching the window.

The daughters came, big girls with jobs in insurance companies,
wardrobes full of bright clothes and twenty-thousand-pound mort-
gages. They stood over Brenda Case and said she should get out
more. She should go to evening classes, they said, join a health
club, do a language course, learn upholstery, go jogging, take driving
lessons. And Brenda Case sat at the kitchen table and nodded. She
quite agreed, it would be a good thing to find a new interest – jogging, upholstery, French; yes, she said, she must pull herself together,
and it was indeed up to her in the last resort, they were quite right.
When they had gone she drew the sitting-room curtains again and

sat on the sofa staring at a magazine they had brought. The magazine was full of recipes the daughters had said she must try; there
were huge bright glossy photographs of puddings crested with
Alpine peaks of cream, of dark glistening casseroles and salads like
an artist's palette. The magazine costed each recipe; a four-course
dinner for six worked out at £3.89 a head. It also had articles advis-
ing her on life insurance, treatment for breast cancer and how to
improve her love-making.

John Case became concerned about his wife. She had always
been a good housekeeper; now, they began to run out of things.
When one evening there was nothing but cold meat and cheese for
supper he protested. She said she had not been able to shop because
it had rained all day; on rainy days the dog was always outside, waiting for her.

The daughters came again and spoke severely to their mother.
They talked to their father separately, in different tones, proposing
an autumn holiday in Portugal or the Canaries, a new three-piece
for the sitting-room, a musquash coat.

John Case discussed the whole thing with his wife, reasonably.
He did this one evening after he had driven the Toyota into the
garage, walked over to the front door and found it locked from
within. Brenda, opening it, apologized; the dog had been round at
the front today, she said, sitting in the middle of the path.

He began by saying lightly that dogs have not been known to
stand up on their hind legs and open doors. And in any case, he
continued, there is no dog. No dog at all. The dog is something you
are imagining. I have asked all the neighbours; nobody has seen a
big black dog. Nobody round here owns a big black dog. There is no
evidence of a dog. So you must stop going on about this dog because
it does not exist. 'What is the matter?' he asked, gently. 'Something
must be the matter. Would you like to go away for a holiday? Shall
we have the house redecorated?'

Brenda Case listened to him. He was sitting on the sofa, with his
back to the window. She sat listening carefully to him and from time
to time her eyes strayed from his face to the lawn beyond, in the

middle of which the dog sat, its tongue hanging out and its yellow eyes glinting. She said she would go away for a holiday if he wished, and she would be perfectly willing for the house to be redecorated. Her husband talked about travel agents and decorating firms and once he got up and walked over to the window to inspect the condition of the paintwork; the dog, Brenda saw, continued to sit there, its eyes always on her.

They went to Marrakesh for ten days. Men came and turned the kitchen from primrose to eau-de-nil and the hallway from magnolia to parchment. September became October and Brenda Case fetched from the attic a big gnarled walking stick that was a relic of a trip to the Tyrol many years ago; she took this with her every time she went out of the house, which nowadays was not often. Inside the house, it was always somewhere near her – its end protruding from under the sofa, or hooked over the arm of her chair.

The daughters shook their tousled heads at their mother, towering over her in their baggy fashionable trousers and their big gay jackets. It's not fair on Dad, they said, can't you see that? You've only got one life, they said sternly, and Brenda Case replied that she realized that, she did indeed. Well then . . . said the daughters, one on each side of her, bigger than her, brighter, louder, always saying what they meant, going straight to the point and no nonsense, competent with income-tax returns and contemptuous of muddle.

When she was alone, Brenda Case kept doors and windows closed at all times. Occasionally, when the dog was not there, she would open the upstairs windows to air the bedrooms and the bathroom; she would stand with the curtains blowing, taking in great gulps and draughts. Downstairs, of course, she could not risk this, because the dog was quite unpredictable; it would be absent all day, and then suddenly there it would be squatting by the fence, or leaning hard up against the patio doors, sprung from nowhere. She would draw the curtains, resigned, or move to another room and endure the knowledge of its presence on the other side of the wall, a few yards away. When it was there she would sit doing nothing, staring straight ahead of her; silent and patient. When it was gone she moved around the house, prepared meals, listened a little to the radio, and sometimes took the old photograph albums from the bottom drawer of the bureau in the sitting-room. In these albums the daughters slowly mutated from swaddled bundles topped with monkey faces and spiky hair to chunky toddlers and then to spindly-limbed little girls in matching pinafores. They played on Cornish beaches or posed on the lawn, holding her hand (that same lawn on which the dog now sat on its hunkers). In the photographs, she looked down at them, smiling, and they gazed up at her or held out objects for her inspection – a flower, a seashell. Her husband was also in the photographs; a smaller man than now, it seemed, with a curiously vulnerable look, as though surprised in a moment of privacy. Looking at herself, Brenda saw a pretty young woman who seemed vaguely familiar, like some relative not encountered for many years.

John Case realized that nothing had been changed by Marrakesh and redecorating. He tried putting the walking stick back up in the attic; his wife brought it down again. If he opened the patio doors she would simply close them as soon as he had left the room. Sometimes he saw her looking over his shoulder into the garden with an expression on her face that chilled him. He asked her, one day, what she thought the dog would do if it got into the house; she was silent for a moment and then said quietly she supposed it would eat her.

He said he could not understand, he simply did not understand, what could be wrong. It was not, he said, as though they had a thing to worry about. He gently pointed out that she wanted for nothing. It's not that we have to count the pennies any more, he said, not like in the old days.

'When we were young,' said Brenda Case. 'When the girls were babies.'

'Right. It's not like that now, is it?' He indicated the 24-inch colour TV set, the video, the stereo, the microwave oven, the English Rose fitted kitchen, the bathroom with separate shower. He reminded her of the BUPA membership, the index-linked pension, the shares and dividends. Brenda agreed that it was not, it most certainly was not.

The daughters came with their boyfriends, nicely spoken confident young men in very clean shirts, who talked to Brenda of their work in firms selling computers and Japanese cameras while the girls took John into the garden and discussed their mother.

'The thing is, she's becoming agoraphobic.'

'She thinks she sees this black dog,' said John Case.

'We know,' said the eldest daughter. 'But that, frankly, is neither here nor there. It's a mechanism, simply. A ploy. Like children do. One has to get to the root of it, that's the thing.'

'It's her age,' said the youngest.

'Of course it's her age,' snorted the eldest. 'But it's also her. She was always inclined to be negative, but this is ridiculous.'

'Negative?' said John Case. He tried to remember his wife – his wives – who – one of whom – he could see inside the house, beyond the glass of the patio window, looking out at him from between two young men he barely knew. The reflections of his daughters, his strapping prosperous daughters, were superimposed upon their mother, so that she looked at him through the cerise and orange and yellow of their clothes.

'Negative. A worrier. Look on the bright side, *I* say, but that's not Mum, is it?'

'I wouldn't have said . . .' he began.

'She's unmotivated,' said the youngest. 'That's the real trouble. No job, no nothing. It's a generation problem, too.'

'I'm trying . . .' their father began.

'We know, Dad, we know. But the thing is, she needs help. This isn't something you can handle all on your own. She'll have to see someone.'

'No way', said the youngest, 'will we get Mum into therapy.'

'Dad can take her to the surgery,' said the eldest. 'For starters.'

The doctor – the new doctor, there was always a new doctor – was about the same age as her daughters, Brenda Case saw. Once upon a time doctors had been older men, fatherly and reliable. This one was good-looking, in the manner of men in knitting-pattern photographs. He sat looking at her, quite kindly, and she told him how she was feeling. In so far as this was possible.

When she had finished he tapped a pencil on his desk. 'Yes,' he said. 'Yes, I see.' And then he went on, 'There doesn't seem to be any very specific trouble, does there, Mrs Case?'

She agreed.

'How do you think you would define it yourself?'

She thought. At last she said that she supposed there was nothing wrong with her that wasn't wrong with – well, everyone.

'Quite,' said the doctor busily, writing now on his pad. 'That's the sensible way to look at things. So I'm giving you this . . . Three a day . . . Come back and see me in two weeks.'

When she had come out John Case asked to see the doctor for a moment. He explained that he was worried about his wife. The doctor nodded sympathetically. John told the doctor about the black dog, apologetically, and the doctor looked reflective for a moment and then said, 'Your wife is fifty-four.'

John Case agreed. She was indeed fifty-four.

'Exactly,' said the doctor. 'So I think we can take it that with some care and understanding these difficulties will . . . disappear. I've given her something,' he said, confidently; John Case smiled back. That was that.

'It will go away,' said John Case to his wife, firmly. He was not entirely sure what he meant, but it did not do, he felt sure, to be irresolute. She looked at him without expression.

Brenda Case swallowed each day the pills that the doctor had given her. She believed in medicines and doctors, had always found that aspirin cured a headache and used to frequent the surgery with the girls when they were small. She was prepared for a miracle. For the first few days it did seem to her just possible that the dog was growing a little smaller but after a week she realized that it was not. She continued to take the pills and when at the end of a fortnight she told the doctor that there was no change he said that these things took time, one had to be patient. She looked at him, this young man in his swivel chair on the other side of a cluttered desk, and knew that whatever was to be done would not be done by him, or by cheerful yellow pills like children's sweets.

The daughters came, to inspect and admonish. She said that yes, she had seen the doctor again, and yes, she was feeling rather more . . . herself. She showed them the new sewing-machine with many extra attachments that she had not used and when they left she watched them go down the front path to their cars, swinging their bags and shouting at each other, and saw the dog step aside for them, wagging its tail. When they had gone she opened the door again and stood there for a few minutes, looking at it, and the dog, five yards away, looked back, not moving.

The next day she took the shopping trolley and set off for the shops. As she opened the front gate she saw the dog come out from the shadow of the fence but she did not turn back. She continued down the street, although she could feel it behind her, keeping its distance. She spoke in a friendly way to a couple of neighbours, did her shopping and returned to the house, and all the while the dog was there, twenty paces off. As she walked to the front door she could hear the click of its claws on the pavement and had to steel herself so hard not to turn round that when she got inside she was bathed in sweat and shaking all over. When her husband came home that evening he thought her in a funny mood; she asked for a glass of sherry and later she suggested they put a record on instead of watching TV – *West Side Story* or another of those shows they went to years ago.

He was surprised at the change in her. She began to go out daily, and although in the evenings she often appeared to be exhausted, as though she had been climbing mountains instead of walking subur-ban streets, she was curiously calm. Admittedly, she had not appeared agitated before, but her stillness had not been natural; now, he sensed a difference. When the daughters telephoned he reported their mother's condition and listened to their complacent comments; that stuff usually did the trick, they said, all the medics were using it nowadays, they'd always known Mum would be OK soon. But when he put the telephone down and returned to his wife in the sitting-room he found himself looking at her uncomfortably. There was an alertness about her that worried him; later, he thought he heard something outside and went to look. He could see nothing at either the front or the back and his wife continued to read a magazine. When he sat down again she looked across at him with a faint smile.

She had started by meeting its eyes, its yellow eyes. And thus she had learned that she could stop it, halt its patient shadowing of her, leave it sitting on the pavement or the garden path. She began to leave the front door ajar, to open the patio window. She could not say what would happen next, knew only that this was inevitable. She no longer sweated or shook; she did not glance behind her when she was outside, and within she hummed to herself as she moved from room to room.

John Case, returning home on an autumn evening, stepped out of the car and saw light streaming through the open front door. He thought he heard his wife speaking to someone in the house. When he came into the kitchen, though, she was alone. He said, 'The front door was open,' and she replied that she must have left it so by mistake. She was busy with a saucepan at the stove and in the corner of the room, her husband saw, was a large dog basket towards which her glance occasionally strayed.

He made no comment. He went back into the hall, hung up his coat and was startled suddenly by his own face, caught unawares in the mirror by the hatstand and seeming like someone else's – that of a man both older and more burdened than he knew himself to be. He stood staring at it for a few moments and then took a step back towards the kitchen. He could hear the gentle chunking sound of his wife's wooden spoon stirring something in the saucepan and then, he thought, the creak of wickerwork.

He turned sharply and went into the sitting-room. He crossed to the window and looked out. He saw the lawn, blackish in the dusk, disappearing into darkness. He switched on the outside lights and flooded it all with an artificial glow – the grass, the little flight of steps up to the patio and the flowerbed at the top of them, from which he had tidied away the spent summer annuals at the week-end. The bare earth was marked all over, he now saw, with what appeared to be animal footprints, and as he stood gazing it seemed to him that he heard the pad of paws on the carpet behind him. He stood for a long while before at last he turned round.

Rosemary Pardoe

THE CHAUFFEUR

Courtham House, in its present form, was mostly built during the reigns of Henry VII and his notorious, much-married son; although portions of earlier work are incorporated into its walls. The building is generally considered to be the best Tudor Manor in Cornwall, and since being taken over by the National Trust twenty years ago, it has become a popular spot with day-trippers. In summer the courtyards and lovely tiered gardens are thronged with holiday-makers; and their cars block the small country lane which runs past Courtham Quay on the River Tamar, and forms the only access to the House. In winter, however, and especially in the evenings, it is a beautifully lonely and isolated place, despite the fact that Plymouth is no more than fifteen miles away.

My friends Edwin and Marion Farrow live in a rambling con-temporary cottage attached to the main building. It was converted several years ago from two diminutive dwellings, one formerly occu-pied by the chauffeur; and thus the ground-plan is very peculiar and confusing, making it all too easy to lose oneself when on a visit.

The Farrows are a pleasant, middle-aged couple with a quiet sense of humour and a good line in conversation. Edwin is a writer on antiquarian matters, which is how I came to know him. I have an open invitation to stay at Courtham at any time, but until one chilly March a year or so ago, I'd had no opportunity to take up the offer. Therefore when I managed to get down to Cornwall for a week's holiday, I was determined to spend part of it with Edwin and Marion. As it turned out, they were kind enough to ask me to stay for the whole week.

My days were devoted to leisurely drives in the surrounding countryside, stopping whenever I came to a church, and sometimes taking photographs for my collection of post-1600 wall paintings. I've been told on many occasions that I miss the most interesting examples by confining myself to those produced after 1600, but my retort is always that earlier work is well covered by other researchers, and anyway my area of study is just as fascinating, not only historically but artistically too. No one who has seen, for instance, the lovely twentieth-century paintings in Denton church, Northamptonshire, could doubt that. However, this is not the subject of my story, and I am in danger of getting sidetracked.

Each evening during my holiday, the Farrows and I would sit snugly around their fragrant log fire – a necessity with the frosty weather we were having then – and enjoy a sherry while we chatted about the places I'd visited that day. One night, just before we started thinking about making a move to go to bed, the subject of ghosts came up.

'Courtham has a ghost, you know,' smiled Edwin, 'but I'm afraid it is a very traditional one: in the House there is supposed to be a blood-stain which magically appears and disappears on the anniversary of a particularly nasty murder. It's unfortunate for the veracity of this legend that, as far as anyone knows, there have been no murders or violent deaths at the Manor; and I for one have never seen the blood-stain! It should definitely be taken with a pinch of salt . . .'

'But, Jane,' interrupted Mrs Farrow, 'we must tell you about our very own phantom. It's much more interesting.'

'Yes, please,' I said eagerly, sleep forgotten for the moment.

'Well, sometimes when I'm in the house on my own,' Marion began in her delightfully musical voice, 'I hear a car drive up and go into our garage – it's the one just outside our gate, by the way; close to where you park your Mini. The first few times it happened, soon after we moved here, I naturally assumed that it was Edwin returning home unexpectedly, but when I went outside to look there was no one about and the garage was empty. Once, I remember, I thought I heard him come home, and I went to the gate, only to see him drive up, three or four minutes later. In those days I was too embarrassed to tell anyone about my experiences, and when Edwin asked why I was waiting for him I made up some silly story about a premonition. He must have wondered whether I'd gone mad!'

'But not long afterwards,' her husband added, 'I also heard the mysterious noise when I was alone in the cottage and Marion had the car. Since then it has recurred countless times.

'Our theory is that the ghost is Mr Watkins, the old chauffeur who lived here when Courtham was still in private hands. He loved his job so much, and was heartbroken when he had to retire at the age of sixty because of arthritis. He died a few years before we came down here in 1964, so we never knew him, but there are many accounts of his single-minded devotion to work. We think that his death gave him the opportunity to return to his duties in spirit form.

'Your bedroom, Jane, was once part of Mr Watkins's cottage, but nobody has ever seen anything odd or sensed any unnatural atmosphere, either there or in the garage. In fact one often gets a warm feeling of peace and contentment. If we have a ghost he is obviously very happy, and neither of us would dream of trying to get rid of him.

'Now I come to think of it, though, I haven't heard him for some months now – have you, Marion?'

'No, it's been nearly a year since the last time,' Mrs Farrow pondered, 'I'm starting to miss him . . .'

The conversation moved on to other topics and shortly thereafter we all went to bed.

When I awoke next morning, light was pouring in through the little diamond-paned window in my room. Inexplicably I was still

incredibly tired and an extra half-hour's lie-in seemed very invit-
ing – I didn't even have the energy to check what the time was. It
was when I tried to turn over that I became aware of something
worse than normal, early-morning lethargy. My limbs felt as though
lead weights had been placed on them, and I had an unpleasant feeling of dizziness. I was not even quite sure of my own identity . . . my
one overpowering emotion was of frustration. Whoever I was, I
knew that I should be getting up – I had a job of some sort to do,
and people were relying on me. However, try as I might I could not
move an inch. Then quite suddenly, the weight lifted and my confusion disappeared along with it.

Over a lone breakfast a little later (the Farrows having eaten an
hour earlier, at eight o'clock), I tried to account for what had happened to me. I was positive that it had not been a dream, and as far
as I knew I was not ill: certainly I felt fine now. The suspicion grew
that the old chauffeur was involved. But *how*? Perhaps there was a
slight chance that I might get a clue from his grave, although it
seemed unlikely. Still, there could be no harm in paying it a visit, so
when Marion came in to see me off on my day's expedition, I asked
her where Mr Watkins was buried. As anticipated, it was in
Lanstock churchyard, only ten minutes' drive away and the closest
village to Courtham. I had already been to the church once, on the
previous day, but it would be easy enough to drop in again on my
way north to the area on my morning's itinerary.

Lanstock graveyard was larger than I had expected, and finding
the tombstone took me some time. Eventually I spotted it – a small
grey tablet inlaid with plain black letters. The inscription was
unspectacular:

Joseph Watkins
1885–1960
Blessed are the meek

'That doesn't tell me much,' I sighed, disappointed in spite of
myself: it had been foolish to hope for an explanation of my strange

experience. There was little point in staying, but I remained for a few moments gazing at the well-kept plot, with its neatly cut grass and vase of fresh daffodils wilting slightly in the cold air. 'Someone still loves the old man,' I thought.

Towards the middle of the grave was a patch of some herb or decorative weed; self-seeded rather than deliberately placed there, by the look of it, but apparently tolerated by the person who tended the plot. I'm no botanist and I could not recognize the plant, but its scanty dark-green leaves were quite attractive and a little like those of a primrose in shape and texture. Of course, in March there were no flowers to aid identification.

Suddenly I felt an irresistible urge to bend down and pull out the entire patch by its roots. I was completely unable to control my actions and, almost before I realized what I was doing, there was not a single stem left in the earth. An ugly area of bare soil about ten inches in diameter, and a small pile of uprooted, aromatic herbs at my feet, bore witness to my misdeed. I stepped back, stunned – why had I done such a thing? Normally I would never dream of picking a wild flower, let alone killing it by removing it bodily from the ground. That, to me, is unwarrantable vandalism.

Only for a minute did I feel this self-doubt, and then a flood of happiness and satisfaction washed over me. I *had* done the right thing. Why, I did not know, but there was a good reason for the removal of the plants. I extracted one from the forlorn pile, wrapped it carefully in tissues and put it into my bag for later identification – if my memory served me right I had seen a small paperback book on herbs in Edwin Farrow's extensive library.

As the day wore on I had other things to think about, including an unseasonable snowstorm which trapped me in Callington church for an hour; and Joseph Watkins and his grave slipped my mind completely. So, at tea-time, as I drove through the slush into my usual parking position tucked around the side of Courtham House, I didn't think twice when I saw Marion Farrow leaning on the cottage gate, looking around with a curious expression on her face.

'You just missed our ghost,' she called out, as I waved and went to unload my camera equipment from the boot. Apparently five minutes earlier she had heard a car driving up and thought it was me, until she realized that the distinctive sound which tyres make as they splash through melting snow was absent.

'It's good to have the old fellow back,' she said happily. 'I wonder where he's been.'

I suspected that I knew why the chauffeur had not been about his usual duties, and more than ever I was convinced that I'd acted correctly in taking the herbs from his grave. Now all I needed to do was to name them and discover why they'd had such an effect.

After tea I borrowed Edwin's book on the subject: *British Herbs* by Florence Ranson; and after some initial difficulty caused by the fact that the book contained only line drawings, I managed to identify the plant with a fair degree of certainty. It was wood betony, and Miss Ranson's description included the following relevant information: '. . . it is . . . often found around old churches and ruined abbeys. The reason for its cultivation in these places is that it was considered a sure charm against "evil spirits . . . and the forces of darkness" . . .'

I would add that as well as keeping evil revenants in their graves, betony is evidently also capable of restraining good and harmless spirits. After I explained my thoughts to the Farrows they agreed to convince whoever was looking after Mr Watkins's plot that all suspect weeds should be removed as soon as they appeared.

That night and for the rest of my holiday I slept better than I have ever done, and I awoke full of energy. I cannot truthfully say that I felt any sort of 'presence' in my bedroom, but there was an atmosphere of peace and joy which had not been there before. My one regret is that I personally did not hear the ghostly car. Perhaps I will be more fortunate next time I go down to Cornwall.

LISA ST AUBIN DE TERÁN

DIAMOND JIM

They call it Tarlojee, that grey stretch of land that fans out from the Esequebo, and it's got a strange history buried under every rock and tree. It's a stony place, and where the fields have been cleared and the sugar grows and flowers with its grey fluff, the piles of stones make little hills like shrines in places. No wonder, then, that people forget the past when there's so much of it and all heaped up like that. So, who came and when, and whether they were Dutch or Scots or Portuguese, and whether they were good or bad, or stayed or died, nobody really cares or knows on Tarlojee.

The sun is too hot there to go filling your head with tales. It's enough to remember where the shifting sands lie along the river, and where the snakes are worst, and which of the many paths and tracks through the estate are safe. Everyone knows that the lands belong to the Hintzens, and they know they always have; and they can't help knowing that the Hintzens are mean and hard. And then, everyone knows about Diamond Jim and old man Hintzen's daughter, Miss Caroline.

That Caroline was wild, so they say. She didn't seem to have that boiled water and steel filings for blood that Germans often do, especially the old ones who've been out pushing back the jungle for so many years they forget to be properly human. She didn't even have the soft blood of the other rich folks, with their mixing of Spanish and Dutch. I've heard say that her mother somehow put the eye of the hurricane in her little girl's eye, and dead-hour sun in her blood and a goatskin drum in her heart. Not even New Amsterdam on a Saturday night was wild like her. She could make a bean stew into a banquet by laughing over it. I think the reason why those two lovers didn't get caught at first was because they were so wild no one could even imagine what they were getting up to. The last person to know about it on the whole of Tarlojee was old man Hintzen himself, and that was because he didn't know what imagination was, let alone possess any. So Miss Caroline and Diamond Jim spread two years of harvest of diamond seed over the fields and in the sheds, and, for all I know, in some of those empty rooms along the top of the big house where nobody ever goes.

It seems the good Lord didn't want to waste that fine seed, and Miss Caroline started growing big under the red sash round her middle.

Things like that will happen anywhere, and there's always trouble when it happens to rich folk. People liked Diamond Jim though, they liked the style of him, the way he'd sit and hum under the guava tree with that diamond pin as big as a child's eye, fixing the bandanna round his neck. He had rum for everyone, real rum and not even dregs. And he had city stuff in his pockets. There were a lot of black men working in the fields, a lot of black men going home dusty and grey – with dirt. There were some brown men too, all the shades of the earth: red, brown, grey; and I suppose we all looked much the same with our trousers cut from the same bolt of cloth and tied round with lengths of the same string. There were ways of being different, mind you, in the shades of a bandanna round your neck, or the tilt of a fibre hat, or even the cut of your shirt. But when it came to who had what, we were all poor and we all had a lot of mouths to feed, and we used to joke that the cane hairs that stuck in our backs were the iron filings old man Hintzen had for spit because he talked so rough. Which made it only natural that we should all admire Diamond Jim. He wasn't just black, he

shone. I swear his skin shone like the rings on his fingers and the
great stone at his throat. And, when he smiled, he looked like he
could swallow up the whole of Tarlojee in that smile. The kids used
to say he could take anything and spit it out as diamonds.

I don't know why we called him Jim, because his name, I believe,
was Walter. I don't know either, who his family were. He must have
been somebody's son, and if they were about they would surely have
claimed him when he came striding home with all his money and
his confidence. Some say he must have seen Miss Caroline somewhere in town and followed her to Tarlojee and that was why he was
there. But nobody knew for sure. The fact is he came and stayed,
and, when he started messing with Miss Caroline, everyone just
waited and held their breath for the deal that they liked that
Diamond Jim for, and the dread they all had of old man Hintzen.
Miss Caroline had so much charm, it was a weight for her to carry
it about. It was as though she was born knowing what was to happen
to her. All her high spirits seemed bottled up, and when she laughed
it came out like an explosion of locked-away things. She used to say
she liked the feel of the sun on the back of her neck. People who
work with cane can't understand a thing like that. And she liked to
lie in the grass and sit on the prickly cane leaves, and she never had
any fear of snakes. That's all I know about her as a girl, just how
strange she was and fanciful for the outdoors and full of life and
laughter. She must have really loved to be alive to have lived on
those twenty years in the tower, with nothing to see but the cracks
of light through her boarded window and the walls cracking as the
years went by.

I've heard talk of people dying of laughter, and I think that's just
what killed that mismatched pair. When Caroline Hintzen laughed
it unsettled everything from the Big House down to the river. It
even made old men shudder and hold themselves, and the little kids
were scared. It had a strange effect. The sound of it carried far and
wide like the crashing of boulders along the river bed of a flood. She
was said to look like an angel and to laugh like a witch.

I don't know, and I don't expect I ever shall, who did bewitch the other out in the orchard under the noses of the whole world, and Tarlojee was a world in those days. Whoever it was who began that crazy love affair, it soon reached such a pitch that it was just burning up worse than a cane fire with a following wind. There wasn't anyone left who didn't know about it. If they'd have run away, who knows how far they would have got. Maybe they knew that not all the diamonds that Jim owned or even all the diamonds left in the hills could save that white girl and her big black lover. Maybe they could have made a dash into the Dutch countryside and hid out there, but black is black and Diamond Jim wasn't exactly inconspicuous anywhere. Then, maybe they thought they were invisible, protected somehow by the Lord himself in their great love from the vengeance of a man so cold he didn't even know that love existed.

It seems the lovers lasted longer than anyone dared hope for, because of Hintzen's stubborn negation of the thing. While every night as the sun sank into the river and the stars signalled across the fields, Miss Caroline's frenzied laughter was like a flare to some and a map reference to others. No matter where they went, the whole work force of Tarlojee, and even her sisters, knew where they were tumbling because of that manic braying that she did. There were times during the day, with no respect for the sun or the dead hours and no sense of a Sunday or rest, when the same thing would rise from field or hut as their lovemaking gathered pace.

Why, every day those two fools could have been caught. But it seems that time was suspended over Tarlojee while Miss Caroline nearly cloyed in the sweetness of her feelings for big Jim, while he sat of an evening and hummed with his back up against the grey bark of a guava tree, staring up at the stars with his eyes half closed, passing messages, it seemed, from his big diamond up into the sky. Whatever it was he learned from that, it seemed to keep him there and vulnerable, for all the months when he could have fled, alone or with the girl and saved his life. He must have known that Hintzen would kill him when he knew. He must have known that, but didn't seem to care. Perhaps that's what the stars were telling him, that long after Hintzen died and his dust was spread, he, Diamond Jim, would still be sitting under his favourite tree, still humming his old tunes.

The rains came first, and they didn't look like the heaven-sent rain of other years because the storms kept coming down red. Then it must have been July when the bats died one night and everywhere around the house their thin furry bodies made a stretched grey layer like a carpet of tiny hidden bones. Later, it must have been in September, the yucca crop failed and the cane itself was slow to grow. That was when it became apparent that Miss Caroline was growing in its stead. Some girls get pregnant and they can conceal the thing for months on end, but Miss Caroline wasn't just big, she was massive.

There were some good people out on Tarlojee around her, and some of them worked hard to cover up her tracks. But she herself seemed to have set her face against her fate and not to care, because she flaunted her great belly as though she was the proudest mother-to-be. And that went on until her father locked her up. I don't believe a mother would have let the old man drive her mad like he did. Maybe no mother could have saved poor Jim, but anyone with a heart could have helped Miss Caroline. It was her misfortune to be orphaned of any kindness in that house.

On that first night, Miss Caroline was locked up in the liquor room. It was always cold in there, windowless, with just a grid and a heavy-bolted door. For a working man, that would be paradise, not punishment; but for the girl in love, used to a soft bed and company, it must have been hard. People said she called all through the night. Called and called, they said, with her great high voice winding through the cane and over the ridges.

Diamond Jim could have run away then, but he didn't. Instead, he stayed out all night long with his bright eyes glazed over, looking at the sky and humming fit to bust like a vibrating engine. Even the cicadas and the tree frogs stopped eventually and there was just the wailing from inside the big house and that one chord buzzing in Big

Jim's throat. That was how he calmed her down. So the sun rose over the crest of the high fields, the ones that hillocked up beyond the dykes, with only the throbbing of Jim's voice to beckon it out of its sleep. He made the sun rise for him that day, willed it to set his stones in its gold because his own sun was going to set over Tarlojee before the day was out.

Eight o-clock saw the children passing by, scuttling past Jim as he sat waiting. They held the billycans close to their chests and looked away, giggling shyly, and then looked back at the black giant they'd heard was going to die. They regrouped behind him, dawdling on the dust track, disappointed. He'd looked the same. He'd even smiled. Condemned men shouldn't smile. Dying was a serious matter.

People knew that Hintzen would never settle for a shooting. He'd want a proper lynching. So the work force dwindled to the old and the boys that day, with a few women standing in for their men. All the strong ones stayed away drunk or feigning sickness, or just plain sick at the thought of helping to string up their hero. They couldn't do it. Well, Hintzen never had trusted his men, he hadn't counted on them before and he didn't count on them then. He sent away to New Amsterdam in the night, and four big mulattos rode into the forecourt that morning, with hats and spurs and their eyes red with greed and rum.

Diamond Jim watched them coming and he didn't stir. That was when the mystery happened. Those four mulattos swore that when they rode by, Jim's diamonds glistened and sparkled in the sun. But just moments later, when they went to get him, all his diamonds had gone. Now, no one passed by to take them, and the ground around him was dug and scratched and sieved and dug and no diamonds were ever found there . . . The mulattos said they thought Jim had hid the stones in his clothes, but after he died they stripped him bare and shredded the cloth. Nothing.

Before Jim died, Miss Caroline started calling again. But this time it wasn't just sounds and moans, it was straight words:

'Jim, don't ever leave me, Jim, Jim . . .'

Then he stood up and his big voice gathered that was rarely heard except to sing, and he called back to her, 'Caro, honey, I ain't going nowhere.'

The man never spoke again, as such. I don't really know what happened next. Some say they cast the rope around his neck and hanged him but he wouldn't die, so those four riders shot him through. Some say they had to shoot him to get the noose on him at all. One thing's for sure, though, the diamonds never were found. All down the years, vandals have been turning over Jim's bones to see if he swallowed those diamonds, but no good ever came of it, and no stones were ever found.

And no good ever came from hanging Jim. Before the year was out, the four mulattos who did it were jinxed, and they drank themselves to their ruin, haunted, they said, by the big smile on his face. And Hintzen? Even Hintzen wished he'd waited with his hanging, because four months later, when Miss Caroline gave birth to a huge grey baby girl, he wanted to kill Jim all over again and there was nothing left of him to hurt. Being a Christian, he couldn't destroy the child, but he took her away one night and returned a week later without her. That's what the towns were like, they'd swallow up the living and the dead. The baby must have been two weeks old then, and already turned as black as the man who made her.

After the baby went, Hintzen shifted his daughter into the stone tower, and that was when Miss Caroline started some serious calling. It seemed that she'd got the idea that all she had to do was cry out hard enough and Big Jim would answer her. Well, Miss Caroline stayed in that tower for twenty years calling out across the cane fields for the man she loved. She never gave up in all that time trying to summon him back to her. It must have been about a year later that her tired, sad voice cracked and turned into bouts of crazy laughter.

Her call had come to be a part of Tarlojee, like the animal call of the bush, and the keening of circling birds. It carried through the lanes between the sugar, and it settled in the daubed mud on the huts. People seemed to stir it in with their bean stew and corn. The dregs of her wailing sat with the pineapple rinds and fermented in pitchers of water. Jim's name was everywhere.

A lot happens in a lifetime, and things get forgotten. Details blur and disappear, and facts merge until only a few events stand out. Sometimes they're not events at all, just passing images, and sometimes they're so powerful they stop your blood from running for a while. That was how the laughter sounded after a year of tears. To hear Miss Caroline braying again chilled all of Tarlojee to the bone. It was her mating call, and, I suppose, it was all part of what held Jim to her because the night she started rattling her wild laugh about, Diamond Jim came back. He had his diamonds on again – the rings and the big one at his throat that communed with the stars. He sat all night under his guava tree and he hummed, a loud throbbing hum, and although no one touched him – because no one dared – he was there, smiling like he could, as though he knew something special, with his big teeth shining out and almost competing with the eye-diamond, the diamond that started it all, and gave him his name, and made him a myth.

A lot of nights have passed since then, and a lot of years, and Miss Caroline has been dead now for a long time, but Big Jim still sits out sometimes, waiting, and he still hums. And, although he's never done any of us any harm, there's no one goes down to the ruins of the Big House on a full moon. The kids nowadays laugh about him too, but there's not one of them eats guavas on Tarlojee or ever hums like a lost tune finding its way out of the sugar cane.

ANGELA CARTER

ASHPUTTLE: OR, THE MOTHER'S GHOST

A burned child lived in the ashes. No, not really burned – more charred, a little bit charred, like a stick half-burned and picked off the fire; she looked like charcoal and ashes because she lived in the ashes since her mother died and the hot ashes burned her, so she was scabbed and scarred. The burned child lived on the hearth, covered in ashes, as if she was still mourning.

After her mother died and was buried, her father forgot the mother and forgot the child and married the woman who used to rake the ashes, and that was why the child lived in the unraked ashes and there was nobody to brush her hair, so it stuck out like a mat, nor to wipe the dirt off her scabbed face and she had no heart to do it for herself, but she raked the ashes and slept beside the little cat and got the burned bits from the bottom of the pot to eat, scraping them out, squatting on the floor, by herself in front of the fire, not as if she were human, because she was still mourning.

Her mother was dead and buried but still felt perfect, exquisite pain of love when she looked up through the earth and saw the burned child covered in ashes.

'Milk the cow, burned child, and bring back all the milk,' said the stepmother, who used to rake the ashes and milk the cow before, but now the burned child did all that.

The ghost of the mother went into the cow.

'Drink some milk and grow fat,' said the mother's ghost.

The burned child pulled on the udder and drank enough milk before she took the bucket back and nobody saw and time passed and she grew fat, she grew breasts, she grew up.

There was a man the stepmother wanted and she asked him into the kitchen to give him his dinner, but she let the burned child cook it, although the stepmother did all the cooking before. After the burned child cooked the dinner the stepmother sent her off to milk the cow.

'I want that man for myself,' said the burned child to the cow.

The cow let down more milk, and more, and more, enough for the girl to have a drink and wash her face and wash her hands. When she washed her face, she washed the scabs off and now she was not burned at all, but the cow was empty.

'You must give your own milk, next time,' said the ghost of the mother inside the cow. 'You've milked me dry.'

The little cat came by. The ghost of the mother went into the cat.

'Your hair wants doing,' said the cat. 'Lie down.'

The little cat unpicked her raggy lugs with its clever paws until the burned child's hair hung down nicely, but it had been so snagged and tangled that the cat's claws were all pulled out before it was finished.

'Comb your own hair, next time,' said the cat. 'You've taken my strength away, I can't do it again.'

The burned child was clean and combed but stark naked. There was a bird sitting in the apple tree. The ghost of the mother left the cat and went into the bird. The bird struck its own breast with its beak. Blood poured down onto the burned child under the tree. It ran over her shoulders and covered her front and covered her back. She shouted out when it ran down her legs. When the bird had no more blood, the burned child got a red silk dress.

'Bleed your own dress, next time,' said the bird. 'I'm through with all that.'

The burned child went into the kitchen to show herself to the man. She was not burned any more, but lovely. The man left off looking at the stepmother and looked at the girl.

'Come home with me and let your stepmother stay and rake the ashes,' he said to her and off they went. He gave her a house and money. She did all right for herself.

'Now I can go to sleep,' said the ghost of the mother. 'Now everything is all right.'

ELIZABETH FANCETT

THE GHOSTS OF CALAGOU

Regus stood in the grey of dawn beneath the great tree on the edge of the empty corral.

Empty now, but not for long. Soon his horses would come and his ranch would begin.

He could not see his shadow, but he did not worry. He knew that it would reveal itself later when the sun came up. He was glad the day was ahead of him, a sunny day, when he would have the surety of his shadow.

He looked about him at his lands and blessed the wealth that had made it possible. *His* gold, though they had sought it together, he and his erstwhile partners. They had worked as hard for it, suffered for it, died for it. And by their greed they had nearly killed him too.

But he had survived, and they had hated him for it. Beyond the grave they hated him. They tried to make him think he too was dead. Had they believed such tricks could drive him to madness, to take his own life maybe – when he really would have been one of them?

He cursed the day when he had taken them on.

He had come into the little town of Calagou, the last stop on his way to the legendary mountains that towered above the intervening valleys and prairies. He knew he would need more help, more hands, strong backs, but held little hope of getting them. For as legends told – indeed, as living men still said – there was more than gold in the high and haunted hills of Calagou.

Many had gone there in the past, few had stayed more than a night there, and many more had not returned. And those who had returned – without gold, though the hills were rich with it – had told their eerie tales in the comfort of lighted cabins or the cosy warmth of saloons, and had shuddered in the telling and in the remembering of the sounds they had heard there and the things they said they had seen there. And they had recalled, with the respect that terror brings, the legendary warning that no man takes gold from Calagou and lives!

Then Regus came, himself something of a legend in this part of the West. Regus could divine gold as some could find oil or water. And Regus was bound for the hills of Calagou.

He made his choice – three young strong men, Talley, deSeegar and Carney. They were willing, they said, but had Regus heard the legends?

Yes, he had heard the tales and scorned them. Tales of disappointed men, he had told them. Excuses for their failures and their stupidity. The voices they claimed to have heard were nothing but coyotes calling from the surrounding hills, the ghosts no more than fevered imaginings of gold-greedy men – not legendary dead men jealously guarding their treasure.

Dead men there were, no doubt. Buried in the mountains, trapped by their own stupidity, their own greed, when they refused to leave before the fierce, unmerciful summer came to the hills of Calagou, when the sun scorched their backs to cinder and fried their heads to madness.

But he, Regus, would be going in the springtime and would quit before the summer came.

They had agreed to go, were eager to go, for they were strong and courageous men. But above all, they were greedy men, possessing the one essential quality to override all fear, to scorn all tales, to laugh at all legends. They had the perfect combination – guts, and the greed for gold – and this pleased and suited Regus.

Calagou was to be his final venture, and his ultimate challenge. For the mountains were enormous, cragged and sheer, the canyons deep. One false move and hell could be waiting. But the rewards were greater than the dangers for any man brave enough – or fool enough – to try.

He'd been a fool! reflected Regus grimly. A fool to trust, a fool to take them. He should have gone alone. But how was he to have known?

And they had worked so hard. They had worked cheerfully, powerfully, pouring out their young strength into the great mountains, mining the areas where he had told them to dig and find.

And they had found – time and again, and again, and again . . .

The weeks had been gruelling, packed tight with work, but they had also packed their storehouse tight with gold, harrowed out of the hills from dawn till dusk and after, and in all that time no ghostly voices called them from the heights, no spectres rose to haunt their work-filled days and they found no signs of the legendary long-since dead guarding their gold from all who dared to come to the hills of Calagou.

They had even stood on the mountain tops, Talley, deSeegar and Carney, and called in strong and mirthful voices if ghosts there be to show themselves. They had laughed about the legends in the cool nights when they rested from their labours or counted their growing sacks of gold.

But they had laughed too long! thought Regus. And they had worked too long. They should have quit when he'd said, gone when he'd decided they should leave. They had a magnificent store of gold, beyond even his wildest hopes. They should have quit when they were ahead, packed up and ridden out.

The long hot days were coming, he had warned them. The heat would be unbearable, the days unendurable, the nights unsleepable. They had not believed him. Not with the golden fire in their veins, not with the dust of gold grimed in the sweat of their calloused hands, clinging to their tattered clothing, not with the bright knowledge of the gold as yet uncovered, the riches untouched. They knew it was there, as he knew it was there. More and more and more . . .

They had enough, he had urged them. Far, far more than enough, more than any man would need in his lifetime. But for them, enough was not sufficient. They wanted more. They had stayed for more. They had stayed one day too long, one week too many, one month too late.

The sun rose higher and fiercer in the long, hot days with no shade anywhere to receive them in rest from their labours. And at night even the shelter of their cabin was an oven for their baked and sweating bodies, a furnace of heat instead of a refuge.

At night, not even the coyotes called from the high hills about them and no birds flew in the fierce, bright scorch of days above the hills of Calagou.

Regus had begged them to pull out, but they would not. Then he himself would go, he had told them. He would take his share of gold and leave the mountains. But they needed him, they had said, to find more gold, and they would kill him if he tried to go. And he knew that they would have, without qualm or hesitation, for by this time they were all not a little mad.

At night, exhausted yet unrelenting, they took it in turns to guard him, lest in the dark he should take his share of gold and pull out on them.

But the day came when they could work no more, when their scorched and blistered bodies bowed beneath the increasing burn of the day. Their young strength broke and madness came upon them. Regus had done his best for them, though his own strength too was failing, but he buried them all eventually in the gold-flecked dirt of the mountains, in the last rich vein he had just uncovered before their strength gave out and the sun had robbed them of their reason.

And in the voiceless, windless, soundless silence, when the last echo of the last clod of earth upon their graves had died away, they came and stood before him, hating him, taunting him, reviling him, cursing him because they were dead.

Assuming that madness had come upon him too, he had crawled

into the cabin and lain there. And all the while they cried to him and cursed him and tried to make him think that he was one of them, willing him to die – no, not to die – telling him, *telling* him, that he was already dead, that he, like them, would never leave the golden, ghostly hills of Calagou.

But he knew that he was not dead. Sick he was, delirious without doubt, but he was alive – and he had his shadow to prove it! And when his fever abated a little he had crawled out into the hot dust, that he might see his shadow and draw comfort from it, and by it know that he still lived.

But when the hot night brought its darkness again his shadow was no longer with him. And they came with their grey, gaunt faces, their dead voices, hating him, crying out for vengeance to which he knew they had no right. He had warned them, hadn't he, he'd told them. Had he not pleaded with them to leave? It had been their own fault they had died, their fault that he was stranded here, all food and water gone, the horses and pack mules dead.

His fever left him, but they did not. They walked with him or stood about him – gaunt, grey, haggard, dead. They stood on the high peaks at sunrise and looked down upon him. They stood on the edge of the canyons at sundown and cried to him and cursed him. They walked the beds of the dried-up creeks and mocked him.

But gradually his strength had returned, enough for him to make a rough sledge from the wood of the storehouse, to load it painfully and slowly with as much of the gold as it could bear – the gold garnered by four pairs of once willing hands throughout the cool sweet springtime of the hills of Calagou .

He had spent a night loading the sledge, dragging the gold bag by bag, inch by inch, until all was stacked and ready. He used his saddle rope to pull it by and he came down from the mountains, carefully, slowly, taking a full day, lest his precious load be spilled into the clefts and chasms of the hills of Calagou. And at night he had set out on his long, slow journey across the parched prairie, dragging his burden through the hot darkness, without his shadow . . . but not alone.

For *they* came with him. Shapes in the darkness, moving mists that called to him and taunted him and screamed at him that he was dead – dead with the gold, dead though he walked, dead though he hoped, dead though he thought that he lived.

'One of us, Regus! One of us! One of the walking dead!'

He had flung their taunts back at them, giving them shout for shout, curse for curse.

'Don't waste your eternity trying to drive me mad! I know that I live! For as long as I can cast my shadow I cannot be dead! As long as my shadow lives – *I* live!'

But they had not left him, they had not ceased to cry.

'One of us, Regus! One of us! Can you see your shadow, Regus? Tell us, Regus, where is your shadow?'

But he had lived. He had won through.

When the town was in sight he had hidden the gold. They had watched him as he buried it, silently grouped around him, ghosts in the sunlight, phantoms in the bright, bright day. But his shadow was with him now, and he drew strength from it.

He wondered if they would enter the town with him, if others would see them too. He knew that if he stayed, if they talked, if they cursed him, he must be careful not to show his awareness of their presence lest the townsfolk think that he was mad.

But at the prairie's end they faded as if the cooling air of the little valley town had blown away their images.

The inhabitants had believed him readily when he told of the greed of the others, their determination to stay on, their eventual deaths, his own sickness and the loss of their animals. Yes, they had believed him. Too many in the past had died defying the sun, too many had not come back. The fact that he had walked the long, dry prairie back, they had no trouble in believing either. Big Regus, strong, indomitable Regus, could outwork and outlive many a younger man.

But most of all they believed him because he had no gold. If he had come into town, dragging his laden sledge, he knew they would not have taken his word about the others' deaths. And because he was

Regus they loaned to him fresh horses and mules, the necessities of his trade, accepting his promise to repay them as soon as he hit gold.

And at night he had returned to the desert, loaded the gold and ridden away – without his shadow, alone. His ghosts had left him. And there had been no sign nor sound of them, no sight nor breath nor cry of them . . . until yesterday.

He had thought he was safe here – a two-months' ride and more from Calagou. They belonged in the hills there for they were dead there, Talley, deSeegar and Carney, buried there among the gold. *That's* where their ghosts belonged. But they had come the previous sundown, when his shadow had left him, they had come in the night, calling his name. And there was more than malice in their voices, more than cursing in their callings. There was triumph . . . exultation . . .

The sun was high now, warm, bright, comforting. Regus turned his eyes to his shadow and was reassured. No man could be dead and yet not know it. That was madness, against all reason – if reason still held, if he was still *able* to reason, if madness had not yet come upon him! For how does one know if one is mad? Maybe he was, and saw ghosts where there were none, heard voices calling when none called. Maybe it had started, his madness, back there in the mountains of Calagou, when he had buried them?

Maybe.

One thing he knew – he was not dead.

Regus paced the ground and his shadow walked beside him. And they came and stood about him, waiting . . .

He looked at his shadow, his precious sentinel of hope. As long as he could see it he was safe. But his soul was weighted down with an unaccustomed dread.

Then there was the sound of hoofs pounding, of distant riders coming. Regus looked beyond the ranch gates for a glimpse of the horsemen. They rode, hard, rode fast.

And still they stood there, Carney, deSeegar and Talley transparent in the sunlight, silent and waiting, watching and waiting, and through them he could see the riders beyond the gates.

As they approached, Regus looked hard at the three men in the saddles. Their faces were grey with the stubble of many nights and days, their clothes white with prairie dust. They dismounted and strode towards him.

'You Regus?' asked one.

The eyes of his questioner were hard, cold, familiar, reminding Regus of someone. He glanced at the second man, at the also familiar features, and he looked at the third man and he knew that all three must be the fathers of the three men he had buried, of the three ghosts in the sunlight, silent, watching, waiting . . .

And he knew why one of the men had a coil of stout rope in his hands as they stood before him in the sunlight, blotting out his shadow, their eyes accusing him.

He tried to deny that he was Regus, but the words would not come. And he could only shake his head.

'He's Regus sure enough!' said the second man. 'The description tallies.'

'We trailed you, Regus!' said the third man, who held the rope. 'For two months and nigh on eighteen days we trailed you, Regus!'

'Then state your business,' said Regus defiantly.

The rope twitched in the man's hand.

'If it's about the animals I borrowed,' went on Regus, 'I long since paid my debts to Calagou.'

'Not *all* your debts, Regus!' snarled the man. 'Regus the great gold hunter, Regus the robber, Regus the killer!'

Regus glanced swiftly at the three ghosts standing silent, watching. He looked at Talley, gaunt and haggard, at deSeegar, his wild eyes fever-bright, at Carney, staring evilly, and on the faces of all three – triumph, a devil's leer of victory, of a battle about to be won. And he knew that *they* had guided their fathers here, in ways known only to the ghostly heart.

'Only *you* came back, Regus! Our sons were with you – but only you came back!'

'We don't know how you worked it, Regus, how you managed to

get out of those mountains on foot and with all the gold, but we're sure you found a way, Regus! You found a way!'

'We don't care about the gold, Regus. But our sons were with you – and only you came back!'

He began to protest, to tell them how it was, but the rope was uncoiled now, swung high over a branch of the great tree, and the noose was about his neck and he was up on a horse and the sunlight exploded into darkness from which the morning would never break.

The three men turned from their deed, mounted their horses and rode out past their watching phantom sons. Before the sounds of the horses' hoofs had died away, the three ghosts moved towards the tree.

'One of us, Regus! One of us!' they chorused, and with that final triumphant cry they faded in sunlight and troubled Regus no more.

In the warm, bright sunny day, on the edge of the empty corral, Regus swung beneath the great tree.

And in the last companionship of death, his shadow swung beside him.

But Regus could no longer see it.

JOAN AIKEN

THE TRAITOR

Oh yes – I once lived in a house with a ghost (said the old lady, gazing steadfastly into the red fire) – in fact with several ghosts. And they took no notice of me. It taught me a most painful lesson, one that I am not likely to forget.

It happened in the year when a great many small local libraries closed through lack of funds, and a lot of librarians were suddenly looking for jobs. I was one of them. Middle-aged lady librarians were two a penny, and nobody seemed particularly anxious for my services. I have always been rather solitary, from childhood on, without friends or relatives – I will explain why in a minute; and in this difficulty I hardly knew where to turn. But fortunately, just at that point, I saw the advertisement in *The Lady*: 'Elderly gentle-woman seeks pleasant Companion with a predilection for reading aloud.'

Now reading aloud has always been one of my greatest pleasures; first, with my dear mother when we had very few other resources; and then in Birklethwaite Library, where I ran a regular Reading Circle in the children's section twice a week, for I don't know how many years, and enjoyed it fully as much as any of my listeners.

So I wrote to the Box Number of the elderly gentlewoman, was interviewed, and happily we both took a liking to one another. She was, indeed, a most delightful person, wholly alert, although in her eighties, intelligent and humorous, in appearance a mixture of owl and eagle, with piercing dark eyes, a small beaky nose, and wayward hair standing up on end like white plumes. What she thought of me, I do not know, except that it was sufficiently well to offer me the post, above a number of other applicants; what I thought of *her* was that I should immensely enjoy her company, and probably learn a great deal from her too. It was arranged that I should commence my duties in two months' time.

Mrs Crankshaw's surroundings were as pleasing as her personality: she lived in a Georgian mansion called Gramercy Place under the slopes of the South Downs, and I looked forward to unlimited walks in the surrounding countryside during my free hours; but to my disappointment, before it was time to take up residence with my new employer, I had a letter informing me of a change of plan.

The poor lady had suffered a slight stroke. 'Nothing of consequence, I am already better, apart from being confined, at present, to a wheelchair,' she wrote with characteristic firmness, 'but I have decided that it would be practical to move to a less solitary environment – better for you, too, my dear Miss Grey. My lawyers are hard at work on the purchase of another house in a small agreeable town – in fact, the purchase of *three* houses which will be converted into one, so that, if we have less outdoors, we shall have plenty of indoors, and shall not be on top of one another, which I think is most important. The builders are only waiting for completion to start tearing down partitions, and I trust that our original plans will be put back by no more than a month or two.'

She did not mention the name of the small agreeable town, and I waited with interest to learn where it was, confident that our tastes would coincide in this, as they had in other matters.

The purchase went through, but the building work dragged, as such work always does, and it was more like nine weeks before Mrs Crankshaw was able to transfer herself from the nursing-home, and her furniture from Gramercy Place, and write to me that she was ready for me to come and take up my duties in the new residence.

When she did so, the address gave me a shock – the first of several.

For she wrote from The Welcome Stranger, Stillingley; and Stillingley was the town where I had spent my childhood, after my father had gone to prison.

And when I reached my destination I received the second shock. For The Welcome Stranger turned out to be the house where my mother and I had lived, now joined together with the houses on either side of it.

'They were all for sale, so I bought the whole little old Tudor row,' said Mrs Crankshaw comfortably. 'Luckily my brother's legacy gave me plenty of leeway. (I told you, didn't I, that he had died, and left me some money?) And it is right that the houses should be joined together again, for apparently, back in the seventeenth century, the whole building was one large inn; only in those days it was called The Bull. But since there is already a Bull Inn in the town, I thought I would choose another old coaching-house name. Besides, it is prettier. The coach entrance was that archway that runs through to the yard at the back.'

I could have told her that. I could have told her a great deal more. I had spent thirteen years in that street, in the middle house, and knew every crooked step in it, every beam and cranny, as well as the palm of my own hand. It was wonderful how little the builders had changed; as Mrs Crankshaw said, the building had been one house two hundred years before; all they needed to do was to knock down a few partitions.

The third and worst shock came as we were having our first cup of tea in the white-panelled parlour – which had been my mother's study where, three days a week, she worked at translation, and read proofs for publishers (on the other three days she had an editorial job on the local paper).

I had asked Mrs Crankshaw why she picked this particular town – did she have any connections with it?

'Oh yes,' she said, tranquilly sipping her Lapsang Souchong. 'My brother lived here, in Pallant House, for a number of years. I used to visit him, and always thought it would be a pleasant place in which to settle if, for some unfortunate reason, one was debarred from living out in the real country. My brother was a judge, you may have heard of him: Sir Charles Sydney.'

And of course I had heard of him. He was the judge who had sentenced my father. That was why my mother had moved to the town, after Father had gone to prison. First we had to give up our own house, we could not afford it. Secondly, visiting would be easier – only an hour's bus ride to the jail where Father was serving his twenty-five-year sentence. But also, having learned, during the trial, that Stillingley was where Sir Charles lived, my mother, apparently at that time, nursed some obscure notion of meeting him in the street or in the Pallant Gardens, or after church on Sunday, and trying to make an appeal to him. 'For anyone can see that he is a *good* man,' she repeated over and over, with tears in her eyes, 'and your father is a good man too; nobody denies that. Somehow, somehow, there *must* be some way of getting his sentence annulled, or at least reduced – I am sure there must be.'

But this plan came to nothing, because, first, she never ran into Sir Charles or plucked up the courage to approach him. I think he was a very busy man, hardly ever to be seen in the streets of the town, mostly up in London. And, secondly, after serving only two years of his sentence, my father died; of a broken heart, Mother said. I sometimes think it is just as well that he did not live on into the times of glasnost and perestroika and the end of the Cold War; all that has happened since his conviction makes what he did – sending some not very important scientific information to a colleague in Moscow – seem so pitifully trifling. My father was a civil servant, and of course what he did was strictly forbidden, and counted as treason. But he was a man of tremendously high principles, a pacifist and a conscientious objector; and he felt strongly that all scientific information should be shared equally all over the world. So he was prepared to go to prison for his beliefs. He took himself and his principles to prison; and he left me and Mother out in the cold. Or rather, he left me in prison too . . .

I often thought that he had behaved very unfairly to Mother and me. Either he should not have married and had a family, or he should have chosen some other job. I was only five when he was taken off, and I missed him dreadfully for a number of years. He had been a kind, affectionate father, and used to play lots of games with me. One was called Treasure Islands, a guessing game, trying to find out about each other's treasures; and we told long sagas, each taking up the story in turn; or we did cookery, inventing new dishes from a list of ingredients all beginning with the same letter: apples, anchovies, artichokes, arrowroot . . . Heartburn holidays, father used to call those afternoons.

So it was an incurable grief when he vanished away to prison, and a worse one when he died. Mother never married again. She and I reverted to her maiden name of Grey when we moved to Stillingley, because she used to get a lot of hate letters from people who said that Father was a traitor. People seem to have unlimited time for acts of spite to other people who have never done them any personal harm. And about ten years after Father's death, Mother also died. And I took a course in Librarianship with the small amount of money she left me, and became a librarian, and worked in libraries for twenty-five years. After Mother's death I never went back to Stillingley. We had no close friends there, because of the quiet life she chose to lead, so it was not at all probable that anybody in the town would recognize me. (Nobody did; partly because the town had changed a great deal. All the little old corner shops had gone, and instead there were tourist boutiques. Walking about the familiar streets, I felt like a ghost myself.)

So, my dears, I expect you can understand why, when Mrs Crankshaw said, 'My brother was a judge: Sir Charles Sydney,' I did not at once and honestly exclaim: 'Why, he was the judge who sentenced my father to twenty-five years for sending treasonable communications to Soviet Russia,' but instead gulped, bit my tongue, knelt to lay another log on the fire, and kept quiet.

Oh, what a difference it would have made if I had not done so! If I had told her that this house was my childhood home. For, once having embarked on a policy of concealment, I was, of course, obliged to go on; there never came an opportunity to change my mind, toss discretion aside, and proclaim: 'Oh, by the way, Mrs Crankshaw, I forgot to mention, when we moved in, that your brother sent my father to prison.' That seemed out of the question. And, although I had never in any way blamed her brother – who was only doing his duty, acting on his principles, as Father had acted on his – there was no slightest hint of resentment or anything of that kind – yet, nevertheless, the fact that I was keeping this major secret from her had some kind of crimping or smothering effect on our relationship; happy and friendly although that became.

Well – it *must* have, mustn't it?

But the worst result of all was what I am now going to tell you.

When Mother and I first arrived to live at Middle House, we were busy carrying baskets and jugs and suitcases in through the back door, when I was a little dismayed to observe an eye carefully scanning us from the window of the house next door. And when I say an eye, I mean literally nothing *but* an eye: the bottom left-hand corner of the lace curtain was twitched aside, leaving just room for one muddy grey optic to peer sharply over the window-sash and study our possessions.

This gave a decidedly chilly, sinister impression; it could not have been more misleading.

After a day or two spent in getting settled, we began to receive the impression that there was a tremendous amount of back-and-forth, come-and-go, to-and-fro, between the two little houses on either side of us. Upper House, Middle House, and Lower House, the row was called. We occupied Middle House; Upper and Lower Houses appeared to be inhabited by two couples who could not have enough of each other's company. Mr and Mrs Brown, Mr and Mrs Taylor were their names, we learned from the postman; and we soon discovered why they all lived in one another's pockets – it was because Mrs Taylor and Mrs Brown were sisters. In no time at all they had invited us into their highly polished front rooms, resplendent with pot plants and cage birds, and they had given us their life histories. Mrs Taylor and Mrs Brown – Di and Ruby – were Cockneys, had originally been evacuated to Stillingley in World

War One, had fallen in love with local boys, married them, and never returned to London. Their husbands, Fred Taylor and Jim Brown, were, respectively, a bus conductor and a builder's foreman. By the end of three weeks, they were playing a very important part in our lives. Fred, every two days, used to bring us fish from Portsbourne, which was at the end of his bus run, and was a monument of sense and experience when it came to practical matters. Jim could deal with any household emergency, could fix leaking taps or loose wiring, mend windows, replace fallen tiles. Ruby and Di supplied the light relief; especially Di. She was a stand-up comic, a harlequin of a woman. Not at all good-looking, she was lean and rangy, with vigorously permed pale-grey locks and skin like uncooked frozen pastry. It was her eye that had peered from under the curtain in Ruby's kitchen. The sisters were perpetually in and out of each other's houses, exchanging pots or clothes, borrowing salt or soap, telling jokes or gossip. 'Roo? Are you there, Roo? Got a minute? Come and take a look at this! Di! Di! Got a pinch of bicarb – a few mothballs – a forty-watt bulb – a spoonful of honey?'

Although the husbands had relatives in the town – plenty of them – the two couples formed such a compact group in themselves that they hardly required other company. But they were immensely, infinitely kind to Mother and me. They became our family – surrogate uncles, aunts, grandparents, cousins. 'You're so *different* from us!' Di sometimes said wonderingly to Mother. That was because Mother spoke several languages and could translate from German and Russian. Our neighbours themselves had the unassuming modesty, the simple unobtrusive diffidence, of completely happy people. They saw no need to assert themselves; they already had all they required.

It was not long before Mother had told them everything about Father's prison sentence. She had resolved never to mention this circumstance to a single soul in Stillingley; she disclosed it all to Ruby and Di, Jim and Fred, without the least hesitation. She did not even ask for their discretion; she knew by instinct that they would never mention the matter to anybody; and they never did.

They listened to her tale with wondering sympathy, wholly without passing judgement.

'Well; he had to do what he thought right, didn't he?' said Fred.

'And so did the judge; all the same, it does seem a proper shame,' said Jim.

'All that time away from you; it's like as if you were a widder,' sighed Ruby.

'And poor little Snowball here, so many years without her dad,' grieved Di.

From then on they were even kinder to us.

Trip-trap and clitter-clatter through my childhood run the feet of Ruby and Di back and forth outside our dining-room window. 'Di! Ruby! Listen to this! Can you let me have a lump of dripping? Come and look at the bird, Di! D'you think he's poorly?'

They insisted on our sharing in the products of all their activities: marmalade, chutney, pickled onions.

Soon it was: 'Missis Grey? Are you busy? Can you spare a minute?' And quickly the Mrs Grey gave way to 'Ianthe' (which they shortened to 'Ianth'). But, scrupulously, delicately, they never dropped in on my mother during the hours of daylight; Fred, the chieftain of the tribe, had decreed this. 'She's the breadwinner, see? You gotta respect that and not go bothering her, you two, mind, while she's workin'.'

Fred and Jim, Di and Ruby; they were like the biologist's ideal, a completely self-sufficient society without the need of any outside agency or supplies.

Only once a year, at Christmas, did they summon huge hosts of other relatives whose arrival was heralded, weeks before, by monumental piles of Christmas cards which, as soon as they arrived, were slung on zigzag strings across and across the front rooms, in among the cyclamens, the tinsel, poinsettias, mistletoe, and folding paper bells. Then they had a Christmas party. After the first occasion we carefully avoided those parties, which could last for six, seven, eight hours at a stretch; Mother explained that she really had to go on working over Christmas and could not afford all that time off.

'But what about the liddle 'un? *She* don't have to work.'

'She's shy,' said Mother firmly.

Those parties did indeed have a numbing, shattering effect, as one munched one's way through more and more sausage rolls and sandwiches, drank more and more lethal mixtures of alcohol and fruit juice, while trying to keep up a continuous fixed smile at the tireless crackle of repartee from cousins, nephews, uncles, and indestructible great-aunts. All these relatives adored and respected our quartet, and would have liked to be invited much more often than once a year. 'But we don't want 'em,' said Fred, Ruby, Di, or Jim. 'We're comfortable just on our loney-own, thank you *very* much – with Ianth and the young 'un.'

So time passed for us, peacefully enough; we were buttressed, comforted, and contained by the strong dependable structure on either side.

When I was seven my father died in jail and, during that time, Fred was of silent, sterling support to my mother. He rented a car and drove her to and fro during Father's illness; he drove her to the crematorium, sternly excluding his wife, brother-in-law, and sister-in-law. 'No, she don't want you lot; it's a family occasion, see?' And he himself would have stayed outside the chapel if she had not insisted on his coming in, and then he stayed firmly on his own at the back. A surprising number of other people turned up, Mother told me (I was in bed at the time with measles); there were quite a few journalists, and old friends from past days. Mother was glad to dodge them after the ceremony and take refuge with Fred in the rented Rover.

That night my mother and the four neighbours held a kind of wake for Father. I expect she felt she owed it to them; it was what they would have expected. Fruit cake, cold ham, sherry, and whisky; lying upstairs in bed, feverish, with painfully aching ears and throat, I heard the subdued hum and grumble of voices down below gradually grow more cheerful, an occasional laugh ring out.

'How can they?' I thought, thrashing and tossing in bed, wretched, sick, and furious. Fred came up with a jug of lemonade and found me so, tears hissing on my hot red cheeks like water on the surface of an iron.

I glared at him, kept by manners and convention from saying what I felt.

But he understood perfectly well.

'I know, I know,' he said, settling his stocky bulk down with caution on my cane-seated chair. 'You think we're all heartless down there, don't you, tellin' jokes to your mum and makin' her laugh? But she's done a deal of sorrowin' already, and she's got a deal more to do; she needs a bit of a break. It ain't unfair to your dad; I expect he'd do the same. I dare say he liked a bit of a laugh in his time, didn't he? I expect he told you a good few jokes?'

Reluctantly I nodded.

'Well then,' said Fred. 'Just you remember, dearie; death ain't all black plumes and caterwauling. You got to carry on as best as you can.'

Fred saw us through various other troubles. When our cat died, he helped bury her; when my first boyfriend dropped me, left me a stricken thirteen-year-old grass widow, he managed to make me believe there were as good fish in the sea, which helped at the time, though in fact he was wrong, for I never acquired another.

And then, when I was fifteen, Ruby died. She had been growing gradually thinner and more gaunt; there was less vivacity in her jokes. She underwent an operation; spent painful weeks in bed at home, tended by Mother and Di. Then Fred said to me one day: 'I've got to tell you this fast – we're going to lose her,' and bolted blindly out of our kitchen. He himself was losing weight at a rapid rate; after her death he became, suddenly, a shrunken thread of a man. Di and Jim took him into their house, as they said he should-n't be on his own. By this time I was sixteen, about to go off on a residential course at the other end of England. Fred was in bed, ill, when I left, I kissed him goodbye and never saw him again. Jim soon followed; it was as if, once the structure and symmetry of the group had been damaged, its individual members were vulnerable, badly at risk. Jim died of bronchitis, coughing his lungs away. He had been a heavy smoker. Poor Di could not bear her life without the others around her.

'It just don't seem right,' she said to Mother. She developed heart trouble and died in the ambulance on the way to hospital. Now the houses on either side of us were up for sale; and one day, at my residential college, I received a telegram to say that my mother had died of pneumonia, very suddenly, in the local hospital. Like Di, she was unable to manage without the rest of the group to support her.

After letting Middle House for a couple of years, to support me through my training, I sold it, having no wish to return there. New neighbours were installed on either side. The thought of Upper House without Fred and Ruby, of Lower House without Jim and Di, of our own house without my mother, was not to be borne; I would have felt like a survivor from a holocaust. I found a plain job elsewhere, in a plain library in a plain provincial town, and entrenched myself in books, catalogues, indexes, and reading aloud.

Until the day, over twenty years later, when I found myself back there, installed in The Welcome Stranger, with Mrs Crankshaw.

She, in her wheelchair, professed herself wholly delighted with the three houses fashioned into one. The builders had made ramps for her, so that her domain was entirely on the ground floor – bedroom at one end, living space in the middle, kitchen at the other. So her living quarters were constructed from Mother's and my old kitchen-dining-room, where Ruby and Di had clattered continually past the window. Her bedroom was Ruby's front room, where the terrifying Christmas parties had taken place. I could sit reading *Dr Thorne* aloud to Mrs Crankshaw and think of all those spangled cards fluttering overhead, and Fred's nephew Peter rolling his eyes under the mistletoe. My bedroom was upstairs (my own old bedroom, as it fell out) and there I lay at night, listening to the house creak and rustle gently round me; Mrs Crankshaw had installed gas-fired central heating.

After a few weeks, Mrs Crankshaw said to me, 'Miss Grey –

Lucy – I am quite delighted with this house, and with our arrangement; I hope that you are too? But would you say – entirely without prejudice – that the place is slightly haunted?'

'No one has said anything of the kind to me, Mrs Crankshaw,' I fenced.

'Oh, won't you call me Moira, my dear, don't you think we have reached that stage by now? No, of course I had no such intimation from the agents or the lawyers or the builders – but then, one never does, does one? Just the same, I do begin to wonder. During the last twenty years there seem to have been a great many occupants. Do you think it was because no one cared to stay very long?'

It was true that since the time of Ruby and Fred, Jim and Di and my mother, the three little houses had changed hands repeatedly. Nobody seemed to have stayed more than a year or so.

'But that need not mean a thing,' I argued, quite truly. 'The whole town is in a – a state of transition. House prices are rising so fast, people buy them as investments, do them up, and move on. Also, the place is becoming more of a tourist centre than it – than it probably was twenty years ago.'

It was becoming harder and harder to maintain my pretence of never having lived in the town before. I felt worse and worse about it. Because our relationship – Moira's and mine – was, in all other respects, so happy, open, and free; she was beginning to seem like a beloved aunt, or cherished older sister; one of those relatives I had never been blessed with. We were able to talk to one another about every possible topic – except one; and our reading-aloud sessions were periods of calm, undiluted pleasure.

'What is giving you the idea that the place might be haunted?' I asked with caution.

'Why, there are times – especially when you are reading to me, my dear – when I am almost convinced that I can hear *voices* – voices perhaps in the next room, or somewhere else about the house, or perhaps in the little lane at the back.'

'Perhaps they are real voices?' I suggested hopefully. 'Echoes, you know, from the lane.'

The little lane – along which Ruby and Di used to run to and fro all day – was a right of way and led to the public library, my long-ago haunt of comfort and instruction.

'Well, yes, sometimes they might be real,' agreed Mrs Crankshaw, 'but not always. Not late at night. And the voices inside the house *must* be ghosts – mustn't they? Unless I am going potty.'

'And that you certainly are not, dear Mrs Crankshaw,' I said fervently.

'Moira, my dear – Moira.' Her hawk-eyes gleamed.

'What *kind* of voices do you think you hear?'

'You are sure you don't hear them yourself?' she inquired wistfully.

'No, I'm afraid I don't. Not at present. Perhaps I shall, by and by.' Oh, how I wished this! For she said, 'Well, there are several different voices. That's why I'm sure it can't be just my imagination – for I never was very imaginative, you know, even as a child, I was the most prosaic little creature, and never cared particularly for pretend games or fairy stories. How could I invent something like this? What I hear is most often women's voices – quite raucous and cheerful, with a Cockney twang to them. Not a bit like our good neighbours up and down the hill.'

The good neighbours up and down the hill were nearly all antique dealers, who went in for a good deal of packaged refinement and ersatz chumminess; the females wore tweeds, and the males neatly trimmed beards.

'And you hear the voices particularly when I am reading to you?'

'Yes, is that not curious? It is precisely like – you know when you tune into a radio station, and at first it comes through perfectly clear, and then, by degrees, some foreign station comes in and jams it; though that is not quite the case here, for I can always hear you, my dear Lucy, perfectly well – but then in the background the voices begin.'

'Always women's?'

'No; the women are the most frequent, but occasionally I get male voices farther back – two different ones, I am fairly sure, one quite deep-toned and gruff, the other higher and more nasal.'

'Can you hear what they *say?*' I asked with quivering interest.

'Not yet, my dear. But let us hope that in due course I shall! Really, nothing so interesting has happened to me for years – and I am sure that I owe it all to your company in this pleasant place, my dear Lucy; I am so very happy that we had the luck to find each other.'

Her words filled me with mingled guilt and relief. Relief that she appeared to be deriving so much pleasure and interest from the phenomenon – many old ladies might have felt very differently – guilt that it was too late for me to be more candid and forthcoming about my friends; I felt I was doing them serious injustice by not telling her all about them.

Oh, what a tangled web we weave! . . .

While Mrs Crankshaw kept exclaiming in her satisfaction at what a warm, welcoming atmosphere the place had – 'Just like its name! I christened better than I knew!' – I, perhaps because I found myself in such a curious moral dilemma, felt the house curiously cold and unresponsive. No echoes came back to me, not a sound, not a signal, from the happy childhood hours I had passed there. And some of them *had* been happy: moments of hope, before my father died, moments of peace and companionship when my mother and I read aloud *Villette* or *War and Peace* in late spring evenings with a pale moon looking solemnly in at my bedroom window; moments of triumph when I had done well at school; or moments of pure fun when Di and Ruby were clowning and Fred and Jim, with us, were laughing at them.

I could not escape the impression that the house was displeased with me. I should have come clean; and I had not.

Mrs Crankshaw began to have remarkable dreams.

'I see such faces! Such real characters! Can they be people whom I have met, at some point during my life, and completely forgotten? They seem so extremely real. There is one extraordinary woman – a tall, bony, angular creature, with false teeth, and such a laugh! I have dreamed about her several times. Her name is Vi or Di – something like that. I must say, she is very entertaining. I wonder if I can be developing mediumistic powers in my old age? I must talk to the Vicar about it.'

She talked to the Vicar, but he was new and young; had come to the town long since the days of Fred and Jim and Ruby and Di. He could make nothing of Mrs Crankshaw's dreams. He assured us that, so far as he knew, nobody had experienced anything of this kind in the house.

I thought, also, that Mrs Crankshaw might be developing mediumistic powers. Was what was happening a kind of telegraphic flash passing over from my memory to hers? Was she picking up scenes from my past – my carefully suppressed past – and, as it were, printing them off in the darkroom of her mind? Did she see these things because I was there?

Or was she receiving entirely new impressions? Were the ghosts of Jim and Fred, of Di and Ruby, still floating around, still present in the house – disturbed, perhaps, by my arrival, by the builders' work – available to Mrs Crankshaw because she was so happily, generously ready to receive them – but not choosing to reveal themselves to me?

That was indeed a chilling thought.

I could imagine – all too easily – Fred's quarter-deck voice. (He had been a petty officer once, long ago, before he retired from the navy and took to bus-conducting.) I remembered how sternly he had said: 'She's the breadwinner, see? You gotta respect that and not go bothering her, you two.' I imagined him saying: 'You shoulda told the lady the whole story, Snowball, right from the start. Now you put yourself in what they call a false position. And you put *us* in one too.'

Oh how I longed to apologize, to confess, to have matters somehow set right!

One morning Mrs Crankshaw called to me, in a voice of pure astonishment:

'Lucy! Somebody pushed my wheelchair!'

Contrary to her hopes, she had never recovered the use of her legs; her upper body was active, but below her hips she was motionless. Because of the ramps, all the ground floor of the house was accessible to her; she had a self-propelled wheelchair with an inner and an outer wheel.

She could spin herself around, very easily, through her downstairs domain, and did so, all day long. It was only when we went out of doors that I pushed her. But the wheelchair had a self-activating brake, a locking device which automatically engaged when the chair came to rest, so that it could never accidentally roll.

'Somebody,' said Mrs Crankshaw, with absolute conviction, '*some*body disengaged the brake and pushed me over to the front window.'

'You are quite sure that you didn't, almost unconsciously, do it yourself?'

She thought about it. 'No, my dear. Because my tiresome old fingers are growing so arthritic and stiff these days that when I heard a horse's hoofs go clopping past outside, I did just wonder, would it be worth unlocking the brake and rolling myself over to take a look out of the window. But I decided not to bother – and then, you see, some kind agency did it for me!'

I felt – believe it or not – a prickle of jealousy.

I said, 'Dear Mrs Crankshaw. I am so very sorry about your hands. Let me give them a rub with embrocation. And you know that wherever I am about the house, if you give me a call, I'll always *gladly* come and move your chair—'

'Oh, my dear, I know you will! And my hands are nothing – a trifle. With so few disabilities, in this charming house and with your company, I am a very lucky old person. And now, it seems, I have a friendly ghost to push me about as well.'

She laughed with real pleasure.

But I felt nervous. Bitterly ashamed, of course – for how could I possibly mistrust my kind friends enough to suppose that they might do Mrs Crankshaw any harm? Just the same, from then on I kept a very sharp eye on the position of her chair, and would casually move stools or small tables into its possible path, so that it could never roll very far.

Several times during the next few weeks the chair was moved

again, always to anticipate some vague wish that Mrs Crankshaw had hardly yet expressed, even to herself. 'They positively forestall my needs,' she said, laughing. 'It really is *most* interesting, my dear Lucy. I am so *sorry* that you can't see them.'

For now she was beginning to get a glimpse of them – in odd, short flashes.

'Rather like a flickering, faulty television screen,' was how she expressed it. 'And, yes, sometimes in colour, sometimes black and white. Colour comes most often at twilight – black and white during full daylight. At night they seem to fade completely – just the reverse of what one expects of ghosts.'

Bit by bit, she described them.

'There is the tall, rangy woman. These are all quite modern spectres, my dear. No ruffs, or crinolines, or nonsense of that kind. The tall woman wears high-heeled leather kneeboots and a long narrow tube of a skirt, with an apron over it, and layers and layers of cardigans. Very often she has her hair in curlers. She is always the strongest image. Then there is a shorter woman, who nearly always has a piece of knitting in her hand.'

Dear Ruby! The number of hideous fancy-stitch sweaters she had knitted me! Which I was obliged out of politeness (and need also) to wear until I had outgrown them.

'Then there is a stocky thickset man who wears a dark-blue uniform. Perhaps he is a postman? I get a feeling of great kindness and dignity. And a little gnomelike fellow who spends hours poring over a folded-up square inch of newspaper, and always has a cigarette dangling from his lip. He is the faintest of them – but still, he is growing clearer as the days go by.'

'Just those four? No others?'

No grey-haired, thin-faced woman with horn-rimmed glasses, busy at her typewriter?

'No, you greedy creature,' said Mrs Crankshaw, laughing. 'Aren't four well-constructed honest-to-goodness spooks enough for you? *How* I wish my dear brother Charles were still alive; he used to be such a sceptical materialist, would never admit even the possibility of ghosts. What a good time I should have, telling him about mine! I really begin to feel as if they were my own family – my family of phantoms.'

To hear her say that gave me a terrible twinge. And then she began to speak of writing to *Psychic News*. 'This is such an interesting phenomenon, my dear. I feel it should be shared with experts.'

'But', I argued, 'then they would want to come down and inspect and investigate, and put in watchers and try to take pictures with infra-red light – or however people do photograph ghosts; do you really want all that going on in your peaceful house?'

She glanced round the pleasant white-panelled parlour.

'Well, no,' she conceded. 'Perhaps not.'

In fact, to me, the house was *not* peaceful any longer. It seemed to throb with reproof and reproach. I knew that the time had come when I must, I absolutely must confess all, and make a clean breast to Mrs Crankshaw.

And what a poor figure I was going to cut! Deceitful, dishonest, hypocritical, cowardly, dishonourable – but, above all, shabby and perfidious to my good friends. Was it so surprising that they seemed to have turned against me?

I decided to make my confession one evening, after our reading-aloud period, between tea and supper. That was our easiest, happiest time, when we were most completely in tune with one another; then, I thought, I would have the best chance of winning forgiveness and understanding from Mrs Crankshaw for my long course of deceit.

All day my heart rattled painfully inside my ribcage. Mrs Crankshaw occupied herself as usual, in reading newspapers and political journals, in writing letters to her bedbound friends, with sketching and solitaire and petit point; she was a most self-sufficient person. Occasionally she would raise her eyes from the card table or embroidery pillow to remark, 'There goes the tall lady past the window, carrying a birdcage with a canary in it. Do canaries have ghosts too, poor little things?' Or, 'Now I see the man in blue. He is carrying one of those rush baskets that fish used to be sold in; do you remember them? Do ghosts eat fish?'

Oh Fred, I thought. He would be bringing the fish for my mother and me. Oh dear, *dear* Fred, why can't I see you too? I'll tell her this very evening. The minute that we have finished our stint on *Wuthering Heights*. And then perhaps, perhaps they will show themselves to me.

We had our reading session, installed as usual: Mrs Crankshaw on the sofa, comfortably snugged in, with cushions behind her and a rug over her knees; myself in the rocker with the table lamp at my side. Twilight was falling fast.

I read aloud several chapters. We were very close to the end.

'Shall I stop here?' I said nervously, clearing my throat.

'Oh no, *do* go on, my dear – if you are not becoming hoarse? Do finish the book. I don't know *how* many times I have read *Wuthering Heights*,' said Mrs Crankshaw with satisfaction. 'And it gets better every time.'

'Are you – are you hearing the voices?' I asked.

'Just a little. They are chatting comfortably in the background. Not intrusively, you know – but like people in the next room who know that we shall stop our reading and talk to them by and by.'

So I read on; read the last two chapters, came to the last line: '*I wondered how anyone could ever imagine unquiet slumbers for the sleepers in that quiet earth.*'

Closing the book, I let a silence of a few moments elapse. The room was almost dark now, apart from the bright circle of my reading light. I glanced about – hoping for a glimpse of a long tube skirt, a head of curlers, a pair of leather kneeboots, a dark-blue uniform jacket. But there was nothing.

'Mrs Crankshaw: there is something I have to tell you. Something I should have told you long ago, at the very beginning of our friendship. *Listen . . .*'

But I had left it too late.

Mrs Crankshaw's head had fallen back peacefully on her cushion; her hands, relaxed, lay open on the rug. She had gone for good, and left me all alone in that silent, silent house.

DOROTHY K. HAYNES

REDUNDANT

He had always taken jobs that nobody else wanted.
'Taken' was perhaps the wrong word. It implied choice, and
Hamish never chose anything. He simply accepted what was left.

He had always been a shy and lonely man, a man who didn't
make friends easily. Girls never looked at him, dumb and awkward
as he was, and he had nothing to offer in conversation with men.
Mostly, people treated him with a kind of ribald affection, a humorous shake of the head, an exasperated but delighted, 'And what's
Hamish been up to now?'

Hamish had usually been up to something laughable. He was a
willing worker, first to clock on and last to leave, but he had a reputation for doing the wrong thing, little mistakes, small
inefficiencies which mounted up, in time, to minor catastrophes.
Sooner or later, every job he took would end. He was never fired, or
angrily dismissed; he was too well-meaning for that. Simply, he was
made redundant, but not nobly redundant, with a handsome settle-
ment as a reward for years of service; merely unwanted after a period
so short that there was no time for benefits to accrue.

That was his life. As he grew older and less able, less confident,
the jobs he was offered became more and more humble; from a trial
period in a pool of janitors to a dustman, a temporary picker-up of
rubbish in the park, and once a kitchen porter, hefting bins full of

fish guts and cabbage leaves and wads of sodden paper. Always, redundancy came in the wake of his well-meant enthusiasm. As a janitor he mistimed the heating cycle, and left the school gates unlocked; as a dustman he spilled rubbish on the road; in the park, boys upended his litter bag in a high wind, and in the kitchen he was too weak to handle bins more than half full.

The job he liked best had been a watchman's; not a posh security officer, with a uniform and a dog to guard him and keep him company, but an ordinary watchman by a hole in the road, with a brazier by the door, and red lamps round the hut. This job lasted longer than all the others. It was a pleasure to him, because he was on his own, with no one to criticize or sap his confidence; but the work came to an end, the holes in the road were filled, the lamps and cones and his little hut carried away on a council lorry, and he was redundant all over again.

It was some time after this, after a spell of being out of work, that he wakened feeling feverish and ill. The days came and went, his head ached, his stomach heaved, and then one day there was a thumping and crashing at the door, and people all around him. The neighbours had missed him, the milkman had had no answer to his knock, and the police had broken in and carted him away to hospital.

It was comfortable there, everyone was kind, and the mates who had worked with him on the building site came in to visit him; but they would not let him lie in peace. They seemed to think that he was ready to give up and die. 'And you don't want that, lad, do you?' they coaxed. 'You know what that would mean? You'd be last in the churchyard. You'd be the *Watcher of the Dead*!'

It didn't sound so very bad, but his mates explained it very clearly, as everything had to be explained to Hamish. It would be a job he couldn't escape from. It would be his, a cold and lonely vigil, until he was released by the next one to die, the next reluctant candidate; and that might be a very long time.

It didn't matter. He was beyond choice and effort. Hamish, cold and giddy, whirled unresisting down a dark echoing tunnel; and at the end of it was his new job, his last job, the one which nobody else wanted.

As he drove in state to the graveyard, spruced and formal in the tight enclosing coffin, he felt he had never started work in such style. The men who had visited him stood around in dark suits and black ties as words of cheer and encouragement were read over him, but all the time there was a shaking of heads and a murmur of sympathy. 'Fancy this happening to Hamish!'

He didn't care. He had a new job, a job with responsibility and a title to go with it. *The Watcher of the Dead*. It was like having his name in gold on an office door.

Patiently, he got to his feet to begin his first perambulation of the night. The gates were locked, the walls were high, and there was no one to see him as he half hirpled, half glided on feet which left no mark on the damp grass.

It was a calm night. Whoever would have thought the sky could be so blue at midnight? Little gold clouds like puffs of smoke reflected late sunshine or early moonshine – he couldn't be sure which – and the whole cemetery was visible, dim and dark blue. Here, in a low iron railing, was the grave of Mrs Swan, who had run out burning and birling when her home went on fire. *She* wouldn't have been much use as a watcher, poor mutilated thing. And there was Isaac Prosser, who had served ham and cheese at the front of his shop, and taken betting lines at the back. He had fallen dead of a stroke, and been buried with great ceremony, but there had been no reprieve for him. He had had to do his stint at the cemetery; and here was little Billy Slater, who had been picked up in pieces after falling over the cliffs on holiday looking for gulls' eggs.

Billy had never served his time. His parents saw to that. Hamish remembered it now with a new understanding. His funeral had met up with the corpse of Torquil McLachlan, who ran the Stag Hotel, and died of drink, and from that minute it had been a neck-and-neck race. It was not decent, the two hearses roaring and edging each other off the road, but Billy's parents were damned sure their laddie was not going to be landed with such a gruesome job, and him not twelve years old. Torquil's driver had had a dram or two before setting out, and his Rover squashed its wing at the church-yard gates. So Billy Slater nursed his bandaged body in peace, and Torquil became Watcher of the Dead.

There had been many after him, and now Hamish had taken over. He was keen, but lonely, lonelier than he had ever been work-ing on his own. It was what the men had warned him about, telling him the disadvantages of the job – long hours, no pay, and no one ever to talk to – but it was not as bad as they had made out. He was not quite sure to whom he was responsible, but he was determined to give full satisfaction.

Never were the graves guarded so well. Crosses and cherubs, urns and hourglasses, he knew them all, the weather-blasted sandstone, the gilt-lettered granite, the upended jam jars, and the marble books open at consolatory texts. He checked them all, in the hours between dark and dawn, and as a bonus to Those Over Him, he sometimes did voluntary overtime in the daytime.

He leaned against the headstone, his feet following the line of the grave, his shoulders level with the last inscription, HAMISH McDONALD McCLURE. He had watched the men carving it, fit-ting the name and date beneath the names and dates of the other McClures, but they had not seen him. No one could see him in sun-light. The bright day hid him as it hides flames, so that they could talk about him as if he did not exist, though they looked over their shoulders and lowered their voices as the marble chips flew and passed through him.

'I thought Hamish would have been at rest by now. Tommy Bain was gey far through with the pneumonia, but it seems he's got the turn. His mother was tellin' me this mornin'.'

'Just as well. How could a wee laddie like Tommy manage the watching?'

'How does *Hamish* manage?'

It raised a laugh, though an uneasy one. Hamish, standing diffi-dently aside, wanted to answer back, and say that he was managing fine. He had nothing to complain about; only, when the men packed up their tools and moved away, he felt for a moment as if the sun had gone in; that was all.

He had another task to perform: the task of summoning those to die.

To begin with, he worried about this. Without instruction or supervision, he had no idea how or where to go about it, or whom to call. In the past, there had always been someone to take him in hand, with a few dos or don'ts, a quick runthrough of rules he couldn't always take in, but on which he could always get advice if he asked. Now there was nothing but a sensing in the midst of his nothingness, a compulsion which told him it was time to set out on a journey; and there by the gate was a black cab, an old black cab with a tired horse with hair as grey as cobwebs; and he knew to go into the driving seat and take up the reins and let the old horse go on its way.

They went through the gate like dissolving steam, and ambled on slowly along the empty road. Such an old cab it was, creaking and trundling, but the man inside was elated. It was the first time he had ever had a job with transport laid on for him. He let the horse go where it willed, and it plodded on past cottages and farms, where people pulled back the curtains furtively and peeped out at the noise. They could see nothing. They shook their heads and let the curtains drop, but Hamish knew that their faces were white and their hearts sinking to their stomachs. The death coach had passed; but if it was not for them, this time, who knew how long it would be before it stopped at their gate?

And then the coach did halt at a big house, a prosperous stone house with carriage lamps at the door and music behind lighted windows. The grey gravel crunched and ground under the wheels, and suddenly the music stopped and the lights went down. Inside, people were wailing. They had heard the sound, and knew what it meant. The horse stood for a while, patient in the grey moonlight, and then clopped away over the churning stones; and they went on and on, dreamlike, to a broken-down steading where the animals set up a terrified clamour, though there was nothing to see; and Jimmie

Gow's wife choked over a scream, because though her husband was now past hearing, he heaved in the bed as if he wanted to be away.

They stopped at many places after that: a closed shop in the town, a new bungalow, and a hospital with dim lights burning. People out late, or up early before dawn, paused and covered their ears and prayed; and Hamish was neither sad nor sorry. He was only doing his job, and he had put in a good night's work.

He repeated his errand many times – he did not know how many; the nights were long, and colder now, and time was no longer a matter of day or night. He knew that if he had done his task properly, it would bear a harvest of souls, but he did not connect the harvest with himself. So far, nothing had happened. The strong took a long time to sicken, and the sick to die.

He was confident now, on top of his job, and no longer lonely. The mourners who came to lay flowers and stand in silence or merely sit and think in the quietness were company for him. He learned, considerately, to keep out of their way, because they had enough to bear without the grue that gripped them when he passed. Anyone meeting him would have screamed. He would have screamed himself at his own reflection, his face all hollowed and wasted away, hair in long wisps on a yellow skull, and his loose robe hiding a transparency of skin over skeleton; but what he wore he thought of as his uniform, clothes for the job, a suitable outfit for what he had to do; and he did it willingly, prowling the paths, inspecting the lairs and memorials, and making way, all the time, for those he still thought of as his betters.

Thus, when the gravediggers arrived with their planks and spades, he did not resent their talk, and the disturbance they made in his territory. They began to delve, deep and narrow, and worms crawled fatly out of the mounded soil. Hamish had an uneasy familiarity with worms; he imagined them . . . somewhere . . . wriggling and . . . he turned away, and the diggers paled as he passed.

The next people who arrived came in more seemly manner, carrying a new box of elm, bright with brasses, and gift-wrapped with ribbons and coloured wreaths. Hamish relaxed into gratification.

For once, he had done everything properly. One of those he had bidden had come, according to plan, and this time no one could fault him. He had always known that, given time, he could work as well as the next man.

The last of many words were spoken, the coffin lowered, the last earth pattered down. The mourners left, with wet hankies, looking back with grief and regret. Hamish settled himself against a yew tree, almost inflated with job satisfaction. Tonight he would make another foray, transport laid on, and the job progressing at his own pace and discretion.

The shade beside him shouldered him away, snivelling soundlessly. Misery and dejection, resentment and terror surrounded him like a smell. As he was edged farther and farther away, Hamish realized now where his zeal had led him. Of all the corpses, one had to be last; and the last one would supplant him.

It was all wrong. This thing beside him dreaded his task, and he, Hamish, did not want to relinquish it. Surely they could come to some arrangement? Surely . . .? But there was no appeal. Slowly, he felt himself seep and settle into his grave like water into a sponge, the trust, the routine, the responsibility of time unmeasured gone as if it had never been. Once again, he was redundant.

NOTES ON THE AUTHORS

Charlotte Brontë (1816–1855), the author of *Jane Eyre*, began writing poems and fantasy stories at the age of twelve, and several of these pieces were rediscovered and published many years after her death. 'Napoleon and the Spectre' was one of a number of fragments preserved by her widower, the Rev. Arthur Bell Nichols. Extracts appeared in *Poet-Lore* (Autumn 1897), and its first separate edition was printed for private circulation by Clement Shorter in February 1919, limited to only twenty-five copies. The story was later published for a wider audience in the Brontë collection of juvenilia, *The Twelve Adventurers* (1925). It was originally written in 1833, nearly thirty years after the mysterious death of French general Charles Pichegru, who Charlotte Brontë apparently believed had been strangled at the instigation of Napoleon – hence the identity of the ghost, 'Piche', which returns to haunt the French Emperor.

Elizabeth Gaskell (1810–1865), née Stevenson, is best known for her novels *Cranford*, *North and South*, and *Mary Barton*. It was while *Cranford* was appearing serially (and anonymously) from 1851 to 1853 in *Household Words* magazine that the editor Charles Dickens asked Mrs Gaskell to write a ghost story for the first special Christmas issue in December 1852. This was 'The Old Nurse's Story', her most powerful and best-known tale in the genre. The best collection of her Gothic stories is *Mrs Gaskell's Tales of Mystery and Horror*, edited by Michael Ashley (1978).

Amelia Ann Blandford Edwards (1831–1892) is now best remembered for her invaluable work in creating the Egypt Exploration Fund, and her excellent travel books A *Thousand Miles Up the Nile* (1877) and *Untrodden Peaks* and *Unfrequented Valleys* (1873). She was also a gifted novelist and short story writer, with over a dozen fine ghost stories to her credit. Only a few of these, notably 'The Phantom Coach', have been reprinted with any regularity; one of her finest, but lesser known, tales is 'The Story of Salome'. This first appeared (anonymously) in the *Tinsleys* Christmas Annual entitled *Storm-Bound* (1867), and was reprinted in her collection *Monsieur Maurice* (1873). All her ghost stories were collected in *The Phantom Coach* (Ash-Tree Press, 1999).

Mrs Henry Wood (1814–1887), née Ellen Price, achieved her first great success with *East Lynne* (1861), and by the time of her death she had reached sales of five million copies from her various popular works. Ghosts and the supernatural often featured in her short stories, but they were never collected into a single volume. Many of them can be found in her much loved '*Johnny Ludlow*' series of which the *Spectator* wrote: 'We regard these stories as almost perfect of their kind.' 'Reality or Delusion?' originally appeared in the *Argosy* magazine, December 1868.

Charlotte Riddell (1832–1906) née Cowan, was a very popular Victorian writer, acclaimed as 'the Novelist of the City'. Like several of her contemporaries, she wrote many fine ghost stories (often for Christmas annuals), and several of these were collected into *Weird Stories* (1882), *Idle Tales* (1888), and *The Banshee's Warning* (1894). Her biographer S.M. Ellis (writing in 1931) declared that *Weird Stories* 'comprise some of the best ghost tales ever written'.

Mrs Margaret Oliphant (1828–1897), a prolific novelist, biographer, and historian, was the author of that brilliant series of novels of English provincial life, 'The Carlingford Chronicles'. She was also one of the greatest writers of ghost stories this country has ever produced. 'Who has ever achieved the same variety of literary work with anything like the same level of excellence?' declared one of the many appreciative tributes after she died. According to her *Autobiography and Letters*, the idea of 'The Open Door' was first suggested to her by part of the grounds belonging to Colinton House, near Edinburgh, where William Blackwood (her publisher) was then residing. This story, which originally appeared in *Blackwoods Magazine* (January 1882), is generally considered to be one of the best ghost stories ever written.

Ella D'Arcy (1857–1937) was one of the select *fin-de-siècle* group associated with the celebrated *Yellow* Book in the mid-1890s, with Wilde, Beardsley, Beerbohm Dowson, and Henry James. She wrote many fine short stories, collected in *Monochromes*, *The Bishop's Dilemma*, and *Modern Instances*. 'The Villa Lucienne', her delicate ghost story set on the Riviera, first appeared in Volume X of *The Yellow Book* in 1896, and was reprinted in *Modern Instances* (1898).

Mary Eleanor Wilkins (1852–1930), was an American author who wrote with sympathy and realism about New England village life. Apart from many novels, she wrote more than two hundred short stories including several classics of the supernatural. The best of these appeared in *The Wind in the Rose-Bush* (1903). Her later works appeared under her married name, Mary E. Wilkins Freeman. The American Academy of Arts and Letters awarded her the Howells medal for fiction in 1926.

Edith Nesbit (1858–1924), the writer of such celebrated children's books as *The Railway Children* (1906), *The Magic City* (1910), *The Treasure Seekers* (1899) and *The Enchanted Castle* (1907), was a woman of enormous energy. In the years following her marriage to Hubert Bland she wrote, painted, recited poetry to earn money for the household, and became an active socialist, and a founder member of the Fabian Society. She broke from convention by wearing her hair short, smoking, and dressing in unfashionably loose and flowing clothes. Her fine supernatural tales appeared in leading magazines and the best including 'The Violet Car' were collected in *Fear* (1910). The story reprinted here is one of the earliest in the genre to feature a car.

Edith Wharton (1862–1937) spent her early years in New York, but for most of her adult life she lived in Europe, mainly in France. She was one of the leading writers of her generation; her novels have been extensively reprinted by Virago, and include *The House of Mirth* (1905), *The Fruit of the Tree* (1907), *The Custom of the Country* (1913), *The Age of Innocence* (1920) and *The Children* (1928). Her supernatural short stories are among the best to be found in American literature. 'The Eyes' first appeared in *Scribner's Magazine* (June 1910), and her collection *Tales of Men and Ghosts* (1910).

May Sinclair (1863–1946), philosopher, biographer. novelist and short story writer, was a keen supporter of women's suffrage and an early devotee of psychoanalysis. She began her long writing career with *Nakiketas and other Poems* (under the name 'Julian Sinclair') in 1886. In her novels, which have been compared to those of Gissing, like *The Divine Fire* (1904) and *Three Sisters* (1914), she displayed considerable understanding of the lives of men and women in cramped and difficult circumstances, while in *May Olivier* (1919) and *Life and Death of Harriet Frean* (1922) she was one of the pioneers of the 'stream of consciousness' technique. Her collection, *Uncanny Stories* (1923), with illustrations by Jean de Bosschere, is now a collectors' item.

Richmal Crompton (R.C. Lamburn, 1890–1969) earned worldwide fame as the creator of the immortal schoolboy 'William'. This eclipsed her impressive *oeuvre* of adult fiction, which included several tales of horror and the supernatural (including 'Rosalind', 'Hands' and 'The Haunting of Greenways'), collected in the volume

Mist and Other Stories (1928). 'Rosalind' was first published in *Sovereign Magazine*, April 1925.

Margery Lawrence (1889–1969) was a devout believer in the supernatural, who wrote a fascinating book on the occult *Ferry Over Jordan* (1944) as well as over sixty ghost stories (several based on reported incidents). Among her many novels, the best-known was *The Madonna of Seven Moons* (1931), made into a film starring Phyllis Calvert. The story reprinted here is taken from her very scarce book *Nights of the Round Table* (1926), in which twelve members of a club relate 'strange tales'.

Margaret Irwin (1889–1967) won many admirers not only for her long series of historical novels but also for her supernatural classic *Still She Wished for Company* (1924). She claimed to have written her first ghost story at the age of five, and often returned to the genre with tales collected in *Madame Fears the Dark* (1935) and *Bloodstock* (1953). 'The Book' originally appeared in the *London Mercury* in September 1930. The critic Joanna Russ described this story (in *How to Suppress Women's Writing*) as 'one of the most interesting stories of the supernatural I ever read'.

Flora MacDonald Mayor (1872–1932) is now attracting a steadily increasing number of admirers after years of neglect. Her important theme of the woman alone occurs in all three of her novels, *The Third Miss Symons* (1913), *The Rector's Daughter* (1924), and *The Squire's Daughter* (1929). Also long ignored, and worthy of revival, are her short stories – many with uncanny and ghostly elements – which were published posthumously in *The Room Opposite* (1935).

Ann Bridge (pseudonym of Mary Dolling Sanders, later Lady O'Malley, 1891–1974) spent a varied and colourful life with her diplomat husband, Owen O'Malley, in China, Turkey, Dalmatia and other locations, all used to great effect in her best novels: *Peking*

Picnic (1932), *The Ginger Griffin* (1934), *Illyrian Spring* (1935) and *The Dark Moment* (1952). Her ghost stories, which include 'The Buick Saloon', 'The Accident' and 'The Station Road', were collected in *The Song in the House* (1936).

Stella Gibbons (1902–89) achieved instant fame with her first novel, *Cold Comfort Farm* (1932), a witty parody of the Mary Webb/Sheila Kaye Smith school of regional fiction. Many other novels and short stories followed. This unusual and memorable tale is taken from her collection *Roaring Tower and other short stories* (1937).

Elizabeth Bowen (1899–1973) is one of the finest writers to come out of Ireland in the past hundred years, her best-known novels being *The Death of the Heart* (1938) and *The Heat of the Day* (1949). Among her varied collections of short stories – *Encounters*, (1923), *The Cat Jumps* (1934), *The Demon Lover* (1945) from which 'The Happy Autumn Fields' is taken – are some of the best weird and supernatural tales ever written. Several were inspired by the Second World War and most of them use uncanny elements indirectly to explore human reactions to fear.

Rosemary Timperley (1920–88), author of nearly fifty novels, was one of Britain's most prolific writers of ghost stories. She produced well over a hundred short stories since her first, 'Christmas Meeting', appeared in *The Second Ghost Book* in 1952. Although her highly respected tales have been published in innumerable anthologies, they have sadly never been collected together in book form. The majority of her stories feature ghosts of the gentle and non-horrific variety. 'The Mistress in Black' is taken from *The Fifth Ghost Book* (1969).

Celia Fremlin (b. 1914) is one of Britain's most gifted writers of suspense novels, noted for special psychological twists and her gift for seeing horror in the ordinary. Her first novel won an Edgar Award from the Mystery Writers of America. 'Celia Fremlin's excellent English mysteries always centre on some apparently average, "normal" family situation gone terribly wrong', commented *Publishers Weekly*. Besides her elegant thrillers she has also written several excellent ghost stories, including 'The Combined Operation', 'The Locked Room' and 'Don't Tell Cissie', from her collection *By Horror Haunted* (1974).

Lady Antonia Fraser (b. 1932), daughter of Lord Longford and wife of the playwright Harold Pinter, has been equally successful as biographer and novelist. Her first historical biography, *Mary Queen of Scots* (1969), received instant acclaim and won the James Tait Black Memorial Prize. She has also written mystery stories including *Quiet as a Nun* (1977; adapted for the television series *Jemima Shore Investigates*), *The Wild Island* (1978) and *A Splash of Red* (1981). 'Who's been Sitting in my Car?', from Giles Gordon's anthology *Prevailing Spirits* (1976), was her first published short story.

Ruth Rendell (b. 1930) has explored the darker regions of the human psyche in a highly acclaimed run of books alternating her series detective Inspector Wexford (introduced in her first novel, *From Doon with Death*, 1964) with other suspense novels focusing on psychotic and obsessed minds. She has been awarded the Edgar for her collection *The Fallen Curtain* (1974) and the Gold Dagger for *A Demon in My View* (1976). 'The Haunting of Shawley Rectory' first appeared in *Ellery Queen's Mystery Magazine* on 13 December 1979.

Antonia Susan Byatt (b. 1936) is noted both as novelist and as literary critic. She has written two books on Iris Murdoch, and a study of *Wordsworth and Coleridge in Their Time* (1970). Her novels include *Shadow of a Sun* (1964), *The Game* (1968), *The Virgin in the Garden* (1979), *Still Life* (1985) and the 1990 ManBooker prizewinner, *Possession*. 'The July Ghost' was first published in *Firebird 1* in 1982.

Audrey Lilian Barker (1918–2002) achieved early success with her first collection, *Innocents*, which won the Somerset Maugham Award in 1947. Her subsequent titles include *Apology for a Hero* (1950), *The Joy-Ride* (1963), *Lost Upon the Roundabouts* (1964), *Femina Real* (1971), *Any Excuse for a Party* (1991) and *Submerged* (2002). She wrote over a dozen memorable tales of the supernatural, notably 'Lost Journey', 'The Little People' and 'The Dream of Fair Women', which originally appeared in the anthology *Stories of Haunted Inns* (1983).

Penelope Lively (b. 1933) has been equally successful as a writer for both children and adults. Her brilliant evocations of the supernatural may be found in *The Whispering Knights* (1971), *The Wild Hunt of Hagworthy* (1971), *The Ghost of Thomas Kempe* (winner of the 1973 Carnegie Medal for an outstanding book for children), *A Stitch in Time* (winner of the 1976 Whitbread Award) and *The Revenge of Samuel Stokes* (1981). Outstanding among her adult novels is the 1987 Booker Prizewinner *Moon Tiger*. 'Black Dog' was first published in *Cosmopolitan* in 1986, and reprinted later that year in her collection *Pack of Cards 1978–86*.

Rosemary Pardoe (b. 1951) has helped to keep the ghost-story tradition alive and well through her longrunning series of *Ghosts & Scholars* (33 numbers from 1979 to 2001; succeeded by *The Ghosts & Scholars M.R. James Newsletter*, 2002 to date) and related titles issued by her Haunted Library imprint. She has also written several fine supernatural tales (under the *nom de plume* 'Mary Ann Allen') narrated by the church restorer Jane Bradshawe. These stories were collected under the title *The Angry Dead* (1986), from which 'The Chauffeur' is taken. Her learned study of Joan, *The Female Pope* (co-written with Darroll Pardoe), was published by Aquarian in 1987.

Lisa St Aubin de Terán (1953–), novelist and poet, lived for seven years in the Venezuelan Andes. Winner of the Somerset Maugham Award for her first novel, *Keepers of the House* (1982), and the John

Llewellyn Rhys Prize for her second, *The Slow Train to Milan* (1983). She has written seven other novels, a collection of poetry, two collections of short stories and four memoirs. Her latest novel *Otto*, was published by Virago in 2005. Much of her fiction, including the story published here for the first time, is rooted in her South American experience, combining powerful narrative with a strong sense of the fabulous.

Angela Carter (1940–92), was one of the most inventive and original writers of fiction during the past three decades. Amongst her novels are *The Magic Toyshop* (1967), *Heroes and Villains* (1969), *The Passion of New Eve* (1977) and *Nights at the Circus* (1985). Her short stories, which include *Fireworks* (1974) and *The Bloody Chamber* (1979), frequently draw on – and radically transform – traditional fairytales. 'Ashputtle' was first published in *The Virago Book of Ghost Stories* (1987).

Elizabeth Fancett has been one of Britain's most talented and original writers of ghost stories during the past twenty years, and has contributed to many anthologies in addition to Capital Radio's *Moments of Terror* series. 'The Ghosts of Calagou' was first published in *The Virago Book of Ghost Stories: Twentieth Century, Vol. II* (1991).

Joan Aiken (1924–2004), daughter of the distinguished American poet Conrad Aiken, wrote nearly a hundred books, ranging from adult mystery novels to a wide range of titles for children. *The Whispering Mountain* won the 1969 Guardian Award, and *Night Fall* won the 1972 Mystery Writers of America Award. Her series of 'horror, suspense and fantasy' collections, which attract an overlapping readership of both adolescent and adult readers, include *A Bundle of Nerves* (1976), *A Touch of Chill* (1979), *A Whisper in the Night* (1982), *A Goose in your Grave* (1987), *A Fit of Shivers* (1990) and *A Creepy Company* (1993). These nerve-tingling fables mix paranormal events with compassion and wisdom in exemplary fashion. 'The Traitor' was first published in *The Virago Book of Ghost Stories: The Twentieth Century, Vol. II* (1991).

Dorothy Kate Haynes (1918–87) first made her name with *Winter's Traces* (1947) and the collection *Thou Shalt Not Suffer a Witch* (1949), with illustrations by Mervyn Peake. A later collection, *Peacocks and Pagodas*, subtitled 'The Best of Dorothy K. Haynes', was published in 1981. Pamela Hansford Johnson wrote that her stories 'send fascinated readers back to the library in search of other books by the same cunning and delicate hand'. 'Redundant', one of several ghost stories by Haynes left unpublished at her death, made its debut in *The Virago Book of Ghost Stories: Twentieth Century, Vol. II* (1991).

THE GHOST STORIES OF EDITH WHARTON

Edith Wharton

In these powerful and elegant tales, Edith Wharton evokes moods of disquiet and darkness within her own era. In icy New England a fearsome double foreshadows the fate of a rich young man; a married farmer is bewitched by a dead girl; a ghostly bell saves a woman's reputation. Brittany conjures ancient cruelties, Dorset witnesses a retrospective haunting and a New York club cushions an elderly aesthete as he tells of the ghastly eyes haunting his nights.

REBECCA

Daphne du Maurier

'Last night I dreamt I went to Manderley again . . .'

Working as a lady's companion, the heroine of *Rebecca* learns her place. Life begins to look very bleak until, on a trip to the South of France, she meets Maxim de Winter, a handsome widower whose sudden proposal of marriage takes her by surprise. She accepts, but whisked from glamorous Monte Carlo to the ominous and brooding Manderley, the new Mrs de Winter finds Max a changed man. And the memory of his dead wife Rebecca is forever kept alive by the forbidding Mrs Danvers . . .

Not since Jane Eyre has a heroine faced such difficulty with the Other Woman. An international bestseller that has never gone out of print, *Rebecca* is the haunting story of a young girl consumed by love and the struggle to find her identity.

THE BIRDS AND OTHER STORIES

Daphne du Maurier

'How long he fought with them in the darkness he could not tell, but at last the beating of the wings about him lessened and then withdrew . . .'

A classic of alienation and horror, 'The Birds' was immortalised by Hitchcock in his celebrated film. The five other chilling stories in this collection echo a sense of dislocation and mock man's sense of dominance over the natural world. The mountain paradise of 'Monte Verità' promises immortality, but at a terrible price; a neglected wife haunts her husband in the form of an apple tree; a professional photographer steps out from behind the camera and into his subject's life; a date with a cinema usherette leads to a walk in the cemetery; and a jealous father finds a remedy when three's a crowd . . .

www.virago.co.uk

virago

To find out more about other Virago authors,
visit: www.virago.co.uk

Visit the Virago website for:

- Exclusive features and interviews with authors,
  including Margaret Atwood, Maya Angelou,
  Sarah Waters and Nina Bawden

- News of author events and forthcoming titles

- Competitions

- Exclusive signed copies

- Discounts on new publications

- Book-group guides

- Free extracts from a wide range of titles

PLUS: subscribe to our free monthly newsletter

You can order other Virago titles through our website: *www.virago.co.uk*
or by using the order form below

☐ The Ghost Stories of Edith Wharton   Edith Wharton   £10.00
☐ Rebecca   Daphne du Maurier   £7.99
☐ The Birds and Other Stories   Daphne du Maurier   £7.99
☐ The House on the Strand   Daphne du Maurier   £7.99
☐ Angela Carter's Book of Fairy Tales   Angela Carter   £12.99

The prices shown above are correct at time of going to press. However, the publishers reserve the right to increase prices on covers from those previously advertised, without further notice.

Please allow for postage and packing: **Free UK delivery.**
Europe: add 25% of retail price; Rest of World: 45% of retail price.

To order any of the above or any other Virago titles, please call our credit card orderline or fill in this coupon and send/fax it to:

Virago, PO Box 121, Kettering, Northants NN14 4ZQ
Fax: 01832 733076   Tel: 01832 737526
Email: aspenhouse@FSBDial.co.uk

☐ I enclose a UK bank cheque made payable to Virago for £ . . . .
☐ Please charge £ . . . . . . to my Visa/Delta/Maestro

☐☐☐☐☐☐☐☐☐☐☐☐☐☐☐☐☐

Expiry Date ☐☐☐☐   Maestro Issue No. ☐☐

NAME (BLOCK LETTERS please) . . . .

ADDRESS . . . .

. . . .

. . . .

Postcode . . . . Telephone . . . .

Signature . . . .

Please allow 28 days for delivery within the UK. Offer subject to price and availability.